30119 022 214 722

CH

**This book is to be returned on or before
the last date stamped below.**

This book is to be returned on or before
the last date stamped below.

- 9 OCT 2004
27 DEC 2005
- 7 JAN 2005
1 0 JAN 2006
2 5 JAN 2005
1 9 FEB 2005
- 9 MAR 2005
2 5 JUL 2006
1 5 AUG 06
- 7 JUN 2005
2 3 SEP 2006
1 6 SEP 2005
- 8 DEC 2005
1 8 OCT 2006

RENEWALS   Please quote:
date of return, your ticket number and
computer label number for each item.

**RENEWALS   Please quote: date of return, your ticket number
and computer label number for each item.**

D1297584

PARTNER IN CRIME

By the same author

PARTNER IN CRIME

J. A. Jance

HarperCollins*Publishers*

This novel is entirely a work of fiction. The names,
characters and incidents portrayed in it are the work of the
author's imagination. Any resemblance to actual persons,
living or dead, events or localities is entirely coincidental.

HarperCollins*Publishers*
77–85 Fulham Palace Road,
Hammersmith, London W6 8JB

www.fireandwater.com

Published by HarperCollins*Publishers* 2002
1 3 5 7 9 8 6 4 2

First published in the USA by
William Morrow
an imprint of Harper Collins*Publishers* 2002

Copyright © J. A. Jance 2002

J. A. Jance asserts the moral right to
be identified as the author of this work

ISBN 0 00 714835 6

Printed and bound in Great Britain by
Clays Limited, St Ives plc

For Mr. Bone. For Sunny, Huck, and Zeke.

For the Nickkis (both of them). For Tess and Mandy.

Azalea and Scratch. Boots and Barney.

Daphne and Ag.

And last but not least, for Daisy Mae.

PARTNER
IN
CRIME

Prologue

"WELL?" DEIDRE CANFIELD ASKED, as she mopped her dripping forehead and straightened the last picture. "What do you think?"

Rochelle Baxter stood back and eyed the painting critically. It was one of sixteen pieces in her first-ever gallery showing. With occasional heavy-lifting help from Dee's boyfriend, Warren Gibson, the two women had spent the previous six hours hanging and rehanging the paintings in Dee's recently remodeled and—for anyone doing physical labor—incredibly overheated Castle Rock Gallery in Bisbee, Arizona. For Dee it was a new beginning. For Rochelle, it was something else.

"It's fine," she said. Then, seeing how her lack of enthusiasm caused a cloud of concern to cross Dee's broad face, Rochelle added quickly, "It's great, Dee. Really, it's fine."

"I'm glad you like it," Dee said. "And don't worry. I know this show is going to be a huge success. You heard the phone calls that came in about it just today. I'm betting we'll have an overflow crowd for tomorrow's grand opening."

Deidre Canfield may have been convinced, but Rochelle wasn't so sure. "I hope so," she said dubiously.

Dee grinned. "What's wrong, Shelley? Sounds like you're suffering from a case of opening-night jitters."

"Maybe so," Rochelle admitted. "In fact, probably so."

"Take my word for it," Dee assured her. "I've been managing art galleries for years. I know what people like, and I'm telling you, they're going to love your stuff. What worries me is that we'll sell out so fast that some people will go away disappointed. I'm a lot more concerned about that than I am about no one showing up."

Turning away, Dee walked over to her desk and picked up her purse. "Warren wants me to give him a lift to the house, and I have to stop by the bank before it closes. Want to ride along?"

Rochelle shook her head. "You two go ahead. If you don't mind, Dee, I'd rather stay here. I want to be alone with the paintings for a little while."

Dee smiled sympathetically. "It must seem like saying goodbye to a bunch of old friends."

Rochelle nodded, but she kept her face averted so the tears welling up in her eyes didn't show. Dee's comment was far closer to the mark than Rochelle Baxter wanted to admit. "Something like that," she murmured.

Dee shrugged. "Suit yourself," she said. "Stay as long as you like. I'll be back in forty-five minutes or so. I also need to do some last-minute consulting with the caterer. I'll lock the door and put up the CLOSED sign. If someone wants in, ignore them. Don't bother opening the door. Eventually they'll get the message and go away. If you have to leave before I get back, pull the door shut behind you."

"Will do," Rochelle replied.

Dee and Warren left then, walking out into the warm autumn weather of a late-October Arizona afternoon. They made an incongruous, Jack Sprat sort of couple. Warren was tall and lanky and looked as though he'd never eaten a square meal in his life. Dee was short and almost as wide as she was tall. He wore a faded denim shirt, frayed jeans, and equally worn tennis shoes. Dee's roly-poly figure was swathed in a flowing tie-dyed smock that covered her from her plump neck to the toes of her aging Birkenstocks. The only similarity lay in their hairdos. Both wore their hair pulled back into single braids, although Dee's gun-metal-colored plait was a good two feet longer than Warren's.

The afternoon temperature was a mild eighty-three degrees. Nevertheless, Dee insisted on keeping a reflective sunshade inside the windshield of her elderly Pinto station wagon. Rochelle watched as Warren pulled the sunshade out of the window and stowed it in the backseat. Then he climbed into the rider's side of the multicolored rattletrap vehicle whose dented panels had been painted in vivid shades of lacquer that almost rivaled Deidre's equally multicolored smock. Dee crammed herself behind the steering wheel.

After three separate tries, the touchy old engine finally wheezed to life. Driving with little-old-lady concentration, Dee eased the Pinto into what passed for rush-hour traffic in Bisbee and headed down Tombstone Canyon, leaving Rochelle to marvel at how a plump, wide-faced, oddly dressed white woman had, in the last few months, become both her good friend as well as an enthusiastic and unflagging artistic booster.

It was Dee Canfield who, after seeing Rochelle's paintings, had decided on mounting a one-woman show. "Reminiscent of Norman Rockwell," Dee had pronounced upon viewing Rochelle's collection of work. "People won't be able to keep from buying it. It has that same old-fashioned, uncomplicated look and feel to it. There are a lot of people out there who are sick and tired of so-called artists who throw globs of paint on canvas and pronounce it 'fine art.'"

Rochelle didn't entirely share Dee's confidence about the salability of her work. There was good reason that her paintings were "reminiscent of" Norman Rockwell. As a child growing up in Macon, Georgia, Rochelle had pored over a book—one of her grandmother's coffee-table books—that was chock-full of Norman Rockwell's paintings. She had paged through each picture one by one, focusing all her attention and wonder on the occasional black people she saw depicted there—children and old people and ordinary adults whose appearance resembled her own.

Those few dark-skinned people in the paintings, like Rockwell's other subjects, were caught while engaged in the most mundane of behaviors—standing outside a barbershop, riding in a wagon, playing with a ball, blowing on a harmonica. She had studied each picture with painstaking care, noticing how the artist had used light and dark to create the subtle variations of skin color. She had marveled at how Rockwell had captured intimate scenes in a way that made her feel as though she, too, knew the people depicted there. But most of all, seeing Rockwell's work had made her want to emulate him—to paint her subjects with the same respect and dignity he had accorded those he had painted.

Now Rochelle had. Her paintings were finished and framed and hanging on the walls of Dee's gallery. But would anyone buy them? That she doubted. In a community populated by precious few African-Americans, Shelley wondered how much commercial appeal her work would have. Based on demographics alone, it seemed unlikely to her that there would be an overwhelming demand for the paintings. Still, she had allowed herself to be dragged along by Dee's unbridled enthusiasm as well as by the encouragement and stubborn-minded insistence of her new friend, LaMar Jenkins.

As far as Rochelle knew, LaMar was the only other African-American currently living in Bisbee. Everyone else called him Bobo, but Shelley preferred the quiet dignity of his given name.

If Deidre Canfield was Rochelle's booster and cheerleader, LaMar Jenkins was her champion. It was no accident that the picture she turned to now was one of him, grinning amiably and leaning, with studied ease, against the back gate of his prized bright yellow El Camino. LaMar was a man in his late forties. His well-conditioned, muscle-hardened body may have belied his age, but there was wisdom in the lines that etched his face, and a sprinkling of gray peppered his short-cropped hair. Behind him and just overhead hung a wooden sign that said BLUE MOON SALOON AND LOUNGE, the Brewery Gulch watering hole he had recently sold.

Of all the portraits hanging in the gallery, that was the only one with the telltale red dot that indicated it was already sold. LaMar, subject and purchaser, hadn't wanted the painting to be exhibited at all, but Dee had insisted. For her, having sixteen pieces represented some kind of magic number. Without LaMar's portrait, entitled simply *Car and Driver,* the show would have been one painting short. So there it was.

Looking at it—seeing LaMar's engaging grin and the reined-in strength of his powerful forearms—caused a lump to grow in Rochelle's throat. She had done something she never should have done, something she had countless times forbidden herself to do—she had allowed him to get too close and, as a result, had become too involved. That kind of involvement was dangerous for both of them now that LaMar "Bobo" Jenkins was about to run for mayor of Bisbee.

The next municipal election was almost a year away, but Rochelle understood the necessity of distancing herself now rather than later. Once LaMar Jenkins officially declared his candidacy, he would be newsworthy. He would be an African-American running for office in a town where everyone considered himself part of an oppressed minority. That was bound to attract attention to LaMar as well as to anyone connected with him.

During the months Rochelle Baxter had lived in the community of Naco, Arizona, a few miles outside of Bisbee, she had noticed how the lady county sheriff, Joanna Brady, and her family were routinely covered in both local and statewide media venues. When the sheriff had remarried, the wedding itself had made headlines in the local paper, *The Bisbee Bee*. Sheriff Brady was, after all, a public figure. Several months earlier, when the sheriff's young daughter and a friend had stumbled over the body of a murdered woman while on a Girl Scout campout, that, too, had been front-page fodder—and not just in Bisbee, either.

Rochelle couldn't afford to live in the unblinking focus of a media microscope. Being a part of that kind of associated publicity—where a picture of Rochelle accompanying LaMar to some campaign event might well be beamed all over the country— was something she could ill afford. She had made up her mind. No matter how much it hurt, she would break off the relationship. And the breakup had to come soon. Now. While she could still do it and make it stick.

Sighing, she turned away from LaMar's portrait and wandered through the building to view the other pictures hanging on the freshly painted stuccoed walls. Castle Rock Gallery occupied a series of small buildings that had been cobbled together over time.

Rochelle theorized that a previous owner or owners had added on and stitched the pieces together in a haphazard fashion, as both spirit and funds had allowed. As a result, the rooms—of various sizes and shapes—were arranged with wildly varying floor elevations. With an eye to forestalling a potential lawsuit from some crusading Americans with Disabilities Act activist, Dee and Warren had installed a complex series of ramps that linked the rooms and uneven floor levels together.

Around the corner from LaMar's grinning portrait but in another room altogether hung Rochelle's favorite piece, one titled *A Boy and His Dog*. The two figures sat side by side on the edge of a large porch overlooking a sun-drenched front yard with a tree-lined paved street beyond a picket fence. One of the boy's arms was flung casually across the golden Lab's sturdy shoulder. Sitting with only their backs showing, they were framed by a doorway as though the artist, standing just inside the shadowy house, had painted them from that vantage point.

Of course, the boy was not really "a boy" at all. It was really Tommy, Rochelle's younger brother. And "his dog" was really Scooter. Rochelle remembered coming out through the front door one summer's day and seeing them sitting together like that. Tommy had been only ten at the time and Rochelle twelve. What hadn't shown then—and what didn't show now in the painting—was the leukemia that was already robbing Tommy of his childhood and obliterating his ability to play outdoors on that carefree summer's day. What also didn't show on that warm and lazy Georgia afternoon was how, a few months later, when an ambulance carrying Tommy to the hospital was speeding away from the house, lights flashing and siren blaring, Scooter went racing after it down the street, where he was struck by a car two intersections away. None of that showed in the picture, but it was all there, twenty-three years later, etched deeply into Rochelle's still-grieving heart.

Two pictures away was another favorite. In it, Rochelle's niece, Jolene, crouched, ball in hand, beneath a basketball hoop fastened high over her grandfather's garage door. Her skin gleamed with sweat and her dark eyes glittered with clear determination. Her cornrows shone in the sunlight. The painting was titled *Making a Basket,* although the ball was still poised on the ends of Jolene's fingertips as she prepared to spring upward.

A viewer would simply have to take it on faith that she had actually made the ball swish effortlessly through the hoop, but Rochelle didn't. She knew for sure. She had been there, home on leave after Operation Desert Storm, playing a predinner pickup game with her sister's teenage daughter. Jolene was married now and had two children of her own. Maybe three, for all Rochelle knew, but in her artist's eye, Jolene was still young and innocent and with a world of possibility open to her.

Rochelle moved from one room to another, strolling up and down the various ramps. Standing in front of each painting, she allowed the images she had captured there to speak to her once more. In *The Pastor and the Lamb* she saw her father again. Roundly middle-aged and dressed in his bright red summer preacher's robe, he leaned down to shake hands with a shy little boy who gazed worshipfully up at him over the grubby white Bible he clutched tightly in his other hand.

Next to that picture was one called *Napping.* In it, Rochelle's grandmother, Cornelia, drowsed peacefully in her rocking chair while rays of early-afternoon sunlight streamed in through the sheer window curtains and transformed her silvery hair into a glowing halo.

Around the corner from *Napping* was the *The Carver.* An old man—Rochelle's grandfather, his vitality not yet drained and his mahogany skin not yet tinged with the jaundice of kidney disease—sat on a kitchen chair and sharpened his knife on a soapstone while curls of newly whittled wood littered the floor around his feet.

A few feet away from *The Carver* was *Homecoming*. In that one, Rochelle's mother, dressed in a suit and looking determinedly elegant, walked toward the front steps late one afternoon carrying her leather-bound briefcase balanced effortlessly in one hand. The slight smile on her lips showed that although she loved her work, she was nonetheless grateful to be coming home to her family— to her husband and children.

Concealed under the paint of that picture and three of the others in the gallery was a never-finished self-portrait. Rochelle had tried to paint that one over and over again. Each time she had given up in frustration and covered the unfinished work over with some other painting. That was the magic of working with oils. If a painting didn't come together, you could always render it invisible by burying it under layers of other colors. Gazing at her mother's well-remembered and equally well-rendered features, Rochelle realized why she had never succeeded in painting herself. She knew who her mother was, but when it came to Rochelle Baxter, the artist wasn't so sure.

Sighing, she turned away. Dee had been absolutely right when she said selling the paintings must be like saying good-bye to a group of old friends, but for Rochelle it went far beyond that. In painting the portraits, she had recalled those loved ones from the past and remembered why she had loved them. Now, knowing she would never see any of them again, it seemed as though she was letting go of them forever at the same time she was letting go of their portraits. Hail and farewell.

Finally, it was all too much. Walking through the empty gallery, a half-sob escaped Rochelle's lips and she knew she was about to lose it. That shook her. If it could happen to her when she was all alone in the gallery, how would she manage to maintain her composure tomorrow night at the opening-night party, when the place would be crowded with people, all of them—according to Dee—potential buyers? What would she do if some nice lady asked the artist who that little boy was, sitting on the porch with his dog? And what if someone else wanted to know about that nice old lady napping so peacefully in her rocking chair?

Feeling the first subtle heart-pounding, breath-robbing symptoms of an oncoming panic attack, Rochelle bolted out of Castle Rock Gallery, slamming the door shut behind her. Anxiously she scanned the parking lot, afraid Dee and Warren might return before she could make good her escape. Her closed Camry had been sitting in full afternoon sunlight. Shivering and sweating at the same time, she sank, gasping for breath, into the cloth seat and welcomed the comforting warmth that surrounded her. She grasped the steering wheel and held on, hoping the heated plastic would help still her quaking hands. After a few long minutes, the panic attack subsided enough to allow her to start the car and drive away.

Leaving Old Bisbee behind, she drove past the remains of Lavender Pit, around the traffic circle, and then southwest out of town toward Naco. When her case manager had asked her where she wanted to go—where she would care to settle—Rochelle had chosen the Bisbee area for two reasons: It was known as a place where artists were welcome. It was also surprisingly affordable.

After only a day or two of prowling around, she had stumbled on the tiny border community of Naco, seven miles south of Bisbee proper. She had spotted the FOR SALE sign on a crumbling but thick-walled adobe building that had, in previous incarnations, served as a customhouse, a whorehouse, and—most recently—a nightclub. She had purchased the place and had then remodeled it into part studio, part living quarters. That's where Rochelle headed now—home to Naco.

Mexico's towering San José Mountain loomed in solitary majesty over the valley floor below. Behind it arched a cloudless blue sky. The summer rains had barely materialized that year, leaving all of Arizona brittle and dry. Naco was no exception. Turning off the short and poorly paved main drag, Rochelle entered a dusty dirt alleyway that ran parallel to the paved street. She parked in the makeshift carport that had been tacked on to the back of the building. Bullet holes from the Mexican Revolution still scored some of the adobe bricks that passing time had denuded of countless layers of stucco.

Once out of the car, she hurried to the studio's back entrance. Unlocking the dead bolt, she hurried inside and punched in the code on her alarm keypad. The system had been installed by the previous tenant. In the interest of saving money, she had kept the existing equipment, merely reactivating it and changing the code. Having a security system made her feel safe and allowed her to sleep easier at night.

The interior of the building consisted of two rooms—a bathroom dominated by an old-fashioned claw-footed tub and a large open space that Rochelle had divided into work, sleep, and eating areas by the strategic placement of a series of rustic used-wood screens. Eating, sleeping, and working in that one huge, high-ceilinged room suited her simple needs. In the months since she had moved here from Washington State, while waiting for the other shoe to drop, she had buried herself in her work, toiling at her easel almost around the clock, stopping only when exhaustion finally overwhelmed her now-chronic insomnia. Eating, too, had taken a backseat to feverish work.

A skylight in the middle of the ceiling suffused the white walls and the broad planks of the wooden floor with the soft pink glow of late-afternoon light, but with all the paintings hauled off to Castle Rock Gallery, the studio seemed strangely empty.

Ignoring the loneliness that threatened to engulf her, Rochelle stripped off her clothes and hurried into the bathroom, where she spent the better part of an hour soaking in the long, narrow tub. She had climbed out and was wrapping her hair in a turban when she heard a persistent knocking on the front door. It was times like this when living and working in the same place had its disadvantages. Pulling on a robe and leaving her hair wrapped, she hurried to the door and used the peephole to check on the identity of her visitor. She was dismayed to find LaMar Jenkins standing outside on the makeshift sidewalk. With his hands stuffed deep in his pockets, he rocked back and forth on his heels and looked distinctly unhappy. Sighing, Rochelle unlatched the dead bolt and let him in.

"We were supposed to have dinner tonight," he reminded her in an aggrieved tone as he stepped inside. "You left a message on my machine saying that you couldn't come. What happened? Did somebody make you a better offer?"

"Dee and I hung the show today," Rochelle said lamely. "I knew I'd be tired and probably not very good company."

"I would have been happy to help with the hanging," LaMar said. "Why didn't you ask me?"

Rochelle shrugged and didn't answer. They were standing only inches apart. LaMar Jenkins was a tall man, but his eyes and

Rochelle's were almost on the same level. Feeling guilty and embarrassed, Rochelle was the first to look away.

"Can I get you something to drink?" she offered. "Iced tea? A beer?"

"No fair changing the subject," he said. "But a beer would be fine."

Rochelle walked away from him and disappeared behind the wooden screen that marked the line of demarcation between studio and kitchen. He followed her and took a seat at the old-fashioned Formica-topped table she had purchased from a nearby consignment store. She set a bottle of Bud in front of him, then went to the refrigerator and poured herself a glass of iced tea.

Without being asked, LaMar opened two packages of sweetener and poured them into her glass. It was exactly that kind of unasked courtesy and thoughtfulness that was driving Rochelle away from the man.

It disturbed her to realize that in the few months they had known each other, LaMar Jenkins had learned far too much about her. He knew, for instance, that she took two packets of sweetener in her iced tea, but none at all in her coffee. He knew that she preferred root beer to Coke and smooth peanut butter to any flavor of jelly. He knew she wanted her eggs fried hard and hated refried beans. Those were all little secret things she hadn't wanted anyone to learn about her ever again. That had never been part of her game plan.

"How about a sandwich?" she offered. "Bologna, BLT, tuna. I've got the makings for any or all."

Shaking his head, LaMar reached out, caught her by the wrist, and drew her toward him. "I'm not hungry," he said, pulling her down onto the chair next to his. "And I sure as hell don't want a sandwich. Talk to me, Shelley. Tell me what's wrong."

"Nothing," she said. "I'm just nervous—about the show, I guess."

LaMar studied her, his hooded eyes searching her face. "It's not about the show, is it?" he said accusingly. "You and I have a good thing going, but now you're pulling away from me, shutting me out. I want to know what's going on, and how come?"

"I need some time for myself," she said.

LaMar had been holding her hand. Now he released it and she let it fall limply into her lap. "That's bullshit, and you know it," he growled back at her. "But even if it's true, you still haven't told me why."

Because knowing me is dangerous, Rochelle wanted to say. Because when they come looking for me, they might come looking for you, too.

"You're too intense," she said instead. "And I'm not ready for that." Even as she said the words, her body, in absolute betrayal, longed for nothing so much as to have LaMar Jenkins take her into his strong, capable arms and hold her tightly against his chest. Afraid she might yield to that temptation, she added quickly, "You'd better go."

"Why? Don't you trust me?"

I don't trust myself, she thought. "Something like that."

Taking a long drink from his beer, LaMar Jenkins showed no sign of leaving. "You never talk about the past," he said. "Why is that?"

"The past doesn't matter," she said flatly. "There's nothing to talk about." She tried to sound cold—as though she didn't care—but, like her body, her voice betrayed her. The past mattered far too much.

"Somebody hurt you, Shelley." LaMar's voice was suddenly kind, concerned. "Whoever it was and whatever they did to you, it wasn't me. Let me help fix it. Talk to me."

"You can't fix it," Rochelle said, shaking her head and fighting back tears. "Just go, please."

Without another word, LaMar Jenkins carefully put down his beer bottle and stood up. He walked as far as the first wooden screen before he turned back to her. "I'll see you tomorrow," he said. "At the show. And afterward, we're having dinner. No excuses."

She capitulated. "All right," she said. "We'll have dinner."

"Promise?"

She nodded. "Yes."

He left then. She followed him as far as the door, made sure the dead bolt was locked, and double-checked the alarm system. Then she returned to the kitchen table. For the next half hour, Rochelle Baxter sat at the gray Formica tabletop and thoughtfully sipped her iced tea while rehashing every word that had been said. She didn't bother making herself a sandwich. She wasn't hungry. Instead, she sat and wondered whether or not she would really go to dinner with LaMar after the show. Maybe by then she'd be able to find the resolve to tell him once and for all that she had to break it off.

When her tea was almost gone, Rochelle left the nearly empty glass and half-finished beer bottle sitting on the kitchen table and returned to her eerily denuded studio.

To combat the loneliness left by all the bare walls, Rochelle wrestled a new canvas out of storage and put it on her easel. It sat there staring back at her, waiting for her hands to fill it with color and give it life. Turning away from the empty canvas, she settled down at her drafting table and went through her sketchbooks trying to decide what she would paint next. Finally, around nine or so, she went to bed.

In her dream, she was back in Desert Storm. Oil-well fires,

burning all around her, filled the air with evil-smelling smoke. She couldn't breathe. She felt as if she were choking; her eyes were tearing. What woke her up, though, wasn't the dream. It was a terrible cramping in her gut. Writhing in pain, Rochelle attempted to get out of bed, but before her feet touched the floor, her body heaved. The involuntary spasm hurled a spray of vomit halfway across the room. Falling back onto the bed, she grasped blindly for the phone. Somehow she reached it. Her stabbing fingers seemed numb and out of control, almost as though they belonged to someone else. Struggling desperately to manage her limbs, she finally succeeded in dialing.

"Nine one one," the calm voice of an emergency dispatcher responded. "What is the nature of your emergency?"

By then Rochelle Baxter was beyond answering. Another wild spasm of vomiting hit her and sent her reeling back onto the bed. As she lay there, retching helplessly and unable to move, the phone clattered uselessly to the floor.

"Ma'am?" the operator said more urgently. "Can you hear me? Is there anyone there to help you? Can you tell me your location?"

There was no answer. By then Rochelle Baxter was beyond hearing as well. A few minutes later, medics dispatched by the Cochise County emergency operator arrived at the scene. When no one responded to their repeated knocking, they finally splintered the sturdy front door to gain entry. While a noisy burglar alarm squawked its insistent warning in the background, a young EMT located Rochelle in her vomit-splattered bed. Gingerly, he felt for a pulse, then looked at his supervisor and shook his head.

"We may have already lost her," he said.

One

As Sheriff Joanna Brady drove through the last thicket of mesquite, the house at High Lonesome Ranch lay dark and still under a rising moon. Usually her daughter Jenny's two dogs—Sadie, a bluetick hound, and Tigger, a half golden retriever/half pit-bull mutt—would have bounded through the undergrowth to meet her. This time, Joanna surmised, they had chosen to accompany Butch on his appointment with the contractor at the site of the new house they were planning to build a mile or so away.

Butch had bugged out of St. Dominick's immediately after the service, while he and Joanna waited for the sanctuary to empty. "I'll stay if you want," he had whispered. "But I really need to go."

"Right," she had told him. "You do what you have to. I'll be fine."

"I'll stop by the house and do the chores first," he said. "Don't worry about that."

Joanna had simply nodded. "Thanks," she said.

By then Yolanda Ortiz Cañedo's grieving husband, her two young sons, her parents, brothers, and sister were walking out of the church through two lines of saluting officers made up of both police and fire department personnel. Joanna could barely stand to watch. It was all too familiar, too close to her own experience. As her green eyes filled with tears, Joanna glanced away, only to catch sight of the prisoners. That forlorn group—eleven county prisoners, freshly barbered and dressed in civilian clothes—stood in respectful silence under the watchful eyes of two jail guards and Ted Chapman, the executive director of the Cochise County Jail Ministry.

Ted had come to Joanna's office the day after the young jail matron had died of cervical cancer at a hospice facility in Tucson. "Some of the inmates would like to go to the services," Chapman had said. "Yolanda Cañedo did a lot of good around here. She really cared about the guys she worked with, and it showed. She helped me get the jail literacy program going, and she came in during off-hours to give individual help to prisoners who were going after GEDs. Some of the people she helped—inmates who have already been released—will be there on their own, but the ones who are still in lockup wanted me to ask if they could go, too. The newer prisoners, the ones who came in after Yolanda got sick, aren't included, of course. They have no idea who she was or what she did."

"What about security?" Sheriff Brady had asked. "Who's going to stand guard?"

"I already have two volunteers who will come in on their day off," Chapman answered. "You have my word of honor, along with that of the prisoners, that there won't be any trouble."

Joanna thought about how good some of the jail inmates'

words of honor might be. But then she also had to consider the notebook full of greetings—handmade by jail inmates—that Reverend Chapman had brought to Yolanda and her family as the young woman had lain gravely ill in the Intensive Care Unit at University Medical Center in Tucson. Sheriff Brady had been touched by the heartfelt sincerity in all those clumsily pasted-together cards. Several of them had been made by men able to sign their own names at the bottom of a greeting card for the very first time. Other cards had names printed by someone else under scrawled Xs. Their good wishes had seemed genuine enough back then. Now, so did the Reverend Chapman's somewhat unorthodox request.

"How many inmates are we talking about?" Joanna had asked.

"Fourteen."

"Any of them high-risk?"

"I don't think so."

"Give me the list," Joanna had conceded at last. "I'm not making any promises, but I'll run the proposition by the jail commander and see what he has to say."

In the end, eleven of the proposed inmates had been allowed to attend the service. In his eulogy, Father Morris had spoken of Yolanda Cañedo as a remarkable young woman. Certainly the presence of that solemn collection of inmates bore witness to that. And, as far as Joanna could tell, the prisoners' behavior had been nothing short of exemplary.

They stood now in a single straight row. With feet splayed apart and hands clasped behind their backs, they might have been a troop of soldiers standing at ease. Seeing them there, dignified and silent in the warm afternoon sun, Joanna was glad she had vetoed the jail commander's suggestion that they attend the funeral wearing handcuffs and shackles.

Chief Deputy Frank Montoya came up behind her then. "Hey, boss," he whispered in her ear. "They're putting the casket into the hearse. Since we're supposed to be directly behind the family cars, we'd better mount up."

Nodding, Joanna left the inmates to the care of the two guards and Ted Chapman and walked back toward Frank's waiting Crown Victoria. Even in heels, the five-foot-four sheriff felt dwarfed as she made her way through the crush of uniformed officers. A light breeze riffled her short red hair.

"Looks like the members of Reverend Chapman's flock are behaving themselves," her chief deputy observed, as he started the Civvie's engine.

"So far so good," Joanna agreed.

"But they're not coming to the cemetery?"

Joanna shook her head. "No. Having them at the church is one thing, but going to the cemetery is something else. If there's any confusion, I was afraid one or more of them might slip away."

"You've got that right," Frank agreed. "We don't need to give your friend Ken Junior anything else to piss and moan about."

"Since when does he need a reason?" Joanna returned.

Ken Junior, otherwise known as Deputy Kenneth Galloway, was Sheriff Brady's current problem child. He was the nephew and namesake of another Deputy Galloway, one who had been part of a network of corrupt police officers in the administration that had immediately preceded Joanna's. The elder Galloway had died as a result of wounds received during an armed confrontation with Joanna Brady. Although Joanna had been cleared of any wrongdoing in that incident, the dead man's relatives continued to hold her responsible for Galloway's death.

Although the younger man was the deceased deputy's nephew rather than his son, around the department, he was referred to as

Ken Junior. Fresh out of the Arizona Police Academy at the time of his uncle's death, the younger Galloway had been far too new and inexperienced to have taken an active part in the police corruption that had marred Sheriff Walter V. McFadden's administration. For that reason, Ken Junior had been allowed to stay on as a Cochise County deputy sheriff. Never a great supporter of Joanna's, he had quickly gravitated to union activism and had recently been elected president of Local 83 of the National Federation of Deputy Sheriffs.

In recent months Joanna had clashed with Ken Junior twice regarding Yolanda Cañedo's illness. The first confrontation had occurred when Joanna suggested that members of the union ought to do at least as much for the Cañedo family as the jail inmates had. The second had happened only a few days earlier, as the Cañedo family had struggled to make arrangements for Yolanda's funeral.

Deputy Galloway had balked at Joanna's insistence on giving Yolanda the honor of an official Fallen Officer funeral. Ken Junior had taken the position that, as a mere jail matron, Yolanda Cañedo didn't qualify as a real Fallen Officer. Joanna had gone to the mat with him on that score. Only over his vociferous objections had two lines of smartly saluting officers greeted Yolanda's grieving family as they exited St. Dominick's Church after the funeral.

Led by two Arizona Department of Public Safety motorcycle officers, the hearse pulled away from the curb. One by one the other members of the funeral cortege formed up behind them for the slow, winding trip down Tombstone Canyon to Bisbee's Evergreen Cemetery two miles away. The ceremony in the cemetery was the part of the service Joanna had steeled herself for. She dreaded the symbolic Last Call and the moment when she would be required to take a carefully folded American flag and deliver it into Leon Cañedo's hands.

She remembered too clearly another bright fall afternoon, not so different from this one, when Walter V. McFadden had placed a similarly folded flag in Joanna's trembling hands at the close of Andy's graveside services.

During the ride down the canyon and around Lavender Pit, Joanna was glad her daughter, Jenny, wouldn't be at the cemetery. Once again she had reason to be thankful for her former mother-in-law's kindness and wisdom. Eva Lou Brady had called High Lonesome Ranch early that morning.

"Let Jenny come stay with Jim Bob and me tonight," Eva Lou had urged. "After what happened to Andy, Yolanda's funeral is going to be difficult enough for you. It'll be even harder on Jen. I'll have Jim Bob pick her up after school so she's here with us before the service gets started. That way she won't have to see the hearse and the cars pulling into the cemetery. We'll take her out for pizza and try to keep her occupied."

Lowell School, where Jenny attended seventh grade, was situated directly across the street from Evergreen Cemetery. Not only that, Joanna had been dismayed the day before when she drove by the cemetery and noticed that the plot Leon Cañedo had chosen was fully visible from some of Jenny's classroom windows.

Bearing all that in mind, Joanna had readily agreed to her former mother-in-law's suggestion. Now, driving into her own front yard and seeing the darkened house, Joanna was even more grateful. This was a night when she needed a buffer between home and work. The killer combination of funeral, wailing bagpipes, graveside service, and church-sponsored reception afterward had stretched Sheriff Joanna Brady's considerable resources to the breaking point. Had Butch or Jenny asked about Yolanda Cañedo's funeral, Joanna would likely have dissolved in tears.

The motion-activated light above the garage flashed on, illu-

minating Joanna's way from the car to the house. The afternoon
had been warm, but as soon as the sun went down, there was a
hint of fall in the air. Once inside, Joanna hurried to the bedroom,
where she stripped off her clothing and weapons. She locked away
her two Glocks and pulled on a thick terry-cloth robe. Headed for
the kitchen, she was stopped halfway there by a ringing phone.

"How did it go?" the Reverend Marianne Maculyea asked.
"And how are you doing?"

Joanna's friendship with Marianne dated from when the two
of them had been preadolescent students at the same school Jenny
now attended. Married and the mother of two, Marianne was also
pastor at Tombstone Canyon United Methodist Church, where
Joanna and Butch were members. She was the only person to
whom Joanna had confided her concerns about attending and par-
ticipating in Yolanda Cañedo's funeral service.

"I'm all right," Joanna replied grimly. "But it was tough."

"You don't *sound* all right," Marianne observed.

"No, I suppose not," Joanna said. "The Last Call was bad, but
when I had to give Leon the flag, I really choked up. If I could have
come home right then, maybe it wouldn't have been so bad.
Instead, I had to go back up to the church and stay through the
whole reception. That almost killed me, Mari. Yolanda's sons,
Manny and Frankie, were there in their white shirts and blue
slacks and little bow ties. They're such cute kids, but they're so
lost and hurt right now, I could hardly stand to look at them, to say
nothing of speak to them. What do you say to kids like that? What
can you say?"

"You say what's in your heart," Marianne Maculyea replied.
"I'm sure seeing them bothered you that much more because it
made you think about what it was like for Jenny during Andy's
funeral."

Marianne Maculyea's on-the-money comment left Joanna with nothing to say. After a moment of silence, Marianne added, "Speaking of Jenny, how is she?"

"Fine, I'm sure," Joanna replied. "She's with Grandma and Grandpa Brady. Eva Lou called this morning and invited her to spend the night. They're going out for pizza. I wish Eva Lou had asked me to join them. For two cents I would have ditched the reception and eaten pizza instead."

"You *had* to go to the reception, Joanna," Marianne reminded her. "It's your job."

"I know," Joanna said hollowly. "But I sure didn't like it."

There was another pause. In the background on Marianne's end of the phone, Joanna heard a murmur of voices. "I'd better run," she said. "Jeff needs help with baths. I just wanted to be sure you're okay."

"I'm fine," Joanna said with more conviction than she felt, because she wasn't fine at all. And what was bothering her most was something she wasn't ready to discuss with anyone—including Marianne Maculyea. Or with Butch Dixon, either, for that matter.

Putting down the phone, Joanna wandered into the kitchen, where she opened the refrigerator door and peered inside. The ladies' auxiliary of St. Dominick's had put on an amazing spread, but Joanna had eaten none of it. And now none of Butch's carefully maintained leftovers looked remotely appetizing, either. Giving up, she pulled a carton of milk out of the fridge and then rummaged in the pantry for a box of Honey Nut Cheerios. Armed with cereal, a bowl, and a spoon, she settled into the breakfast nook. After a few bites she lost interest in the cereal and found herself staring, unseeing, at the game CD taped to the outside of the box.

"Damn Ken Galloway anyway!" she muttered.

He was the main reason she had been heartsick at the funeral reception. Joanna was sure it was due to arm-twisting on his part that so few deputies from her department had been in attendance. In addition to Frank Montoya, only one other deputy—a relatively new hire named Debra Howell—had defied peer pressure and come to the reception.

Not that the Cochise County Sheriff's Department hadn't been represented. All jail personnel who weren't on duty had turned up, including the two guards who had escorted the inmates to the funeral earlier. And there had been plenty of representation by support staff—the clerks and secretaries who worked in the offices, crime lab, and evidence room. Casey Ledford, Joanna's fingerprint technician, had been there, along with all but one of the emergency dispatch operators. And there were plenty of officers from other jurisdictions who had shown up out of courtesy. As a group, however, the deputies from Cochise County were notable in their absence.

Only half of Joanna's detective division had shown up, but that was understandable. Jaime Carbajal's eleven-year-old son, Pepe, played on the same Little League team as Yolanda Cañedo's older son, Frankie. So Jaime and his wife, Delcia, had both been there. Detective Ernie Carpenter's absence had nothing to do with Ken Galloway's political machinations; he was on vacation. Ernie had reluctantly agreed to take his wife, Rose, on a weeklong trip to Branson, Missouri, in celebration of their thirtieth wedding anniversary.

So Ken Galloway hadn't managed to keep everyone away. Still, at a time when Joanna needed the entire department to pull in the same direction, she was upset that the head of the deputies' union local seemed determined to drive wedges among members of her department. She worried that eventually those small wedges might splinter her employees into warring factions.

The phone rang. As Joanna picked up the extension on the kitchen counter, she caught sight of the Cochise County Dispatch number on the caller ID. "Sheriff Brady here," she said. "What's up?"

"A 911 call came in a little while ago from down in Naco," Dispatch operator Tica Romero reported. "When the EMTs arrived, they found a nonresponsive African-American female. They transported her to the hospital and did their best to revive her, but she was DOA."

Joanna Brady felt the familiar clutch in her gut. Something bad had happened in her jurisdiction. It was time to go to work. "Any sign of foul play?" she asked.

"No. The general assumption is natural causes. The victim had evidently been terribly ill. There was no sign of forced entry—until the EMTs had to break in to get to her, that is. The place was locked up tight, and the screeching security alarm almost drove the medics nuts while they were working on her."

"They closed everything back up once they left?" Joanna asked.

"The night-watch commander is sending a deputy out to make sure that's taken care of."

"Good," Joanna said. "What about the body?"

"The woman's young," Tica Romero replied. "Somewhere in her thirties. The hospital has asked Doc Winfield to take charge of the body and do an autopsy, just to make sure that whatever she had isn't transmittable. Since the ME's been called out on the case, he'll handle next-of-kin notification."

Joanna allowed her body to relax. Dr. George Winfield, Cochise County's medical examiner, was married to Joanna's mother, Eleanor. Unfortunately, George would have more on his hands than simply unmasking the cause of death, communicable or not, and locating next of kin. He'd also have to explain to his demanding wife why he was going back to work at eleven o'clock on a weekday evening.

"Better him than me," Joanna murmured.

"Have to go," Tica said urgently. "Another call's coming in."

Joanna took the phone back over to the table with her. By then, her once-crispy Cheerios had turned soggy. She went out to the laundry room and dumped the remainder, dividing it evenly between the two dog bowls. She was straightening up from doing that when Butch's Outback pulled into the yard. She waited on the porch, watching as he opened the luggage-gate door, letting Sadie and Tigger bound out onto the ground. Together the dogs raced to the water dish and eagerly lapped up what sounded like a gallon of water each.

"You're spoiling them," she said, kissing Butch hello. "Sadie and Tigger are ranch dogs, remember? They're supposed to run, not ride."

"They ran from here over to Clayton's place," Butch said.

That was how they still, months after his death, referred to the ranch Joanna's octogenarian handyman, Clayton Rhodes, had left them in his will.

"When it was time to come home," Butch continued, "Tigger was the only one hot to trot. Sadie wasn't interested. Once I let her into the car and Tigger figured out she was riding, he wanted a ride, too."

"Sibling rivalry," Joanna said with a smile. "But like I said, you're spoiling them. Did you eat anything?"

"I had a sandwich when I got home from the funeral. What about you?"

"I just fixed myself a bowl of cereal."

"Not very substantial," Butch observed.

"It was all I wanted."

He studied her face closely. "Are you okay?" he asked.

Joanna shrugged. "Going to law enforcement funerals isn't exactly my favorite afternoon pastime."

Butch opened the refrigerator and took out a beer. "Do you want anything?"

"Nothing," Joanna said. "Thanks. I'm fine."

"You don't look fine."

"I just got off the phone with Dispatch," she replied. "The EMTs hauled a DOA up to Copper Queen Hospital from Naco a little while ago."

"Does that mean you have to go back out?"

Joanna shook her head. "No. Tica Romero said it looks like natural causes. The woman was evidently terribly sick. She's George's problem now, not mine."

"Thank God for small favors," Butch muttered.

"What's going on with the house? Have you been working with Quentin all this time?"

Quentin Branch was the contractor Joanna and Butch had hired to build their new rammed-earth home.

"No," Butch said. "The meeting didn't last that long, but there were things I needed to do. Puttering, mostly. Making myself useful."

While Joanna was having trouble at work with Ken Galloway, Butch Dixon was dealing with his own identity crisis. He had yet to adjust to his relatively new role as stay-at-home spouse. He had completed writing his first mystery novel, but now, while he lived through the interminable months of waiting to see if a literary agency would agree to handle his work, Butch had tackled the job of overseeing construction on the house.

Quentin Branch would be in charge of the major aspects of the job. Butch was doing some of the hand excavation and finish carpentry. It was a way of passing time and keeping his hand in. Joanna had seen Butch's previous remodeling projects. She had no doubt as to his ability, and his do-it-yourself skill would wring more than full value out of their home-building dollars. Her only qualm had to do with how long the process would take.

Butch finished his beer, and they went to bed. Within minutes, Butch was snoring softly on his side of the bed while Joanna lay awake and wrestled with the Devil in the guise of Ken Galloway. She was sorry now that she hadn't answered truthfully when Butch had asked what was bothering her. He might have had some useful suggestions about dealing with the recalcitrant president of Local 83. Still, Ken Junior was Joanna's problem and nobody else's. If she hauled him on the carpet again and made an issue of the deputies' collective snub of the funeral reception, it would probably do more harm than good. For all concerned. It certainly wouldn't make things any easier for Leon Cañedo, and it wouldn't improve intradepartmental relations, either.

The last time Joanna looked at the clock, it was nearly two in the morning. A ringing telephone jarred her awake at ten past seven. Butch was already long gone from his side of the bed when Joanna opened her eyes and groped for the bedside phone.

"Hope I didn't waken you," George Winfield said.

"That's all right," Joanna mumbled sleepily. "It's time for me to be up anyway. What's going on?"

"It's about that DOA from last night," the medical examiner said.

Joanna forced herself to sit up. "What about her?" she asked.

"The name's Rochelle Baxter," George returned. "Her driver's license says she's thirty-five. My preliminary examination says she was in good health."

"What did she die of?"

"I don't know. I thought you might want to have a detective on hand when I do the autopsy, just in case."

"In case of what?"

"In case she was poisoned."

Joanna was wide awake now. "You think she was murdered?"

"I didn't say that. But for an apparently healthy woman to become as violently ill as she was, I'm thinking she may have ingested something."

"What about the water?" Joanna asked. "Could contaminated water have made her that sick?"

For years the local water system had been under investigation by the Arizona Department of Ecology due to sewage from across the line in Old Mexico that had been allowed to seep into the water table and possibly contaminate the wells that provided water for the entire Bisbee area. Lack of money, combined with lack of enthusiasm, had resulted in nothing much being done.

"It could be, but I doubt it," George replied.

"What are you saying—it's a homicide?"

"At this time I won't say anything more than it's a suspicious death," George said. "But if you're not treating the victim's place as a crime scene, Joanna, you probably should."

"Thanks," Joanna said. "I'll get right on it. When are you planning to do the autopsy?"

"As soon as you can have one of your detectives up at my office. I'm here now. I'd like to get started as soon as possible."

"Ernie's on vacation, so it'll have to be Jaime," Joanna said.

"I'll get ahold of him at home and give him a heads-up. Thanks for the call, George."

"Just doing my job."

Butch appeared at the bedroom door carrying a mug of coffee. "What's up?"

"The DOA from last night just turned into what George is calling 'a suspicious death.' In case it turns out to be a homicide, I've got to get Jaime to witness the autopsy. The victim's home down in Naco needs to be designated as a crime scene and then investigated."

Butch glanced at the clock, which now showed twenty past seven, and shook his head ruefully. "Sounds like a full day to me. Joey, don't you sometimes wish you had a regular nine-to-five job?" he asked, handing Joanna her coffee.

She shook her head.

"Okay, then. Breakfast in fifteen minutes, whether you need it or not."

Chief Deputy Frank Montoya usually arrived at the department by seven in order to get incident reports lined up for the morning briefing at eight-thirty. Joanna dialed his direct number and was relieved to hear his cheerful "Good morning."

"You know about the DOA from Naco?" she asked.

"I was just reading the report," Frank replied. "The EMTs made it sound like natural causes."

"Doc Winfield doesn't think so," Joanna replied. "We need Casey and Dave down there right away." Dave Hollicker, having just completed a strenuous course of training, had moved out of patrol into the newly created position of crime scene investigator.

"I'll get right on it," Frank told her.

"Anything earth-shattering for the morning briefing?"

"Nothing."

"Good," Joanna said. "In that case, we'll put it off until afternoon. You hold down the fort there. When I leave the house, I'll go straight to the crime scene."

"Fair enough," Frank said.

Once showered and dressed, Joanna hurried into the kitchen, where eggs and bacon and freshly squeezed orange juice were already on the table. Butch stood at the kitchen counter buttering toast with the smooth economy of a well-practiced cook.

"Jenny called while you were showering," he said. Joanna reached for the phone. "Don't bother trying to reach her," Butch told her. "Jenny said Jim Bob was taking her to school early. Something about play practice. There are two rehearsals today, both before school and again this evening."

"She's all right then?" Joanna asked.

Butch shrugged. "She sounded okay to me."

He brought a plate of toast over to the table and set it down. "I suppose this means we won't be having lunch at Daisy's," he added.

"Why not?"

"Come on, Joanna," Butch said, rubbing his clean-shaven head with one hand. Joanna recognized the gesture for what it was—unspoken exasperation. "You know as well as I do. If there's a murder investigation under way, you won't pause long enough to breathe, let alone eat."

Butch's complaint sounded familiar—like something Eleanor Lathrop might have said to Joanna's father when D.H. Lathrop was sheriff of Cochise County.

"We don't know for sure it's a homicide," Joanna countered. "Right this minute, I don't see any reason to call off lunch."

"When you call to cancel later," Butch said, "I won't forget to say 'I told you so.'"

DR. GEORGE WINFIELD DIDN'T LIKE making next-of-kin notifications over the phone, but hours of fruitless searching for Rochelle Baxter's relatives had left him little choice. DMV records had yielded a bogus address with a working phone number.

"Washington State Attorney General's Office," a businesslike voice responded.

Hearing that, Doc Winfield was convinced the phone number was wrong as well. "I'm looking for someone named Lawrence Baxter," he said.

There was a long pause. "One moment, please," the woman said. "Let me connect you with Mr. Todd's office."

"Did you say Mr. Todd?" Doc managed before she cut him off.

"Yes." She was gone before he could ask anything more. After an interminable wait, a man's voice came on the line. "O.H. Todd," he said brusquely. "To whom am I speaking?"

"My name's Winfield. Dr. George Winfield. There's probably been a mistake. I'm looking for someone named Lawrence Baxter, but they connected me to you instead."

"Baxter!" O.H. Todd exclaimed. "What do you want with him?"

"You know him then?" George asked hopefully.

"Why do you need him?" Todd demanded. "Who are you again?"

"Dr. George Winfield," he explained patiently. "I'm the medical examiner in Cochise County, Arizona. I'm calling about Mr. Baxter's daughter, Rochelle. If you could simply tell me how to reach him—"

"Something's the matter with her?" the man interrupted. "Why? What's happened?"

George Winfield sighed. This was all wrong. "I'm sorry to have to deliver the news in this fashion," he said finally. "Over the phone, I mean. But Ms. Baxter is dead. She died last night."

For a long moment, all George heard was stark silence. Just as the ME was beginning to think he'd been disconnected, O.H. Todd breathed a single word.

"Damn!" he muttered, sounding for all the world like he meant it.

Two

D RIVING PAST THE Cochise County Justice Center on
her way to the Naco, Arizona, crime scene, Joanna wondered
about her own motives. Had she opted to go to the crime
scene in order to avoid the members of her department who
had boycotted the funeral reception? She had anticipated that
countywide politics was a necessary part of being elected to the
office of sheriff. What she hadn't expected were the political
machinations within the department itself.

She had managed to dodge the obstacles her former chief
deputy Dick Voland had rolled into her path. Once he resigned
from the department, Joanna had thought her troubles were over.
She knew now that had simply been wishful thinking. Politics was
everywhere—inside the department and out. She had to accept
that reality and learn to work around it.

Fifteen minutes after leaving High Lonesome Ranch, Joanna
pulled in behind a fleet of departmental cars parked at the corner

of South Tower and West Valenzuela in the tiny hamlet of Naco. The front door of an aging stucco building stood ajar. When Joanna knocked, Detective Carbajal appeared in the doorway.

"Morning, boss," he said.

"What are you doing here?" she asked. "I thought you were with the ME."

Jaime nodded. "I thought so, too. Then Doc Winfield called to say there would be a slight delay. I had an extra forty minutes, so I thought I'd come see what's what." He moved aside and allowed Joanna to enter. "We left the door open in hopes of airing the place out," he added, handing her the crime scene log. "You may not want to come in."

As Joanna stepped into the large open room, she understood at once what Jaime meant. The all-pervading stench of stale vomit assailed her nostrils. When she finished signing the log, Jaime passed her a mask and a small jar of Vicks VapoRub.

"Thanks," she said, dabbing some on her upper lip. "Now where?"

"Dave Hollicker is over there in what passes for a bedroom," Jaime Carbajal said, pointing. "That's where the EMTs found the victim. She'd been sick as a dog all over her bed and most of the room as well. Casey's in the kitchen lifting prints."

"What's the victim's name again?"

Jaime checked his notebook. "Rochelle Ida Baxter. Age thirty-five. The EMTs found a purse with a driver's license and gave the information to Doc Winfield."

"Any sign of robbery?"

Jaime shook his head. "Negative on that. They found eighty dollars and some change in her purse, along with a full contingent of credit cards. She was wearing two rings when she was taken to the hospital, and nothing around here looks disturbed. No broken glass. It's not looking good for a robbery motive."

"Forced entry?" Joanna asked.

"That's a little harder to tell, but I don't think so," Jaime said. "Both front and back doors were locked when the ambulance arrived, so the EMTs had to break in. If the lock on the front door was damaged prior to that, there'd be no way to separate EMT damage from any that might have occurred previously. There's an alarm system that went off like a banshee while the medics were here. I've already checked with the alarm company. Their monitoring system shows no disturbance prior to the arrival of the emergency personnel."

Following Jaime's directions, and with the smell of vomit no longer actively engaging her gag reflexes, Joanna moved to the bedroom area. The bed had been stripped down to bare mattress, and Dave Hollicker was in the process of rolling up a soiled bedside rug. The place didn't resemble a crime scene so much as it did a hospital room, emptied of one desperately ill patient and awaiting the arrival of another. Joanna was relieved to see that most of the mess had been cleaned up prior to her arrival.

"How's it going, Dave?"

He finished bagging the rug and placed it in a stack of similarly full and tightly closed bags before answering. "I've taken photographs and bagged everything I could. Once I load this stuff into the van, I'll come back and start looking for hair and fibers."

"How's the print work coming?"

Dave Hollicker shrugged. "Beats me. You'll have to ask Casey. I've been in here most of the time."

"I'll go see," Joanna said, heading for the screens she assumed walled off the kitchen. The great room glowed with natural

morning light that streamed in through an overhead skylight. Off
to one side stood a large wooden easel. On it hung a starkly empty
canvas. Joanna paused in front of it, struck by the fact that the person who had placed the canvas there was no longer alive to color
it. Whatever scene Rochelle Ida Baxter had intended to paint there
would never materialize. Next to the easel squatted a paint-
blotched taboret. The top drawer sat slightly open, revealing neat
rows of paint tubes. On the back of the taboret was a collection of
oddly sized jars. In them brushes of various sizes stood with their
bristles up, waiting to be taken up and used once more.

"Our victim's an artist then?" Joanna asked, turning back to
Jaime Carbajal.

The detective nodded. "Evidently," he said, "although you
couldn't prove it by what's here. So far I haven't found anything
but a few sketchbooks and more empty canvases just like the one
on the easel. Maybe she was an artist who hadn't quite gotten
around to actually doing any painting."

Joanna looked at the floor underneath the easel, where more
daubs of paint stained the white planks of the floor. "She'd been
painting, all right," Joanna observed. "There must be finished canvases around here somewhere. Keep looking."

When Joanna poked her head into the kitchen area, Casey
Ledford was carefully brushing fine black powder onto the
smooth gray surface of an old-fashioned Formica-topped table.

"How's it going?" Joanna asked.

Pursing her lips in concentration, Casey smoothed a strip of
clear tape onto the powder before she answered. "All right," she
said. "Good morning, Sheriff," she added.

Carefully peeling it back, Casey smoothed the black-smudged
clear tape onto a stiff manila card. After holding the card up and
examining it, she put it back down. On the top of the card she jot-

ted a series of notations about where and when the prints had been found. Then she tossed the tagged card into an open brief-case that already held many others just like it.

"From what I'm seeing here," Casey said, "I'd say our victim had company last night. We found an almost empty glass and a partially emptied beer bottle sitting on the table. Dave bottled up the remaining contents from the glass. He'll take that back to the lab. I picked up two distinctly different sets of prints from both the bottle and the glass, and from the table, too. Assuming one set belongs to the victim, it's possible the other one could belong to the perp. We'll take the glass, the bottle, and whatever else is in the trash back to the department. Together Dave and I will go through it all. I'll look for prints; he'll look for anything else. Oh, and at Doc Winfield's suggestion, we'll be taking all the foodstuffs from here in the kitchen as well."

Joanna nodded. As she often did these days, she had chosen to wear a uniform. Not wanting to disturb evidence, she stood in the middle of the kitchen area with her hands in her pockets. The room was tiny, but orderly. The cupboards were the kind that come, ready to be hung, from discount lumber stores. The table, a fridge, and a small apartment-size stove made for a kitchen that was functional enough, but one that had been put together by someone focused on neither cooking nor eating.

"Have you collected water samples?" Joanna asked.

"Dave did that first thing."

Just then Joanna heard the sound of a woman's voice, raised in anger, coming from the other side of the screen. "What do you mean, I can't come in? What's going on here? What's happened?"

Back in the studio, Joanna found Detective Carbajal standing in the doorway and barring the entry of a solidly built woman who kept trying to dodge past him.

"I'm sorry, ma'am," Jaime was saying. "This is a crime scene. No one is allowed inside."

"Crime scene!" the woman repeated. "Crime scene? What kind of crime? What's happened? Where's Rochelle?"

Removing her mask, Joanna walked up behind her detective, close enough to glimpse a heavyset woman whose long gray hair was caught in a single braid that fell over one shoulder and dangled as far as her waist. She was swathed from head to toe in a loose-flowing, tie-dyed smock.

"I'm Sheriff Joanna Brady," Joanna explained, stepping into view. "We're investigating a suspicious death here. Who are you?"

"Death?" the woman repeated, wide-eyed. "Somebody died here? But what about Rochelle? Where's she? Certainly Shelley isn't—"

Suddenly the woman broke off. She blanched. One hand went to her mouth, and she wavered unsteadily on her feet. Up to then, Jaime Carbajal had been steadfastly trying to keep her outside. Now, as she swayed in front of him, he stepped forward and grasped her by one elbow. Then he led her into the great room and eased her onto a nearby stool. For a moment, no one spoke.

"I take it Rochelle Baxter is a friend of yours?" Joanna asked softly.

The woman glanced wordlessly from Joanna's face to Jaime's. Finally she nodded.

"I'm sorry to have to tell you this, then," Joanna continued. "Rochelle Baxter fell gravely ill last night. She called 911, but by the time emergency personnel reached her, she was unresponsive. She was declared dead on arrival at the hospital."

The woman began to shake her head, wagging it desperately back and forth, as though by simply denying what she'd been told she could keep it from being true. "That can't be," she moaned. "It's not possible."

By now Jaime had his spiral notebook out of his pocket. "Your name, please, ma'am?"

"Canfield," the woman answered in a cracked whisper. "Deidre Canfield. Most people call me Dee."

"And your relationship to Miss Baxter?"

"We were friends. I own an art gallery up in Old Bisbee—the Castle Rock Gallery. It's where Shelley was going to have her first-ever show tonight . . ." Dee Canfield's voice faltered, and she burst into tears. "Oh, no," she wailed. "This can't be. It's so awful, so . . . unfair. It isn't happening."

For several long moments, Joanna and Jaime Carbajal simply looked on, waiting for Dee Canfield to master her emotions. Finally, pulling a man's hanky out from under a bra strap, she blew her nose. "Has anyone told Bobo yet?"

Joanna knew of only one person in the Bisbee area with that distinctive name. "You mean Bobo Jenkins?" Joanna asked quickly. "The former owner of the Blue Moon Saloon and Lounge?"

Dee nodded. "That's the one."

"What's his relationship to Miss Baxter?" Jaime asked.

Dee shrugged in a manner that suggested she thought Bobo Jenkins's relationship with Rochelle Baxter was nobody else's business. Jaime, however, insisted. "Would you say they were friends?" he asked.

Dee paused for several moments before answering. "More than friends, I suppose," she conceded.

"They were going together?" Joanna suggested.

"Yes."

"For how long?"

"I don't know exactly. Several months now. Bobo is the one who introduced Shelley to me."

"Had there been any trouble between them?" Jaime asked. "Any disagreements?"

"No!" Dee Canfield declared staunchly. "Not at all. Nothing like that."

"You mentioned Rochelle's show is scheduled to open at your gallery tonight," Joanna said quietly. "Is that why you stopped by this morning?"

"No," Dee replied. "Thursday mornings are when I come down to get gas. I have a Pinto, you see," she explained. "It still uses leaded. Once a week I come down here, go across the line to Old Mexico, and fill up in Naco, Sonora. I usually stop by to see Shelley, coming or going. We have a cup of coffee and indulge in girl talk. When Shelley worked, she'd isolate herself completely. A little chitchat is what I used to drag her back into the real world."

"If Rochelle Baxter is an artist, why don't we see any paintings here?" Jaime Carbajal asked.

"Because everything's up at the show. Oh my God!" Deidre Canfield wailed. "What am I going to do about that? Should I cancel it? Have the opening anyway? And who's going to tell Bobo?"

"My department will notify Mr. Jenkins," Joanna reassured her. "We'll need to talk to him anyway. But when it comes to deciding whether or not to cancel the show, you're on your own."

Dee nodded and swallowed hard. "Rochelle was such a talented young woman," she said, dabbing at her tears. "This was her very first show, you see, and she was so excited about it—excited and nervous, too."

"Did she complain to you about feeling ill?"

"Ill? You mean was she sick? Absolutely not. We worked

together all day long yesterday—Shelley, Warren, and I. She certainly would have told me if she wasn't feeling well."

"Who's Warren?" Jaime asked.

"Warren Gibson. My boyfriend. He helps out around the gallery. I'm the brains of the outfit. He's the brawn."

Just outside Dee Canfield's line of vision, Jaime caught Joanna's eye and motioned toward his watch, indicating he needed to head for his autopsy appointment at Doc Winfield's office.

"Detective Carbajal has to leave now," Joanna explained. "But if you don't mind, I'd like to ask you a few more questions."

"Okay," Dee said. "I'm happy to tell you whatever you need to know. I want to help, but I'll have to leave soon, too, so I can make arrangements about the show."

As Jaime hurried out the front door, Dave Hollicker appeared from behind one of the screens lugging two heavy bags. Joanna took Dee's elbow, helped her off the stool, and escorted her outside.

"It might be better if we talk out here," Joanna said, taking her own notebook out of her purse. "Now tell me, Ms. Canfield, how long have you known Rochelle Baxter?"

"Five months or so," Dee answered. "As I said, Bobo Jenkins met her first—I'm not sure how—and he introduced us. He knew I was getting ready to open the gallery. He thought Shelley and I would hit it off. Which we did, of course. She was such a nice person, for an ex-Marine, that is. I'm more into peace and love," Dee added with a self-deprecating smile. "But then, by the time Shelley made it to Bisbee, so was she—into peace and love, I mean."

"Where did she come from?"

Dee Canfield frowned. "This may sound strange, but I'm not sure. The way she talked about being glad to be out of the rain, it could have been somewhere in the Northwest, but she never did say for certain. I asked her once or twice, but she didn't like to talk about it, so I just let it be. I had the feeling that she had walked away from some kind of bad news—probably a creep of an ex-husband—but I didn't press her. I figured she'd get around to telling me one of these days, if she wanted to, that is." Dee frowned. "Now that I think about it, maybe she has," she added thoughtfully.

"What do you mean?"

Dee countered with a question of her own. "What do you know about art?"

"Not much," Joanna admitted. "I had to take the humanities course at the university, but that's about all."

"Remember that old saw about writers writing about what they know?"

Joanna nodded.

"The same thing goes for artists," Dee continued. "They paint what they know. Shelley painted portraits. Her subjects glow with the kind of intensity that only comes from the inside out—from the inside of the subject and of the painter as well. The titles are all perfectly innocuous—*The Carver, The Pastor and the Lamb, Homecoming*—and yet they're all painted with the kind of longing that puts a lump in your throat. Shelley was painting far more than what she saw. She was also painting what she *wanted*—a time and place and people she wanted to go back to, but couldn't. Does that make any sense?"

Joanna nodded. "She never talked to you about any of the people in her paintings?"

Dee shook her head. "Not really. 'Somebody I knew back home,' she'd tell me without ever bothering saying where 'back home' was. But I did notice that there's no rain in any of her pictures. Wherever home was, it must not rain very often, or else she just didn't like to paint rain."

"Maybe Rochelle Baxter didn't tell you where she came from because she had something to hide," Joanna suggested.

"Like maybe she had done something wrong? Something illegal?" Dee demanded.

"Possibly."

"No!" Dee replied hotly. "Nothing like that. I'm sure of it. I'm an excellent judge of character, Sheriff Brady. Psychic, even. Shelley was as honest as the day is long. If she had done something bad, I would have known it."

"You said she was an ex-Marine. Did Rochelle mention anything to you about where she served and when?"

"She'd been in the Gulf War," Dee answered. "I remember something about her being an MP, but again, she wasn't big on details."

"Do you have any idea about the people in the paintings?" Joanna asked. "Who they might be?"

"Maybe you should come up to the gallery and see for yourself," Dee suggested. "I assume they're people from Shelley's past. They're all painted in a wonderful sort of summer light, but not the light we have here in the desert. The shadows don't have the same hard edges that desert shadows do. This is much softer. And speaking of soft, that's how she spoke, too—with a soft drawl that makes me think she must have come originally from somewhere down south, but then she'd say something about being glad her bones were finally warming up, so I really don't know.

"If that's all you need, I'd better go," Dee added, extracting a car key from the fringed leather purse that hung from her shoulder. She edged away from Joanna toward a wildly colored, custom-painted Pinto station wagon.

"I still need to go get gas," she said, "but I've made up my mind. I'm going to go through with the show's grand opening tonight after all. For one thing, it's too late to call off the caterer. Even if I canceled, I'd still have to pay for the food. So we'll have an event anyway, even if it's more like a wake than anything else— a wake with paintings instead of a body. But before it opens, I'm going to redo all the prices."

"Redo them?" Joanna asked. "What do you mean?"

"I'm going to raise them," Dee Canfield returned decisively. "Those fifteen pieces are all I have to sell of Shelley's work. With her gone, that's all there's ever going to be, which makes a big difference to collectors. It means the paintings are more valuable."

"There aren't any others?"

"Only one," Dee replied. "But that one's already sold."

"But I would have thought there'd be others, either here in her studio or in storage. . . ." Joanna began.

Dee shook her head. "Shelley was something of a perfectionist, you see. She'd paint one canvas over and over until she got it right and moved on to the next one. Maybe she was just cheap, but she didn't believe in letting canvases go to waste."

"How do art galleries work?" Joanna asked innocently. "Do you get a set fee and the artist receives all the rest?"

"Of course not," Dee said. "Shelley's and my agreement works on a percentage basis, fifty-fifty."

"So, if you raise the prices on Rochelle Baxter's work, her heirs will receive more, but so will you."

"Believe me," Dee said, "I'll see to it that Shelley's heirs receive the additional proceeds, if that's what you mean." She paused, and her eyes narrowed. "Wait a minute. Are you suggesting that I may have had something to do with Shelley's death—that I killed her so I could make more money off her paintings?"

"I wasn't implying anything of the kind," Joanna replied evenly. "But whenever we encounter a suspicious death like this, we question everyone. It's the only way to find out what really happened."

Joanna's response did nothing to calm Dee Canfield's sudden anger. "You can take your questions and your not-so-subtle hints and go straight to hell!" she fumed.

With that, Dee got in her car and slammed the door behind her. On the second turn of the key, the old engine coughed fitfully to life. Jerking and half-stalling, the Pinto lurched away from the curb and bounced through an axle-bending pothole.

As the Pinto shuddered out of sight, Joanna Brady jotted into her notebook: Who is Deidre Canfield and where did *she* come from?

Three

D AVE HOLLICKER CAME OUTSIDE and heaved yet
another set of plastic bags into his waiting van. "How much
longer do you think you're going to be?" Joanna asked.

"Probably several more hours," he said.

Joanna nodded. "All right, then. I'll leave you and Casey to it.
In the meantime, I'm going back to the department to try to herd
my day into some kind of order."

As she drove toward the Justice Center, Joanna recalled the last
time she had seen Bobo Jenkins. It had been several months earlier, on the occasion of Angie Kellogg's marriage to Dennis
Hacker. The wedding ceremony had taken place in the parsonage
of Tombstone Canyon United Methodist Church, with the Reverend Marianne Maculyea presiding. Bobo Jenkins, Angie's
employer at the Blue Moon Saloon and Lounge, had given away
the bride.

Recalling the event, Joanna remembered that Bobo Jenkins

had seemed buoyantly happy as he told Butch about his plan to sell the Blue Moon to Angie and Dennis. He said he was looking forward to his second early retirement."

Rochelle hadn't been in evidence at the wedding, but Joanna wondered if Bobo Jenkins's happiness then had had less to do with early retirement than with the appearance of a new woman in his life. Now, though, whatever future the two of them might have planned together had evaporated. Rochelle Baxter was dead.

Halfway back to the department, Joanna changed her mind about going there. Bobo Jenkins was a man Joanna knew and liked. He needed to be informed about Rochelle's death in person rather than through one of Bisbee's notoriously swift gossip mills. Plus, if Joanna went to see him right then, she wouldn't have time to think about it for too long, while her own sense of dread kept building. She hated doing next-of-kin notifications—hated having to tell some poor unsuspecting person that a loved one was suddenly and unexpectedly dead.

Picking up her radio, she called in and asked for Bobo Jenkins's address. She learned that he lived on Youngblood Hill in Old Bisbee, only a matter of blocks from his former business, the Blue Moon. Joanna drove directly there and parked in the designated area at the top of the hill. She then hiked down the steep incline to the arched and gated entrance that led back up a steep flight of stairs to a house perched far above the street. It was no accident that people who lived on some of Old Bisbee's higher elevations were regular winners in the annual Fourth of July race up "B" Hill.

Thirty-two steps later found her standing, out of breath, on the wooden porch of a fully renovated 1880s-vintage miner's cabin overlooking Brewery Gulch. The clapboard siding, front door, and porch railings were all newly painted. The broad planks of flooring showed evidence of having been recently replaced.

The period piece of etched glass in the front door had been carefully relined with new putty, and the glass itself sparkled in the morning sun. Sighing with reluctance, Joanna placed her finger on the old-fashioned doorbell and listened while it buzzed inside the tiny house.

When Bobo Jenkins came to the door, he wore shorts, a sweat-soaked T-shirt, and a pair of tennis shoes. A limp towel was thrown around the back of his neck. "Hi, there, Joanna," he said. "I was out back working out. Care to come in?"

Joanna made her way into a brightly painted living room. Hardwood flooring glistened underfoot while huge pieces of leather furniture dominated the space. Looking at the furniture, Joanna shuddered at the idea of dragging those large pieces up from the street.

"Nice place," she said. "But how on earth did you get this furniture up here?"

"I didn't beam it up, if that's what you mean." He grinned. "It helps if you lift weights. It's also a good idea to have a bunch of weight-lifting friends. Have a seat."

Joanna eased herself down onto the soft gray leather couch. She would have preferred keeping up the pretense of polite conversation. Her stomach clenched at the idea of doing what she had come to do. Once she unleashed her bad news, this comfortable, peaceful room would never again be quite so peaceful. Some of her disquiet must have communicated itself. When she turned back to Bobo Jenkins, his easygoing smile had disappeared.

"What's going on?" he asked, perching on the arm of the couch.

"I'm sorry to have to do this," she began. "I understand you're good friends with a woman named Rochelle Baxter. Is that true?"

"With Shelley? Of course it's true. And I hope we're a little more than friends," he added. A concerned frown crossed his face. "Why are you asking me about her? Has something happened?"

Joanna took a deep breath. There was no easy way. "She's dead, Bobo," Joanna said.

The big man's mahogany-colored skin faded to gray. "No!" he exclaimed. "That's impossible!"

Joanna shook her head. "I'm sorry, Bobo," she said, "but it's true. Rochelle Baxter was taken ill and called 911 around ten o'clock last night. She collapsed while talking to the emergency operator. When the EMTs reached her, she was unresponsive. Rochelle was DOA on arrival at Copper Queen Hospital."

Bobo buried his face in the towel. "Shelley, dead?" he murmured. "I can't believe it. She was fine when I left her—perfectly fine. What happened?"

"We don't know," Joanna replied. "At least, not yet. From what we can tell, she became desperately ill. By the time help reached her, it was already too late."

Joanna paused, allowing Bobo to internalize the awful information. Finally she asked, "Did Rochelle have any known medical condition that might explain this sudden attack?"

His face contorted by anguish, Bobo shook his head wordlessly.

"You said she was fine when you left her," Joanna continued. "Does that mean you saw her last night?"

Bobo nodded.

"What time?"

"I don't know exactly," he answered. "Fairly early. It couldn't have been much later than seven or so. I was back here by seven-thirty."

"What was the purpose of your visit?"

Bobo sighed. "Shelley and I were supposed to have dinner last night, but she stood me up. Not stood up, exactly. She just called and canceled. I went to see her anyway—to ask her about it and find out what was going on."

"You say she canceled. What time was that?" Joanna asked.

"What time did she call?"

Joanna nodded.

"Sometime in the afternoon. I don't remember exactly when. I erased the message after I listened to it."

"And why did she?" Joanna asked. "Cancel, I mean. Was something wrong?"

"You mean was she sick?" Bobo asked.

Joanna nodded.

"Sick, but not physically," he said ruefully. "Sick of me is more like it. Still, when I showed up at her place in Naco, she invited me in and offered me a drink. We talked for a little while. She tried to give me the brush-off. Told me she needed time for herself—time by herself. I was afraid she was going to break up with me right then and there, but I talked her out of it. The last thing before I left, she agreed to have dinner with me tonight after the gallery opening."

"You parted on good terms?"

"Of course." Bobo Jenkins frowned. "Wait a minute. What about that opening? Somebody needs to call Dee Canfield right away and tell her what's happened."

"She already knows," Joanna said. "She came by the studio down in Naco while I was still there."

"She's going to cancel, right?"

"I don't think so. She said she intended to go through with the opening after all. The only difference is she plans to raise the prices."

"Raise the prices? What do you mean?"

Joanna nodded. "Dee told me that Shelley's death automatically makes the pieces more valuable."

Bobo Jenkins stood up abruptly. "What is she, some kind of vulture? What the hell is Dee Canfield thinking? You'll have to excuse me, Joanna. There's something I have to do."

He went to the door and held it open, motioning Joanna through it.

"What's the hurry?" Joanna asked, allowing herself to be escorted back outside. "Where are you going?"

"To Castle Rock Gallery," he told her determinedly. "I'm going to go have a heart-to-heart chat with Deidre Canfield."

"Wait, Bobo," Joanna began. "Do you think that's a good idea?"

He ignored her. Without bothering to lock the door, he pulled it shut behind them and loped off down the steep flight of stairs that led to the street. Standing alone on the small porch, Joanna watched him take the steps two and three at a time. When he reached the bottom, Joanna expected him to turn right and head back up the hill to retrieve his waiting El Camino. Instead, he turned left and barreled down Youngblood Hill toward Brewery Gulch on foot.

Stunned, Joanna stared after Bobo Jenkins's retreating figure. She had known him for years, but she had never seen him angry before. Now that she had, she worried about the damage those powerfully muscled arms and fists might inflict once he caught up with Deidre Canfield.

Sheriff Joanna Brady had just brought Bobo Jenkins an entire lifetime's worth of unwelcome news. As sheriff she was charged with protecting the citizens of Cochise County. Instead, by telling Bobo about Dee Canfield's plans, Joanna had inadvertently incited him—possibly to the point of violence.

Not good, Joanna told herself grimly as she, too, started down the stairs. *Not good at all!*

Bobo Jenkins was completely out of sight by the time Joanna reached the arched gate at the bottom of the stairs. She jogged back uphill to her Crown Victoria, then threw herself inside. Panting with exertion, Joanna punched up her radio.

"Sheriff Brady here," she gasped when she heard the voice of Larry Kendrick, her lead dispatcher. "I'm on my way to Castle Rock Gallery. Please advise Bisbee PD that I may need backup."

"What's the problem, Sheriff?" Larry asked. "You sound like you've been running for miles."

"Not miles, just up and down Youngblood Hill," she told him. "I just finished telling Bobo Jenkins that Rochelle Baxter is dead. He's upset with a woman named Deidre Canfield and is on his way to her place of business, Castle Rock Gallery on Main Street in Old Bisbee. Bobo said he was going to talk to her, but he was really off the charts when he left here. I'd say he's more likely to punch somebody's lights out. I'm headed there, too."

By then the Civvie was on the move. Joanna turned on her lights and siren as she careened down Youngblood Hill into the upper reaches of Brewery Gulch. Bobo Jenkins was moving fast. By racing down stairways and cutting through back alleys, it was likely he would reach the Castle Rock Gallery on foot well before Joanna could drive there.

Deidre Canfield's place of business consisted of a series of small, formerly ramshackle buildings that looked invitingly renovated when Joanna drove up. As soon as she opened her car door, she heard a chorus of raised voices coming from inside.

As she pushed open the door to the gallery, a tiny bell tinkled overhead, but neither Dee Canfield nor Bobo Jenkins noticed.

Across the room they stood locked in a fierce, nose-to-nose con-frontation.

"You've got no right barging in here and telling me what I can and can't do," Dee shouted shrilly. "This is *my* gallery. The contract is between Rochelle Baxter and me. It has nothing to do with you, Bobo Jenkins. The terms of that contract allow me to set, raise, or lower prices as I see fit."

Bobo's powerful fists were clenched at his sides. Beads of sweat glistened on his face as he struggled to keep his anger under control. "That was *before* she died," he said pointedly.

"Yes," Dee returned. "And that's why I'm raising the prices. In the world of art, those pieces are all more valuable."

"Not more valuable," Bobo countered softly. "They're price-less. What about Shelley's family?"

"Who else do you think I'm doing it for?" Dee demanded. "If the pieces sell for more money, the family receives more. It's as simple as that."

Bobo stepped closer to Dee. It was a threatening gesture. She blinked, but stood her ground.

"You think that's what Shelley's family is going to want—money?" he demanded, his face bare inches from hers. He waved an arm, motioning at the vividly colored paintings that lined the white-stuccoed walls. "Who the hell do you think those people are, Deidre Canfield? You know as well as I that they must be Shel-ley's family. Having those pictures is going to be far more impor-tant to them than any amount of money. Cancel the show, Dee."

"No. Absolutely not!"

"Then I'll cancel it for you."

A man Joanna hadn't seen before emerged from a backroom, carrying a hammer. "You'd better leave now, Bobo," the newcomer said, tapping the head of the hammer in the palm of his other hand.

"And you'd better stay out of this, Warren," Jenkins growled, his eyes swiveling in Warren Gibson's direction. "This is between Dee and me."

"You'd all better cool it," Joanna ordered, physically inserting herself between Dee Canfield and Bobo. "Now. Before things get out of hand." She turned toward the man with the hammer. "As for you, put that thing down. On the desk. Now."

After a momentary hesitation, Warren complied. Meanwhile, Bobo Jenkins ignored Joanna's presence entirely. "Give me my picture, Dee," he said, speaking over Joanna's head. "You can go on with the damned show if you want, but it won't be with my picture in it."

"All right," Dee said. "Go get it, Warren. Whatever it takes to get him out of here."

Again, Gibson hesitated. "Go," she urged again. Finally, shaking his head, Warren shambled out of the room.

"Look," Joanna said reasonably. "You've all had a terrible shock this morning. No one here is thinking clearly."

"Those pictures shouldn't be sold," Bobo Jenkins insisted. "Or, if they are, it should only be done once Shelley's family members have given permission."

For the first time Joanna took a moment to look around the room. Her eyes fell on a picture of a boy and a dog sitting on a front porch. The heat of a summer's day shimmered around them, but the two figures in the foreground rested companionably in cool, deep shade. The boy and the dog had been lovingly rendered by someone who knew them well; by someone who cared about who they were. Even without looking at any of the other pictures, Joanna knew instinctively that Dee Canfield was right—

that the portraits were those of Rochelle Baxter's loved ones. She was equally sure that Bobo was correct as well. The people painted there would want the pictures to treasure far more than any amount of money.

"Shelley's family!" Dee Canfield spat back at him. "What family? Did you ever meet any of them?"

Bobo shook his head.

"If Shelley's work was so damned important to that so-called family of hers," Dee continued, "don't you suppose one or two of them would have been included in the invitations for tonight's opening party? I asked Shelley specifically if there was anyone she wanted me to invite. She said there wasn't anyone at all."

"Now that Rochelle is dead, her family is bound to turn up," Bobo said.

"Fair enough," Dee replied. "When they do, I'll have a nice fat check waiting for them, and they'll be more than happy to take the money and run."

Warren Gibson appeared in the doorway carrying an almost life-size portrait of Bobo Jenkins. Bobo swallowed hard when he saw it, then he stepped forward and snatched it out of Warren's grasp. He walked back over to Dee and stood there, holding the painting with both hands.

"Do you know what you are?" he demanded. "You're a money-grubbing bitch who doesn't know a damned thing about what's important." With that, he turned and stalked out of the gallery while the little bell tinkled merrily overhead.

Once Bobo was gone, all the starch and fight drained out of Deidre Canfield's face and body. She staggered over to the polished wooden desk where Warren had deposited his hammer. She sank into the rolling desk chair and laid her head on her arms. "I can't believe Bobo would talk to me that way," she sobbed. "He and I have been friends for a long time. How could he?"

Warren Gibson moved to the back of Dee's chair and gave her shoulder a comforting pat. "It's all right, Dee Dee," he said. "He's gone now."

The doorbell tinkled again. A young uniformed police officer wearing a City of Bisbee badge with a tag that said "Officer Jesus Romero" ventured cautiously into the room.

"Everything all right, Sheriff Brady?" Romero asked. "I was told there might be some kind of problem."

Joanna felt embarrassed. The lights, siren, and call for backup had all proved unnecessary. "Sorry about that," she said. "It turned out to be nothing. Everything's under control."

The officer grinned at her. "I'd rather have it be nothing than something any day of the week. Glad to be of service."

With that he left. As the doorbell chimed again, Joanna turned back to Dee Canfield, who looked pale and drawn. There was little resemblance between the woman seated at the desk and the angry hoyden who had raised such hell down in Naco a scant hour earlier.

"Are you all right?" Joanna asked.

"I'm fine," Dee returned, though she didn't sound it. "I've sunk everything I have into getting this gallery up and running. It's fine for Bobo Jenkins to be all sentimental and altruistic with my money. It's no concern of his. He's got his military retirement and now he's sold his business and has payments coming from that on a regular basis as well. But what the hell does he think I'm going to use to pay *my* bills? My good looks? This show is important to me, Sheriff Brady, damned important! It's a chance to make some real money for a change. I'm not going to hand over the paintings for free just because he said so!"

"What about the prices?" Warren said, reappearing behind her. "I started changing them. Want me to keep on?"

"Absolutely."

Joanna sighed. Obviously Bobo Jenkins's visit hadn't altered Dee Canfield's intentions, but at least Joanna had been there to prevent any physical violence.

"All right, then," she said. "Mind if I take a look around before I go?"

"Go ahead," Dee said. "Help yourself."

Joanna spent the next few minutes wandering through the gallery. The lovingly rendered subjects—a young girl shooting baskets, an old man sharpening his knife, a minister leaning down to speak to a young parishioner—were most likely the same living and breathing people who, by now, would be reeling from the terrible news that Rochelle Baxter was dead. Joanna noticed that the paintings in the first two rooms were priced from $850 to $1,000. In the room where Warren was hard at work, they were triple that. Bobo's accusation of her being "money-grubbing" wasn't wrong.

Shaking her head, Joanna returned to the front desk, where Dee Canfield was on the phone. Without saying a word, Joanna let herself out the door. She and her Civvie caught up with Bobo Jenkins halfway through town.

"Hey, Bobo," she called. "That looks heavy. Care for a lift?"

He glared at her briefly, then shrugged his broad shoulders and headed for the car. Between them, they carefully loaded the painting into the Civvie's backseat, then he climbed in the front next to her.

"Thanks," he muttered gruffly. "Appreciate it."

He sat in brooding silence until they started up O.K. Street. "Dee's still going through with it, isn't she—the opening and raising the prices?"

"Yes," Joanna replied.

Bobo slumped deeper into the seat. "Damn!" he said. "What about Shelley's family? Have you found them yet?"

"Not so far. We're working on it."

"Once Dee sells the paintings, Shelley's family will never be able to afford to buy them back."

"Probably not," Joanna agreed. "But you tried, Bobo. You did your best."

He shook his head. "Not good enough."

Joanna stopped the car halfway down Youngblood Hill, right in front of the gate and the steep stairway that led to Bobo's house. For the better part of a minute he made no move to exit the car. The depth of his misery was palpable, and Joanna's heart ached for him.

"I'm sorry about all this, Bobo," she said at last. "I can see Shelley meant a lot to you."

He chewed his lip, nodding but saying nothing.

"And I'm sorry to burden you further," she added. "But we're going to need your cooperation."

"What kind?"

"We'll want you to stop by the department and give us a set of prints. Detective Carbajal is tied up right now. As soon as he's free, he'll need to ask you a few questions."

"You need my fingerprints? Why? I thought you said Shelley was sick."

"She *was* sick," Joanna agreed. "But the medical examiner has labeled her death as suspicious."

"You're saying someone killed her?" Bobo asked incredulously. "Who would have done such a thing? And why?"

"I can't answer those questions, either," Joanna said. "Not yet.

We're working on it, but it's very early in the process. Investigations take time."

"But you want my prints. Am I a suspect?"

"Not at all. Yours will be elimination prints. We print everyone who was known to have been at the crime scene prior to the event. That way we can sort prints that belong from those that don't. From what you've told me, you may have been the last person to see Shelley alive."

Bobo Jenkins nodded morosely. "I see," he said. "Do I need to do that right away—the fingerprinting?"

"As soon as possible," Joanna told him. "Time is always important, but you'll need to call the department before you come by and make sure Casey Ledford is there. She's our latent fingerprint tech. The last I heard, she was still at the crime scene. And Detective Carbajal is busy at the moment, too. I'm sure he'll contact you once he's free."

"Crime scene." Bobo repeated the words and then took a deep breath. "Detectives. I can't believe all this is happening. I can't believe Shelley was murdered."

"Bobo, we don't know that for sure, either," Joanna reminded him patiently. "At this time, her death is regarded as suspicious. For all I know, it could have been a suicide."

"No," Bobo Jenkins declared. "Absolutely not! Whatever killed Shelley, it sure as hell wasn't suicide!"

With that, he opened the car door, got out, and slammed it shut again. Joanna unlocked the back door. Then she exited the car, too, and helped him retrieve his painting.

"It's a very good likeness," she said, once he was holding it upright so she could see it clearly. "Your Shelley must have been a very talented woman, and very special, too."

As Bobo Jenkins looked down at the painting, his eyes filled with tears. He wiped them away with one end of the grubby towel that still dangled, unheeded, around his neck.

"Thank you for telling me about this, Joanna," he said quietly. "For coming in person, I mean," he added. "You're the boss. It would have been easy to send someone else instead of doing it yourself."

Joanna nodded. "You're welcome," she said.

"And thanks for following me down to the gallery, too," he continued. "I was so pissed off when I went down there that I might have done something stupid. I could have hurt somebody."

Joanna looked up at him and smiled reassuringly. "No, Bobo," she said. "I don't think you would have. But for whatever it's worth, I think you're right about the paintings. There's no question—they shouldn't be sold. They should all go to Shelley's family. Deidre Canfield is dead wrong on this one."

"Thanks for that, too," he said.

Carefully holding the painting in front of him, he angled his way through the gate and started up the stairs. Behind Joanna a horn honked impatiently. She jumped back into the Civvie and hurriedly moved it out of the way of the vehicle she'd been blocking.

It was a tough way to start the day, considering she still hadn't had her morning briefing or a second cup of coffee.

STANDING IN THE WARM LATE-MORNING SUN with the heavy pay phone receiver held to one ear, the man waited impatiently for his call to be put through. The receptionist had accepted the charges, so it wasn't a matter of money. Still, he didn't have all day.

Finally someone picked up at the other end. "Good," he said when he heard the voice. "It's you. You'll be happy to know it's done. She's dead. All you have to do now is send money."

four

B Y THE TIME JOANNA ARRIVED at the Justice Center
and let herself in through her private back-door entrance, it
was almost eleven o'clock. As usual, her office was a mess.
The wooden surface of her desk was barely visible under
stacks of neglected files and paper.

Organizing the Fallen Officer portion of Yolanda Cañedo's
funeral had taken far more of Joanna's personal time and effort
than she had expected. She and Frank Montoya had shared the
responsibilities. All essential law enforcement work had been handled, but some of the more routine matters had been allowed to
slide. Now, though, as Joanna dug into the paperwork on her desk,
she discovered items that had been routine on Monday. By Thursday they had moved to the "urgent" column.

Wanting to have some quiet time to attack the daunting back-
log of paper, Joanna set to work without bothering to announce

her presence to anyone, not even to Kristin Gregovich, her secretary in the outside office. Twenty minutes later, as Joanna whaled away at the mess, Kristin came into her office to deliver yet another batch of paperwork. Startled to find Joanna seated at her desk, Kristin almost dropped what she was carrying.

"You scared me to death!" she exclaimed. "Why didn't you tell me you were here?"

"Because my phone would have been ringing off the hook," Joanna answered. "The only way I'm going to make any progress with this mess is to work on it without interruptions."

Kristin nodded and placed a neatly arranged stack of papers on the one part of the desk Joanna had finally managed to clear. Then, instead of taking the hint and returning to her own office, Kristin sighed and sank, uninvited, into one of the two captain's chairs facing Joanna's desk.

In the past two months, Kristin Gregovich had gone from being slightly pregnant to being profoundly pregnant. Her once showgirl-worthy ankles were now severely swollen by the end of each workday. The baby, a girl, wasn't due for another three weeks, but Kristin, rubbing her aching back, was vocal about hoping to deliver sooner than that. On the other hand, money concerns made her want to stay on the job as long as possible.

Hearing Kristin's sigh, Joanna looked at her secretary with concern. She worried that there might be some third-trimester complication brewing. "Are you all right?" she asked.

Kristin nodded, but she didn't look all right.

"Weren't you supposed to see the doctor yesterday?" Joanna asked.

Kristin nodded again. "That's what I wanted to talk to you about, Sheriff Brady. We did go, Terry and I both."

Terry Gregovich, Kristin's husband, and Spike, his German shepherd, comprised the Cochise County Sheriff's Department's K-9 Unit.

Joanna stood up and came around to the front of the desk. "You look upset, Kristin," she said. "What is it? Is there something the matter with the baby?"

"Oh, no, nothing like that," the young woman answered hurriedly. "Shaundra's fine. The thing is, the only time we could get in for the ultrasound was late yesterday afternoon. We went right after the church service ended. By the time we finished up at the hospital, it was too late to go to the graveside service. I was too beat to go to the reception, so Terry and I just stayed home. But I didn't want you to think we didn't come because . . ." Kristin's voice trailed off uneasily.

When Joanna had first taken over the job of sheriff, she and her young secretary had needed to sort out some issues between them. For a time after Joanna's election, Kristin's loyalties had remained with members of the previous administration. With the passage of time, however, the two women had developed a comfortable working relationship. Months earlier, Joanna was the person to whom Kristin had first confided the news of her unexpected pregnancy. And it was Joanna who had helped Kristin and Terry arrange their nice but hurried shotgun wedding.

In the months since, Joanna Brady had taken a kind of proprietary interest in the young couple's situation. She had been more than a little disappointed the day before when she'd been forced to assume that they, too, had boycotted the funeral reception. It had hurt her to think that both Kristin and Terry had aligned themselves with Ken Galloway's malcontents in Local 83. That, of course, had been the other reason Joanna had avoided announcing her presence to Kristin.

"You didn't want me to think you missed the reception because of what?" Joanna asked.

"You know," Kristin said with an uneasy shrug. "Because of what's going on around here."

"You mean because of Deputy Galloway?"

Kristin nodded. "That's right. Neither Terry nor I wanted to have anything to do with him and his buddies," she said quickly. "But four forty-five was the only time we could schedule the ultrasound, and the doctor was later than that. I just wanted you to know, Sheriff Brady—whatever those guys in the union are trying to pull, Terry and I aren't involved. If we had known what was going to happen—that everybody else was going to stay away like they did—we would have come no matter what!"

A wave of relief washed over Joanna. She eased herself into the chair next to Kristin. Maybe things inside her department weren't quite as universally one-sided as she had supposed.

"The baby's welfare has to be your first priority," Joanna said kindly. "Thanks for telling me, though." She paused, then added, "But what exactly do you think Ken Junior and his pals are up to? Any ideas?"

"I don't know," Kristin said, shaking her head. "Not really. I asked Terry the same thing this morning on the way to work. He thinks most of the guys are just messing around and that we shouldn't pay any attention to them. But how could they do something like that—ditch the cemetery and the reception, I mean? And what about Leon Cañedo? How do those jerks think their staying away made *him* feel?" Kristin demanded, her voice quivering with suppressed emotion. "What would they think if somebody did something like that to their wives or kids?"

Joanna leaned back in the chair and thought for a moment before she answered. She didn't want whatever she said to Kristin to add to her department's inner turmoil if it happened to be repeated to anyone else.

"Some people are simply incapable of putting themselves in anybody else's shoes, Kristin," she said finally. "Empathy won't ever be one of Deputy Galloway's long suits. But if it will put your mind at ease, I think Leon Cañedo was so overwhelmed by everything that was going on yesterday, he probably didn't notice who was there and who wasn't. Ken Junior may have drained off everyone he could bamboozle into not showing up, but it was still standing room only in the parish hall up at St. Dominick's for most of the evening."

Kristin heaved another sigh, this one of relief. "Good. I'm really glad." Saying that, she pushed her unwieldy body upright. "Now that I know you're here," she said, "I'll go get your messages."

Joanna felt like saying, *Do you have to?* She didn't. Instead, she watched Kristin waddle out of the room before returning to her own desk. Moments later, Kristin was back with a fanfold of telephone message slips in her hand. "Chief Deputy Montoya wants to know if you're ready for the briefing yet."

"Not yet. Give me a while."

Nodding, Kristin went out, closing the door behind her. Joanna took the messages and shuffled through them. One was from her mother, one from the county attorney's office, and two were from people in the community whose names she recognized but who had somehow failed to mention exactly why they were calling. Pulling all pertinent information from reticent phone callers was one of the essential secretarial skills Kristin Gregovich had yet to master. The bottom message was from Butch. "Daisy's," it said. "Twelve o'clock. DON'T FORGET!"

With an air of impatience she pushed that one aside. After all, it wasn't anywhere near twelve yet. What would make him think she'd forget? She glanced at her watch. It was only twenty past eleven—plenty of time.

When it came to returning phone calls, Joanna was a believer in doing the tough things first. She dialed her mother's number immediately.

"Why, there you are," Eleanor Lathrop Winfield said. "I'm so glad you called back. I just had the strangest conversation with Marliss Shackleford."

The fact that her mother was a longtime bosom buddy of *The Bisbee Bee*'s featured columnist was one of the crosses Sheriff Joanna Brady had learned to bear. Anytime there was a question Marliss didn't want to pose through official channels—like going through the media relations officer, Chief Deputy Montoya—she had no compunction about asking Eleanor instead. Joanna's first thought was that Marliss was on the trail of something to do with the Rochelle Baxter case. That assumption proved wrong.

"Marliss asked me why there were so few Cochise County deputies in attendance at the funeral reception yesterday evening," Eleanor was saying. "I told her she had to be mistaken. I was there myself. It seemed to me there were plenty of people in uniform, all of them plowing through that buffet like they hadn't eaten in days."

Hardly any of those starving uniforms belonged to me, Joanna thought despairingly. It bugged her to realize that, as usual, Marliss Shackleford had focused in on the one critical issue Sheriff Brady had been trying to dodge. Rather than issuing a denial Marliss could easily refute, Joanna played coy.

"Really," she said, feigning as much innocence as she could muster. "Marliss says my deputies weren't there? That's strange. I could have sworn they were all over the place, but I could be wrong. I had a few other details to worry about. There wasn't time for an official roll call."

"See there?" Eleanor responded, sounding relieved. "I tried to tell Marliss that very thing—that she had to be mistaken, but you know her. Sometimes you have to hit that woman over the head with a baseball bat to get through to her."

Hitting Marliss Shackleford over the head with anything sounded like an excellent idea to Sheriff Joanna Brady about then, but she fought down a biting comment that could have turned into additional ammunition. "I've noticed," she agreed.

"I'd best be going," Eleanor went on briskly. "I just spoke to George. He's finished up with whatever it was he had to do this morning. He's coming home for lunch. I should get it on the table. The egg salad is ready, but I haven't made sandwiches yet."

That, too, was vintage Eleanor Lathrop. The "whatever" George Winfield had to do that morning was to perform an autopsy. How like Eleanor simply to gloss over and/or ignore anything remotely unpleasant. Her husband's title might be that of Cochise County Medical Examiner, but in Eleanor's self-centered world, none of his professional duties were any more important than the egg-salad sandwiches she planned to serve for lunch. And if a scheduled autopsy or an unexpected phone call happened to delay him beyond what Eleanor considered reasonable, Joanna knew there would be hell to pay.

Better him than me, she thought.

Even so, Eleanor didn't hang up immediately. "According to Marliss, there was another murder last night," she added.

Here we go again, Joanna fumed. *Another one of Marliss Shackleford's notorious end runs.*

"A suspicious death," she corrected. "I suppose she asked you about that, too."

"Not about the death specifically," Eleanor replied. "She wanted to know if I had noticed how the crime rate has really taken off since you became Sheriff."

That depends on who's counting, Joanna thought. "What did you say?" she asked.

"I told her the truth," Eleanor replied. "I said that no matter who's in charge, the crime rate stays pretty much the same."

Coming from Eleanor Lathrop Winfield, that lukewarm statement constituted a ringing endorsement.

"Thanks, Mom," Joanna said.

"You're welcome."

Next Joanna dialed the county attorney's office. Arlee Jones was a blowhard, deal-making good old boy.

"Glad to hear from you, Sheriff Brady," he said cordially. "Wanted to keep you in the know."

"About what?" Joanna replied.

"Remember Rob Majors?" Arlee asked. "That kid from San Simon?"

Joanna remembered Rob Majors all too well. He was a not-too-bright kid who had spent the summer earning college tuition money by carjacking travelers along I-10 and selling their stolen vehicles to migrant-smuggling crooks from Old Mexico. Joanna's department had spent weeks and far too much valuable overtime before they had apprehended him. They had finally decoyed Majors into trying to lift a car driven by Terry Gregovich with Spike, his German shepherd sidekick, stationed in the backseat.

Majors had been taken into custody at the rest area just inside the Arizona/New Mexico border, but he wasn't jailed until after emergency-room treatment of the numerous puncture wounds on his arm, compliments of an eighty-five-pound police dog.

"What about him?" Joanna asked.

"Thought you'd be relived to hear that I've brokered a deal. Rob Majors pleads guilty to a lesser charge, and he drops the police brutality charge against your K-9 officer."

"How good a deal did he get?" Joanna asked. Arlee Jones's plea bargains usually gave her a headache. This one was no exception.

"He pleads guilty to one count of first-degree assault and goes to Fort Grant until his twenty-first birthday."

Joanna barely believed her ears. "The kid's seventeen. You're letting him off as a juvenile?"

"It's the best I could do," Jones said in an aggrieved tone. "At least it gets your Deputy Gregovich off the hook."

"Thanks," Joanna said. "That's just what I wanted to hear."

She hung up and was still burning with indignation when she dialed the number for Debra Highsmith, the newly installed principal at Bisbee High School. A student office assistant put the call through.

"This is Sheriff Brady," Joanna said when Debra Highsmith answered. "I understand you called earlier."

"That's right. Thanks so much for returning the call," Ms. Highsmith said. "We're trying to do something a little unusual around here. I was wondering if you could help us out."

"That depends," Joanna said. "What are we talking about?"

"I attended an all-girls high school, and an all-girls college as well. This was back in the days when they still had such things," Debra Highsmith added with a chuckle. "I'm trying to create an atmosphere that will challenge and motivate the young women here at Bisbee High. We want to get them thinking outside the box, as it were. For that we need really dynamic role models."

Joanna waited silently for Debra Highsmith to cut to the chase.

"BHS career day comes up the end of next week," Ms. Highsmith continued. "I must apologize for calling you at the last minute. I had made arrangements for an old college chum of mine, Althea Peachy, who works for NASA, to speak to our girls-only assembly. Unfortunately, Peaches found out just this morning that she has to testify before the House Appropriations Committee in D.C. next week. I was wondering if I could prevail on you to pinch-hit."

Suppressing a sigh, Joanna reached for her desktop calendar. "What day?" she asked.

"Next Thursday. We'd like you to speak first thing in the morning—around nine or so. The boys will be in the gym having their own assembly. The girls will be in the auditorium."

Joanna consulted her calendar. The morning after a night of Halloween pranks would be a bad day for her to be out of the office, but encouraging young people was also part of her job.

"All right," she said, penciling it in. "Nine o'clock. Anything else I should know?"

"Well, there is one more thing," Debra Highsmith added. "I need to let you know that we have a zero-tolerance policy about weapons here on campus."

"Wait a minute," Joanna objected. "I'm a sworn police officer, remember? You want me to come to your school and talk to students about the possibility of considering law enforcement as a career, but you don't want me to wear my guns?"

"Right," Debra Highsmith allowed. "It doesn't make sense, but you know how paranoid school boards can be about such things these days. What if a student overpowered you, grabbed one of your weapons, and used it on some other student?"

"And what if one of *your* students shows up at school that day with a weapon of his or her own? What then?" Joanna returned. "Wouldn't it be a good idea to have a properly trained and armed police officer on-site when all hell breaks loose?"

"I don't make the rules," Debra Highsmith returned. "I simply enforce them."

That's the same thing I always say, Joanna thought.

"All right," she said. "Nine o'clock, on Thursday, November first, in the auditorium."

She put down the phone and was still staring at it when her private line rang.

"You're late," Butch said. "It's ten after twelve. You're still in the office."

"Sorry," she said. "Time got away from me. I'll be right there."

Ten minutes later and twenty minutes after the appointed time, she pulled up in front of Daisy Maxwell's café in Bisbee's Bakerville neighborhood. Junior Dowdle, the developmentally disabled fifty-year-old ward of the restaurant's owner, met Joanna at the door. He carried a pile of menus and sported a wide smile. "Time to eat?" he asked.

Junior had been abandoned by his caretakers a year earlier. Daisy and her retired postal worker husband, Moe, had taken him under their wing and assumed guardianship. Junior had blossomed under their care. Working in their restaurant, he took his tasks of clearing tables and washing dishes very seriously. Occasionally he was allowed to serve as host, passing out menus and accompanying guests to tables or booths.

Joanna stood in the doorway of Daisy's and scanned the room for Butch. His Honda Goldwing was parked in front of the restaurant. Butch himself was nowhere to be seen.

"Back," Junior said, pointing helpfully. "Back there. Reservation," he added with an emphatic nod.

Following Junior Dowdle's directions, Joanna made her way to the private back room that sometimes doubled as a meeting room for the local Rotary Club. Pushing open the door, she was surprised to find every available surface covered by unfurled blueprints.

Butch looked up when she entered. "There you are," he said wryly. "I may be your husband, but do you have any idea how hard it is to book an appointment with you these days?"

She looked around the room. "What's this?"

"Our new house," he said. "Or what's supposed to be our new house. The problem is, I can't get you to sit still long enough to talk about and sign off on the plans. In other words, you and I are having a meeting—an official meeting. We're still working through the permit process, but before construction can begin, all the decisions need to be made. Cabinets have to be ordered, plumbing fixtures, appliances, everything. So first we'll have lunch. They made Cornish pasties today, so I ordered two of those. Then we're going to go over each of these papers, one piece at a time."

"I saw the house you redid in Saginaw," Joanna told him. "I'm sure whatever decisions you make will be fine with me."

"Still," he said. "There are things we should talk about. Marriages don't work well when one person makes too many unilateral decisions. I'm not going ahead until you've officially signed off on everything, from countertops to cabinets."

Joanna wanted the new house. She was looking forward to living in it, but she dreaded the process of getting there. If only she could bring herself to tell Butch how she had grown up listening to her parents squabble endlessly over one of D.H. Lathrop's grindingly slow remodeling projects after another.

"All right," she said, and sat down.

They had eaten lunch and were making good progress through the various blueprints until they got to a detailed rendering of the family room. "What's this?" Joanna asked, pointing to a line that went all the way around the room, just above the doorjambs and window frames.

"That's the train shelf," Butch told her proudly.

"The what?"

"Remember the O-gauge Lionel trains I used to have on display up at the Roundhouse? They've been in storage ever since I came to Bisbee. I decided the family room would be a great place to put them out again—in sight but not in the way. And by putting it in now, during the building process, the wiring can be built into the conduit in the walls behind the shelf."

As he spoke, Butch brimmed with enthusiasm. Now he stopped and glanced sharply at Joanna's face. "Don't you like it?"

"A train in the family room?" she asked uneasily.

"Several, actually," Butch answered. "I have six. There won't be enough room to have all of them out at once, but . . ."

"Wouldn't it be better to have just a television set, some sound equipment, and a couch and some chairs in there?" Joanna asked tentatively. "Having pictures on the walls would be fine, but trains?"

Butch's face fell. "All right," he said glumly. "I'll get rid of it, but at this rate, I might just as well get rid of the trains, too."

"I didn't say that."

"Well," he said, "why not? If I've got no place to display them—if I have to leave them packed up and in storage all the time—what's the point of having them?"

"Butch, please, I never said you should get rid of your trains."

"It sounded like it to me."

Joanna's cell phone rang. Butch rolled his eyes and crossed his arms as she plucked it out of her pocket to answer it. Detective Jaime Carbajal was on the line. "What's up?" she asked.

"According to Doc Winfield, we just ran into a problem," Jaime said.

More than one, Joanna thought, looking at Butch. Scowling, he had returned to studying the family-room blueprint. "Like what?" she asked.

"Our victim's name isn't Rochelle Baxter," he said.

"What is it?"

"Latisha Wall, originally from Macon, Georgia."

"Okay," Joanna said. "She went by a different name. How come? Does she have a record?"

"No."

Joanna was losing patience playing Twenty Questions. "What's the deal?"

"The ME tracked down one Lawrence Baxter, supposedly her father and the person the DMV lists as her next of kin. Turns out he doesn't exist, either. Doc Winfield ended up talking to some guy in the Washington State Attorney General's Office in Olympia. His name's O.H. Todd, and he claims he's Latisha Wall's case manager. She was evidently in a witness protection program."

"They gave her a new name and identity and set her up to live down here in Arizona?" Joanna asked.

"That's right," Jaime said. "Except now she's dead. Doc Winfield said the guy in Olympia almost had a coronary when he heard what had happened."

"What was she a witness about?"

"Todd wasn't saying, at least not to Doc Winfield," Jaime replied. "Said he had to check with his superiors before he could release any information to anyone, including us. However, he did request that he be kept informed about all aspects of the investigation. He gave Doc Winfield the name, phone number, and address of Latisha's mother and sister back home in Georgia. The father is deceased, and the mother is in poor health. The ME says authorities from Washington will contact the next of kin."

"Thank God for small favors," Joanna said. "What about the preliminary results from the autopsy?"

"Inconclusive. No wounds of any kind. No bruises or abrasions. No defensive wounds that would indicate a struggle, and no sign of disease, either. Doc's not willing to say she died of natural causes, though. He's ordering a full set of toxicology tests. You know how long those take."

"Weeks," Joanna murmured.

"Right," Jaime said. "So where does that leave us?"

Joanna thought for a moment before she answered. "Okay," she said. "We'll handle this case like a full-blown homicide investigation until we know otherwise. If we learn later that Latisha Wall took her own life or died from some kind of accidental poisoning, all we'll be out are the man-hours we've devoted to the investigation. But we have to pay attention right now, while the evidence is fresh. If someone did murder her and we wait for toxicology reports, the trail will be cold by the time we start looking for the perp."

"What should I do then?" Jaime asked.

"Go back to the crime scene," Joanna said without hesitation. "Make sure Dave and Casey went over every inch of that place without missing anything. I want you to check with the alarm company and see if there was anything the least bit out of kilter in the last few days or weeks. Talk to people. Canvass the neighborhood."

"I'm on it, boss," Jaime said. "Anything else?"

"Yes. You should interview Bobo Jenkins up in Old Bisbee, since he and Rochelle Baxter had something going. Bobo told me he was in her home last evening. He must be the last person to have seen her alive."

"You think he's involved?" Jaime asked.

"He and Shelley Baxter were *romantically* involved," Joanna replied. "But if you're asking if I think he killed her, the answer is no. I personally told him about what had happened. He was absolutely devastated."

"He could have been acting," Jaime suggested.

"Wasn't," Joanna returned.

"All right," Detective Carbajal said. "I'm on my way."

Joanna shut off the phone and turned back to Butch. He had sat down in front of the family room blueprint. The disappointed expression on his face made her feel as though she'd just told some unsuspecting kindergartner that there was no Santa Claus.

"Butch, if you really want to have a train shelf, it'll be fine. I can live with it."

"You're not supposed to *live* with it," he countered. "You're supposed to *love* it."

"The rest of the house is great," Joanna continued. "And I *do* love the kitchen and the bathrooms. There'll be so much more space than we have now. My problem is that I want the house to be sort of . . . well, normal," she said finally.

"Normal as opposed to bizarre," he said. "You're right. It's a dumb idea. I should just grow up."

"We'll find a place for your trains," she assured him. "I promise we will."

"Where? Not in the house. None of the other rooms are big enough."

"We'll sort it out. Isn't that what marriage is all about—compromise?"

"I guess." Butch began reassembling and rolling up the set of blueprints. "Sounds like you need to go," he added.

"I do," she said. "But not like this. Not if we're quarreling."

"We're not quarreling," Butch returned. "You were right; I was wrong. The train shelf's out of there."

"But you really wanted it."

"Look, Joey," he said. "You can't have it both ways. The train shelf was an oddball idea. You happen to want normal. That's reasonable enough. You win. We'll have normal."

"But I don't want to *win*," Joanna objected. "I want us both to be happy with the house."

"I'll be happy."

"How much trouble will it be to take it out of the plans?"

He shrugged. "Not much. The train shelf was a late-breaking brilliant idea I added in just a few days ago or so. All I have to do is take it back out. I'm guessing Quentin will be ecstatic to avoid all that extra electrical work. So there you are. Two to one—I lose."

"It's going to be okay, then? You're not mad?"

"Not terminally mad, but you can buy lunch," he said. "By the time you pay up, chances are I'll be almost over it."

Out at the cash register, Junior took Joanna's money and then painstakingly counted out her change. When he had finished he flashed Joanna a triumphant smile. "Daisy taught me," he said proudly.

"Daisy's a very good teacher."

"Yes," Junior agreed, nodding vehemently. "Very good!"

By then Butch, with blueprints in one hand and motorcycle helmet in the other, had followed Joanna out of the backroom. He arrived in time to watch the end of the monetary transaction. He waited until they were out in the parking lot before commenting.

"Amazing," he exclaimed. "When we first met Junior, I never would have dreamed he'd be capable of making change."

"Kindness and patience go a very long way," Joanna said. "Now kiss me. I have to go back to work."

He gave her a halfhearted smooch and opened her car door.

"Can't you do better than that?" she demanded.

"Not in public," he said.

He grinned when he said it. Even so, a troubled Joanna Brady headed back to the Cochise County Justice Center. Getting married and combining households wasn't easy. She had expected that she and Butch would have tough going over child-rearing practices; over the chores of looking after a ranch full of animals in need of care and feeding.

Whoever would have thought we'd end up fighting over model trains? she wondered. *Compared to that, everything else has been a picnic.*

WASHINGTON STATE ATTORNEY GENERAL Ross Alan Connors had just returned from a meeting with the governor when O.H. Todd came into his office to give him the bad news.

"Damn!" Connors muttered. "You're sure it's her?"

"No mistake, I'm sorry to say," O.H. returned. "What do we do now?"

Connors rubbed his forehead thoughtfully. "We'd better send someone," he said at last. "But who?"

"One of the special investigators?" O.H. Todd suggested.

Connors considered and then nodded.

"Which one?"

"What about that new hire?" Connors returned. "The one who just retired from Seattle PD."

"You mean J.P. Beaumont?"

"Right," Connors said, nodding. "That's the one. He hasn't been on board very long. You should probably check with Harry Ball and see if Beau's up to speed."

O.H. Todd stood up and made for the door. "Right," he said. "Will do."

five

JOANNA AND FRANK MONTOYA FINALLY HAD their much-delayed morning briefing right after lunch. Late in the afternoon Joanna was boning up for her Friday-morning appearance before the board of supervisors meeting when Detective Carbajal knocked on her door.

"How's it going?" Joanna asked.

Jaime shook his head and sank into a chair. "I just finished preliminary interviews with Dee Canfield and Bobo Jenkins. Bobo stopped by so Casey could print him. I caught up with him while he was here."

"What do you think?" Joanna asked.

"Gut instinct?"

Joanna nodded.

"You may be convinced he's in the clear on this, but I'm not sure I agree."

"Fair enough," Joanna said. "We'll agree to disagree. Did anything more turn up at the crime scene?"

"No. I canvassed the entire neighborhood. No one saw or heard anything out of line until the EMTs showed up and started breaking down the door. What about you?"

She told him everything she had learned earlier from both Bobo Jenkins and Dee Canfield.

"Since she's going ahead with the show," Jaime said, "I guess I should be there. One of the guests may be able to fill in some of our blanks on the victim."

"Speaking of blanks," Joanna said. "Have you talked to that guy up in Washington?"

"O.H. Todd?" Jaime replied. "I've tried. I've called his number three different times. All I get is voice mail. So far he hasn't bothered to call me back."

"The man must have a boss," Joanna said. "What's his name?"

"I don't know."

"Find out, Jaime, and get me his number," Joanna said. "I'll give *him* a call. Maybe the big boss can set a fire under Mr. Todd's butt."

Jaime Carbajal grinned. "Works for me," he said. He left the room. A few minutes later he returned with a slip of paper.

"Good luck," he said, handing it over.

Joanna glanced at her watch. "It's already after five. He's probably gone."

"Try anyway," Jaime said.

Picking up her phone, Joanna dialed. "Attorney general's office," a woman's voice answered.

"I'd like to speak to Mr. Ross Alan Connors," Joanna said. "This is Sheriff Joanna Brady of Cochise County, Arizona."

"May I say what this is concerning?"

"Latisha Wall."

There was a noticeable pause. "One moment, please."

As soon as the operator went away, canned classical music began playing, interrupted periodically by a recorded voice apologizing for the length of the wait and assuring Joanna that her call was very important to them and that someone would be with her as soon as possible. The third time she heard the equally canned apology she was ready to blow.

Five minutes later a live voice finally returned to the line. "I'm sorry. Mr. Connors is in a meeting right now."

"Any idea what time he'll be through with it?"

"None at all. Sorry."

Like hell you're sorry, Joanna thought. "What about O.H. Todd?" she asked. "Is he available?"

"He's also in a meeting."

The same one, no doubt.

"Would you like to be connected to Mr. Connors's voice mail?" the woman asked.

"No, thank you," Joanna said. "I'd like you to personally take a message. Tell him Sheriff Joanna Brady needs to speak to him, urgently. Detective Jaime Carbajal, the investigator working Latisha Wall's death, has so far been unable to reach Mr. Todd. Obviously, time is of the essence." After leaving her office, home, and cell-phone numbers, Joanna hung up. Across the desk from her Jaime Carbajal scowled.

"You got the same treatment I did," he said. "Don't hold your breath waiting for a callback."

HARRY IGNATIUS BALL HAD TURNED off the light in his office and was about to close the door and head home when his phone rang. Muttering irritably under his breath, he returned to his desk and grabbed up the receiver.

"Special Unit B," he said. "Ball speaking."

"Harry, glad I caught you," O.H. Todd said, sounding relieved. "I just got cut loose from a meeting that lasted all afternoon."

Harry rattled his car keys, hoping O.H. would get the message. "What's up?" he asked.

"How's Beaumont doing?"

"What do you mean, how's he doing?"

"Is he up to speed?" O.H. asked. "Ready to send out on a case?"

Harry snorted. "He was ready for that the day he got here. Why?"

"We've developed a problem down in Arizona. A place called Bisbee. Ross may need to ship someone down to check it out." Todd paused. "What can you tell me about Beaumont?" he added. "About him personally, I mean. What kind of guy is he?"

"From what I've seen so far," Harry replied, "he isn't exactly a team player."

"Maybe that's okay," O.H. Todd said thoughtfully. "In fact, for this case, that may be just what the doctor ordered."

IT WAS ALMOST SEVEN when Joanna finally pulled into the yard at High Lonesome Ranch. The house was dark and locked up tight. Once inside, she discovered that Jenny and Butch had evidently already eaten. A single place setting remained on the table in the breakfast nook. In the middle of the plate was a note from Butch saying he had taken Jenny back into town for a play rehearsal and that there was a green chili casserole waiting for her in the fridge. All she had to do was heat it up.

After locking her weapons away and changing clothes, Joanna dished up a serving of the casserole and put the plate in the microwave. "Looks like I'm in the doghouse, too," she said to Sadie and Tigger, who sprawled comfortably on the kitchen floor. Other than thumping their tails in unison, the dogs made no further comment.

Joanna picked halfheartedly at the casserole—a dish that was usually one of her favorites. All the while she couldn't help wondering if Butch was still mad at her about the model train situation. *He said he wasn't, but he still must be,* she surmised. After all, he hadn't bothered calling to remind her about having to eat early due to Jenny's rehearsal. If he had, she could have come home earlier rather than waiting for Ross Connors to have the common decency to return her call. Now Joanna was home by herself when she didn't especially want to be alone.

No longer hungry, she divvied the remaining casserole on her plate into two portions and plopped them into the dog dishes. Uncharacteristically, Sadie showed no interest in the proffered treat. She stayed where she was, allowing Tigger to lick both dishes clean.

Joanna leaned down and patted the bluetick hound on her smooth, round forehead. "We're both a little out of sorts today, aren't we, girl," she said.

Joanna spent the evening catching up on reading, watching the clock, and waiting for the telephone to ring. It was after nine before Butch's Subaru finally pulled into the yard. Joanna and the dogs went out to greet the new arrivals.

"How was rehearsal?" Joanna asked.

"Awful," Jenny said. "The show's just two weeks away and most of the boys *still* don't know their lines. It's going to be a gigantic flop, Mom. I wish Miss Stammer would cancel it. We're all going to be up on stage looking stupid."

"It'll be fine, Jen," Joanna reassured her, tousling Jenny's blond curls. Behind Jenny's back, Butch rolled his eyes and shook his head as if to say Jenny's assessment was far closer to the truth than any motherly platitudes.

Jenny took the dogs and went into the house. Joanna turned to Butch. "Is it really that bad?"

"I'll say," Butch said.

Joanna changed the subject. "You should have called and reminded me to come home early."

Butch reached into the car and removed the roll of blueprints that, these days, seemed to be a natural extension of his arm. When he turned to reply, he wasn't smiling.

"I had to remind you to come to lunch today," he said. "I figured you were a big enough girl that you could decide when to come home for dinner on your own."

Ouch, Joanna thought.

She followed him into the house and locked the back door once she was inside. Butch put the blueprints on the dining room table. Joanna thought he would unroll them and pore over them as he did almost every night. Instead he said, "I think I'll turn in."

"You just got home," Joanna objected. "Don't you want to talk?"

Butch shook his head. "I'm beat. Quentin and I have a meeting first thing in the morning. Night."

He gave Joanna a halfhearted peck on the cheek and left her standing in the middle of the dining room. Rebuffed and hurt, Joanna returned to the kitchen. In a bid for sympathy, she had wanted to tell her husband about her day. She had wanted Butch to give her a loving pat and tell her that of course Ross Connors from Washington State was an unmitigated jerk. But Butch Dixon had surprised her. He had given her a cold shoulder rather than one to cry on.

Joanna sulked in the kitchen for a while. Then, wanting to talk and thinking Butch must still be awake, she crept into the bedroom, only to find him snoring softly. *So much for that!* she thought.

It was midnight before she finally went to bed and much later than that before she fell asleep. And overslept. If it hadn't been for the telephone ringing at ten after eight the next morning, she might have missed the board of supervisors meeting altogether.

"Hello," she mumbled into the phone. Staring wide-eyed at the clock, she staggered out of bed. The caller ID box next to the phone said the number was unavailable. Taking the phone with her, she headed for the bathroom.

"Sheriff Brady?"

"Yes. Who's this?"

"My name's Harry Eyeball and—"

"Look, mister," she said, cutting him off. "If this is some kind of joke—"

"Believe me, Sheriff Brady, it's no joke. My name is Harry, initial I, Ball. I'm with the Washington State Attorney General's Special Homicide Investigation Team. I'm returning the call you made to Ross Connors yesterday afternoon."

"Oh, yes," Joanna said. "I called about Latisha Wall."

"Making any progress?"

Joanna bristled. "My call was to Mr. Connors," Joanna said. "I'm not in the habit of discussing ongoing cases with people I don't know."

"I just told you—"

"Yes, yes, I know. Your name is Harry Ball. But I don't know you from Adam's Off Ox, Mr. Ball," she said, resorting to one of her father-in-law's favorite expressions. "My homicide detective, Jaime Carbajal, has been trying to contact Mr. Connors's office for information regarding this case. Up to now there's been no response."

"So Latisha Wall was murdered, then?"

Joanna ignored the question. "What Detective Carbajal needs, I believe, is for someone to fax Latisha Wall's information to us so we'll know where to start. All we have so far is her real name and her family's address in Georgia."

"That file isn't faxable, ma'am," Harry Ball told her.

"What do you mean, it isn't faxable?" Joanna returned. "What is it, chiseled in granite?"

"It's confidential. We have no assurances that it might not fall into unauthorized hands in the process of transmitting it."

"You're implying that someone in my department might leak it?" Joanna demanded. "And why is it so damned confidential? Let me remind you, Mr. Ball: Latisha Wall is already dead. If she was in a witness protection program you guys set up, I'd have to say you didn't do such a great job of it. And I still need the information."

"That's what I'm trying to tell you, ma'am. We're sending it to you."

"How? By pony express?"

Joanna glared at the clock, whose hands were moving inexorably forward. The board of supervisors meeting would start at nine sharp. Even skipping a shower, it was going to be close.

"One of the members of my team, an investigator named J.P. Beaumont, will be delivering it in person. Once he does so, Mr. Connors would like him to stay on as an observer."

"A what?"

"An observer. This is an important case with long-term, serious financial implications for the state of Washington," Harry Ball continued. "We wouldn't want someone to inadvertently let something slip."

Joanna was dumbfounded. "Let something slip?" she demanded. "Connors thinks my department is so incompetent that he's sending someone to bird-dog *my* investigation? I don't believe this! You can give that boss of yours a message from me. Tell him he has a hell of a lot of nerve!"

Slamming down the phone, she hopped into the shower after all. She was too steamed not to. Her hair was still damp and her makeup haphazardly applied when she slid into a chair next to Frank Montoya at the board of supervisors' Melody Lane conference room fifty minutes later. Frank glanced at his watch and sighed with relief when he saw her. The board secretary was already reading the minutes of the previous meeting.

"What happened?" he whispered.

"I overslept."

"Oh," Frank said. "Is that all? From the look on your face, I thought it was something serious."

Sheriff Joanna Brady hated having to attend board of supervisors meetings. For routine matters, Frank Montoya usually attended in her stead. This meeting, however, was anything but routine. The general downturn in the national economy had hit hard in Cochise County, requiring budget cuts in every aspect of county government. Today, with the board's cost-cutting knives aimed at the sheriff's department, she and Frank had decided they should both appear. Within minutes, Joanna knew they'd made a wise decision.

The newest member of the board, Charles Longworth Neighbors, was a man no one ever referred to as Charley—at least not to his face. He was a full-bird colonel who had retired from the army at Fort Huachuca a year or so earlier. He had now been appointed to fill out another board member's unexpired term of office.

Since Charles Neighbors was career army, the United States government had seen to it that he had earned a Harvard MBA while in the service. Now in civilian life, he loved to wield his relatively recent degree as a double-edged sword. He had no compunction about inflicting everything he had learned on the unwashed masses in every branch of Cochise County government, one reluctant department at a time. Today he homed in on the sheriff's department, going over budget items line by line, convinced that there were substantial cuts that could and should be made.

"If it can be done, it should be done," he told Joanna, with a patronizing smile that made her want to grind her teeth.

Three and a half grueling hours later, she and Frank escaped the boardroom, having taken a 10-percent-across-the-board hit. She waited until they were safely outside the building and out of earshot before she exploded.

"If it can be done, it should be done," she grumbled, doing a credible job of imitating Charles Longworth's pedantic, school-principal-like delivery. "If he had said that one more time, I think I would have thrown something! Of course, his should-bes are all one-way streets. Budget items are to be taken out and never put back in."

"Now, now," Frank counseled, "give the man a break. He's new and trying to get a grip on how things work. Supervising county government has to be different from being an officer in the army."

"Right," Joanna agreed. "We can't afford two-hundred-dollar toilet seats. And then there's Harry I. Ball."

"What hairy eyeball?" Frank asked. "I don't remember anyone saying a word about that."

"Not 'hairy eyeball,'" Joanna returned. "That's a man's name," she said, reading off the scrap of paper she had stuffed in the pocket of her blazer. "First name is Harry, middle initial I, and last name Ball. I made him spell it out for me."

"Who the hell is he?"

"Some high mucky-muck with the Washington State Attorney General's Office. He called me at home this morning when I should have been on my way to work." She didn't add that Harry Ball's unwelcome call was the *only* reason she hadn't been even later to the board of supervisors meeting.

"What did he want?"

"His office is sending someone to bring us Latisha Wall's file because the material is too volatile to be sent any other way than in person. Not only that, whoever they send is supposed to hang around and keep an eye on us—an observer to bird-dog us the whole time we're doing the Latisha Wall investigation. I believe the exact phrase he used is that his boss didn't want anyone to 'let something slip.' The good folks up in Washington are evidently convinced that our department is totally incapable of conducting an adequate homicide investigation. If you ask me, Mr. Ball sounded exactly like some of those high-handed yahoos from the *other* Washington, and just as screwed up."

"When does this so-called observer arrive?" Frank asked mildly.

"Who knows?" Joanna shot back. "And who cares? His name's . . ." She paused again to consult her note. "J.P. Beaumont. All I can say is, Mr. Beaumont had better stand back and stay out of my way."

Frank shook his head and unlocked the door to his waiting

Civvie. "Want to stop off and grab some lunch before we head back to the office?" he asked. "Something tells me you're running on empty."

Joanna gave him a sidelong glance. "What makes you say that? Just because I'm ranting and raving?"

Frank nodded. "The thought crossed my mind."

"We've been working together for too long," Joanna said, grinning in spite of herself. "And lunch is probably a good idea. Butch left the house early this morning. I ran late and skipped breakfast."

"I thought so," Frank said.

Minutes later Frank and Joanna turned their matching Crown Victorias into Chico's Taco Stand in Bisbee's Don Luis neighborhood. The building that housed Chico's had once served as the office of a junkyard. The wrecked cars had all disappeared, and now the building itself had been transformed. The tiny restaurant consisted of a counter where people lined up to place their orders. In addition to the counter's four stools, there were five booths that consisted of sagging, cigarette-scarred red vinyl benches with matching chrome-and-chipped-Formica tabletops. All of the furnishings had been purchased secondhand from a soon-to-be-demolished diner in Tucson. Several dusty, fading piñatas and a few unframed bullfight posters provided what passed for interior decor.

Fortunately, Chico's lunchtime clientele was in search of good food rather than trendy surroundings. Customers lined up daily for some of Chico Rodriguez's signature tacos, made from a recipe passed down from his great-grandmother to his grandmother, then to his mother, all of whom had spent decades cooking in various Bisbee-area Mexican eateries. When the last of the Rodriguez women retired, Chico had followed in their footsteps and opened his own establishment, one where his mother still filled in occasionally so Chico could have a day off.

Joanna and Frank went to the counter and placed their order. Taking their drinks, they retreated to a recently vacated booth, where they were obliged to clear their own table. Minutes later, Chico himself delivered their orders. The food came on paper plates accompanied by paper-napkin-wrapped plastic utensils. The shredded-beef tacos, made from crunchy homemade corn tortillas, were piled high with chopped lettuce. The lettuce was sprinkled with a generous helping of finely grated sharp cheese and topped by a dollop of tomato salsa that was more sweet than hot. It was that special combination of ingredients that made Chico's tacos taste better than any Joanna had eaten elsewhere.

As she took her first bite, Frank grinned at her. "As soon as you're no longer a raving maniac, tell me more about your call from the Washington State Attorney General's Office and this so-called observer they're sending."

"I've pretty much told you what I know," Joanna returned. "The guy's name is Beaumont. That's about it."

"When can we expect him?"

"Tomorrow or Sunday, I suppose," she said.

"And the purpose of his visit?"

"Other than spying on us and getting in the way? Beats the hell out of me. Like I said before, talking with Mr. Eyeball, as you called him, was like dealing with feds from back east. He fully expected me to spill my guts and tell him everything we know. But that isn't going to happen, at least not until that file gets here."

"He didn't go into any details as to why the state of Washington is so concerned about Latisha Wall's death?"

"No, and the longer they keep us working in the dark, the easier it'll be for us to make that slip Harry Ball seems to be expecting."

Frank jotted himself a note. "When we get back to the office, I'll go on-line and find out what I can about Ms. Latisha Wall. It must be a pretty high-profile case to garner this much attention from the attorney general's office. There may be newspaper coverage that will tell us some of what we need to know."

"Good idea," Joanna said. "We should also check with Casey and Dave to see how they're doing with processing all the evidence they brought back from the crime scene."

Frank nodded and made another note as Joanna finished the second of her two tacos. She was scraping the last of the *refritos* off her plate when the phone in her purse crowed.

"Hello, boss," Detective Jaime Carbajal announced when she answered. "Sorry to bother you. Kristin said you were at a board of supervisors meeting. Hope I'm not interrupting."

"The meeting's over," Joanna assured him. "Frank and I stopped off at Chico's to grab some lunch. What's up?"

"I still haven't heard a word from anybody in Washington," Jaime complained.

Joanna's laughter barked into the phone. "I have," she told him. "And I can tell you now, you're not going to like it. Meet us out at the department. I'll bring you up to date, and you can do the same."

Jaime Carbajal was waiting in the outside office when Joanna arrived. As predicted, he was irate at the idea of an outsider prowling around on his turf and messing around in his case.

"What about the opening at Castle Rock Gallery?" Joanna asked when she, Frank, and Jaime had exhausted the topic of Ross Connors's unconscionable interference.

"I didn't go," Jaime replied.

"You didn't go?" Joanna asked. "Why not?"

"It was canceled. When I got there last night, I found a sign on the door saying the opening had been canceled due to the death of the artist. Sorry for any inconvenience, et cetera, et cetera."

"Dee Canfield canceled the show after all?" Joanna mused. "She must have come to her senses then. The last I heard she was determined to go through with it. I wonder why she changed her mind. . . ."

Six

AS I PULLED my Porsche 928 out of the Belltown Terrace parking garage at seven that morning, I wasn't thinking about traffic or even about work. I was thinking about my mother and about how fortunate it was that she was dead and had been for more than thirty years. I still miss her, of course, but if I had told her about my new job with the Washington State Attorney General's SHIT squad, she would have been obliged to wash my mouth out with soap no matter how old I was.

Somewhere in the wilds of the state capitol down in Olympia was the out-of-touch Washington State bureaucrat who had dreamed up the name for the Special Homicide Investigation Team of which former Seattle homicide detective J.P. Beaumont was now the newest member. If you say the name word for word like that—Special Homicide Investigation Team—it sounds fine, dignified, even. The same holds true if you print it out on stationery or business cards. And that's exactly what that same dim-witted state official did. He went nuts ordering reams of preprinted stationery, forms, envelopes, and business cards.

There was, however, a fly in the ointment. The world we live in is made up of shortcuts and acronyms—the Seattle PD, the U.S. of A., the U Dub, et cetera. The AG's (see what I mean?) Special Homicide Investigation Team had barely opened its doors for business when people started shortening the name to something a little more manageable. And that's where the SHIT hit the fan, so to speak. While everyone agrees the name is "regrettable" and "unfortunate," no one in the state bureaucracy is willing to take the heat for rescinding that previously placed order for preprinted stationery, forms, and business cards. So SHIT it was, and SHIT it remains.

Getting back to my mother. I don't want you to think Karen Piedmont was some kind of humorless prude. She was, after all, an unwed mother who, in the uptight fifties, raised me without much help from anyone—including her own parents. Her total focus was on turning me into a "good boy." To that end, "bad language" was not allowed. As far as I know, the word "shit" never escaped my mother's lips. Her mother, on the other hand, a chirpy eighty-six-year-old named Beverly Piedmont Jenssen, loves to ask me about my job—acronym included. It's as though, at her advanced age, she's decided she's allowed to say anything she damned well pleases. And does.

Woolgathering as I went, I drove straight to what locals call the Mercer Mess—the Mercer Street on-ramp to I-5. I planned to take I-5 south to I-90 and go east across Lake Washington to the business park in Bellevue's Eastgate area, where the attorney general had seen fit to set his team of investigators up in a glass-walled low-rise building.

But southbound I-5 was where things went dreadfully wrong.

I turned onto the on-ramp and stopped cold. Nobody was moving—not on the ramp, and not on the freeway, either.

This was not news from the front. Seattle's metropolitan area is notorious for gridlock. It's a tradition. For the last several decades our trusted elected public officials have done everything possible to limit highway construction while allowing unprecedented growth. It doesn't take a rocket scientist to figure out that this is a recipe for transportation disaster. Now that it's here, those very same public officials alternately wring their hands and try to blame the problem on somebody else.

I have to confess that while I was both living and working downtown, the increasingly awful traffic situation was easy to ignore. However, now that I had thrown myself into the role of a trans–Lake Washington commuter, I was learning about the problem up close and personal.

So I wasn't especially surprised to find that I-5 traffic was barely moving. At least, that's what I thought—that it was barely moving. Then, when I had advanced only three car lengths in the space of fifteen minutes, I finally switched on the radio in time to hear KUOW's metro traffic reporter, Leslie Larkin, announce that the I-90 bridge was closed in both directions due to "police action."

The I-90 floating bridge is made up of two entirely separate side-by-side structures with eight lanes of traffic between them. During rush hour, the two center lanes are reversible. If there's an accident going one way or the other, it would normally shut traffic down in one direction only. But Leslie had clearly stated that it was closed in both directions, which seemed ominous to me. It made me wish I were still part of the Seattle PD. I could have called in and found out what was really going on. Instead, I concentrated on getting far enough onto the freeway so I could get off again—at the first available exit.

To understand the scope of the Seattle area's traffic woes, you have to imagine a densely populated metropolitan area with a twenty-five-mile-long lake dividing it neatly in half. Now, superimpose a huge pound sign over that body of water, and you can visualize the problem. The two legs are Interstates 5 and 405 running along the western and eastern sides of the lake. Two bridges, I-90 and Highway 520, form the cross-legs. If one of the two lake bridges goes out of commission, all hell breaks loose. Drivers have to choose among three unacceptably inconvenient and time-consuming choices. They can drive around either the top or the bottom of Lake Washington, or else they take a number and get in line to cross whichever bridge is still working.

I chose to go around. I exited the freeway at Stewart and took surface roads, but by then they were stopped up, too. Finally I called into the office to say I was going to be late.

"Special Unit B," Harold Ignatius Ball, my new boss, barked into the phone. "Whaddya need?"

I've had problems with my name all my life. Jonas Piedmont Beaumont isn't a handle any right-thinking woman should have laid on a poor defenseless baby, but that's what my mother did. Once I had a say in the matter, I chose to go by either Beau or by my initials, J.P. But in the troublesome name game, my mother was a piker compared to Harry's mom. By naming him as she did, Mrs. Ball had sentenced her little son Harold to be designated Harry I. Ball for the rest of his life. The words "Special Homicide Investigation Team" look fine on paper, and so does Harry's name. The trouble starts when you string the first together or say the second one aloud.

Harry went to work for the Bellingham Police Department right after returning from Vietnam. I suppose he could have nipped the problem in the bud by using his given name, going by Harold at work, and ditching his middle initial altogether. If he'd just used initials alone, it would have still made him an easy target for teasing. Hi-ball isn't much better. But Harry's a perverse sort of guy. Harry I. Ball is what his name tag said when he was a uniformed cop in Bellingham, and it's what's on his desk right now as Squad B leader of the Special Homicide Investigation Team. Occasionally, someone will look at the name and think it's some kind of joke, but anyone who underestimates Harry I. Ball is making a serious mistake.

"I'm going to be late," I said.

"You and everybody else," he muttered. "Why the hell don't you move to the right side of the lake?"

Harry lives in North Bend, right up against Mount Si on the west side of the Cascades. His commute is even longer than mine. The only difference is, there are no bridges.

"What's going on?" I asked. "I understand I-90 is shut down in both directions."

"Who knows?" he grumbled. "And who cares? When you gonna be in?"

"As soon as I can."

And I was. I arrived at nine-thirty, an hour and a half late, having spent two and a half hours making what is, in the best of circumstances, a twenty-minute drive. Barbara Galvin, Unit B's office manager, hadn't made it in yet, either. Knowing better than to risk my stomach lining on a cup of Harry I. Ball's crankcase-oil coffee, I timed in and then slipped into my tiny cubicle to go to work.

Every new hire in the Special Homicide Investigation Team spends his first few weeks of employment going over cold-case files before being brought on board one of the current investigations. Conventional wisdom dictates that one of us may bring to the table some previously unheeded bit of insight that will magically solve one of those cold cases. As far as I know, it's never happened, but it might.

I had worked my way through most of the files, saving the biggest and, as a consequence, most unwieldy, to last. I was manfully working my way through the Green River Killer Task Force documents when Harry's stocky figure darkened my doorway.

"How's it going?" he asked.

Sorry to be caught with my reading glasses on, I quickly stowed them in my pocket. "Okay," I said. "But it's like slogging though mud."

"I know," he said. "And you're dying to read every word, but I need you in my office. Now."

I followed him back down the hall. Since Barbara was at her desk by then, I stopped into the break room long enough to pour myself a cup of her freshly brewed coffee. Harry sat at his desk, massive arms resting on a file folder as I eased myself into one of the chairs.

"What's up?" I asked.

"I understand you're acquainted with a town in Arizona called Bisbee," he said casually.

I was so dumbfounded that I nearly dropped my coffee in my lap. The Department of Labor and Industries would have had a blast with that workman's comp. claim. Yes, I did know Bisbee. My second wife, Anne, had come from there, along with the money that had once been hers and was now mine.

To say Anne Corley was as troubled as she was beautiful is something of an understatement on both counts. I personally never discuss the circumstances surrounding her death on what was our wedding day, but I knew enough about Harry I. Ball to understand that if he was asking the question, he also knew the correct answer.

"Yes," I said. "I know a little about Bisbee."

He looked at me with a raised eyebrow worthy of Mr. Spock from *Star Trek*. "Ever been there?" he asked.

I had gotten as close to Bisbee as Sierra Vista once—twenty-five miles or so away. At the time I hadn't been ready to face visiting Anne's hometown. I wasn't emotionally equipped to deal with what I might have learned there. Fresh out of treatment at Ironwood Ranch up near Wickenburg, I was smart enough to know that there were some questions I was better off leaving unanswered.

"No," I said. "I never have."

"Would you have a problem going there now?" Harry asked.

I was stronger, older, and hopefully a little wiser. "I don't think so," I said.

"Good," Harry told me. "Because something's come up that needs looking into. It means sending someone out for an undetermined period of time. Since you say you prefer working alone, I thought it would be a helluva lot easier on the budget if we sent one investigator rather than two."

He had that right. I'm not a partner kind of guy. "What needs investigating?" I asked.

Harry sighed. He glared at the folder on his desk, but he didn't open it. "Know anything about UPPI?" he asked.

I shook my head. *Another collection of damnably meaningless letters. Doesn't anything go by its full name anymore?*

"Those initials mean nothing to me," I said. "Give me a clue."

"United Private Prisons, Incorporated."

Then it registered. "Okay, okay," I said. "I remember now.

That's the company the state of Washington contracted with to ease overcrowding in the state juvenile justice system, right?"

"Exactly," Harry agreed, "right up until we fired 'em. Now they're suing the state of Washington's ass for a hundred and twenty-five million dollars—breach of contract."

"Great," I said. "What does that have to do with us—with me, I mean?"

"The state of Washington's star witness, a young lady by the name of Latisha Wall, was murdered in Bisbee, Arizona, the day before yesterday. Or maybe not murdered, because the local sheriff's department down there is playing coy. The point is, Latisha Wall is dead, and we need to know how come."

I was a little foggy on the details of the Latisha Wall situation because I hadn't been directly involved, but I remembered the name. There had been a huge problem at a new, supposedly state-of-the-art correctional facility built near Aberdeen in southwestern Washington. Aberdeen had been given the nod in hopes that locating a new prison there would help relieve some of the long-standing unemployment in the state's lumber industry. Two years after opening, the place was summarily closed.

"Wasn't Latisha Wall some kind of whistle-blower?"

Harry nodded morosely. "That's right, and now she's dead. She begged Ross Connors to put her in a witness protection program. Said she was afraid somebody from UPPI might come gunning for her. We did as she asked, but now it looks like they found her anyway."

Ross Connors, the Washington State Attorney General, was Harry I. Ball's boss and mine as well.

"Didn't you say she was murdered in Bisbee, Arizona? Why should we be involved in the investigation?"

At last Harry moved his arms and opened the folder. "Turns out Latisha Wall didn't actually die in Bisbee proper," he said. "She died in a place called Naco, a little burg that's seven or eight miles outside of town and right on the U.S./Mexican border. Technically, the murder is being investigated by the Cochise County Sheriff's Department."

"So?"

"So. The sheriff's a young woman named Joanna Brady. I talked to her a little while ago. Sounds like she's just barely out of high school. Anyway, as soon as I started asking questions, she got her tits in a wringer and threatened to go to my boss. Of course, that's no problem since Ross is the one who had me call her in the first place."

Did I tell you that Harry I. Ball is an almost terminally unreconstituted male chauvinist? Word has it that when the personnel folks at the city of Bellingham diplomatically suggested he attend a sensitivity seminar, Harry told them to put their sensitivity where the sun don't shine. He then pulled the pin and went down the road, pension in hand. As for Attorney General Ross Connors? I wouldn't call him a beacon of political correctness, either. That goes for me as well, but I like to think I'm trying.

"Once I got off the phone with her, I called Ross myself," Harry continued. "Believe me, he has no intention of leaving a case this big in the hands of some little wet-behind-the-ears cowgirl who probably rides a horse, wears ten-gallon hats, and packs a forty-five on her hip, just for show."

For me, easy acquiescence to that kind of comment has been forever erased by the searing memory of my former partner, a bloodied Sue Danielson, sitting slumped against the wall of her trashed living room, my Glock in her wavering hand. *She* hadn't been holding it just for show. And no matter how much I try to avoid thinking about it, I know she would have used that weapon if she'd had to. She would have used it to save my life.

But sitting there in Harry I. Ball's office, I understood it was hopeless for me to try fixing his outdated view of the world. I've now spent enough time in AA that I understand the meaning of the Serenity Prayer. It says to change what you can and accept what you can't change. Harry wasn't changing—not for me, and not for anybody else. I let it pass.

"What do you want me to do?" I asked.

"When Barbara came dragging her butt in here a little while ago—she was even later than you, by the way—I told her to get on the horn with the AG's travel agent down in Olympia. She's to get you down to Arizona ASAP, before our latter-day Nancy Drew/Annie Oakley can screw up the evidence. In other words, I want you there yesterday, but I suppose that's asking a little much. In the meantime, while you're waiting for your travel packet, you might want to go over this."

With that, he spun the file folder across his desk. I managed to catch it before it skidded onto the floor. "Oh, well," I said, as I collected the file and my coffee cup and stood up to leave. "I guess the Green River Task Force file is going to have to wait,"

"Right," Harry agreed with a grin. "It's just too damned bad."

On the way back to my cubicle I passed the office manager's desk. Barbara Galvin is an attractive, up-and-coming young woman in her late twenties. She's competent and cheerful. She can also type like a maniac on her little laptop computer. In the world of slow-moving civil-service bureaucracies, those qualifications make her some kind of superstar. She wears a modest diamond and a wedding ring on her left hand and an equally modest diamond stud in her left nostril. The only picture that clutters her otherwise immaculately clean desk is one of a knobby-kneed, straw-headed kid about six or seven years old and wearing a red-and-white soccer uniform. He's holding a black-and-white ball and grinning from ear to ear.

I paused momentarily in front of Barbara's desk. She motioned to the earpiece of her phone to indicate someone else was talking, so I went on my way. Back at my desk I opened Latisha Wall's folder and was relieved when the first piece of paper that fluttered out contained a scribbled notation in Harry's virtually illegible scrawl that said Officer Unreadable in Indecipherable, Georgia, had made the next-of-kin notification. I was glad to know I had dodged that particular bullet.

I had only just started on the file's first page when my phone rang. "Beaumont here."

"Good morning," Naomi Pepper said cheerily. "How long did it take you to make it over to this side of the water?"

Naomi Cullen Pepper is a relatively recent widow and a girlfriend of rather brief standing. We had met more than a month earlier on a cruise ship bound for Alaska. Through several strange turns of events, we had found ourselves bunking in the same cabin—a situation that had, almost effortlessly, evolved into our becoming lovers. It was only when we were back home and on solid ground that the new reality hit me.

The first time I asked her out on a date, I spent hours agonizing over where I would take her and what I would wear. Ralph Ames, my attorney and good friend, happened to be visiting my Belltown Terrace condo at the time I was wrestling with that dilemma. He had almost fallen on the floor laughing.

"What the hell's the matter with you?" he had demanded. "You've already spent several nights in a cruise-ship cabin with the woman. How can you be worried about what you're going to wear?"

Believe me, worrying was easy. The truth is, on board the *Starfire Breeze,* where Naomi and I had walked away with the ship's tango prize, everything had seemed amazingly simple. But back on dry land, being involved in a relationship was much more complicated. And a lot more like hard work. What wasn't easy for me right then was carrying on my half of the conversation opposite Naomi's breezy sweet nothings when I was stuck in a tiny open-ended cubicle with God knew how many of my fellow Unit B SHIT investigators lapping it all up.

"Long time," I muttered in response to her question. "Two and a half hours. How about you?"

"I had to be here for a seven o'clock meeting," she said.

Naomi had recently been promoted to assistant manager in the kitchen department at The Bon Marché. Part of the promotion had involved her transferring from the downtown Seattle store to the Bell Square one in downtown Bellevue. This meant we were both now commuting from the west side of Lake Washington to the east side, although our disjointed schedules made carpooling impossible.

"I was already crossing 520 before they shut down I-90," she continued. "I heard they've reopened the bridge," she added. "No bombs anywhere. Are we still on for tomorrow?"

I was lost in Latisha Wall's history. "For tomorrow?" I said vaguely.

"Come on, Beau. Don't play dumb. It's your birthday. We're going out, remember? My treat."

There comes a time, somewhere after forty, when birthdays are best forgotten. Or ignored. In this case, I had forgotten completely.

"Come on," I wheedled. "Am I the kind of guy who would forget his own birthday?"

Of course, the answer was yes. I was and I had, but Naomi was all for giving me the benefit of the doubt.

"Good," she said. "We're going someplace special. As long as you don't mind driving back to Bellevue after driving home from work, that is."

With a dozen top-rated restaurants within walking distance of Belltown Terrace, there wasn't much need to drive all the way to Bellevue for dinner, but Naomi had made it clear that this time she was paying. "I don't mind at all," I told her.

"All right," she said. "I just wanted to confirm. Will I see you tonight?"

"Probably," I said. "I'll give you a call this afternoon."

I looked up to see Barbara Galvin standing in my doorway and giving me a knowing smile. Why wouldn't she? It's no coincidence that the newest kid on the block—me—has the cubicle closest to Barbara's desk.

"Gotta go," I said hurriedly to Naomi. "Somebody's waiting."

"You didn't have to hang up on her like that," Barbara told me. "I would have waited."

She had been listening. My ears turned red. "We were done anyway," I said. "What's up?"

Barbara tossed an envelope onto my desk. "Your travel packet, complete with itinerary," she said. "You're booked on Alaska Flight 790. It leaves for Tucson tomorrow morning at seven A.M."

"Seven A.M.!" I groaned. "Are you kidding? Why so early?"

Barbara grinned. "What's the matter, Beau?" she asked. "Got a hot date? You're on that flight because, even though it's the last minute, the travel agent was able to get us a good deal. She has you scheduled to return next Friday afternoon, but you can always extend if you need to."

Maybe I should go ahead and do it right now, I thought glumly. *When Naomi finds out about this, there won't be any point in coming home.*

Assuming the conversation had ended, I opened the envelope and glanced at the E-ticket itinerary. When I glanced back up, Barbara was still standing in my doorway looking at me with a strange, faraway look on her face.

"What is it?" I asked.

"Nothing," she said with a shrug. "I was just thinking about how much you remind me of my dad."

Words every older guy loves to hear! No longer a hunk, you're someone's dad instead.

With that she was gone. *Poor kid,* I thought in a sudden flash of empathy. *No wonder she can put up with all of Unit B's geriatric cop crap. She must have spent most of her life living with an old troglodyte who is as tough to get along with as we are.*

I picked up the phone and called Naomi right back. "Where were you planning on taking me to dinner tomorrow night?" I asked.

"Why? It's supposed to be a surprise."

"It's a surprise, all right. I just found out I have to be on a plane to Tucson at seven o'clock tomorrow morning."

"Work or pleasure?" Naomi asked.

"What do you think?"

"Bis," she said. "Bis on Main is the name of the restaurant."

"What do you say we go tonight instead? I'll pay."

"I suppose," she agreed, although I could tell she wasn't happy about it. "If you can get a reservation, that is. It's a pretty popular place."

I looked up the number in the phone book, called, and gave whoever answered my tale of woe. "For you, my friend, I believe we can do something," he said. "We're very busy this evening, but if you could come in early, say five-thirty . . ."

"Done," I told him. "It might just as well be early. I have to be up at the crack of dawn tomorrow morning to catch a plane."

I put down the phone. Part of me was sorry to disappoint Naomi. And part of me was pissed at the people in the AG's office for dropping this on me at the last minute. But there was a third part of me—the stubborn old-coot part—that was more than happy to get off his butt, put the cold-case files back where they belonged, and go to work.

Seven

FOR THE SECOND TIME IN AS MANY DAYS, Joanna and Frank Montoya's "early-morning" briefing took place in the early afternoon. Afterward, Joanna started in on that day's worth of correspondence. Almost an hour later and near the bottom of the stack, she discovered the latest edition of *The Bisbee Bee*. The words "See page two!" were scribbled on the top of the front page in Kristin Gregovich's girlish handwriting.

Joanna opened the paper and turned to what she knew would be Marliss Shackleford's latest column. The headline read:

CAN COCHISE COUNTY AFFORD A SOFT-HEARTED SHERIFF?

There can be no question that Wednesday's Fallen Officer memorial in honor of Cochise County Corrections Officer Yolanda Cañedo was moving and inspirational, but here's the question many county residents are asking themselves: Should a dirty dozen of Cochise County inmates have been in attendance with what amounted to minimal sheriff's department supervision?

There can also be no question that, as a corrections officer, Yolanda Cañedo made a difference in the less-than-exemplary lives of some of those unfortunate inmates. Ms. Cañedo used her off-duty hours to work as an unpaid volunteer with an inmate literacy project. She personally tutored a number of inmates who were working toward GED certificates while being incarcerated.

But the fact remains that these men are prisoners. They're in the county lockup for reasons that either a judge or a jury could not ignore or excuse. Why, then, were they allowed to attend Ms. Cañedo's funeral services without any evidence of restraints and with only two off-duty guards and the director of the Cochise County Jail Ministry looking after them?

Not that they did anything bad. From what I could learn, the inmates caused no difficulty. They behaved themselves during the funeral service and afterward were all returned to their cells at the Cochise County Jail without incident. But some people, including yours truly, think that letting those prisoners out at all was a mistake and that having done so sets a bad precedent.

Unnamed sources within the department suggest that Sheriff Joanna Brady herself is the one who made the decision to allow prisoners to attend the service. And why would she do such a thing? Was it a grandstanding effort on her part to let people see that her department is interested in rehabilitating county prisoners, as opposed to locking them up and throwing away the key? Or was it something else entirely?

Since her election, Sheriff Brady has gone to great lengths to prove she's just as tough and hard-nosed as anybody else. But now, with the beginning of what promises to be a hotly contested reelection campaign only months away, I think it's possible she wanted to show potential voters her softer, gentler side.

The problem is, if one of those inmates had decided to take off for parts unknown, any number of people could have been hurt, endangered, or even killed in the process. That's a kind of soft-hearted, soft-headed approach to law enforcement that the people of Cochise County don't deserve and can ill afford.

Finished reading, Joanna wadded up the paper and tossed it into the trash. For a while she tried to return to her paperwork, but it was no use. Distracted and unable to concentrate, she touched the intercom button.

"I'm going home early," she said to Kristin. "If anybody needs me, have them call me there."

"Are you okay?" Kristin asked. "I mean, it's only three o'clock. You're not sick or anything, are you?"

"Lots of people go home at three o'clock," she said. "And today that's me. I've done all I can do, unless there's an emergency, that is."

She left her office via the private door. Once back home at High Lonesome Ranch, she changed into a T-shirt, jeans, and boots. Then she hurried out to the barn, where she started mucking out the stall where Jenny kept her sorrel quarter-horse gelding, Kiddo. It was hot, dirty, smelly work—just the thing to take Joanna's mind off Marliss Shackleford's latest piece of attack journalism.

She became so involved in her shoveling and cleaning that she lost track of time. When Jenny came home from school and spoke to her from a few feet away, Joanna was so startled, she jumped.

"Mom, what are you doing that for?" Jenny demanded. "I told Butch I'd clean the stall out today, as soon as I got home from school. I haven't had a chance to do it before because of play practice and—"

"I just felt like doing it myself," Joanna said. "I was sick and tired of sitting behind a desk. I decided a little physical labor would do me a world of good."

A look of alarm flitted briefly across Jenny's face. She paled. "Nothing bad happened at work, did it?" she asked.

"Not really," Joanna reassured her daughter. "All I'm saying is, my day was rotten. How was yours?"

"Okay, I guess," Jenny said unenthusiastically.

"Let's go wrestle a few bales of hay together," Joanna suggested cheerfully. "Maybe throwing a couple of those around will make us feel better."

Once the chores were done, Joanna came out of the barn to find Jenny leaning against the topmost rail of the corral with Kiddo nuzzling her jacket pocket, searching for the sugar cubes she routinely carried there. With their matching blond manes, girl and horse leaned on each other in an unspoken communion that made Joanna marvel.

Kiddo had come into their lives not long after Andy's death. As a single mother with a demanding full-time job, Joanna had been wary of taking on any more responsibilities. She had objected to the idea of Jenny's having a horse, but on that subject she had been overruled by her in-laws. And rightly so, she realized now.

She had watched in amazement as Jenny and the gelding had bonded. She had also been astonished at how caring for the horse had somehow helped ease Jenny's terrible grief after her father's death. In a way Joanna didn't quite understand, she realized that allowing Jenny to be responsible for this huge, four-legged creature had helped transform her from a child into what she was now—a self-possessed young girl verging on womanhood.

Silently Joanna went over and joined Jenny at the fence, noticing as she did so that she and her daughter stood almost eye-to-eye. Within months, Jennifer Ann Brady would most likely be taller than her five-foot-four mother.

"Did you and Butch have a fight or something?" Jenny asked as Joanna reached out a hand to touch Kiddo's sleek neck.

"Why do you ask that?" Joanna returned.

Jenny shrugged. "He was real quiet last night when he took me to play practice, and he was gone this morning by the time I got up," she said. "He usually cooks breakfast, but today he didn't. I had cold cereal instead."

"We had a disagreement," Joanna conceded after a pause. "Not a fight. And it's all settled now. He said he had a meeting over at the new house this morning. I'm sure that's the only reason he left the house so early."

"What was it about?" Jenny asked pointedly.

"The disagreement?"

Jenny nodded.

"About his trains," Joanna answered, thinking how silly that must sound.

"What about them?" Jenny asked.

"He wants to build a permanent track for them in the family room and run it over the doors and window frames," Joanna replied. "I want a regular family room with a couch, a couple of chairs, a television set, and no trains."

"If he's still mad about it, then I guess you won," Jenny said.

"It's not a matter of winning or losing," Joanna replied. "Being married means you have to discuss things and work out compromises you can both live with. I told Butch we'd find someplace else to put his trains, and we will."

There was a long pause after that. Joanna assumed the conversation was over. It wasn't.

"Did you and Dad have disagreements?" Jenny asked.

This was tougher ground. With Andy dead, it might have been

easier to pretend that everything between them had always been perfect, even if that wasn't true.

"Yes," Joanna admitted finally. "Yes, we did."

"What about?"

Joanna thought about those first stormy years in her previous marriage. She and Andy had both been young, and having a child only a few months after the wedding had added a whole other dimension to the usual newlyweds conflicts. For years, there had always been too little money and too many bills. Thinking back, it seemed to Joanna that she and Andy had fought about almost everything—about whether or not he had filled the car with gas the last time he drove it, about why he was late for dinner or hadn't picked up his dirty clothes, and why he always seemed to leave an unsightly sprinkle of whiskers in the bathroom sink. Then, after five years or so, things had smoothed out. Joanna and Andy had made it to their tenth anniversary and most likely would have made it longer if only . . .

"A lot of little things, I guess," Joanna said finally. "Things that I see now weren't important enough to fight over in the first place."

"I never heard you fight," Jenny said wistfully. "Or if I did, I don't remember."

"Good," Joanna returned, meaning it. Her relationship with Roy Andrew Brady hadn't been all good or all bad. Neither was her relationship with Butch Dixon. Jenny needed to have a more realistic idea of how the world worked.

"It's better to forget quarrels than it is to remember them," Joanna added.

Then, as they stepped off the rail and started toward the house, Butch drove into the yard. Again the dogs rode in the back with their heads thrust out the open windows.

As soon as Butch opened the door, the two dogs leaped out and gamboled over to Jenny. Only after greeting her did they make for their water.

"I see you let them ride again," Joanna said, walking up to kiss him hello. If he was still angry about the train situation, it didn't show.

He kissed her back and then frowned at the dogs. "I remembered what you said about spoiling them," he said. "I tried to get them to run home, but Sadie wasn't having any of it. She lay down in the middle of the road and wouldn't budge. I had to go back and get her. Once she was in the car, Tigger wanted to ride, too."

"It's all right," Joanna said. "I was teasing."

Butch glanced down at Joanna's clothing and then checked his watch. "It's only five now. How long have you been home?"

Joanna shrugged. "A couple of hours. Jenny and I have been cleaning Kiddo's stall and putting out hay."

"Why so early?"

"I gave myself part of the afternoon off," she said.

"How come?"

"Politics," she said.

"I see," Butch said. "Come tell me about it while I fix dinner."

Inside the house, Jenny and the dogs disappeared into her room. Relieved that things were better with Butch, Joanna sat in the breakfast nook and sipped at a soda while he hustled around the kitchen. There was no point in asking if she could help. Years of being a short-order cook made Butch's culinary efforts far superior to Joanna's limited skills in that regard. His movements were quick, decisive, and economical.

Joanna told him everything—about the Rochelle Baxter/ Latisha Wall case as well as the difficult board of supervisors meeting and Marliss Shackleford's hurtful column. Somehow, though, she neglected to mention the heart-to-heart she and Jenny had shared outside Kiddo's corral.

"It sounds like Marliss is throwing her lot in with your opposition," Butch said when she finished relating the part about the column. "Any idea who that's going to be?"

"Not really," Joanna said. "I have my suspicions. It was Ken Galloway who raised such a stink about Yolanda's Fallen Officer funeral. I wouldn't be surprised to learn he's Marliss Shackleford's 'unnamed source.' "

Butch stopped with a half-peeled potato in one hand and the paring knife in the other. "Do you think Galloway might run against you?" he asked.

Joanna nodded. "It's possible."

"That's my guess, too," Butch agreed.

The phone rang, and Joanna hurried to answer it. "Howdy, boss," Jaime Carbajal said. "Sorry to bother you at home."

"It's all right. What's up?"

"I had an appointment to finish my interview with Dee Canfield today. Like I told you, I did a preliminary with her yesterday, but she was so anxious about getting ready for the show that she barely paid attention to my questions. Since she was so distracted, I made an appointment to see her this afternoon at the gallery."

"And?"

"She wasn't there. Her boyfriend wasn't, either. The place is still closed up tight, just like it was last night. The sign's still on the door. There were two notices—one from FedEx and one from UPS—saying they had attempted deliveries."

Joanna felt a twinge of concern. She had been pleased to hear Dee had canceled the show, thinking the gallery owner had come to her senses. Now there was a far more ominous possibility. Only one person in town had been absolutely determined to shut down that grand-opening party.

"Did you go by her house?" Joanna asked. "Maybe she's ill."

"Sure did. She lives on Cochise Drive out in Huachuca Terraces. I stopped by twice," Jaime said. "Nobody was home. The blinds are down and the curtains closed. Something's not right here, Sheriff. I have a really bad feeling about it. If there's still no sign of her or Warren Gibson by tomorrow morning, I should probably get search warrants and go through both the house and the gallery."

"Maybe they decided to take a few days off," Joanna suggested.

"I doubt that," Jaime said. "For one thing, I talked to Gina Dodd at Desert Stairs Catering. Dee hired Gina to supply the food for last night's party. The first Gina knew about the cancellation was when she showed up with a vanful of food and found the sign on the gallery door. Gina says Dee never would have done that without calling. She says that's not the way Dee Canfield does business. Gina's convinced something is terribly wrong."

"Do you think Gina Dodd's word will be enough for you to get a search warrant? And will you be able to get one on Saturday morning?"

"By the time I talked to Phyllis Kelly, Judge Moore's clerk, he was gone for the day," Jaime replied. "He and his wife have a dinner engagement in Tucson. I'll have to catch up with him in the morning. Phyllis says I can bring the paperwork by his house then."

"Did you talk to Bobo Jenkins about any of this?" Joanna asked. "He had a disagreement with Dee Canfield over Rochelle Baxter's show, but I believe he and Dee have been friends for a long time. Maybe he knows where Dee and Warren might have gone off to."

"I didn't actually talk to Bobo today," Jaime said. "What I got instead was a call from Burton Kimball. He says he'll be along for the ride when Bobo Jenkins comes to talk to us at ten o'clock tomorrow morning."

Joanna was surprised. "Bobo's bringing Cochise County's premier defense attorney along for the interview? How come?"

"You tell me. I told Mr. Kimball all we want is to ask Bobo a few routine questions. Burton hinted that he thought our reasons for wanting to talk to his client were possibly politically or racially motivated."

"Politically or racially motivated?" Joanna repeated. "What kind of nonsense is that?"

"I've heard talk that Bobo Jenkins is thinking of running for mayor," Jaime offered.

"He can run for governor, for all I care," Joanna shot back, angered by the implication. "Bobo is one of the last people who saw Latisha Wall alive. He was also raising hell in Castle Rock Gallery yesterday morning, not long before Dee Canfield and Warren Gibson disappeared. Of course we need to talk to him. That's not race or politics; that's police work. If Bobo feels a need to have Burton Kimball along to hold his hand, it's his problem, not ours."

There was a pause. "Are you okay, boss?" Jaime asked.

"What do you mean, am I okay?" Joanna demanded, trying not to sound as irritable as she felt. "Of course I'm okay."

"Kristin told me that you went home early, which, you have to admit, isn't like you," he said. "She thought you weren't feeling well, and you do sound a little . . ."

"A little what?"

"Well . . . cranky," Jaime replied reluctantly.

Joanna didn't want to sound cranky. Or unreasonable. "I'm fine, Jaime," she assured him, deliberately softening her tone. "What time is that Bobo Jenkins interview again?"

"Ten."

When her other homicide detective, Ernie Carpenter, had asked to take a full week of vacation all at once, it hadn't seemed like that big a deal. "When's Ernie due home?" she asked.

"Monday."

"I wish it was sooner, but that's the way it is. All right, then. If Bobo is bringing the big guns in with him, you'd better have some backup as well. Call Frank Montoya and ask him to be there with you."

"Will do," Jaime agreed.

"All the same," Joanna added, "I'll be in the office. When you're done with the interview, come tell me how it went."

"Okeydokey," Jaime Carbajal responded. "Who needs weekends anyway?"

He hung up and Joanna turned back to Butch. "What was that all about?" he asked.

Joanna explained as best she could.

"Dee Canfield," Butch said. "The woman who disappeared. Who's she again?"

"She owns the gallery where Rochelle/Latisha's art was going to be exhibited. Even with the artist dead, she was going to go through with the grand opening last night, but then she didn't. Jaime Carbajal tried to go to the party himself, but the gallery was closed up tight, and it still is, more than twenty-four hours later."

Butch lifted a pot lid to check on the potatoes. "I can hardly wait to read next week's paper," he said. "No doubt Marliss will figure out a way to make all of this your fault as well."

At that moment Jenny meandered into the kitchen. "What's your fault?" she asked, opening the refrigerator door and examining the contents. "What's for dinner?" she added. "It smells good, and I'm starved."

"Pork chops and gravy," Butch replied. "Along with mashed potatoes, string beans, and apple sauce."

"Great," Jenny said. "Everything except the string beans." Butch's fried pork chops were her unqualified favorite. Reaching for a clean glass, she poured herself some milk.

"So what's your fault, Mom?" Jenny asked, sipping her milk and studying her mother's face over the rim of the glass.

"At the moment, one person is dead and two others are missing," Butch explained. "I was saying that in Marliss Shackleford's next column, she'll probably try to blame all of it on your mother. That's Marliss's usual modus operandi."

"Oh," Jenny said, taking her half-empty glass and heading into the dining room. "Is that all? I thought you guys were back to talking about putting a train track in the family room."

Butch shot Joanna a quizzical look. Joanna sighed.

Thanks, Jen, she thought. *You've just provided a perfect ending to a perfect day!*

Eight

IT WASN'T A PARTICULARLY NICE WAY to begin celebrating my birthday. For one thing, I had to be up and out of Belltown Terrace by five in the morning in order to make that 7 A.M. Alaska Airlines flight to Tucson. It was pitch-dark as I climbed into a cigarette-smoke-saturated cab driven by a noncommunicative maniac. I wasn't about to give the state of Washington access to the condo's communal limo.

The rain was pouring down as we headed for the airport, but I didn't regard that as any kind of ill omen. After all, it was the last week in October. Everybody knows it rains like mad in Seattle in October. And maybe that's why the seven-o'clock plane to Tucson was loaded to the gills. It was full of people wanting to trade chill autumn rain for one last glimpse of sun along with a whole wad of purple-and-gold-bedecked rowdy Husky fans on their way to a U Dub/U of A football game.

When I reached my row, I discovered I was in the back of the plane in the middle seat, squashed between two very large men. I'm not exactly a lightweight, but these two guys dwarfed me. One was a twenty-something weight lifter with massive shoulders. The other was in his mid-to-late seventies and had probably never been in a gym in his life. His shoulder muscles had come about the old-fashioned way—by doing hard physical labor. He was an old codger with several missing teeth and amazingly bad breath. He read every word of his in-flight magazine, moving his lips constantly and showing off those missing teeth as he did so.

Resigned to two and a half hours of misery, I settled into my seat as best I could, closing my eyes and hoping to nap my way to Arizona. I willed myself into unconsciousness and thought about the previous evening's night on the town with Naomi Pepper.

We'd had a nice-enough dinner. The food at Bis on Main was wonderful and the service impeccable. Even so, the evening hadn't turned out to be the complete success either Naomi or I had envisioned. I could tell when I stopped by the mall to pick her up after work that Naomi wasn't a happy camper.

"What's wrong?" I asked.

"It's my mother," she said.

In the month or so that Naomi Pepper and I had been hanging out together, I had gleaned bits and pieces of information about her mother, Katherine Foley. Putting those pieces together, I had determined Katherine was something of a handful. Twice widowed and once divorced, she had now been abandoned by her most recent boy toy.

Some of Katherine's wilder antics—like insisting on doing her weekly shopping at midnight in her local Albertson's in full evening-wear regalia—verged on Auntie Mame behavior. It's easier to deal with Auntie Mame when the person in question is some distant relative, preferably a second cousin. When the kook turns out to be your very own mother, all bets are off. That evening I realized that being Katherine Foley's daughter had turned into tough duty for Naomi Pepper.

"What about her?" I asked.

To my surprise, Naomi's eyes filled with tears. "Let's not talk about it right now," she said. "We're having a fun birthday celebration. I don't want anything to spoil it."

"Tell me about your mother," I insisted.

"She wants to move in with me," Naomi said finally, after taking a deep breath. "She's just this week been diagnosed with Parkinson's. She's worried about continuing to live on her own now that Geoff has taken off for parts unknown. I don't know much about Parkinson's disease, but I suppose she has a point. But she's so incredibly bossy, Beau. She's forever trying to run my life by remote control. If I let her move in . . ."

Naomi's voice trailed off, and I could guess at what *wasn't* being said. Naomi Pepper is one of the nicest people I've ever met. Nice as in kind. Nice as in loving. Nice as in giving you the shirt off her back and caring about everyone else first and herself last, often to her own detriment. The problem is, the world is full of not-nice people who prey on the ones who are, people who have zero compunction about taking advantage of their victims. Naomi Pepper's husband, Gary, is a prime case in point.

Gary hadn't quite finished divorcing her when he was diagnosed with liver cancer. His girlfriend wouldn't look after him, so he had dragged his dying butt back home to Naomi. And, because she's a nice person, she had taken him in and cared for him until his death several months later.

Then there's Naomi's daughter, Melissa. She may not be Gary's biological daughter, but she's still a chip off the old block. The hair-raising stories I'd heard about Missy's formative years put her in a class with the rotten little kid in that old movie *The Bad Seed*. From seventh grade on, Missy Pepper had been a mess—in and out of juvie and rehab and on and off the streets. Despite Melissa's propensity for getting into trouble, Naomi loves the girl to distraction and has stuck with her through some very rough times. Naomi may have been introduced to the concept of tough love, but I'm sure she'll be there to bail Melissa out of trouble the next time the girl needs bailing.

What I thought Naomi Pepper herself needed right then was a vacation from troublesome relatives. Here, though, was her mother, prepared to waltz into Naomi's life as yet another patient in need of nursing and attention.

Let me be clear: I wasn't being totally altruistic. I know the younger set is under the impression that adult sex drives disappear completely somewhere around age thirty-seven. But that's not true. At least mine hasn't. Still, the idea of having a sexual interlude in a bedroom where someone's aging mother might possibly burst in on the scene at any moment encourages a degree of sexual malfunction that no amount of Viagra can fix.

In other words, I wanted Katherine Foley to live somewhere else, but I was hoping for subtlety. I tried to avoid saying it in so many words. What I said instead was, "Are you sure you want to do that—take her in, I mean?"

"I don't have a choice," Naomi said. "I'm an only child."

"Does your mother have money?"

Harry I. Ball isn't alone in asking nothing but questions for which he already knows the answers. It's one of the oldest ploys in an experienced interrogator's bag of tricks, one I myself utilized to good effect during the years I worked as a homicide detective at Seattle PD. In this case I happened to know that the answer to my money question was an unequivocal yes. Naomi had mentioned on several occasions—occasions when the mother-daughter guilt card wasn't faceup on the table—that Katherine Foley's various ventures into the world of holy matrimony had left her fairly well off, much better off financially than her daughter, who still had to go to work at The Bon every day to earn her keep.

"Some," Naomi allowed now.

"Couldn't she move into an assisted-living place? Beverly and Lars live in one of those, you know. They're in Queen Anne Gardens, up at the top of the Counterbalance. It's very nice. At least it seems nice to me."

Beverly Piedmont, my widowed, eighty-six-year-old grandmother, had recently married Lars Jenssen, my AA sponsor, who's a spry eighty-seven. After their wedding, they moved into a retirement center on top of Seattle's Queen Anne Hill, where they seem to be enjoying themselves immensely. The common areas of what they call "the home" resemble the lobby of a posh hotel. The rooms and corridors are brightly painted and well-lit. The floors are covered with bluish-green carpets that look new and smell clean.

At Queen Anne Gardens, Lars and Beverly had signed up for a plan that comes complete with linen service as well as three hot meals a day. The food is plentiful and palatable, with no need to shop or cook beforehand or to wash up and put away dishes afterward. Beverly Piedmont Jenssen had spent more than five decades cooking and serving three meals a day, with little or no help from my now deceased grandfather. As far as she's concerned, being relieved of KP duty qualifies as nothing short of heaven on earth. And, since Beverly is happy, Lars is happy, too.

"Does your mother have any pets?" I asked.

Naomi nodded. "A cocker named Spade," she said. "He's eleven."

"According to Lars, some of the residents have pets," I hinted. "There may be a size restriction. You probably couldn't get away with bringing along an Irish wolfhound, but I'm sure a cocker spaniel would qualify."

"Mother won't go," Naomi said flatly.

"How do you know that?" I said. "Have you asked her?"

"No, but I know my mother," Naomi replied. "She'd rather die than have to go live in a place like that."

Watch out, I wanted to warn Naomi. *You're about to be suckered.* But I didn't. I kept my mouth shut because I've learned over the years that when it comes to minding other people's business, I always wind up getting myself in trouble.

Alaska Air Lines Flight 790 had reached what the pilot called a "comfortable cruising altitude." That was easy for him to say. He wasn't jammed into the middle of a three-seat row. About that time the guy in front of me leaned his seat back all the way, crushing both my kneecaps. Is it any wonder I'm not much of a fan of air travel? I don't know many people over six feet tall who are.

The weight lifter next to the window—the guy whose humongous shoulders overlapped my seat by a good three inches—suddenly needed to get up. Climbing over both me and Mr. Moving Lips, he removed a laptop computer from the overhead compartment and turned it on. I thought he was going to work on something interesting. Instead, he began playing solitaire. The only time he paused was during the couple of minutes it took him to plow his way through his English muffin/scrambled egg sandwich. It wouldn't have been so bad if he had been any good at solitaire, but he wasn't. He'd sit there not making moves that I could see and he couldn't.

I would have gone back to thinking about Naomi, but between the lip-moving reader on one side and the solitaire player on the other, it wasn't possible. Finally, with my seatmates seemingly preoccupied with their own activities, I opened my own briefcase, took out the Latisha Wall file, and commenced to reread the reports I found there. As soon as I started working, the weight lifter abandoned his solitaire game in favor of engaging me in polite conversation. Rather than let him read over my shoulder, I put the file away.

Guess what he wanted to talk about? Working out. It seems his father was a championship weight lifter in the age fifty-five-to-sixty-five category. Father and son worked out at the same gym, where all the other weight lifters thought the father-and-son act was cool. Since they had bonded so well this way, the weight lifter felt free to tell me that he thought everybody else should do the same thing. And so on and so on. At tedious length. I was tempted to tell him this would be difficult for me since I never knew my father, but even that probably wouldn't have shut him up.

I was trapped with no means of escape. It reached a point where I would have welcomed a comment from the guy on the other side, but he continued to read his magazine in total, lip-moving concentration.

Eventually—and not nearly soon enough—the pilot announced that we were beginning our gradual descent into Tucson International, which—as far as I could see from my limited middle-seat view—seemed to consist of a vast sea of brown. Brown or not, I was looking forward to landing. That would mean the guy who was crushing my knees would have to put his seat back in the full upright and locked position. I thought my troubles would soon be over. They weren't. Once I managed to escape from the plane, my life immediately got worse.

Compared to Sea-Tac, Tucson International Airport is small potatoes. I collected my luggage and walked down the car-rental aisle, looking for a counter called Saguaro Discount Rental, the car-rental agency listed on my itinerary. I finally stopped at the Alamo desk and asked one of the women working there.

"That's pronounced 'sa-waro,'" she told me, rolling her eyes. "It's Spanish, so the g is pronounced like a w. They're off-site. You have to call on their courtesy phone. It's over there on the wall. They'll send a shuttle to pick you up."

No matter how you pronounce it, the office and lot for Saguaro Discount Rental was more than a mile from the airport. As soon as I saw their fleet of brightly colored KIAs—all of them last year's model—I knew that the Washington State Attorney's penny-pinching travel agent had struck again. My car was a four-cylinder automatic KIA Sportage SUV, a name that sounds a whole lot more sporting and exotic than it is.

I admit to being spoiled. At Seattle PD I often drove vehicles equipped with police pursuit engines. Meanwhile, parked on the P-3 level of the Belltown Terrace garage is my slick guard's red 928. Even so, I do have some experience at driving four-cylinder vehicles. I spent eight years—the whole time I was in college and four years afterward—driving an old-time VW Beetle, but that was a standard four-speed, not an automatic. My rental Sportage did fine as long as I was driving on flat ground. It was only when I started up an incline, even a gradual one, that it lugged down so far that it seemed I was barely moving. Compared to the rest of the seventy-five-mile-an-hour traffic on the freeway, I wasn't.

My printed MapQuest directions said it would take me two hours and twelve minutes to get from Tucson to Bisbee. It actually took forty-five minutes longer than that because the road was uphill most of the way. By the time I came chugging up over the mountain pass just north of Bisbee, I was beginning to think I'd never get there. The good news is, moving that slowly I had plenty of time to survey the scenery. I found myself regretting not having brought along a pair of sunglasses, but in the dark and wet of pre-dawn Seattle, sunglasses hadn't seemed like a pressing necessity.

The mountainous terrain on either side of the highway leading to Bisbee was either reddish brown or gray. The hillsides were dotted with green specks I assumed to be bushes of some kind. Then, as I started up the north side of the Mule Mountains, I realized those bushes were really full-fledged trees after all. They're not the kind of towering, stately evergreens we have in Washington. No, these starved and stunted trees did have leaves on them, but there was no hint that they were about to change colors or drop off.

Every once in a while, winding along what looked like a dry creek bed, I'd see a stand of much bigger trees that had leaves that were beginning to change, but just barely. I've never been much of a botanist, but I found this astonishing. Back home in Seattle, many of the trees that line the avenues were already mostly bare.

I drove through a tunnel—the Mule Mountain Tunnel, I believe it's called—near the top of that range of mountains. When I emerged from the tunnel, the town of Bisbee lay nestled in a red-hued canyon that twisted down the other side. Seeing the town for the first time gave me an odd sensation. It seemed so isolated, as though the entire rest of the world were on the far side of those mountains. The Bisbee side—with a brilliant-blue sky above it—was a world unto itself, like a self-sufficient castle with a wide moat of desert all around it.

That's when it struck me. This place—this small, isolated mining town—had been Anne Corley's world when she was a young, innocent girl. This was where she had grown up and where she had first run off the rails. And that one thought about Anne Corley was enough to wipe all concerns about Naomi Pepper and her aging mother right out of my head.

I had arrived in town shortly after one on Saturday, probably far too early to check in to my hotel. Considering the car I was driving, I was under no delusions that I had been booked into luxury accommodations. And so, since I wasn't on vacation anyway, I followed the next set of incredibly confusing directions that were supposed to take me to a place called the Cochise County Justice Center.

I wound down a long canyon, through an abandoned open-pit mine, and around a traffic circle. It took several turns around the circle and more than one false start before I finally turned off on Highway 80 toward Douglas. For the better part of a mile I drove along a huge flat mound of red rocks that stretched along the highway. I assumed this had to be waste that had been removed from the open-pit mine I had just driven through. Beyond the dump, although the desert near at hand continued to be of that strange Mars-like shade of red, the cliff-lined hills that jutted up a mile or so beyond it were a dull, uninspiring gray that reminded me of Seattle's winter skies.

The Cochise County Justice Center was on the left-hand side of the road a couple of miles out of town. To get into the parking lot, I had to cross a rough metal grating. The cluster of buildings I found there was about as different from Seattle's Public Safety Building as possible. Of single-story construction, they spread across a wide swath of desert. The exterior walls were reddish brown in the early-afternoon sun. They might have been made by simply scooping up the surrounding earth and turning that into building material. The campus was good-looking enough, I suppose. It might even have been mistaken for a school if it hadn't been for the curls of razor wire that surrounded what was evidently the jail.

I drove my panting Sportage into the public parking lot and got out of the car. Missing my sunglasses even more, I went looking for a lady sheriff named Joanna Brady.

JOANNA ARRIVED AT THE OFFICE at nine that Saturday morning. She put down her purse and called Jaime Carbajal. "Any sign of Dee Canfield or Warren Gibson?" she asked.

"Not so far, boss. I stopped by her house again this morning. Nothing's changed since yesterday."

"What about the search warrant?"

"I've got a problem with that, too. Judge and Mrs. Moore must have stayed over in Tucson last night. They're still not home. I won't be able to do anything about a warrant until after the Bobo Jenkins interview."

"That's fine," Joanna said. "The warrant can wait."

Once again she tackled the endless stream of paperwork. At ten o'clock she was studying the latest vacation schedule and shift rotations when she saw Frank Montoya and Jaime Carbajal escort Bobo Jenkins and Burton Kimball into the conference room down the hall.

Dressed in a jacket and tie, Bobo didn't look nearly as intimidating as he had in the Castle Rock Gallery two days earlier. At the time, Joanna had thought she had derailed his anger and that he no longer posed any kind of threat to Dee Canfield. Now Joanna wasn't so sure about that. Both the gallery owner and her boyfriend were presumed missing, and Bobo Jenkins had come to a routine interview with a defense lawyer in tow.

When I'm wrong, I do it up brown, Joanna told herself.

Shaking her head, she returned to the rotation schedule. A few minutes later, Dave Hollicker knocked on the casing of her open office door. "May I come in?" he asked.

"Sure," she said, looking up. "Have a seat. What's going on? And why are you at work on a Saturday morning?"

After the previous day's budget-cutting ordeal with the board of supervisors, Joanna knew that, from now on, she would have to curtail overtime wages.

Dave seemed to read her mind. "I know Casey and I weren't scheduled to work today," he said, "but there's so much crime scene evidence to process, we thought you'd want us to get on it as soon as possible."

I may, Joanna thought. *Charles Neighbors may have other ideas.*

"Next time, you'd better have the overtime authorized before-hand," she said. "But I can see from your face that you've found something, and I'm guessing it's not good news."

Dave sighed. "You know Bobo Jenkins came by the department on Thursday afternoon to see Casey."

Joanna nodded. "Right. I'm the one who told him we'd need his prints. Why?"

"Casey's found Mr. Jenkins's prints on the empty sweetener packets we pulled out of the trash at Latisha Wall's place."

"Of course they are," Joanna agreed. "He told me he'd been to see her Wednesday evening. He also said he'd had a drink. If he had tea or coffee, it's to be expected that his prints would show up on some of the sweetener packets."

"The problem is," Dave said, "they may be sweetener packets, but what's in them isn't sweetener."

Joanna felt a familiar clutch in her gut. If the sweetener pack-ets had been tampered with, it was likely Doc Winfield was right.

"You're saying Latisha Wall really was poisoned?"

"All I'm saying right now, Sheriff Brady, is that some of the packets *appear* to have been tampered with," Dave replied. "They were slit open and then carefully resealed. When Casey was straightening one of them so she could lift prints off the outside, she noticed white powder clinging to something tacky inside. You know how those little packets work. Usually the paper isn't sticky at all. So we checked the other packets, including several of the supposedly unopened ones we took from the crime scene. Most of them are fine. Three of them aren't."

"Do you have the contents from those three unopened packets?" Dave nodded.

"Any idea what it is?"

"None. I tried taking just a little whiff to see if there was any odor. I started feeling woozy. Whatever it is, it's powerful stuff. I've put the remaining packets in stainless-steel containers."

"Good," Joanna said. "You'd better hustle whatever you've got up to the DPS satellite crime lab in Tucson. Get them working on it ASAP. If they give you any grief, have them call me personally, understand?"

Taking that for a dismissal, Dave Hollicker stood. "Yes, ma'am," he said. "I'll get on it right away."

"Wait," Joanna added, holding up her hand. "One more thing. Does Jaime Carbajal know about this?"

Dave shook his head. "As I was coming over from the lab, he was already in the conference room with the OCCUPIED sign showing. A clerk told me he and Chief Deputy Montoya are con- ducting an interview. Rather than interrupt, I came to you instead."

"Thanks, Dave," she said. "I'll take it from here. You get that stuff to the crime lab."

Joanna sat at her desk for a few moments after Dave left her office. Naturally, a mere deputy would have been wary about interrupting an ongoing homicide interview. Under most circum-stances, interrupting detectives at work didn't seem like a good idea to Sheriff Joanna Brady, either. However, she was in posses-sion of vital information that Jaime Carbajal needed to have now, while he was still interviewing Bobo Jenkins, rather than later, when it no longer mattered.

Hustling to the conference room door, Joanna ignored the OCCUPIED sign and let herself in. As she entered, she was greeted by the sound of raised voices.

"Don't keep calling her Latisha Wall, Detective Carbajal," Bobo Jenkins growled. "I'm telling you, I don't *know* anyone by that name. The woman I knew was Rochelle Baxter. Shelley. She's the one I came here to talk about."

Joanna heard the overwrought man's voice falter on the word "Shelley." She winced at the audible hurt in that word. Bobo Jenk-ins was angry and grieving both. He sat still, his powerful arms folded across a massive chest. His jaws were clenched so tightly that the muscles in his cheeks twitched. Burton Kimball, seated next to his client, reached over and touched Bobo's shoulder. The attorney was the first person in the room to notice Joanna's arrival.

He stood and held out his hand. "Good morning, Sheriff Brady," he said politely. "So glad you could join us."

Joanna ignored Jaime's impatient scowl and returned the greeting. Then she turned to her detective. "Could I speak to you for a moment, please, Detective Carbajal?" she asked, beckoning him toward the door.

Jaime rose at once and followed Joanna out into the lobby. "What's going on in there?" she asked.

Jaime shrugged. "You heard some of it. Bobo insists he knows nothing about Rochelle Baxter's other life. As you can see, he's more than a little upset about it."

"Why wouldn't he be?" Joanna returned. "Someone he cared about is dead. It must seem to him as though we're treating him more like a suspect than a witness. No wonder he's upset. But that's not why I called you out here, Jaime. Dave Hollicker and Casey Ledford have come up with something important."

"What?"

"Several of the sweetener packets they removed from the crime scene appear to have been tampered with. They contain an unknown substance Dave is taking to the DPS crime lab in Tucson for analysis and identification. Not only that, Casey found Bobo Jenkins's fingerprints on some of the tampered packets that were empty. When I talked to Bobo right after we found Latisha Wall's body, Bobo told me he had been to her place the evening she died to have a drink."

"In other words, if his prints are on the sweetener packets, why isn't he dead, too?"

"Exactly," Joanna said. "I thought you'd want to know about this as you go forward with the interview."

Jaime nodded. "Thanks," he said. With that, he turned and let himself back into the conference room.

Joanna stared at the closed door and thought about what kind of person would knowingly place a fatal dose of poison in someone else's glass, especially when the unsuspecting victim was someone close—a lover, a friend. Joanna had thought Bobo Jenkins capable of striking out in anger, but that was vastly different from committing cold, premeditated murder.

Just thinking about it was enough to leave Joanna feeling chilled and sick at heart.

Nine

FOR THE NEXT TWO AND A HALF HOURS, Joanna waited impatiently for the Bobo Jenkins interview to come to an end. During that time, she would have welcomed Kristin's waddling into her office to pile another load of correspondence onto her desk. Unfortunately, an hour into the process, her jungle of paperwork was entirely cleared away. All e-mails had been answered, all memos duly signed off on. Desperate to keep herself occupied, Joanna rummaged through a stack of previously unread issues of *Law Enforcement Digest* and the *Arizona Sheriffs' Association Newsletter*, where she actually scanned several of the articles. By twelve-thirty she had been reduced to the rarely performed task of cleaning her desk.

When someone knocked on the doorjamb a while later, Joanna looked up eagerly, hoping for Jaime Carbajal or Frank Montoya. Instead, Lupe Alvarez, one of the public lobby receptionists, stood in the doorway.

"Yes?" Joanna said.

"There's someone to see you, Sheriff Brady. Do you want me to bring him back?"

"Who is it?"

"He gave his name and showed me a badge. He's Special Investigator Beaumont, J.P. Beaumont, from Seattle, Washington."

So, she thought, *Mr. J.P. Bird Dog has arrived.*

No doubt the big-city cop who was here to screw up her investigation and look down his nose at her department would expect to find a small-town sheriff in a squalid office with her shirtsleeves rolled up and her feet planted on her desk. She was glad to be in uniform that day and grateful that her office was, for a change, in pristine order.

"Thanks, Lupe," she said. "I'll come out and get him myself."

Lupe disappeared. Joanna checked her makeup and hair in the mirror before venturing into the lobby. As she stepped through the secured door, she glanced around the room. The only visible visitor was a tall, broad-shouldered man with a gray crew cut and a loose-fitting sport coat. He stood at the far end of the room, examining a glass case that contained a display of black-and-white photos of the current sheriff of Cochise County along with all of her male predecessors.

The photos of the men were all formal portraits. Most of them had posed in Western garb that included visible weaponry. Their faces were set in serious, unapproachable expressions. Joanna's picture stood in stark contrast to the rest. The informal snapshot, taken by her father, showed her as a grinning Brownie Scout pulling a Radio Flyer wagon loaded front-to-back with stacked boxes of Girl Scout cookies.

As Joanna's uninvited visitor lingered in front of the display case, Joanna wished for the first time that she had knuckled under to one of Eleanor Lathrop Winfield's never-ending bits of motherly advice. Eleanor had tried to convince Joanna that she should do what the previous sheriffs had done and use her official, professionally done campaign photo in the display. She realized now that it wouldn't be easy for her to be taken seriously by this unwelcome emissary from the Washington State Attorney General's Office if his first impression of Sheriff Joanna Brady was as a carefree eight-year-old out selling Girl Scout cookies.

"Mr. Beaumont?" she asked, holding out her hand and straining to sound more cordial than she felt. She wasn't especially interested in making him feel welcome, since he was anything but. As he turned toward her, she realized he stood well over six feet. Naturally, at five feet four, she felt dwarfed beside him. She held herself erect, hoping to appear taller.

"I'm Sheriff Brady," she said.

As he returned her handshake, Joanna realized J.P. Beaumont wasn't a particularly handsome man. Despite herself, though, she was drawn to the pattern of smile lines that crinkled around his eyes. *At least smiling isn't an entirely foreign activity,* she thought.

"Glad to meet you," he said, pumping her small hand with his much larger one. "I'm Beaumont—Special Investigator J.P. Beaumont. Most people call me Beau."

"What can I do for you?" she asked.

"I believe we need to talk," he replied.

"In that case," she said, "we'd better go to my office."

I HAD BEEN WAITING for Sheriff Brady for several minutes, but she surprised me when she walked up behind me without making a sound. Her bright red hair was cut short. The emerald-green eyes that studied me could have sparked fire. She wore a dark olive-green uniform, which looked exceptionally good on her since she filled it out in all the right places. If it hadn't been for the forbidding frown on her face, she might have been pretty. Instead, she looked as if she had just bitten into an apple and discovered half a worm. In other words, she wasn't glad to see me.

I followed Sheriff Brady from the public lobby into her private office, realizing as I did so that I hadn't expected her to be so short, in every sense of the word. She waited until she had closed the door behind us before she really turned on me. "What exactly do you want?" she demanded.

I know how, as a detective, I used to hate having outside interference in one of my cases, so I didn't expect her to welcome me with open arms. But I hadn't foreseen outright hostility, either.

"We have a case to solve," I began.

"We?" she returned sarcastically. "*I* have a case to solve. My *department* has a case to solve. There's no *we* about it."

"The Washington State Attorney General's Office has a vested interest in your solving this case," I said.

"So I've heard," she responded, crossing her arms and drilling into me with those amazingly green eyes.

In that moment Sheriff Joanna Brady reminded me eerily of Miss Edith Heard, a young, fearsomely outspoken geometry teacher from my days at Seattle's Ballard High School. At the time I was in her class, Miss Heard must have been only a few years older than her students, but she brooked no nonsense. After suffering through two semesters of geometry that I barely managed to pass, I had fled in terror from any further ventures into higher math.

Like Joanna Brady, Miss Heard had been short, red-haired, and green-eyed, and she had scared the hell out of me. But a lot of time had passed since then. I wasn't nearly as terrified by Joanna Brady as I was annoyed. And it wasn't lost on me that she hadn't offered me a chair.

"Look," I said impatiently, "today happens to be my birthday. There are any number of ways I'd rather be spending it than being hassled by you. So how about if we cut the crap and get our jobs done so I can go back home."

She never even blinked. "Your going home sounds good," she said. "Now, if the Washington State Attorney General is so vitally interested in this case—"

"The AG's name is Connors," I interjected. "Mr. Ross Connors. He's my boss."

"If Mr. Connors is so vitally interested in this case, why can't I get any information about Latisha Wall out of his office?"

I set my briefcase down on a nearby conference table and flicked open the lid. "You can," I said, extracting Latisha Wall's file from my briefcase. "That's why I'm here." I handed it over to her. She took it. Then, without opening the file or even glancing at it, she walked over to her desk and put it down.

"I'm delighted to know that Mr. Connors's office has the financial wherewithal to have files hand-delivered by personally authorized couriers. It seems to me it would have made more sense for him to fax it. All we needed were straight answers to a few questions. Instead, we got stonewalled, Mr. Beaumont. And now we have you," she added. "When you get around to it, you might let Mr. Connors know that the Cochise County Sheriff's Department doesn't require the assistance of one of his personal emissaries."

The lady was getting under my skin. I pulled out a business card and handed it to her.

"I'm not an emissary," I said. "As you can see, I'm an investigator—a special investigator—working for the attorney general. Latisha Wall was in our witness protection program. Mr. Connors needs to know whether or not her death is related to her being in that program. If not, fine. What happened is on your turf. It's your problem and not ours. But if it *is* related," I added, "if Latisha Wall died because someone wanted to keep her from giving potentially damaging testimony in a court of law, then it's our problem as much as it is yours. Whoever killed her should never have been able to find her in the first place."

"In other words, your witness protection program has a leak, and you're the plumber sent here to plug it," Sheriff Brady returned.

"Exactly," I said.

She recrossed her arms. "Tell me about Latisha Wall," she said.

I had read through the file several times by then. I didn't need to consult it as I related the story. "After graduating from high school, Latisha Wall did two stints in the Marines where she worked primarily as an MP. Once she got out of the service, she went to work for an outfit from Chicago called UPPI. Ever heard of them?"

"I know all of that," Sheriff Brady said.

"You do?"

She smiled. "We only look like we live in the sticks, Mr. Beaumont. Have you ever heard of the Internet? My chief deputy, Frank Montoya, was able to glean that much information from newspaper articles. What else?"

Score one for Joanna Brady.

"Mind if I sit down?"

"Please do," she said. She motioned me into a chair and then sat behind a huge desk that was so impossibly clean it was frightening. I worry about people with oppressively clean desks.

"So in the nineties," I continued, "United Private Prisons, Incorporated, saw coming what they thought was a long-term prisoner-incarceration boom. They set out to corner themselves a piece of that market. The state of Washington went for them in a big way, and when it came to picking up one of those lucrative state contracts, it didn't hurt to have an African-American female on board to help deal with all those pesky EEOC considerations.

"UPPI won the bid to build and run a boot-camp juvenile facility near the town of Aberdeen in southwestern Washington. Once the Aberdeen Juvenile Detention Center opened, UPPI appointed Latisha Wall to be its first director. On the surface of it, I'm sure putting an African-American female who was also an ex-Marine MP in charge of a place like that must have seemed like a good choice all around."

"What went wrong?" Joanna asked.

"According to subsequent investigations, UPPI had cut some serious corners in order to get costs low enough to win the contract. Some of those cut corners were in basic building materials. Only the cheapest and shoddiest materials were used during the construction phase. Subsequent investigations show that basics like insulation and wiring didn't even meet code, but they somehow had passed all required building inspections. Consequently, the deficiencies came to light only after the building was occupied, at which point they were passed off as the fledgling director's fault."

"We had a few jail-construction problems of our own," Sheriff Brady said thoughtfully. "So they turned her into a fall guy."

"Or girl," I suggested.

Sheriff Brady didn't return my smile. "Whatever," she said.

"UPPI's corner-cutting at the facility didn't stop with construction of the physical plant. UPPI budgets expected to provide for food, medical care, bedding, and personnel were too low to sustain a livable environment. Even with a boot-camp-style existence, the available monies and feeding the inmates nutrition loaf three meals a day, seven days a week, wouldn't have stretched far enough.

"The state had situated the facility in an economically depressed part of southwestern Washington in hopes of creating living-wage jobs for people after the lumber industry pretty much disappeared. Only UPPI didn't budget for living wages, either. Nor did they make any effort to turn new employees into trained correction officers. As a result, people who ended up working there weren't necessarily the best or the brightest. That caused real problems, too, in terms of lack of discipline, inappropriate sexual interactions, gang activity, drug and alcohol abuse—all the things a boot-camp environment is supposed to prevent.

"Aberdeen Juvenile Detention Center opened in the spring three years ago and was operating at full capacity within three months. By the time fall came along and the rains started, the walls began weeping moisture and forming mold. Latisha Wall immediately reported the facility's shortcomings to her supervisor. When inmates complained that the food they were given was full of bugs and wasn't fit to eat, she passed that information along as well. Nothing happened. No corrective measures were taken, and no additional expenditures were allowed. Finally, Latisha was told that dealing with the ongoing difficulties was her problem. At that point, she went to her supervisor's supervisor, with the same result.

"The final straw came when Ms. Wall discovered that her assistant—her second in command—had been routinely covering up prisoner complaints of misconduct on the part of a number of guards. The inmates were troubled kids who had been put in her charge in hopes of straightening them out. Rather than getting help, they were being abused both sexually and physically. When Latisha tried to fire the guards involved, along with the guy responsible for the cover-up, UPPI cut her off at the knees. They told her she wasn't allowed to fire anybody. That's when she finally figured out that not only had she been suckered but so had the state of Washington.

"Latisha Wall was underqualified for the position she held and was being very well paid to do it. UPPI expected her to take her money, go with the flow, and keep her mouth shut. Instead, Ms. Wall went to Ross Connors's office and told her story there. She resigned. The facility was shut down completely a few months later."

"She was a whistle-blower, then."

"Right," I answered. "What wasn't in the papers—what Ross Connors did his best to keep out of the media—was that once the scandal went public, Latisha Wall was subjected to numerous death threats. None of them could be traced back to UPPI Head-quarters in Chicago, but that's where the AG theorized they came from. Latisha Wall thought so, too."

"So your boss put her in a witness protection program and shipped her here, to Bisbee, under the name of Rochelle Baxter."

"Right," I told her.

"And you think someone from UPPI came here to kill her?"

"That's certainly a possibility," I said.

"Why's that?" she asked.

"Because there's a civil trial coming up in Olympia in a little more than a month. Based on lack of performance at the Aberdeen facility, Washington State has terminated all contracts with UPPI, and they're suing for breach of contract. Latisha Wall was scheduled to be the state's star witness. Without her, UPPI may walk away with a bundle."

Finished with my recitation, I paused. "So what's the deal, then?" I asked.

"What do you mean?"

"What have your guys found out?" I asked. "We need to know—the attorney general's office needs to know—what's going on."

"My 'guys,' as you call them—my investigations unit," she corrected stiffly, "which isn't all male, by the way—has been working the problem. As far as your need to know or your boss's need to know, Mr. Beaumont, that's up to me."

I could see that I had stepped in it big time without really knowing how. Sheriff Brady had been chilly when she had first escorted me into her office. Now she was downright frosty.

"Please, Sheriff Brady, I don't want you to think I'm taking anything away from your people—"

"Oh?" she said, cutting me off. "Is that so? You could have fooled me. I thought that's *exactly* what this is about. What you've told me just now is what your office could and should have told me two days ago. Right this moment, Special Investigator Beaumont, I can't think of a single compelling reason to tell you any of what my people have learned so far. Not until that information is in some kind of reasonable order. Give me a day or two to think it over."

She smiled coolly, then added, "Actually, two days sounds just about right. Let me know where you'll be staying. I'll give you a call, say Monday or Tuesday, and let you know what's happening. After all, that's how long it took you to get to us. Now, if you don't mind, I'm somewhat busy."

In other words, "Here's your hat, what's your hurry?" And I did mind. I minded very much, but there didn't seem to be much point arguing about it. I heard people's voices out in the hall. The way her green eyes darted toward the door, I could tell Joanna Brady was far more interested in what was going on outside than she was in talking to me. There are times when pushing works and times when it doesn't. I had a feeling that Sheriff Joanna Brady would react badly to pushing. I took the hint, stood up, and headed for the door.

"One more thing," I said. If I wasn't going to be doing anything for Ross Connors for the next two days besides sitting on my butt, I could just as well be doing something for me.

"What's that?" Joanna Brady asked.

"How long have you lived in Bisbee?"

"All my life. Why?"

"Did you ever know of someone named Anne Rowland?"

It took a moment for Anne Corley's maiden name to register in Joanna Brady's mental database, but it did eventually—with visible consequences. "I didn't know her personally," the sheriff said guardedly. "I know *of* her. Why?"

"She was my wife," I said. "I was hoping maybe I could meet someone who knew her when she was growing up and maybe talk with them for a little while."

Joanna Brady blinked. "I can't think of anyone right off," she said.

"All right."

"Where will you be staying?" she asked.

"At a place called the Copper Queen Hotel."

"Good," Sheriff Brady said distractedly. "If anything comes up, I'll call you."

I reached out, took her hand, and shook it. Her handshake was firm, but that was to be expected. Not only was she the sheriff, she was also a politician. I opened the door and let myself out, leaving

Joanna Brady standing in what looked for all the world like stunned silence.

·········

ONCE THE DOOR CLOSED BEHIND HIM, Joanna went back to her desk and sat down. Of course she remembered Anne Rowland Corley. Who wouldn't? People in Bisbee thought about Anne Rowland Corley's guilt or innocence the way lots of people think about O. J. Simpson's: She was a killer who had gotten away with it.

It had happened only a year or so before Joanna's father had been elected sheriff. The saga of the Rowland family's series of tragedies was one that wouldn't go away. Anita and Roger Rowland had two daughters, Patricia and Anne. The older girl, Patty, was developmentally disabled and died after an accidental fall in their Warren neighborhood home. Shortly after that, Roger Rowland too was dead of a single gunshot wound to the head. Because both deaths had occurred inside the city limits, the cases had been investigated by the Bisbee Police Department. Joanna remembered her father fussing about that.

"Roger Rowland and Chuck Brannigan have been asshole buddies for years," Joanna remembered D.H. Lathrop complaining. "If Chief of Police Brannigan were actually smart enough to think his way out of a paper bag, he would have recused himself and let someone else take charge of the investigation."

But Brannigan hadn't removed himself from either case, and neither had the then Cochise County Coroner, Bill Woodruff, who was another of Roger Rowland's cronies. Brannigan and Woodruff were two good old boys working together. Their hasty but official determinations of "accident" and "suicide" had stuck despite the fact that, shortly after Roger Rowland's funeral, his younger daughter, Anne, had claimed she had fired the shot that had killed her father. That claim had never been investigated. Instead, Anne had been packed off to a private mental institution somewhere in Phoenix.

One of the city detectives from that time, a man named Dan Goodson, had left Bisbee PD shortly thereafter to work for Joanna's father, Sheriff D.H. Lathrop. He had told his new boss that he had quit Bisbee PD partly out of disgust at the way the Rowland cases had been handled.

"Anne Rowland isn't crazy," Joanna's father had reported an outraged Danny Goodson as saying. "Not a bit of it. She's a killer, and with Chuck Brannigan's and Bill Woodruff's help, she's getting off scot-free."

Although rumors about Anne Rowland's guilt continued to swirl around town, the coroner's rulings had remained unassailable.

Joanna vaguely remembered hearing or reading that Anne Rowland Corley had died a violent death somewhere out of state several years earlier, but she couldn't recall any details. Now it turned out that this same woman had once been married to Detective J.P. Beaumont?

Lost in thought, Joanna jumped reflexively when the phone on her desk rang.

"Mom?" a tearful Jenny sobbed into the phone.

"Yes. What's the matter?"

"It's Sadie," Jenny wailed. "Something awful's wrong with her. I just got home from Cassie's. Her mom dropped me off. Sadie's lying on the back porch. She won't get up."

"Where's Butch?" Joanna asked.

"At the other house. He left a note that he'd be back by one, but he isn't. I need someone here now. She's real sick, Mom. Is she gonna die?"

Joanna closed her eyes and remembered how, the last few days, Sadie hadn't been quite herself. How she hadn't wanted to run home to the ranch. How she hadn't wanted to eat the Cheerios or the green chili casserole. No doubt something *was* wrong with Sadie. Joanna hadn't paid enough attention to notice.

"I don't know, Jen," she told her daughter. "But you hold tight. I'll be there as soon as I can."

With everything else forgotten, Joanna grabbed her purse and dashed out the back door into the parking lot.

Ten

J OANNA PULLED INTO THE YARD at High Lonesome
Ranch and stopped the Civvie in a cloud of dirt and gravel. As
she raced home, she had expected to find Jenny in hysterics,
but that wasn't the case. She found her daughter and both
dogs grouped on the back porch. Tigger leaped off the porch and
came to greet her while neither Jenny nor Sadie moved. Jenny sat
with the dog's head cradled in her lap, gently stroking Sadie's long,
floppy ears. The dog's sides heaved as she struggled to breathe.

Stepping close to her daughter, Joanna saw there was ample
evidence that Jenny had been crying, but she wasn't crying now.

"She doesn't like it when I cry," Jenny explained. "It upsets her,
so I stopped. And I already called Dr. Ross's office. She says we
should bring Sadie right over."

Sadie was a big dog—seventy-five pounds at least, Joanna esti-
mated. "How will we get her to the car?" she asked.

"We have to, that's all," Jenny replied.

"Wait here while I go get the keys to the other car," Joanna said. "Sadie will be more comfortable in the Eagle than in the Civvie."

Jenny nodded. "Hurry," she said.

Joanna dashed into the house, grabbed the keys to the Eagle, and hurried back outside. Sadie and Jenny hadn't moved.

"I tried giving her some water, but she wouldn't drink it," Jenny said. "That's a bad sign, isn't it."

It was a statement, not a question. Joanna blinked back her own tears. "Probably," she agreed.

Years of hefting hay bales had served both mother and daughter in good stead. As soon as they lifted the dog, though, it was clear Sadie no longer weighed what she once had.

When did she lose so much weight? Joanna wondered. *Why didn't I see what was happening?*

Once Sadie was loaded into the car, Tigger wanted to go along. "No!" Jenny told him. "You stay."

With his tail between his legs, the dejected mutt retreated into the yard and curled up, moping, on the porch. Joanna got in and turned the key in the ignition. The Eagle was driven so seldom nowadays that she worried if the battery was charged, but it started right away. Once the engine was running, Joanna expected Jenny to clamber into her seat. Instead, blond hair flying behind her, she darted back into the house. She emerged moments later carrying Sadie's blanket.

"Good thinking," Joanna said. For the remainder of the drive into town, neither mother nor daughter said a word.

Veterinarian Millicent Ross's office was only a mile or so past the Cochise County Justice Center. Joanna was there less than ten minutes after leaving home. Millicent was a broad, more-than-middle-aged woman who had returned to college to become a vet only after her three children had graduated.

She came out to the parking area to meet them, bringing along a gurney that had been designed with animals in mind. Sadie, who had never liked going to the vet, started to struggle as Dr. Ross began to transfer her to the gurney. Jenny held Sadie's head and spoke soothingly until Dr. Ross was able to strap the dog down. As they rolled the gurney toward the building, Joanna's cell phone rang. She stayed outside to take the call and was grateful to hear Butch's voice.

"Where are you?" he asked. "I came home and found your Civvie here, but no Eagle, no Joey, no Jenny, and no note. What's going on?"

"It's Sadie," Joanna said brokenly. "She's sick. We've brought her to Dr. Ross's office. I'm afraid she's not going to . . ." Her voice faltered. She couldn't continue.

"I'll be right there," Butch said.

Hanging up, Joanna turned off her phone. For once her family's needs would take precedence over the people of Cochise County. If something important came up, somebody else would have to handle it.

Inside the office waiting room, Jenny sat disconsolately on a chair, clutching Sadie's blanket to her chest. "Dr. Ross took her into the back for X rays," Jenny explained matter-of-factly. "To see if she can find out what's wrong."

Joanna sat down on the chair next to Jenny's. "That was Butch on the phone," she said. "He's back at the house. He'll be here as soon as he can."

Jenny nodded. "Okay."

Since Jenny wasn't crying, Joanna didn't either. Instead, she thought about how many years the long-legged bluetick had been part of their lives. Jenny was barely a year old when Andy brought the gangly, ill-mannered six-month-old puppy home from work. Another deputy had bought it for his son but had subsequently discovered that both his wife and son were allergic to dogs. Or perhaps just to that particularly energetic and rambunctious dog. He had been on his way to drop Sadie off at the pound when Andy had intervened.

Initially, Joanna had voiced the same kinds of objections to Sadie that she would attempt to use years later when Jenny wanted Kiddo. They didn't need a dog. Dogs were too much trouble, too much work. But Andy had insisted, and Jenny had been ecstatic. "Mama" or "Dada" may be the first words most children speak, but for Jennifer Ann Brady, it was "'Adie." It would be another two years before she'd be able to get her little tongue around that initial S.

And if Jenny was crazy about the dog, the feeling was mutual. The two were inseparable. Joanna could recall few family snapshots of Jenny that didn't have Sadie lurking, lop-eared and panting, in one corner or another. Only in more recent ones had Sadie been joined by Tigger's clownish presence.

Fifteen minutes after his phone call, Butch drove up and parked beside the Eagle. When he entered the waiting room, a buzzer in the back of the office announced the newcomer's arrival. The sound of the buzzer reminded Joanna of the jangling bell over the door of the Castle Rock Gallery. Determinedly, she shut the thought away. Now was not the time.

Butch took the chair on Jenny's far side. "What's happening, Tiger?" he asked.

Jenny looked at him for a long minute before she answered. Then her long-lashed blue eyes filled with tears and she threw herself into Butch's arms. "It's Sadie," she croaked. "She's sick. I think she's going to die."

Butch held her and stroked her hair. "There, there," he said, while his eyes sought Joanna's over the weeping child's head.

Joanna bit her lip, nodded in confirmation, and wondered why Jenny had gone to Butch for comfort rather than to her own mother. The obvious snub hurt Joanna in a way that surprised her.

"I'm sorry, Jen," Butch continued, holding her tightly. "I'm so very sorry."

Jenny's desperate sobs subsided finally, but they were all still sitting that same way—with Jenny in Butch's arms and Joanna off to one side—a few minutes later, when Dr. Ross emerged from the backroom. "Joanna, if you'd like to come with me and . . ."

Seeing the grim expression on the vet's face, Joanna knew it was bad news. By taking Joanna aside, Millicent Ross hoped to spare Jenny further heartache. But in this instance, Joanna decided, Jennifer Ann Brady had earned the right to be treated as a grown-up.

"Sadie is Jenny's dog," Joanna said, shaking her head. "Whatever's going on—whatever has to be decided—we'll all hear about it together."

Millicent sighed and nodded. "Very well," she said. She eased her stocky frame into another of the waiting-room chairs. "I've looked at the X rays. Sadie has a large tumor on one of her lungs and a smaller one on the other. The larger one is affecting her heart."

"Tumors?" Jenny asked. "How can that be? She hasn't been sick or anything."

"It's like that with animals sometimes," Millicent Ross explained gently. "Tumors come on swiftly. A few months ago, when Sadie was here because of that poisoning incident, there was no sign of a tumor. Now there are two. Her lungs are filling up with fluid. That's why she's having such difficulty breathing."

Jenny's lower lip trembled. "What can you do?"

Dr. Ross shrugged her shoulders. "Nothing, really," she said. "Sadie's in pain and she's suffering. The longer we wait, the harder it will be for her."

"You mean we should put her to sleep?"

While Joanna found herself unable to speak, Jenny had asked the questions.

"Yes," the vet replied.

"When? Now?"

"There's no sense in prolonging it, Jenny. I can do it this afternoon—as soon as you leave."

"No," Jenny said at once. "We're not leaving. I want to be with her."

"That's really not necessary," Dr. Ross said. "She's still strapped to the gurney. . . ."

"Sadie doesn't like being at the vet's, and she hates those metal tables," Jenny said determinedly. "They scare her. I have her blanket right here. Let's take her off the gurney and put her on that. I'll sit on the floor and hold her while you do it. That way she won't be afraid."

Millicent Ross nodded. "Good thinking," she said. "If you'll come with me, then . . ."

Still clutching the blanket, Jenny stood up. She glanced briefly at Joanna, then she stiffened her shoulders. "Okay," she said. "I'm ready."

As the door to the back office closed, Joanna burst into tears. She fell into Butch's arms. As he moved to comfort her, his eyes, too, were brimming.

"Jenny knew it was coming," Joanna managed in a strangled whisper. "That's why she brought along the blanket."

"She's one smart kid," Butch said admiringly. "I wonder where she gets it."

⁙⁙⁙⁙⁙⁙

I MADE MY WAY back uptown and located the Copper Queen Hotel. The closest parking place was two perpendicular blocks away. There was no bellman, but my room was ready. I checked in and then took myself downstairs to the restaurant. My scanty airline breakfast had long since disappeared. I was more than happy to mow my way through one of the Copper Queen's generously greasy hamburgers. I hadn't had one that good since Seattle's old Doghouse Restaurant closed up shop years ago.

Joanna Brady may not have won any Miss Congeniality awards, but something she had said stuck with me. She had called me a plumber, and I supposed that was true. The sheriff of Cochise County wasn't pissed at me so much as she was at Ross Connors for taking so long in getting back to her department with the needed information. I admit I was puzzled by that, too.

None of the information in Latisha Wall's file had seemed so volatile or critical or even confidential that it couldn't have been faxed back and forth to Cochise County without a problem. Due to that AG-enforced lag time, Joanna Brady was going to make me cool my heels for a while. I had told her I would spend my downtime looking for people from Anne Corley's past. And maybe I would, but there was something almost physically addictive about once again sinking my teeth back into an active homicide investigation. Being benched and put on the sidelines by the likes of Sheriff Brady wasn't how J.P. Beaumont played the game.

And so, using a paper napkin from the other, unused, place setting at my table, I began making notes. There were really only a few possibilities. One: Rochelle Baxter/Latisha Wall had died of accidental or natural causes. In either of those instances, no one was responsible, and both Joanna Brady's department and mine were off the hook. Two: The victim had indeed been murdered. Why? A: She had died as a result of something that had happened while living in Bisbee. If that was true, the solution was entirely Joanna Brady's responsibility. Whatever her "investigators" might or might not have discovered had nothing to do with me.

Or B: The woman Bisbee knew as Rochelle Baxter had been murdered because she was really Latisha Wall. The trail there would likely lead back to her having blown the whistle on UPPI. In that case what had happened to her definitely *was* my business. Ross Connors had blundered along and dragged his feet for two days. Homicide cops call those first forty-eight hours after an incident the magic time. It's then, right after the death and before the trail goes cold, that most homicides are solved. In Latisha Wall's case, those hours had been allowed to elapse with no help from the state of Washington.

So who all had information concerning Latisha Wall's whereabouts? I asked myself.

As far as I know, I'm not on a nodding-acquaintance basis with anyone currently or formerly in a witness protection program. Even so, I understand that programs like that can operate successfully only so long as the fewest possible people know details of the arrangements. Cumbersome bureaucracies leave behind paper or computer trails with far too many opportunities for unauthorized personnel to access the same information. Computers are susceptible to hacking. Stray pieces of paper can end up damned near anywhere.

I remembered that among the supposedly confidential pieces of paper Harry I. Ball had given me before I left town was one with a list of telephone numbers scribbled on it. I had been directed to guard that scrap of paper with my life. It contained all the confidential phone numbers that belonged to Washington State Attorney General Ross Alan Connors.

"Home, office, and mobile phones," Harry had said, pointing at each of them with the tip of his pen. "Whatever you do, don't lose them. You're to report directly to him by phone on this. No intermediaries. No left messages. No e-mail. Understand?"

"Got it," I had said, reveling in the first case I could ever remember that came complete with an actual prohibition against writing reports. "This is my kind of case."

"We'll see," Harry I. Ball had muttered in return.

"Ask the AG who knew," I jotted on the napkin.

There was a stir in the room. Two guys at the table next to me and a woman one table away peered at the dining room entrance with avid interest. As the door swung shut, a hint of flowery perfume wafted through the room. The hostess, carrying a single menu, strode past my table leading a tall, heavyset African-American woman wearing low heels and a gray silk suit that rustled as she walked. The hostess seated the newcomer at a table for two next to a lace-curtained window.

"Can I get you something to drink?" the hostess asked.

"Coffee," the woman said in a thick Southern drawl. "Coffee and water, please."

"It takes one to know one," my mother used to say, and on this occasion that trite old saying was true. I was a stranger in Bisbee, Arizona, and so was the black woman seated three tables away. A single photo of Latisha Wall had been in the file I'd handed over to Sheriff Brady. It had been taken on the occasion of Latisha's graduation from USMC boot camp. Except for an extra hundred pounds or so, the woman seated across from me could have been Latisha's older twin.

A waitress brought coffee and water. While the woman studied the menu, I studied her. Long black hair was drawn back into a cascade of neatly braided cornrows that flowed past her shoulders. Her teeth were large, straight, and very white. The fingers that held the menu were topped by long scarlet-tipped nails. Everything except the nails spoke of solemn dignity—and unspeakable sorrow.

"What can I bring you, ma'am?" the waitress asked.

"What's the soup today?"

"Tortilla/green chili," the waitress offered cheerily. "It's really very good."

The woman look unconvinced. "I'll have the tuna salad," she said.

The waitress took my plate away and dropped off the bill. It was a subtle hint for me to move along. "Could I please have another cup of coffee?" I asked.

For some time I sat and wondered about my next move. Clearly this was a relative of Latisha Wall's—an aunt or a much older sister perhaps—come to bring the dead woman's body home for burial. Most likely the woman had been summoned by a local coroner or medical examiner's office in order to make a positive identification. After all, if none of the people in Bisbee knew that Rochelle Baxter was really Latisha Wall, they could hardly be counted upon to make a positive ID.

The woman's tuna salad arrived at the same time my coffee refill did. She picked at her food with faint interest, as though she was going through the motions of eating because she knew she should rather than because she was hungry. By the time she put down her fork and pushed away her still-laden plate, I had made up my mind.

I stood up and walked over to her table. "Excuse me," I said. "I couldn't help noticing. You look so much like Rochelle that you must be related. Please accept my condolences."

She nodded. Her eyelashes were thick and almost as long as her fingernails. "Thank you," she said. "You're very kind. And, yes. Her real name was Latisha, you know. She was my sister, my younger sister." She held out her hand. "My name is Cornelia Lester. And you are?"

I wondered if, to maintain the subterfuge, I should ask about the Rochelle Baxter alias, but decided against it. At that point, the less said, the better.

"Beaumont," I told her, returning her solid handshake. "J.P. Beaumont."

"Have a seat." She motioned me into the table's other chair. "I hate eating alone," she said, as if to explain her uneaten salad. After a pause she added, "Did you know her?"

I sat down and shook my head. "Not really," I lied. "But I know about her. Bisbee's a very small town."

"Yes," Cornelia agreed. "Small towns are like that. Did you know she was an artist?"

"No."

"Tizzy was always sketching away when she was a kid. That's what we called her back home, Tizzy. Other kids would be out playing ball or swimming, or just hanging out, but Tizzy always had a pencil in one hand and a piece of paper in the other. Even back then we all knew she had a God-given talent, although our parents weren't much in favor of art for art's sake. They wanted us to have jobs that would actually pay the rent. It's bad enough that she's gone, but to die like that, the night before her first show . . ." Cornelia Lester shook her head and lapsed into silence.

"Show?" I asked.

"Yes. A one-woman exhibition of her paintings at a place called Castle Rock Gallery. The opening party was to be held Thursday night, but Latisha died on Wednesday. I'd really love to see the paintings, but I haven't been able to. The gallery isn't open. I checked on my way through town."

I glanced at my watch. "It's after one," I suggested helpfully. "Maybe they're open now."

Once again Cornelia Lester shook her head. The beads on her cornrows knocked together with a sound that reminded me of a baby's rattle. "No," she said. "I don't think so. I talked to a man who owns the antique store next door. He said this is the second day in a row the gallery has been closed. He's heard rumors that something bad may have happened to the owner. Dee Canfield, I think her name is. She's been missing for two days now, ever since she posted the notice canceling the show and locked the place up on Thursday afternoon."

"That's odd," I said.

"Yes. I thought so, too," Cornelia Lester agreed. "Since this Canfield woman and Latisha were evidently friends, I intend to ask Sheriff Brady about this the first chance I can."

"You haven't spoken with Sheriff Brady then?" I asked.

"No. I tried calling a few minutes ago and was told the sheriff is currently unavailable. I left a message, but she hasn't called back. That's all right. There's plenty of time. I'll be here until Tuesday at least. That's the very soonest the medical examiner may be able to release the body."

This was all very interesting. It would have been nice if Joanna

Brady had bothered to mention that another woman was missing, especially since she was someone closely connected to Latisha Wall, making it more than likely that the two incidents were related. Since Sheriff Brady hadn't said a word, I decided it was time to follow up on my own leads.

"If you'll excuse me," I said, standing up, "I really must go. It was rude of me to barge in on you this way."

"Not at all," Cornelia Lester said. "I enjoyed the company. I was glad to have a chance to talk."

"Same here," I said.

I charged lunch to my room and then hurried out to the desk, where I borrowed a local telephone book. Castle Rock Gallery wasn't listed in the dog-eared copy the clerk handed me, so I asked him instead.

"Oh, that," he said. "No wonder. The phone book came out last spring. Castle Rock Gallery is brand-new—too new to be listed, but it's not hard to find. Go straight out here, cross the street, cut through the park, and then turn right on Main Street. The gallery is several blocks up on the right. If you find yourself walking past a big chunk of gray limestone two or three stories tall, that's Castle Rock. It means you've missed the gallery and gone too far. Come back down and try again."

The uncomplicated directions made it sound fairly close, so I left the Sportage parked where it was and set out on foot. Getting there took me just ten minutes, but it was real walking—all of it uphill. I remembered seeing a sign that said Bisbee's elevation was over five thousand feet. By the time I arrived at Castle Rock Gallery, I felt every damned one of them.

I was out of breath and sweating up a storm by the time I reached the place. Cornelia Lester had been right. Castle Rock Gallery was locked up tight even though the posted hours said the gallery was open from ten to six on Saturdays. A hand-lettered sign taped to the inside surface of a window next to the door said the grand opening of Rochelle Baxter's one-woman show had been canceled until further notice.

I looked around. Cornelia Lester had mentioned speaking to the man who ran an antique shop next door. Because the gallery meandered down the street and filled three adjacent storefront buildings, next door was actually three doors away in a place called Treasure Trove Antiques.

I went there and let myself into a musty, dusty place stacked high with mountains of junk some people had thrown out of their lives. No doubt other people would be happy to part with far too much of their own hard-earned cash to bring the cast-off crap into theirs.

A bow-legged guy in cowboy boots and a Western shirt sat in a faded leather morris chair with a thousand-dollar price tag. He took off a pair of wire-rimmed glasses as he looked up from the paperback he was reading. "Howdy," he said. "Let me know if I can be of any help. Don't like to smother people. Not my style."

I pulled out my badge and held it up for him to look at it. I hoped the combination of bad lighting and slightly below-par eyesight would fix it so he didn't get that good a look. "Actually," I said, "I understand the lady who owns the gallery next door has gone missing."

"Sure enough," he said. "Dee's gone, and so is that jerk of a boyfriend of hers—Warren something or other. They've been gone almost two full days now. If Dee's come to any harm, I'm guessing that Bobo Jenkins from up Brewery Gulch way might've had something to do with it. He was in there raising so much hell the other day—Thursday morning, it was—that the sheriff had to show up with her siren screaming and lights flashing just to calm things down. This here's a quiet little town," he added. "Don't get a lot of that—lights and sirens, I mean."

I jotted down the name. "You said Bobo Jenkins?"

"Yup. Used to own a place called the Blue Moon Saloon up in Brewery Gulch. I believe he sold it a couple of months back. I was outside having a smoke Thursday morning. That's the thing with all the dad-gummed rules and regulations we have nowadays. A man can't smoke in his own shop even when he ain't hurtin' nobody but his own damned self. So I was outside smoking when ol' Bobo comes charging up the street like the devil hisself is after him. I do mean he was movin'. Not jogging. Not trotting along, but outright running. Looked mad enough to chew nails. Next thing I know, he's in the gallery and him and Dee are screaming at each other something fierce."

"Did you hear what was said?"

"I'm not one of them eavesdroppers. Even if I had heard, I pro'ly wouldn't say. But it was loud, I can tell you that much. And they didn't stop carrying on until Sheriff Brady showed up and made 'em. I didn't vote for her, you understand, but I got to give her credit. She's no bigger 'n a minute, but the sheriff's a feisty one, I'll say that for her. She busted that argument right up. The next thing I know, Bobo was walkin' down the street carryin' this big old picture, and lookin' like someone'd just told him to shut up and get the hell out."

Sheriff Brady may be feisty, I thought, *but she's also one closed-mouthed little bitch!*

"Thank you," I said. "I appreciate the help. Your name is?"

"Harvey," he replied. "Harvey Dowd. Most people call me Harve. And you?"

"Beaumont," I told him. "J.P. As I said, you've been a big help,

Mr. Dowd. Now, if you could direct me to the place you told me about. The one that Mr. Jenkins owns . . ."

"The Blue Moon?"

I nodded.

"Sure. That's no trouble. You walkin' or drivin'?"

"Walking."

"Well, sir, you just go right down this here hill. Stick to the main drag. You'll go through town and past the park. Turn left at the end of the park and just walk straight ahead until you get there. It'll be on the left. Believe me, you can't miss it."

You'd be surprised, I thought, but I set out with a spring in my step. Part of the spring was due to the fact that I'd finally gotten around to having the bone spurs removed from my heels. And it helped that it was all downhill. But something else—something perfectly simple—made me feel downright gleeful as I walked back down through the narrow two-lane street Harve Dowd had called Bisbee's "main drag." Nothing could possibly have improved my state of mind more than having a lead Sheriff Joanna Brady hadn't given me and obviously didn't want me to have.

Now, before she had a chance to stop me, I was going to see what I could do with it.

Eleven

I F YOU'RE A STRANGER IN TOWN and want to dig up a few pertinent details about someone local, it's a good bet to go where his friends might possibly hang out, keep a low profile, and listen like crazy. Which is why I left Treasure Trove Antiques and headed immediately for the Blue Moon.

As far as I could tell, Brewery Gulch is actually a street rather than a gulch. It looked a bit bedraggled and worn around the edges. In fact, it could easily have doubled for an old-time movie set. Brewery Gulch evidently did once boast a working brewery. In fact, there was a decrepit building bearing a sign that said BREWERY. But professional beer making in Bisbee, Arizona, had long since passed into oblivion. A single restaurant survived inside the brick-fronted hulk, but little else.

Other buildings along Brewery Gulch were similarly ramshackle. Many storefronts exhibited faded FOR RENT signs. Others were entirely boarded up. Not so the Blue Moon Saloon and

Lounge. That establishment was hopping. Thirty or so big, honking Harleys sat angle-parked outside along the curb. I'm an officer of the law. I don't generally feel welcome in places of business frequented by bikers.

Looking at the building, I saw no reason the Blue Moon, unlike its nearest neighbors, hadn't closed down years ago. I stepped inside, hoping the place wouldn't fall down around my ears.

My eyes had to go from bright sunlight to hardly any light at all. When my pupils finally had adjusted, I saw that the interior of the Blue Moon was in better shape than the exterior. Reasonably new linoleum covered the floor. Pedestal cocktail tables scattered throughout the room were jammed with leather-clad, chain-wearing bikers, all of them drinking and smoking. A few were clearly well on their way to being drunk while others were just gearing up. Ironically, the atmosphere reminded me of a Twelve-Step biker bar a friend of mine used to run up on Eighty-fifth in Seattle's Greenwood District. This establishment, however, was definitely not alcohol-free—not even close.

Beyond the tables, a magnificent wooden bar that dated from the eighteen hundreds ran the length of the long, narrow room. The bar, like the tables, appeared to be fully occupied except for a single seat three stools from the end wall, where dreary, painted-over windows obscured all trace of outside light.

Grabbing that one empty stool, I immediately understood why it had been left unoccupied. My neighbors to the right were two crippled old geezers who looked like escapees from a low-rent retirement home. Two walkers were stowed in what I had thought to be available leg space. Unfortunately, I noticed the walkers the hard way—by banging my kneecap, full force, into the handle of one of them.

"Sorry about that," the guy nearest me said. "Let me haul that thing out of your way."

"No," I said, rubbing my bruised knee. "It's fine where it is."

"Hate having to drag that thing around with me everywhere I go, but it beats being locked up at home."

"What can I get you?" someone asked.

I turned away from the old man to find myself facing what had to be the Blue Moon's greatest asset—a killer blond bartender. She was a gorgeous young woman whose lush good looks would have turned heads at a Miss America Pageant.

"O'Doul's," I replied.

"Sure thing," she said. I watched as she walked briskly away. My obvious admiration didn't pass unnoticed.

"Look but don't touch," my neighbor advised. "Angie's happily married, and she don't take nonsense off nobody."

I scanned the room for evidence of another bartender, cocktail waitress, or bouncer who might lend Angie a hand if the band of bikers started acting up. I saw no one. Filling glasses at the distant tap, Angie seemed totally unruffled by her roomful of tough customers. Obviously Angie was more than just a pretty face. And body.

When she returned with my bottle of alcohol-free O'Doul's, Angie brought along two brimming glasses of beer. She set those in front of my neighbors, picked up their two empties, and then turned to me.

"That'll be three bucks," she said.

I pulled a ten out of my wallet and handed it over. As she walked back down the bar to the cash register, my neighbor leaned over to me. "It's getting close to the end of the month," he confided in a beery-breathed whisper. "Angie's real good about carrying me an' Willy till our checks catch up with us the first of the month, if you know what I mean."

So Angie wasn't above running a tab. The practice was most likely illegal, but it was something the two guys at the end of the bar really appreciated.

"You from around here?" I asked.

The man's loud burst of laughter was punctuated by an equally loud belch. "You hear that, Willy?" he demanded, clapping his buddy on the shoulder.

"Hear what?" Willy asked.

"This fella wants to know if we're from around here."

Willy grinned at that, and they both laughed uproariously. Since they thought my question utterly hilarious, I took that to mean they were natives.

Angie returned with my change and laid it on the polished surface of the bar. "Are these guys bothering you?" she asked, giving my two bar mates a searing look.

"No," I said. "Not at all."

She raised a warning finger. "You and Willy behave yourselves, Arch," she said. "You bother any of the other customers and you two are out of here."

"Yes, ma'am," a seriously chastened Archie replied. "We'll be good."

"Wha'd she say?" Willy asked.

"We got to behave," Archie shouted.

"Right," Willy agreed, raising his glass. "Absolutely."

It seemed unlikely that I would glean any useful information from this pair of doddering old drunks, so I turned hopefully toward my neighbors on the other side. No luck there. The person next to me—someone I had actually thought to be a guy—turned out to be a leather-booted, leather-jacketed babe whose face was almost as well-tanned as the cowhide she wore on the rest of her body. When I glanced in her direction, the man next to her glowered back at me in the mirror. Resigned, I returned to Archie.

"Who owns this place?" I asked.

Archie frowned. "Why'd you want to know?"

I shrugged. "Maybe I'm thinking about making some investments around town," I offered. "Maybe I'd like to buy it."

"No way!" Archie glowered. "The Blue Moon's not for sale."

"Wha'd he say?" Willy asked. The man must have been stone-deaf. As far as I could tell, that was his only line.

"If you know it's not for sale, you must be the owner then," I remarked casually.

"Angie and her husband own it," Archie allowed, nodding toward the shapely blonde. "Bought it off Bobo Jenkins a couple of months ago, and it's a good thing, too. Bobo was tired of running it. Can't blame him there. Workin' too hard's not good for you. 'Sides, I hear he's thinking about running for mayor. You ask me, he'd do a helluva job. If I ever get a chance, you can bet I'll vote for him, too.

"Bobo might've just closed up the place and walked away. Locked the door and throwed away the key. Lucky for us, Angie come along and saved our bacon. She and that husband of hers offered to buy it off him, and he sold, just like that. The place runs a little irregular now. You can't always count on it being open."

"Does Angie's husband work here, too?" I asked.

Archie sipped his beer and shook his head. "Hacker's an odd duck. He's a Brit and a bird-watcher besides. Does something with birds. I'm not sure what. So when he goes out into the boonies to do whatever it is he does, Angie sometimes shuts the place down and goes with him. Who can blame her? They're newlyweds, after

all. Why shouldn't she? But that's mostly during the week. Weekends the place is open regular, like it should be.

"It's like I told my good friend Willy here. So what if we can't
always count on the hours? It's better than having no Blue Moon
at all. Me and Willy've been coming here for what, forty years
now? I'd hate like hell to see it shut down and boarded up."

"What?" Willy asked.

"Never mind," Archie told him. "Just drink your beer. The
man's deaf as a post, you see," Archie explained unnecessarily to
me. "Too many years of working with dynamite in the mines. You
ever been in a mine?"

"No," I said. "I never have." *And never wanted to, either,* I
thought.

"They've got theirselves a underground tour over across the
way, in case you're interested," he suggested. "Takes you right
back into the mountain."

"Thanks, but no thanks," I said.

What I really wanted was information about Bobo Jenkins. If I
could manage to prime Archie's pump, I guessed he'd turn out to
be a veritable fountain of information, some of which might be
useful.

"I hear there's been some trouble around town the last few
days," I suggested innocently.

Archie took a sip of beer and then slammed his glass onto the
bar, splashing beer in every direction. "Boy howdy!" he exclaimed.
"If that ain't the truth! Poor old Bobo. Me and Willy've knowed
that man for years and years, ever since he come to town and
bought this joint. In all that time, he wasn't never sweet on anybody before that Shelley Baxter woman showed up. They just
seemed to click, know what I mean?

"Not that I'm prejudiced or nothing," he continued, "but I like it when whites stay with whites, blacks stay with blacks, and Mexicans stay with Mexicans. That's how God Almighty meant for things to work. But there weren't hardly no black women in town for Bobo to hook up with, so he was sort of a lone wolf. Then she turned up and put a smile on his face."

If Archie wasn't prejudiced, then Willy wasn't deaf, either. I kept my mouth shut and let him talk.

"But now Bobo's girlfriend, this Shelley, up and died at her place down in Naco. That's Naco, Arizona, not Naco, Sonora, you see. So what do the cops do? This morning they haul poor ol' Bobo's ass into the sheriff's office for questioning. Like they think maybe he did it. Like maybe he's responsible for what happened to her. I was telling Angie a little while ago, it's all so much BS. I didn't use that word, of course, not in front of the lady. But between you and I, that's what it is. All bullshit—and knee-deep, too.

"Bobo Jenkins may be what they call a African-American, and strong as a mule, but he's definitely not the violent type. Wouldn't hurt a fly. Willy and me, we've seen him break up some pretty bad fights in this place over the years. Bobo's so big he could scare shit out of you by just lookin' at you crooked, but I never saw him hurt nobody—not even when they were raising hell and really deserved it."

Once Archie got started talking, there was no turning him off, but I was no longer paying attention. I was thinking about a closed-mouthed lady sheriff named Joanna Brady, damn her anyway! All the while she was playing coy with me, her detectives were questioning a suspect. That's all right. The next time I saw her, I planned to ask her straight out what her investigators had learned in their interview with Bobo Jenkins. And I intended for "next time" to be soon. Now, if at all possible.

Angie had left my change lying on the bar, and so had I. Now I left a dollar tip and pushed the remainder over to Archie.

"Take this," I said. "You and Willy have one on me. It'll help tide you over until next month's checks arrive."

Archie looked at the money gratefully, as though he'd just won a lotto jackpot. He gave me a heartfelt grin. "Thanks," he said. "Thanks a lot."

For a change Willy didn't bother asking what had been said. He'd seen the money pass along the bar and had figured out on his own what that meant.

"Thanks, fella," he mumbled, once again raising a glass that still had a few modest dregs of beer in it. "You're a gentleman," he said. "A gentleman and a scholar."

WHEN A DRY-EYED JENNY EMERGED from Dr. Ross's back office, she was carrying Sadie's blanket and collar. "Ready?" she asked.

"Which car do you want to ride in?" Butch asked.

"I'll go with Mom," Jenny said.

Butch nodded. "You two go on, then," he said. "I'll stay here to settle up with Dr. Ross."

Joanna unlocked the Eagle, and they both climbed in. "Dr. Ross asked if we wanted to bring Sadie home to bury her," Jenny said. "I told her no. There've been too many funerals. I didn't want another one. That's okay with you, isn't it?" she asked.

"Jenny, sweetie, whatever you decide," Joanna said. "It's entirely up to you."

"Okay, then," Jenny said. She settled back in the car seat and closed her eyes. "Will you tell the Gs?" she asked.

"Yes," Joanna said. "I'll be glad to," although "glad" wasn't at all the right word.

Several times on the drive home, Joanna had to brush unbidden tears out of her own eyes. Sadie had been a beloved family pet. But it was more than just losing Sadie. Joanna was losing her daughter as well, losing her baby. Because Jenny must have known what was coming when she went racing back into the house to get Sadie's blanket. Even then, she was thinking about Sadie first—putting the dog's comfort and well-being before her own.

No, Jenny wasn't Joanna's baby anymore. She was a thoughtful, caring, wonderful, surprisingly mature person who put others' needs ahead of her own. *She could probably give me lessons,* Joanna thought bleakly. And grateful as she was for all that—for the kind of human being Jennifer Ann Brady was becoming, there was a tiny corner of Joanna's heart that wanted to turn back the clock so Jenny could once again be the cute, cuddly little girl she had been before.

Once out of the car at home, Tigger raced around the Eagle several times, sniffing eagerly. "He's looking for her, isn't he?" Jenny said.

Joanna nodded. "Yes. I suppose he is."

Jenny called the dog to her and knelt down to hug his neck. "Come on, boy," she said finally. "Let's go get Kiddo. We'll go for a ride."

Alone, Joanna went into the house. While Jenny was with Dr. Ross, she had called in to the department to let Frank and Dispatch both know what was going on, that she would be out of radio, phone, and pager contact for the next little while. When she picked up the phone, the broken beeping of the dial tone announced that there were messages waiting. For a change she didn't bother checking them. Instead, she dialed her former in-laws' number.

"How terrible for Jenny," Eva Lou Brady said when she heard the news. "Do you want Jim Bob and me to come out and spend some time with her? We'd be glad to."

"No," Joanna said, "that's not necessary. She's handling it amazingly well. She's out saddling up Kiddo right now. A long ride will do both her and Tigger a world of good."

"Sounds just like her daddy," Eva Lou offered. "That's the way Andy always was, too. Whenever there was a crisis, he'd go off by himself to think things over and come to terms with whatever it was. Don't you worry about Jenny, Joanna." Eva Lou added. "She's one tough little cookie. She'll be fine."

Joanna's next call was to her own mother. "Oh, dear," Eleanor Lathrop Winfield said. "Is Jenny all right?"

"She's fine," Joanna said.

"That's the problem with having dogs," Eleanor went on with barely a pause. "You just get used to them and before you know it, they get old and die on you. Of course, Jenny can always get another one. Heaven knows there are enough unwanted dogs in this world, although why you'd want to have two, I can't imagine."

Joanna Brady closed her eyes and wished her mother could somehow be different than she was.

"I just heard Butch drive up," Joanna said. "Have to go."

"All right," Eleanor said. "You let Jenny know I'm thinking about her."

You may be thinking about her, Joanna thought grimly, *but we're all better off with her not knowing what you're thinking.*

Butch came into the house and dropped his keys on the counter. "I thought we'd bring Sadie home and bury her somewhere out here on the ranch, but Dr. Ross said Jenny didn't want us to. So I let it go. What do you think?"

"Jenny told me she was tired of funerals."

"You can hardly blame her for that," Butch replied. "Where is she?"

"Out riding," Joanna told him. "She took Tigger along. I thought it was probably the best thing for both of them."

Butch nodded. They were standing in the kitchen with their arms wrapped around each other when the phone rang.

"Don't answer," Butch said. "Let it go to voice mail."

"I'd better not," Joanna said, pulling away. "I've been unavailable all afternoon. It could be important."

She plucked the cordless phone off the counter. "Brady/Dixon residence," she said.

"Sheriff Brady?" Dave Hollicker asked. He sounded excited.

"Hi, Dave," she told him. "How's it going? Are you back from Tucson already?"

"No, I'm still here. At the crime lab. But I've got something for you."

"What?"

"Ever hear of sodium azide?"

"Never. What is it?"

"It's the propellant they use in cars to make air bags work. It ignites, and the resulting explosion inflates the bag."

"So?"

"It's a white, odorless compound that resembles salt. Or sweetener. And it dissolves readily in liquids."

Joanna felt her pulse quicken. "I suppose it's also poisonous?" she asked.

"Very," Dave agreed. "More poisonous than cyanide."

"And tasteless?"

"I wouldn't know about that," Dave answered. "And I don't know how you'd find out for sure. Who'd be willing to taste it, and how would they tell us what they'd found out after they died? But since it evidently ended up in Rochelle Baxter's iced tea and since she emptied the glass without noticing, we pretty much have to assume it's tasteless."

"If sodium azide is that deadly, how come she didn't die right away?"

"Ingested poisons don't work until they're assimilated into the bloodstream. If you breathe it in, it can kill almost instantly. I'm lucky I just got woozy when I did. Otherwise, you'd be having another Fallen Officer funeral in a day or two," Dave went on.

"Thank God," Joanna said. "But tell me, where would somebody get this awful stuff?"

"That's the really bad news," Dave Hollicker replied. "The answer is, almost anywhere. It's not a controlled substance, so you could buy a whole barrel of it if you wanted. You could also rip the air bags out of your car and claim somebody stole them. Or else you could go to your local junkyard. If a car wrecks and the air bags are deployed, it's not a problem. Once the air bag inflates, what's left after the sodium azide oxidizes is totally harmless. It's the undeployed air bags with their canisters of unused sodium azide that are the problem."

"Don't junkyards strip the air bags out and sell them?" Joanna objected. "My understanding is that they can be parted out and reused."

"That's how everybody *assumed* it would work," Dave said. "In actual practice, it's not that simple. People don't want to ride around in a vehicle where their life and the lives of their loved ones depend on the effectiveness of somebody else's secondhand air bag. And, if death or injury occurs in a vehicle fitted with a used air bag, there's always a potential liability problem. All of which leaves this country with millions of unrecycled air bags sitting in junkyards everywhere."

"The sodium azide is loose, then?" Joanna asked.

"No. It comes in little aluminum canisters about the size of tuna-fish cans. I'm guessing there are stacks of dozens of those little hummers sitting on used-parts shelves in junkyards in Cochise County alone."

"Wait a minute," Joanna objected. "You've told me this is a deadly poison. Do you mean somebody could just walk in off the street and pick a can of it off a shelf?"

"You ever been to a junkyard, boss?" Dave Hollicker asked.

"Not recently."

"Well, that's pretty much how they work. Around here, junkyards are long on self-service."

"Can sodium azide be traced?"

"You mean have the manufacturers put markers in it the way they do with explosives?"

"Exactly."

"I suppose it's possible, but I'm guessing the automobile industry would be dead-set against it."

"Because they don't want to admit the stuff is a potential problem?"

"You've got it," Dave agreed.

"Great," Joanna said. "It's readily available, totally untraceable, and deadly."

"And that's what was in those tampered sweetener packets that Casey and I brought back from Latisha Wall's place down in Naco. I've got the DPS crime lab's printed analysis right here in my hand."

"Have you told anyone else about this?" Joanna asked.

"Not yet. I've been cooling my heels around here all day waiting for test results. They dissolved some and ran it through an ion chromatograph. That's what I have right now—a preliminary report and a tentative identification of sodium azide. They'll do a confirmation test using mass spectrometry. The lab manager told me we won't have tentative results on that for another day or so. Official results will take another week. The criminalist I talked to says they can use the same technique on vomit samples if Doc Winfield sends them along, but that takes up to two weeks longer. I thought you should be the first to know."

"Thanks for calling," Joanna said. "I'll get on the horn and tell everyone else."

"Do you want me to come by the office with this when I get back to Bisbee, or can it wait until tomorrow?"

Joanna thought about the board of supervisors meeting and the looming overtime issue. "No, since it's just a preliminary copy, have the lab fax one to the department tonight. Nobody will be able to work on it before tomorrow or Monday anyway. Good work, Dave," she added. "You and Casey deserve a lot of credit for being on top of this."

"Thanks, boss," he said, "but isn't that what you pay us to do?"

Joanna heard the unmistakable pleasure in his voice at having been given a compliment. "You're right," she returned. "That's exactly why we pay you the big bucks."

By the time she hung up, Butch had gone over to the fridge and pulled out a beer. "I can hear it already," he said. "They're sucking you back into work, aren't they?"

"Not really," Joanna said. "But now that we know what killed Rochelle Baxter, I have to tell people. I'll make some calls. It won't take more than a few minutes."

She went into the living room. Butch, tired of having the dining-room table constantly littered with work-related papers, had redesigned the living room. Eva Lou Brady's little fifties-era telephone table had been replaced by a secondhand cherry secretary, where Joanna's papers could be spread out and the hinged desk surface closed up over them when necessary.

Joanna retreated there and picked up the phone. The first call she made was to Jaime Carbajal.

When Jaime's wife, Delcia, said, "Hold on, I'll get him," Joanna glanced guiltily at her watch. It was only a few minutes past four. *Good*, she thought. *At least it's too early for me to be interrupting dinner.*

When Jaime came to the phone, he sounded out of breath. "Pepe and I were out doing batting practice," he said. "Frank told me earlier about Sadie. Is Jenny okay?"

"She's fine," Joanna returned. "In fact, she's handling it better than I am at this point, but tell me about the interview with Bobo Jenkins. How did it go?"

"No surprises there," Jaime said. "Bobo insists he had nothing to do with what happened to Latisha Wall. He claims the two of them were in love and that he had no reason to harm her."

"Did he mention being afraid that she was about to break up with him?"

"He said something about it, but he claimed things were fine between them when he left her place on Wednesday night. As far as I'm concerned, that remains to be seen."

"Did you let him know we found his prints on the sweetener packets?"

"No. That's a holdback. I didn't want to say anything about that until I had a chance to talk to both Dave and Casey."

"Makes sense," Joanna said.

"Did you ask Bobo about Dee Canfield?"

"Affirmative. He claims the last time he saw her was in the gallery on Thursday morning. He said you were there at the same time. He says he has no idea what happened to her afterward, and he has no clue where she and Warren might have gone."

"He's right," Joanna said. "I was there when he was. Now what's the deal on the search warrant?"

"Not yet," Jaime said. "I finally found out why the judge didn't come home last night. Mrs. Moore ended up in TMC with an emergency appendectomy. I talked to their house sitter. She says Judge Moore is supposedly coming back to Bisbee tonight. The soonest I'll be able to get the warrant and serve it will be later this evening."

"That'll have to do, then," Joanna said. "If you want someone along when you serve it, check with Frank."

"Will do," Jaime said. "Now, what about Dave Hollicker?"

The detective listened in silence while Joanna told him what the crime scene investigator had learned. "Does Frank know about any of this?" Detective Carbajal asked.

"He's my next call."

She tried Frank's home number and got no answer. Next she called the department.

"He's in," Lupe Alvarez told her. "But he's got someone with him at the moment. That guy from Washington."

Beaumont again, Joanna thought. *Good enough. Let Frank deal with him.*

"Have Chief Deputy Montoya call me when he's done," Joanna said. "I'm at home. Anything else I should know about now that I'm available?"

"Yes," Lupe said. "You've had three calls from someone named Cornelia Lester. She says she's . . ."

Joanna remembered the name from the next-of-kin contact

sheet in Latisha Wall's file. "I know who she is. Is she here in town?"

"Yes. She's staying at the Copper Queen, room five-twelve."

Joanna picked up a pen. "Do you have the number?"

"Yes."

"You'd better give it to me, then," Joanna said, once again dreading the thought of having to speak to yet another grieving relative. "I'll call her back while I'm waiting to hear from Frank."

Twelve

B
Y FOUR O'CLOCK THAT AFTERNOON I was back at
the Cochise County Justice Center. "I'm sorry, but Sheriff
Brady has had a family emergency," the same public lobby
receptionist told me. "She's not available at this time."

"What about her second-in-command?" I asked.

"Chief Deputy Montoya is on his line at the moment. When
he's free, I'll let him know you're here."

"And my name is—"

"I know," she returned. "You're Special Investigator Beaumont. I remember you from earlier."

I wondered about that. Did she remember my name because
she just happened to remember it, or had her boss passed the
word that I was persona non grata? For the next ten minutes, I
cooled my heels in the lobby. The longer I waited, the more I
fumed. It wasn't as though I was in a hurry or had anywhere else

to go. It was the principle of the thing. So far, Sheriff Brady and her department had been something less than cooperative.

I found myself once again studying the picture montage in that glass display case. Joanna Brady may have been cute as a button when she was a little kid, dressed in a Brownie uniform and selling Girl Scout cookies like mad. Maybe she still was, but cute wasn't working on me.

Eventually the secured door to the back offices opened and out walked a late-thirty-something Hispanic guy. He wore the same kind of uniform the sheriff had been wearing when I last saw her, although his was free of curves. And his head was shaved absolutely smooth.

"Hello," he said as he approached my chair. "You must be Special Investigator Beaumont. I'm Chief Deputy Frank Montoya. What can I do for you?"

He escorted me back to his office, which was in the same wing of the building as the sheriff's private office. I thought maybe I could pull out the good ol' boy card and jolly Chief Deputy Montoya out of some useful information. But Sheriff Brady had her people firmly in line as far as J.P. Beaumont was concerned. Montoya gave me diddly-squat.

"Look," he said in answer to my direct question about the Bobo Jenkins interview. "I can appreciate your wanting to know about that, but our department is conducting what is becoming a more and more complicated investigation. Without Sheriff Brady's express permission, I'm not authorized to give out any information. Period."

"It is complicated," I agreed, "what with the addition of not one but two missing persons cases."

Montoya's eyes narrowed when I said that. He didn't like my knowing about the missing art dealer and her boyfriend.

Too bad, I thought. *I found that out on my own, Mr. Chief Deputy Montoya. If you don't like it, you'll just have to lump it.*

"If I were Sheriff Brady," I said aloud, "I think I'd be glad to have an extra detective show up and lend a hand with all this."

Frank Montoya's lips curled into a tight smile. "I don't think that's quite how she views the situation," he said. "And until I have a chance to talk to her about it . . ."

By then I had pretty well decided that Sheriff Brady's supposed family emergency was nothing but a smoke screen to keep me out of her hair.

"When will that be?" I asked. "When will you be able to talk to her again? And how long is this so-called family emergency scheduled to last?"

That one pissed him off. "As long as it takes," he replied, standing up. "Now, if there's nothing else, I'm quite busy at the moment."

With that he escorted me to the door, down the hall, and back into the public lobby. As he booted me out I realized that, years ago when I had the chance, I should have coughed up the six hundred bucks and taken myself through the Dale Carnegie course.

⁞⁞⁞⁞⁞⁞⁞

JOANNA DIALED THE HOTEL and was relieved when Cornelia Lester didn't answer. She left word with the desk clerk and had just put down the phone when Frank called her back. "Losing a dog is tough," he said. "How's Jenny faring?"

Joanna liked the fact that everyone who knew about Sadie asked about Jenny. "Better than I would have expected," Joanna told him. "She took Kiddo and Tigger and went for a ride. Now, tell me. What did Mr. Beaumont want?"

"Anything and everything," Frank replied.

"I'm not surprised, but what exactly?"

"He asked about the Bobo Jenkins interview."

It was something Joanna hadn't anticipated. "How did he know about that?" she demanded.

"Who knows?" Frank replied. "I sure as hell didn't tell him. He also asked if we were making any progress in locating Dee Canfield and her boyfriend."

"So he knows about the missing persons part of it, too," Joanna mused. "Who all has he been talking to?"

"Beats me, boss," Frank said. "Remember, though, the man's an ex–homicide detective. He's probably been all over town asking questions. You know how people here love to talk."

Joanna knew that very well. Bisbee was a small place where everyone had a finger in everyone else's pie.

"What did you tell him?" she asked.

"Nothing. Not without your approval."

"Which I'm not in danger of giving anytime soon," Joanna said. "Now let me tell you what Dave Hollicker found out."

When she finished explaining about sodium azide, Frank Montoya was aghast. "Geez!" he exclaimed. "That stuff sounds scary!"

"You've got that right," Joanna told him grimly. "It's scary as hell."

"You're saying this sodium azide crap is lying around all over the place where any nutcase in the universe can lay hands on it?"

"That's the deal," she told him. "And," she added, "unlike cyanide or arsenic, there aren't any limits on who can have it."

"There should be," Frank said.

"Amen to that," Joanna agreed.

There was a pause. "Maybe I should go on the Internet and check this out," Frank suggested. "I'll see what more I can find out about it."

"Good idea," Joanna said. "Unfortunately, we have no idea how much of it the killer still has in his or her possession. I'm guessing there's some left over after loading up the sweetener packets in Latisha Wall's kitchen." Then, as an afterthought, she added, "While you're surfing the Net, there's something else I'd like you to check out, Frank. I want you to do some research on Anne Rowland Corley."

"Wait a minute," Frank said. "Isn't she the young girl from Bisbee who, years ago, supposedly killed her father and then skated?"

At the time, the two Rowland deaths had been high-profile cases in southern Arizona, and they still were. Joanna wasn't surprised to learn that, years later, their outcomes continued to be common knowledge in local law enforcement circles.

"She's the one," Joanna replied.

Frank frowned. "I seem to recall she died several years ago."

Joanna nodded. "I vaguely remember that, too," she said. "But the details escape me. That's why I want you to check it out."

"This Rowland thing is ancient history," Frank objected. "Why the sudden interest?"

"Because Special Investigator Beaumont told me he used to be married to Anne Rowland Corley," Joanna told him. "I believe he said she was his second wife, although he's probably on number three or four by now."

"Beaumont was married to her?" Frank asked. "That's interesting."

"Isn't it, though," Joanna agreed. "Very interesting."

EARLIER AT THE HOTEL I had tried using my laptop to check my e-mail. Years ago, when Seattle PD dragged me kicking and screaming into the twentieth century and forced me to start using a computer, I hated the damned things. Now that I'm used to them, I can see they have some advantages. I've adjusted. On this day, however, not being able to make my connection work in the twenty-first century drove me nuts.

Frustrated, I had turned to my cell phone. I wanted to talk to Ross Connors and ask him who all had been in the know when it came to witness protection living arrangements for Latisha Wall. To my astonishment, I found that my cell phone didn't work, either—not in Bisbee. The call wouldn't go through. When I went downstairs and asked the desk clerk about the problem, he explained that maybe my cell phone's poor signal strength was due to the hotel's location deep inside the steep walls of what he called Tombstone Canyon.

Now, having been thrown out of Frank Montoya's office, I sat in my Sportage in the Justice Center parking lot and considered my options. Reflexively checking the readout on my cell phone, I was delighted to see that I had full signal strength. Again I dialed the Washington State Attorney General's home number. The phone rang once and was immediately answered by a woman speaking in a torrent of rapid-fire Spanish. After a couple of futile attempts to get her to switch to English, I realized I was talking to a recording.

Thinking I must have dialed the wrong number, I dug the list of Ross Connors's phone numbers out of my wallet and checked to be sure I hadn't transposed some of the digits. No such luck. The number I had dialed was correct. I had no idea what was going on with my cell phone now.

Cochise County, Arizona, has to be the black hole of the telecommunications universe, I told myself.

I drove back into town and wandered around until I finally located a pay phone at a Chevron station by the selfsame traffic circle that had given me such fits when I had been trying to reach the sheriff's office the first time. With the proliferation of cell phones, it seemed like years since I'd been reduced to using an outdoor phone booth. It felt a little weird to be standing there in the open—practically in public—and dialing Ross Connors's super-secret unlisted phone numbers. Since it was Saturday, I tried the cell phone first. No answer. Then I tried the office and reached a machine. Finally I dialed his home number, where a woman answered after the third or fourth ring. To my eternal delight, she spoke English. "Is Mr. Connors there?" I asked.

"No. He's out," she said. "This is his wife, Francine. Who's calling, please? Can I take a message?"

I recalled Harry I. Ball's stern admonition. "No messages."

"Please tell him Beau called," I said. That seemed innocuous enough. "Tell him I'll call back later. Any idea when he'll be home?"

"It's sunny today," she said. "He's playing golf."

That figured. The rain had cleared up in Seattle and Ross Connors was out having himself a nice Saturday afternoon while J.P. Beaumont—the birthday boy—was stuck spending a very long day in Bisbee, Arizona, being kicked around by a pushy small-town sheriff and her entire department.

In the old days, that kind of feeling-sorry-for-myself misery would have sent me straight to the nearest bar, but the Blue Moon wasn't calling me. Instead, I decided to stay right where I was and exercise the prepaid phone card the Washington State travel agent had thoughtfully placed in my travel packet. It certainly wasn't my fault that none of my nearest and dearest could reach me by telephone to wish me many happy returns.

First I talked to Kelly, my daughter. She and her husband live in Ashland, a small town located in southern Oregon. When Kelly dropped out of school and ran away from home mere weeks before her high school graduation, I wouldn't have bet a plugged nickel that she'd ever go back and finish, especially since she had taken up with a young actor/musician and was pregnant besides. But it turned out marriage and motherhood were good for her. She picked up her GED right after the baby was born. Kelly's now two years into a bachelor of fine arts program at Southern Oregon University. Not only that, my son-in-law, Jeremy, seems to be a pretty good sort, too—for an actor, that is. At least he's gainfully employed.

Kelly wished me a happy birthday and told me about her midterm exams before turning me over to three-year-old Kayla, who spent the next several minutes babbling incoherently to her "Goompa."

Next I called my newly graduated and only recently gainfully employed son, Scott. He's a neophyte electronics engineer who lives and works in the Bay Area. He and his girlfriend, Cherisse, are up to their eyeballs in plans for a wedding that is scheduled to take place sometime next spring. As we chatted on the phone, he gave me some of the pertinent wedding details, but I forgot them as soon as he told them to me. As Father of the Groom, I know all I have to do is show up, pay for the rehearsal dinner, and keep my mouth shut. It's a far better deal than the one you get as Father of the Bride.

Finally, I called Naomi Pepper. If I thought she'd be glad to hear from me, I should have had—as my mother would have said—another think coming. She was distant, to say the least.

"What's going on?" I asked.

"I did what you said," she told me.

"What's that?"

"I suggested to Mother that maybe we should look into an assisted-living sort of arrangement for her. I told her about the one you mentioned, the place up on Queen Anne that takes dogs."

"And?"

"She hung up on me. She even left the phone off the hook so I couldn't call her back. I was so worried, I finally got in the car and drove over to check on her, just to make sure she was okay. When I got there, she had a whole line of pill bottles set out on the kitchen counter. She told me that if that was how I felt about it—if I didn't care for her any more than that—there was no reason for her to go on living. If I hadn't been there, Beau, I can't imagine what she might have done."

I was fairly certain that the pill bottles had been strictly for show. *She wouldn't have done a damned thing,* I wanted to say, but Naomi was crying now, and I knew the poor woman had been totally outfoxed and outmaneuvered. As I said before, Naomi's a nice person; her mother isn't. There was no need for me to add to Naomi's misery by telling her so.

"What are you going to do?" I asked.

"The only thing I *can* do," Naomi replied shakily. "She's coming to stay with me. Mother says she'll call and start getting estimates from moving companies first thing Monday morning. I'll have to put some of my stuff in storage to make room for hers. You're not mad at me about this, are you, Beau?"

Heartsick, I thought. *And disappointed, but not mad.*

"No," I said. "I'm not mad at all. You have to do what you have to do."

"Thank you," she said gratefully. "Thank you so much for saying that." She seemed to gather herself together. "And now," she added, "tell me all about your birthday. How's it going?"

"About as well as can be expected," I said.

⁙⁙⁙

JENNY CAME BACK FROM HER RIDE and headed directly for her room. "Are you going to want dinner?" Butch asked as she passed through the kitchen.

"I'm not hungry."

"There's plenty of food in the fridge if you want something later."

"Okay," she said.

"What about you?" he asked Joanna.

"I'm not hungry, either," she said.

"In that case, the cook is taking the night off. We'll all make do with leftovers."

Joanna stretched out on the couch and covered her eyes with one hand. She was about to doze off when Cornelia Lester called. It was painful to have to tell the woman that although Joanna's investigators were making progress on the case, they still had no idea who had murdered Latisha Wall.

"You say she was poisoned?" Cornelia asked in what sounded like disbelief.

"That's what we believe," Joanna said.

Cornelia absorbed that information. "What about her paintings?" she asked. "The ones in the gallery. Will I be able to see those anytime soon?"

"I'll try to make arrangements for you to be allowed inside the gallery," Joanna said. "But I'm not sure when that will be."

"In other words," Cornelia said, "you still haven't located the gallery owner."

Cornelia Lester was a stranger who *wasn't* a former detective, yet she, too, seemed to be as privy to what was happening inside the Cochise County Sheriff's Department as J.P. Beaumont was. *What would it be like to work in a big city?* Sheriff Brady wondered. *To be able to do this job in a place where everyone didn't mind everyone else's business?*

"No," Joanna had admitted with a sigh. "We still haven't located Dee Canfield."

"What if you don't?"

"If we don't find her?"

"Or what if you do and she's dead, too?" Cornelia persisted. "What happens to the paintings then?"

"As far as I know, they belonged to your sister," Joanna said. "If something unfortunate has happened to Dee Canfield—and I'm certainly not saying it has—then the paintings would, either by will or by law, go to Latisha's heirs. I'm assuming her heirs would be her family members, but let me remind you, Ms. Lester, that we won't be able to release them to anyone so long as they're part of an ongoing investigation."

"Of course not," Cornelia said. "But I'd still like to see them."

"I'll see what I can do."

"Thank you."

Joanna put the phone down and had actually fallen asleep before it rang again. This time Butch answered.

"It's for you," he said, scowling at the receiver as he handed it over. "Tica Romero."

"Hello?"

"We just got another 911 call from Naco," the dispatcher said. "Some kids were playing around in one of the old cavalry barracks down there. They've reportedly found a body—a woman's body. Chief Deputy Montoya and Detective Carbajal are already on their way. Deputy Montoya wanted me to let you know as well."

"Thanks, Tica," Joanna said, sitting up and shoving her aching feet back into her shoes. "I'll be right there."

Joanna went into the bedroom and slipped on her soft body armor as well as her weapons. Once she was dressed she stopped by Jenny's room. The door was ajar. When she peeked in, she saw Jenny and Tigger curled up together on the bottom bunk, both of them sound asleep.

Leaving them be, Joanna returned to the kitchen where Butch was at work on his house file.

"Duty calls," she said when she bent over to collect a good-bye kiss."

"Don't say I didn't tell you so," Butch said, but Joanna was relieved to see that he was smiling.

"I won't," she said.

I HAD HUNG UP after talking with Naomi and was wondering what to do next. It sounded like the Naomi Pepper door in my life was about to be slammed shut in my face. It came as no surprise that I immediately went back to thinking about Anne Corley.

I recognized I'd gone slinking off to Bisbee, Arizona, without mentioning it to my friend Ralph Ames. If I had been willing to ask him questions about Anne Rowland Corley's history, I'm sure he could have given me answers, chapter and verse. As her attorney, he had known everything about her. Well, almost everything.

The problem with asking Ralph about Anne is that he knew her too well. Not only that, he had cared for her almost as much as I had. Ralph and I are friends, good friends, so whatever he might tell me would automatically go through those two distinctly separate filtering processes. I had no doubt that Ralph would tell me the truth—up to a point—but I suspected he might leave out a detail or two, if only to spare my feelings.

I was wavering between calling him and not, when I heard a siren. I looked up as a patrol car came racing up to the traffic circle from Highway 80. I'm always conscious of cop cars. It's something I notice wherever I go. While in town, I had spotted several city of Bisbee patrol cars. They were white with a blue shield on the door. The fast-moving Crown Victoria making its way around the traffic circle sported a gold star on the door. That meant it belonged to the Cochise County Sheriff's Department.

I watched it go and wondered about it, but then I heard a second siren coming from the direction of Old Bisbee. This one was a cumbersome Ford Econoline van, but the same star was emblazoned on the outside. Something was up, something serious. The sheriff's department was being summoned en masse.

Should I follow or not? I wondered.

Then, barely seconds later, a third vehicle came along—this one a second Crown Victoria. It followed the same path as the first one. As it slowed to negotiate the curve of the circle, I caught a glimpse of bright red hair behind the wheel. This Crown Vic was being driven by Sheriff Brady herself. Whatever had happened was serious enough to summon her away from her family emergency. That did it. Moments later I was in the Sportage and trying to catch up.

Of course, there was never any question that the underpowered Sportage *would* catch up. The best I could hope for was to keep the Crown Vic in sight. It rounded the traffic circle and took off in what I judged to be a southwesterly direction. As I turned off the traffic circle myself, I thought at first that I'd lost her. Then, after coming through two subdivisions, past a mysterious no-visible-reason stoplight and through what looked like a genuine slum, I caught sight of her again.

From what I could tell, Bisbee is made up of little separate knots of tumbledown buildings strung together by strips of failing blacktop. In between are big chunks of undeveloped desert. By the time Sheriff Brady made it to the next little burb, I had closed some of the distance between us. Signaling for a left-hand turn, she paused at yet another traffic light. That slight delay gave me time enough to draw even nearer.

I, of course, had to stop at the light, too, and wait for what seemed an interminable length of time. Eventually, though, when the light changed, I could still see Joanna Brady's car, speeding away on a straight downhill stretch. We seemed to be headed toward a solitary mountain that rose up in front of us some distance away.

Going downhill, the Sportage did a little better. After a few more little pieces of town, we were in desert again. What I wouldn't have given to be driving my 928 about then. Barring that, it would have helped to have a police radio with me. At least I would have had some idea what was happening.

The next time the Crown Vic made a turn it was onto a smaller road that bordered a golf course. I guess I was surprised to see a golf course sitting there like a little emerald-green oasis in the middle of an otherwise unremittingly brown desert. There was a marked golf-cart crossing at the entrance. Naturally I had to stop and wait for not one but two golf carts to dawdle their way into the small but jam-packed RV park that faced the course. In the process I really did lose sight of Joanna's Crown Vic.

Cursing under my breath, I drove to the far end of the course and looked around. Still I saw nothing. Then I stopped the car, got out, and listened.

The place was quiet. At first all I heard was a stiff breeze blowing from the west. But then, carried on by the wind, I heard the faint but familiar chatter from a nearby police radio. Even if the radio wasn't Sheriff Brady's, she wouldn't be far from the one I was hearing.

I got back into the Sportage and drove. I roamed through several blocks of gravel-topped streets where a series of very old wooden and red-dirt buildings seemed intent on melting back into the desert. I found what I was looking for when I came to where a patrol car with flashing lights was parked astride a red-dirt trail. The officer signaled for me to stop. I pulled up next to a big bony dog who lay beside the road, unconcernedly observing the action. His shaggy black coat was tinged red by a layer of dust. The officer, who was now engaged in putting out a string of flares, booted the dog out of the way. Shaking off a cloud of dust, the dog sauntered off.

With the dog gone, the scowling deputy turned his ill-tempered gaze on me. "Sorry, buddy," he said. "This is a crime scene. No unauthorized personnel allowed beyond this point."

"My name's Beaumont," I said, passing him my badge. "Special Investigator Beaumont. It's okay," I added. "Sheriff Brady knows I'm here."

He squinted at the badge and compared my face to the picture on my ID. "All right, then," he said. "Pull over to one side so your vehicle's not blocking emergency access."

Poor guy, I thought, feeling almost guilty as I followed his instructions. *She'll have his butt for letting me through.*

I decided my best course of action was simply to act as though I belonged. I left the car with the keys in it. Mimicking the dog's unconcerned attitude, I sauntered past the deputy who, by then, was busy turning someone else away. I walked through several blocks of what looked like old-time military barracks. And I do mean old. The place came complete with a long, dilapidated building that had clearly been a stable. It took a few minutes for me to realize that I hadn't wandered into a moldering Western movie set. This was truly the genuine article—an old U.S. Cavalry station.

By then I could see Sheriff Brady. She stood in a huddle with Frank Montoya and a plainclothes guy I hadn't seen before.

She caught sight of me while I was still fifty feet away. Breaking out of the huddle, she marched toward me, furious and practically breathing fire.

"What have we got?" I asked casually, thinking that my well-placed "we" might mollify her just a little.

It didn't. "What the hell are you doing here?" she demanded.

I expect women to yell when they're upset. That's what I'm used to, anyway—ranting and raving, if not outright screaming. That wasn't Joanna Brady's style. She barely whispered her question, but the effect was the same.

"Look," I said reasonably, "I'm trying to do my job. Your deputy back there told me there's been another homicide. I thought maybe it might have something to do with those two missing—"

"Get out!" she ordered.

"But Sheriff Brady, I thought we were supposed to be working together on—"

"I said, 'Get out!' and I meant it."

"I just—"

"You just nothing! Go!"

More officers were showing up by then, and I could see she wasn't going to change her mind. So I left. I put my tail between my legs and beat it back to the Sportage. A woman wearing golf course duds was chatting with the unfortunate deputy. No one could have overheard what Sheriff Brady was saying to me, but her hand gestures had spoken volumes. By then the deputy had figured out that he had made a potentially career-stopping mistake in letting me through. He shot me a disparaging look as I passed, but I ignored it. What did he expect me to do? Apologize?

I had folded myself back into the Sportage and was wondering what to do next when somebody tapped on my window. When I rolled it down, the lady in the golf clothes, who wore her blond hair in a wild frizz of curls, gave me a bright smile.

"Yes?" I said.

She reached in through the opened window and handed me a card. "Marliss Shackleford," the card said. "Columnist. *The Bisbee Bee.*"

"Glad to make your acquaintance," she said, batting her eyes.

Under normal circumstances, I wouldn't be caught dead talking to a reporter. But I was currently at war with Sheriff Joanna Brady. That meant all bets were off.

I held out my hand. "Special Investigator J.P. Beaumont," I said. "Glad to make your acquaintance."

Thirteen

W
HEN I INVITED MARLISS SHACKLEFORD to come up to the Copper Queen Hotel so we could talk, she jumped at the chance. "If you don't mind, though," she said, "I'd like to go home and change first."

"Sure," I said. "I'll see you there."

As I walked into the lobby, the desk clerk caught my eye and waved to me before I could step into the elevator. "There you are," he said. "A call for you. I was about to take a message. If you want, there's a house phone over there."

He pointed to an old-fashioned black phone hidden away in the corner, right next to a darkened hotel-lobby jewelry stand that was evidently closed for the evening.

"Is that you, Beau?" Attorney General Ross Connors asked. "Francine told me you called. How's it going?"

"Let's just say Sheriff Brady didn't exactly welcome me with open arms."

"I didn't expect she would. Are her people making any progress?"

"They brought a suspect in for an interview today. He was accompanied by his attorney. As far as I know, however, no arrests have been made."

"Who's the suspect?" Connors demanded impatiently.

I glanced around the lobby to see if anyone was listening. No one seemed to be. Still, talking on a house phone in a hotel lobby, I didn't want to say too much. "Boyfriend," I said. "Could be a lovers' spat of some kind."

Ross Connors breathed a sigh of relief. "Let's hope," he said.

His heartfelt reaction jangled a nerve that had been niggling at me ever since Harry I. Ball sent me off on this wild-goose chase.

"Would Latisha Wall's presence really have made that big a difference?" I asked. "In the upcoming trial, I mean. Surely you have depositions and so forth from her that can be placed in evidence even if she's not there to testify in person."

"Believe me," Ross said. "It makes a huge difference."

In other words, I'd have to take his word for it.

"Listen," he went on, "if the boyfriend angle pans out—and I'm sure you'll know that within a day or two—then you can put yourself on a plane and come on home."

"*If* it pans out," I returned. "There's no guarantee that it will. In the meantime, though, while we're still looking at all the *other* angles, I have a question for you."

"What?"

"Who knew about the arrangements?"

"What arrangements?"

What the hell did he think I meant—arrangements for his next day's tee time? "For Latisha Wall," I said. "I know enough about witness protection programs to realize they cost money, lots of it. I also know you don't jar that kind of money loose from the Washington State budget without having to jump through a bunch of hoops."

"Dale Ahearn," Ross answered. "And O.H. Todd. O.H. is the actual case manager. He was in charge of making all financial and living arrangements. He's also the one who put together her supporting documents."

"His telephone number is the one that's listed for Lawrence Baxter, the guy who's named as next of kin in Rochelle Baxter's DMV file."

"Right," Ross agreed.

"What about Dale Ahearn? Who's he, and what does he do?"

"He's my chief of staff. Like I said, O.H. made the arrangements, but Dale signed off on them and passed them along to me for final approval."

I didn't know O.H. Todd and Dale Ahearn from holes in the ground, but Ross Connors did. "You think these two guys are trustworthy?" I asked.

"I certainly thought so," Connors replied. "And that's why this thing has me so spooked. I've worked with O.H. and Dale for years. Until all this came up, I would have trusted either one of them with my life. Now I'm not so sure. That's why it's so important for me to know exactly what happened. It's also why I'm counting on your discretion."

So that's what this is all about, I told myself. *I'm not down here on the state's nickel to fend off UPPI's upcoming breach-of-contract dispute with the state of Washington. I'm here because Ross Connors is having a crisis of confidence with some of his minions.*

My enthusiasm for having signed up with Ross Connors and his outfit took a sudden nosedive. I had thought the purpose of the Special Homicide Investigation Team was to investigate murders. Now it sounded as though someone in the attorney general's office might actually be causing homicides here and there rather than simply solving them. That being the case, could a cover-up be far behind?

"I've just come from another crime scene," I said into the phone. "I'm pretty sure it's another homicide. There's a possibility that it could be related to what happened to Latisha Wall."

"Could be?" Ross repeated. "You mean you don't know for sure? That's why I have you on the scene, Beaumont. It's also why we paid to fly you down there. We need to know for sure what's going on."

As Attorney General Ross slipped into the old blame-game routine, I bristled. "I'm not exactly working under optimal conditions," I growled.

"Why not?"

"Because Sheriff Brady ordered me to leave the scene the minute I showed up."

"Why would she do that?" Connors asked. "What is she, some kind of prima donna?"

You're the problem, I wanted to say. And I did, in so many words. "Sheriff Brady is ripped because it took so long for us to get her any information."

"I was trying to get a handle on the situation," he said.

Handle, my ass! I thought. *What you really mean is spin.*

That was about the time Marliss Shackleford waltzed into the lobby. "Sorry to have cut you off," I told the attorney general. "Someone's here to see me. I've gotta go."

"HOW MANY TIMES DO I have to tell you boys to stay away from those houses?" an outraged Velma Verdugo railed. "'The places are falling down,' I say. 'They're dangerous. The ceilings could cave in on you. A floor could collapse. You never know what you'll find. You're bound to end up getting in trouble.' That's what I tell them, but do they listen? Not on your life!"

Unfortunately, Joanna knew exactly how this exasperated mother felt. It hadn't been that many months ago when Jenny, while breaking a similar prohibition and doing something she shouldn't have, had stumbled on the body of a murder victim. This time the boys in question—two brothers ages eight and nine—had found the body of a woman Joanna presumed to be the missing Deidre Canfield.

As their mother shrieked at them and shook her finger in their faces, the two boys shrank away from her. Cowering just out of reach, they looked so thoroughly humiliated that Joanna felt sorry for them, just as she did for Velma. Joanna suspected that the woman's shrill tirade had far more to do with her being frightened for her sons—over what might have happened to them—than it did with genuine anger.

"If you'd allow us to speak to them for a few minutes, Mrs. Verdugo," Joanna said soothingly. "It shouldn't take long."

"It better not," Velma returned. "Their daddy will be off work soon. Believe me, when Gabe gets here, he'll do more than talk."

Faced with the old wait-till-your-father-gets-home threat, the boys exchanged wary glances but they didn't speak. The look that passed between them wasn't lost on Joanna.

"I hope he won't be too severe," Joanna said. "It's really fortunate for my investigators that Marcus and Eddie found the body when they did."

Chief Deputy Montoya ambled over to where Joanna stood talking to the Verdugos. Taking in the situation, he winked at the boys and then began speaking to their mother in Spanish. Joanna had taken years of both high school and college Spanish, but the classes had left her something less than fluent. Nevertheless she was able to follow enough of what Frank was saying to realize he was simply expanding on much of what Joanna had said moments earlier and praising the two boys for reporting their find rather than concealing it.

Frank's words seemed to have a calming effect on the agitated woman. Velma listened in silence. When he stopped speaking, she turned back to her sons. Squeezing her eyes tightly shut and with tears streaming down her face, she pounced on the two boys and then hugged them to her in a desperate embrace.

Jaime Carbajal appeared just then with his crime scene camera still in his hand. "Sorry for the interruption, Sheriff Brady. Could you please come with me?"

Excusing herself, Joanna followed Detective Carbajal. She had visited this deserted, crumbling cavalry post with her father years earlier. D.H. Lathrop, an amateur historian, had explained to her how Pancho Villa had attacked Columbus, New Mexico, in 1916. Camp Harry J. Jones in Naco, Arizona, named after a murdered Army guard, had been part of a network of military posts maintaining border security during the Mexican Revolution. With her father, Joanna had explored the adobe-walled stables and the fallen-down barracks. Now Jaime Carbajal led her toward what had once been the officers' quarters. The house—a small, graffiti-marred wreck—was missing all its windows and doors.

"You'd better come inside and take a look," the detective said. "And you're going to need these." Once again he handed her a mask, evidence-preserving Tyvek booties, and his much-used vial of Vicks.

"Dee Canfield?" Joanna asked. She paused on the small front porch long enough to apply the menthol and don the mask and booties. Meanwhile Jaime nodded grimly in answer to her question.

"Any sign of Warren Gibson?" the sheriff added.

"Not yet," Jaime reported. "But we haven't searched the whole place yet. There could be another body hidden in one of the other buildings. We just haven't found it yet."

Joanna nodded. "Has Frank called for extra deputies?"

"He has," Jaime said. "Dispatch tells me two of them are on their way."

Joanna nodded. "Good. We'll give one of the deputies to you for the crime scene. The other we'll send with Casey Ledford when she goes through Dee's house and the gallery, assuming you did manage to pick up those search warrants," she added.

Jaime nodded. "Dave's on his way to pick them up."

Long before Joanna stepped through the open doorway into the gloomy, dusty interior, and even through the barrier of menthol, her nostrils detected the unmistakably rank odor of human decomposition. A woman's fully clad body lay on the sagging wooden floor of what had once been a kitchen. Joanna immediately recognized the distinctive hues of Dee Canfield's tie-dyed smock. After maneuvering far enough around the body to have a complete view of the victim's face, Joanna saw that the dead woman's fleshy features were drawn up in a horrific grimace.

"Any signs of violence?"

Jaime shook his head. "No apparent bleeding or bruising as far as I can see."

Joanna looked at him closely. "Are you thinking the same thing I am, that maybe we're dealing with another poisoning?"

The detective nodded. "The thought did cross my mind."

"Damn," Joanna said.

She made her way outside.

Velma Verdugo was now seated in the front passenger seat of Frank's Civvie while her two sons leaned against the front fender a few feet away. The chief deputy crouched before them. Holding a clipboard, he was asking questions and making notes.

Frank glanced over his shoulder as Joanna approached. "You boys may have seen Sheriff Brady a while ago," he said, "but I doubt you were introduced. This is Eddie," Frank explained to Joanna, indicating the taller of the two. "That one is Marcus."

Joanna held out her hand, and the boys took turns shaking it.

"Here's what we have so far," Frank continued. "Eddie and Marcus told me that they discovered the body earlier in the day, probably between three and four this afternoon. Because their parents have declared this whole place off-limits, they didn't want to let on about their discovery for fear of getting in trouble. They talked it over, though, and finally decided to tell anyway. Mrs. Verdugo found out about it around forty-five minutes ago. That's when she called 911."

Joanna turned to the boys herself. "Did either of you touch anything while you were inside?" she asked.

"No, ma'am," Eddie replied at once. "We were both too scared. Besides," he added, "Marcus was about to puke because it smelled so bad and he's such a sissy. We got out of there and ran home."

"The woman whose body you found has been missing since Thursday," Joanna told them. "It's likely she's been here since then. Did either of you see any unusual activity between then and now—any unusual vehicles? Any people who looked out of place and who maybe had no business being here?"

"*Nada,*" Eddie Verdugo answered.

"Me, either," Marcus chirped.

Joanna turned to Velma. "What about you, Mrs. Verdugo?" she asked. "You must live nearby, don't you?"

Velma nodded and pointed toward a mobile home parked on a lot a block or so away. "That's where we live."

"Did you notice any unusual activity?"

"No."

Just then, a man dressed in a Border Patrol uniform passed through the checkpoint and strode toward them.

"Daddy," Marcus cried. Darting away from Frank's car, the boy broke into a run and raced to meet the new arrival. The man caught Marcus in midstep, lifted him off the ground, swung him around in a circle, and then hugged him close. It was only as they came nearer that Joanna recognized Gabe Verdugo, a Border Patrol officer she had encountered on previous occasions when her officers and those from the Border Patrol had been involved in joint operations.

"What's going on?" Gabe Verdugo demanded. "Is everyone all right?"

While Frank explained what had happened, little Marcus clung like a burr to his father's neck. Joanna guessed that if Velma expected someone to ream her boys out for their willful disobedience, she was out of luck as far as Gabe Verdugo was concerned.

Fortunately, Gabe, a law enforcement officer himself, knew what would be expected of his sons now that they had blundered into a homicide investigation.

"When will you want them to come in for the official interview?" he asked.

"Good question," Joanna told him. "We're one detective short at the moment. Right now Detective Carbajal has his hands full. We won't be ready to talk to the boys anytime before Monday morning, when Detective Carpenter comes back."

"Hey, great!" Eddie crowed, his face breaking into a wide grin. "If we go Monday morning, we'll get to miss school."

That was more than his mother could stand. "Oh, no, you don't," Velma Verdugo said fiercely. "The detectives can interview you during lunch." Then, after a long moment, her troubled face collapsed into a smile. Seconds later, the entire Verdugo clan was laughing and hugging.

Joanna Brady understood that, too. Something awful had happened. Like Jenny finding the body at camp, the Verdugo boys, while just being kids, had stumbled unwittingly into a homicide. Their lives had been touched by an evil that had left them all feeling vulnerable and scared. But now, while that vulnerability was still fresh, there was much to be thankful for in just being alive. In that situation, even a mother's fierce anger could be cause for celebration.

"Sheriff Brady?" Deputy Howell said, announcing her arrival. "They told us to report to you or Chief Deputy Montoya."

Joanna turned away from the people clustered around Frank Montoya's Civvie to greet the two uniformed officers who had just arrived on the scene. Although Joanna was glad to see Deputy Debra Howell, she was less than thrilled when she realized the second deputy was Kenneth Galloway.

"What should we do?" Debra asked.

"We've got another homicide," Joanna told them. "I want you to work with Detective Carbajal and Dave Hollicker on the crime scene investigation here, Deputy Howell. Deputy Galloway, you'll be assisting Casey Ledford."

"Doing what?" Ken Junior asked.

It wasn't outright insubordination, but it was close—more in tone of voice than anything else.

"Whatever Casey needs," Joanna told him. "From keeping the

evidence log to lifting prints. She's over there talking with Detective Carbajal. Ask her."

Galloway walked away, muttering something unintelligible under his breath. "What's wrong with him?" Frank Montoya asked.

"I'm not sure," Joanna said. "But I suspect Deputy Galloway has a few issues about working with women."

Within minutes, the medical examiner arrived. While Detective Carbajal led Doc Winfield to the body, Deputies Howell and Hollicker were sent to search other nearby buildings for a second possible victim. Meanwhile, Joanna and Frank Montoya consulted with Casey Ledford while Galloway lounged in the background.

"What do we know about the missing boyfriend?" the fingerprint tech asked. "How long has he been around?"

"According to Jaime, he's been in town for several months," Frank responded. "Working for and living with Dee Canfield most of the time. The DMV tells me that no one named Warren Gibson currently holds a valid Arizona driver's license, and I haven't been able to find any other official record of him, either."

"All right," Joanna said. "We have search warrants for both Dee Canfield's house and her gallery, but let's check the gallery first. There may be employment records or something else there that'll make it possible for us to find out more about Warren Gibson. Something's out of whack here."

<hr />

IT DIDN'T TAKE LONG for me to figure out that Marliss Shackleford hadn't agreed to talk to me because she'd been charmed by my boyish good looks and overwhelming charm. She was after something. No, make that someone. She was out to get the goods on Sheriff Joanna Brady.

We retreated from the lobby to the bar. I had O'Doul's. Marliss had a tall gin and tonic.

"I should have thought you'd be more interested in hanging around a homicide crime scene than in talking to me," I said for openers.

Marliss gave me a flirtatious smile. She was fortyish and not all that bad looking. She had what my old partner, Sue Danielson, once referred to as big hair. Ash blond and crinkly, it stood out from her head like a massive halo.

"That's the reporter's job," she explained. "Like my card says, I'm a columnist. I write a thrice-weekly piece called "Bisbee Buzzings." The paper is called the *Bee,* you see," she added, as if she thought me a bit dim. *"The Bisbee Bee."*

I have a long-term, not-so-cordial relationship with a man named Maxwell Cole who's a columnist for the *Seattle Post-Intelligencer.* Marliss Shackleford didn't know it, but being in the same league with Max wasn't the best kind of third-party referral.

"As I understand it, you're a detective."

"Used to be," I told her. "Now I'm a special investigator with the Washington State Attorney's Special Homicide Investigation Team. That's spelled S-H-I-T," I added helpfully.

Marliss Shackleford's face changed. She looked shocked. "I beg your pardon?"

"That's what my unit is called, the Special Homicide Investigation Team."

"Oh," she murmured. "But since this is a family newspaper, we'll probably have to write the whole thing out." She fumbled to an uneasy stop and then started over. "And you're here in Bisbee because . . ."

"Why do you think I'm here?" I asked in return.

She shrugged. "I presume it's because of the woman who died

down in Naco on Wednesday night. I've learned that her real name was Latisha Wall. I've also been told she was in the Washington State Witness Protection Program."

Marliss obviously had sources inside the Cochise County Sheriff's Department. I wondered who those sources might be. Rather than asking, though, I simply raised my bottle of O'Doul's and clinked it on her glass.

"See there?" I said. "Since you already know so much about it, I don't understand why you need to talk to me at all."

"All right," she admitted, dropping her ploy of fake innocence for the moment. "I know who you are and where you're from, but I still don't know why you're here. Is it because your boss . . . ?"

"Ross Connors," I supplied. "He's the Washington State Attorney General."

"Are you here because Mr. Connors has no faith in Sheriff Brady's ability to bring this case to a successful conclusion?"

Marliss Shackleford waited for my answer with her pen poised over a small notebook and with her eyes sparkling in anticipation, like a cat ready to spring on some poor unsuspecting sparrow. She clearly wanted me to say that I thought Sheriff Joanna Brady was incompetent. And, much as I might have liked to—much as I thought Joanna Brady to be an arrogant little twit—I couldn't bring myself to do it. I was incapable of saying so to a reporter, much less to a newspaper columnist.

"From what I can see," I told her guardedly, "Sheriff Brady is doing a credible job, especially since her department is so shorthanded. She seems to have only one detective on the job, and he's having to deal with two separate homicides. Her plate is pretty full."

Marliss's eager expression faded to disappointment. She put down her pen. "Ernie's on vacation," she told me unnecessarily.

"Ernie?" I asked.

"Ernie Carpenter. He's the sheriff's department's other detective. He and his wife, Rose, are off on an anniversary trip—their thirtieth."

Bully for them, I thought. *God spare me from living in a small town.*

"So you think the county investigators are doing a good job?" Marliss continued.

"Yes," I said. "I do."

"And your function is?"

"I'm here as an observer," I told her. "An interested observer; nothing more."

"I see." She frowned briefly, then added. "I understand Latisha Wall's sister is in town. Have you talked to her?"

"I'm not sure there's any reason for me to talk to her," I fudged. "As I said, I'm observing, not investigating."

Marliss tried coming at me from another direction. "I believe the sheriff's department investigators interviewed a suspect today."

The columnist certainly did have an inside track. Now it was my turn to play innocent. "Really?" I asked.

She nodded. "The guy's a local, someone who's lived around here for years. His name is Bobo Jenkins—LaMar Jenkins, actually. He and Latisha were a romantic item for several months. I suppose there's a possibility that Latisha Wall's death could have resulted from some kind of domestic dispute. What do you think of that idea?"

Cops don't talk to the press about critical aspects of ongoing investigations. Those are words I've lived by for most of my adult life. Joanna Brady's actions may have provoked me beyond endurance, but I couldn't bring myself to do that much of a flip-flop.

"I don't think I should comment about that one way or the other." I said.

"You think it's true then?"

"No. I said, 'No comment.' There's a difference."

The desk clerk came through the doorway and poked his head into the bar. "Hey, Marliss," he said, "I've got a call for you. Want to take it here or in the lobby?"

"Lobby," she said.

Marliss got up and left me sitting alone. On this cool Saturday night the bar was filling up with people, most of whom seemed to know one another. I was relieved that none of the bikers from the Blue Moon were in evidence. Alone in that crowded room, I thought about what it might be like to be a homicide cop in a small burg like this—a place where almost every victim and suspect would be someone known to you and where every move you made would be accomplished under the glaring spotlight of local reporters who knew you, the victims, and the perps. That kind of case-solving was definitely not for me.

And I also thought about having a drink, just one, maybe, in honor of my birthday. But before I made up my mind one way or the other, Marliss returned looking flushed and excited.

"That was Kevin," she explained breathlessly. "He's our reporter. He just heard that the second victim has been identified. Tentatively, of course. Not officially."

"Really," I said nonchalantly.

If I had acted as though I were vitally interested in the information, I doubt Marliss would have told me. Since I gave every indication that I couldn't care less, she eagerly filled me in.

"Her name is Deidre Canfield," Marliss said in a stage whisper that was entirely unnecessary since no one in the bar was paying us the slightest visible attention. "Dee owned an art gallery here in town. She and Latisha Wall were friends. This is all confidential, of course. It's totally on the QT until there's been an official notification of next of kin. You won't tell anyone, will you?"

"Of course not," I agreed.

"But I have to go back to the paper and check something out," Marliss added. "I did a profile of Dee Canfield a year or so ago, when she first came to town. I'll be able to reuse some of that material. I won't print anything prematurely, you understand, but if I write it right now while it's all still fresh, then the column will be ready the moment the coast is clear."

As I said before, between living in big cities or little towns, give me the city any day of the week.

Fourteen

FTER MARLISS SHACKLEFORD LEFT, I found I needed either a drink or some air and space. Upon reflection, I took myself for a walk.

It was well after dark by then and much chillier than the toasty daytime temperatures would have led me to expect. I was glad I was still wearing my wrinkled blazer as I wandered through narrow, crooked streets. The two- and three-story buildings I saw reminded me of those in downtown Ballard back home in Seattle. I wondered what Bisbee must have been like back in its heyday, back when domestic copper production was still a moneymaking proposition.

Here and there streetlights revealed ghostly traces of old signs painted on the sides of brick buildings, just barely still legible. They testified to the more abundant and diverse commercial past in small-town America—Western Auto, Woolworth's, JCPenney. But those bedrock businesses had long since deserted Bisbee, just as they had deserted countless other communities across the nation. Now the buildings had different occupants. It looked as though the current crop of merchants and organizations catered to tourism—a mining museum, an antiques mall, and a mostly used bookstore. The bars, of course, hadn't gone away. Maybe you couldn't buy a hammer and nails on Main Street in Bisbee, Arizona, anymore, but Coors on tap was readily available.

Naturally, as I walked, my mind strayed back to Anne. Had she walked this winding canyon street as a little girl? Had she bought an Etch A Sketch in Woolworth's or an Easter outfit in JCPenney?

And, as often happens when I think of Anne, I see her again as I did that very first time. It's a cloudless spring afternoon in Seattle's Mount Pleasant Cemetery. Wearing that bright red dress, she's striding across the green grass toward Angela Barstogi's open grave. The dowdily dressed mourners from Faith Tabernacle all stand aside to let her pass, parting before her commanding presence as the waters of the Red Sea did for Moses.

She stops only when she reaches the grave. Her hair is long and dark. A slight breeze ruffles it around her face, and I realize I've never seen anyone more beautiful or so undeniably sad.

The crowd is dumbstruck, and so am I. No one moves. Even the overbearing Pastor Michael Brodie is stunned to silence. Then slowly, gracefully, she raises her hand. A single rose drifts away from her open fingers and falls gently onto the casket of a small, murdered child.

And then the scene shifts. The funeral is over and when I see her again, she is coming down the hill. She is walking purposefully, with a certain goal in mind. Eventually I realize she's coming to me—directly to me. I am her goal, and my life will never again be the same.

Lost in thought, I nearly blundered into Cornelia Lester, who was making her way down Main Street.

"Sorry," I apologized. "I was thinking of something else. Mind if I join you?"

"But you were going in the other direction," she objected.

"That's all right. I was about to turn back anyway."

She laughed. "Help yourself, then, Mr. . . . I'm sorry. You'll have to forgive me. I seem to have forgotten your name."

"Beaumont," I supplied, falling into step beside her. "J.P. Beaumont. You can call me Beau."

Once again, Cornelia Lester's clothing rustled as she walked. Despite her ample girth, she set a brisk pace, moving much more swiftly than I had been on my own. Only the fact that we were now going downhill made it possible for me to keep up.

"I went up to the art gallery again," she explained. "I keep hoping someone will show up there and let me in."

I wrestled with whether or not I should tell her what Marliss Shackleford had just told me—that Dee Canfield had now been identified as a murder victim as well—but I decided against it. A reporter's unsubstantiated tip might very well be wrong. That kind of information needs to come from someone officially connected to the investigation. Marliss Shackleford certainly wasn't official and, as far as this latest incident was concerned, neither was I.

"There were lights on inside," Cornelia continued. "They must be on a timer so they come on automatically. I was able to catch a glimpse of a couple of Tizzy's paintings through the window. The one of Daddy . . ." She stopped talking abruptly, swallowed hard, and wiped at her eyes.

"Did you know our father was a minister?" she asked finally when she found her voice again. "He was a United Methodist minister at a mostly black church in Macon, Georgia. You ever been to Georgia?"

"Never," I said.

"Macon's a quiet place. Comfortable. But Tizzy couldn't wait to get out of town, and out of Daddy's church, too. We both did that, Tizzy and I, left home and neither of us set foot inside a church for years." She shrugged. "That's kids for you. They *have* to rebel. Daddy was a man of prayer. Tizzy loved action. He believed in nonviolence. He wanted his daughters to go to church and get educated. What did Tizzy do? She joined the Marines and went off to war. I finally got over what was bugging me. I went back home to Macon for keeps and to Daddy's church as well. I made my peace with our parents. Tizzy never did, and it broke Daddy's heart. I think that's part of what killed him, but that one picture . . ."

Again she paused, overcome by emotion.

"Which picture?" I asked.

"It's one of Tizzy's paintings in the gallery. Have you seen them?"

"No."

"Well, one of them shows Daddy standing outside his church on a sunny Sunday morning. He's wearing that old robe of his—the bright red one that he loved so much and wore every summer until it was so thin you could practically see through it. Tizzy captured everything about it, even the little patch Momma darned into the arm. I could almost smell it, reeking of Daddy's Old Spice.

"The picture was so true to life that it took my breath away. It might have been a photograph. And there's little T. J. Evans, standing there looking up at Daddy with those big brown trusting eyes. I'd know that boy anywhere; he was such a cute little thing. T. J.'s gone now, of course. Died in a car wreck three or four years ago, but Tizzy painted him just the way he was back then when he was a little-bitty sprout. It's like her mind was a camera, with everything stored there just like it used to be."

We walked the distance of a block in silence, although with no cross-streets, it's hard to measure blocks in Bisbee.

"That picture just got to me, I guess," Cornelia Lester continued eventually. "Made me think maybe she was intending to come back after all. Not home, of course. I know she couldn't have done that, but maybe she was ready to come back to the fold. Like she was finally ready to make peace with Daddy and with all he stood for. What do you think?"

"I wouldn't know," I said. "But maybe so."

"Did you happen to notice that United Methodist Church back there, just across the street from the gallery?" Cornelia asked.

I hadn't. "No," I said.

"Tombstone Something, I think. The sign says services start at ten-thirty. I believe I'll go there tomorrow morning. I like to do that—visit other churches when I'm traveling."

I've never had a sibling, but if I had just learned one of them had been murdered, I doubt I would have been out looking for Sunday-morning services in a strange church in a strange town. Cornelia Lester had a depth of belief that made me half envious.

We had come to a small plaza, an almost level spot in an otherwise up-and-down town. We crossed a one-way backstreet and were making our way through a postage-stamp-size park when three Cochise County patrol cars came roaring past us, one right after the other. None of them had their flashers or sirens on. Even so, they were moving at a good clip. I was pretty sure one of them belonged to Sheriff Brady, and I theorized that they had come from the crime scene in Naco and were probably headed for Castle Rock Gallery.

I really wanted to turn on my heel and go there, too. But I didn't. I was certain that if I showed up somewhere uninvited, Sheriff Brady would send me packing. Again.

Call me a slow learner, but I've finally figured out that sometimes I'm better off not going where I'm not wanted.

Cornelia Lester and I made our way up the steps on the far side of the park and then across a narrow side street and up into the hotel lobby. By the time we topped the last set of stairs, we were both huffing and puffing. I fully expected Cornelia Lester to head directly for the elevator and her room, but she didn't. Instead she made her way toward one of the leather couches.

"Wouldn't you mind sitting with me awhile?" she asked. "I'd really appreciate it. I feel a need to talk to someone tonight, but it's past midnight back home by now. Everyone there is probably sound asleep."

"Sure," I agreed.

After all, it may have been my birthday, but I had nothing else to do but listen. And with memories of Anne Corley haunting me once more, it was either that, find an AA meeting, or go to the bar and have a drink. Faced with those three alternatives, listening to Cornelia Lester was by far the best choice.

WHILE FRANK MONTOYA STAYED with the crime scene investigation in Naco, Joanna took her Civvie and followed Casey and Ken Junior back into town and up to Castle Rock Gallery in

Old Bisbee. Joanna had parked her car and was locking the door when a man smoking a glowing cigarette materialized unexpectedly next to her.

"Oh, Harve," she said, recognizing the owner of Treasure Trove Antiques. "You startled me. I didn't see you there."

"Wasn't," he said. "Came down when I heard them other two cop cars drive up. See you've got some officers in there now," he added, nodding in the direction of the gallery. "Did you find her? Something bad must have happened."

Joanna nodded. "Dee Canfield is dead, Harve," she said. "Some boys found her body in an abandoned house down in Naco several hours ago, but that's not for public knowledge just yet. We need to notify her family."

Harve sighed and nodded sagely. "I was afraid of that," he said. "In fact, I pro'ly should have said as much to that other detective of yours when I talked to him earlier this afternoon, but I'm no gossip. I didn't want to cause trouble."

"You talked to Detective Carbajal today?" Joanna asked.

"Oh, no. Not Jaime—that other fellow, the big one with the salt-and-pepper crew cut. He must be new. I don't remember ever seein' him around before. Can't tell you his name, but I'm sure you know who I mean."

Joanna knew exactly whom Harvey Dowd meant. *Mr. Beaumont, I presume,* she thought.

"What all did you tell him?" she asked.

"Nothin' much. About that fight the other day, the one you had to break up. I was surprised that he didn't seem to know nothin' about it."

I'm not, Joanna thought.

"I haven't had a chance to talk to him this afternoon," she said innocently. "Did you tell him anything else I should know about?

Or have you seen anything unusual going on around the gallery in the last day or two?"

Harvey Dowd took a final, thoughtful drag on the end of his cigarette, then he dropped the stub into the gutter and ground it out with the sole of his boot. "Had a long talk again this evening with that nice black lady, the one whose sister was killed down in Naco earlier this week. She keeps coming by hoping to get a look at her sister's paintings, but, of course, nobody's been there."

Cornelia Lester, Joanna thought.

"She was all wore out from walking so far uphill," Harve Dowd continued. "She's from Georgia, you see. She's not accustomed to this here elevation of ours. My shop was closed for the day, but I let her come in and sit a spell in one of my old rockers until she got her breath back. I offered to bring my car down from the parking lot and give her a ride back to the hotel, but she wouldn't hear of it. She said walking was fine."

Harve paused long enough to shake another cigarette out of his pack of Camels. "What about that boyfriend of Dee's?" he asked.

"So far there's no sign of him," Joanna answered.

Sheltering a flickering match with his cupped hand, Harvey Dowd lit his next cigarette. "Not surprised," he drawled when he finished. "I'm guessing you're not gonna find him, either. Never did like Warren Gibson much. Struck me as sort of underhanded, know what I mean? Didn't seem like the type who'd stick around if there was any sign of trouble. I knew as soon as I heard the ruckus that Bobo Jenkins meant trouble."

"You think Warren Gibson is underhanded?" Joanna asked. "What makes you say that?"

"When I'm out prospecting in the desert, which I do every now and again, I sometimes get this funny feeling. I call it feeling snaky. It's like my body is picking up signals that I can't see or hear, but it's tryin' to let me know all the same; tryin' to tell me there's a rattlesnake out there somewhere, and I'd best be careful. First time or two it happened, I ignored it and damned near got myself bit. Then I learned to pay attention. Now I stop and look around until I find the snake before it finds me.

"Warren Gibson's the first human being ever who gives me that same kind of snaky feeling. It happened right off, the first time Dee introduced us, and for no real reason I can explain."

"He makes you feel snaky?" Joanna asked, trying keep the disbelief out of her voice.

Harvey Dowd nodded. "Not exactly the same, but sort of. Like he's dangerous or somethin', although he never done nothin' to me and never said anything out of line, so I could be mistaken about the man. Like I said, it's just a feelin'."

"Did you ever mention any of this to Deidre Canfield?"

Harve shook his head. "Did you ever have any dealings with that woman?"

"A few," Joanna replied.

"I liked old Dee well enough, but she could be a screaming meemie when she wanted to. She seemed to think the sun rose and set on that man of hers, so far be it from me to try to tell her otherwise. Like I told you before, I'm not the gossipin' kind. If I'd a told Dee Canfield that Warren was two-timing her, she would've bit my head clean off."

"Two-timing?" Joanna asked. "Are you saying you saw Warren Gibson with another woman?"

"Didn't see," Harvey Dowd corrected. "Heard. Maybe not even heard, either, as far as that goes, but I'm as sure of it as I'm standing here. Why else would someone, with a perfectly good phone at home and another one right there in the gallery, spend so much time standing around on Main Street yakkin' away on a pay phone? Maybe I'm all wet. Maybe it's not a girlfriend, but I saw him talking on those pay phones down by the post office a lot—well out of Dee's sight, you see. And what crossed my mind at the time was that, whoever it was he was talking to and whatever he was up to, he sure as hell didn't want Dee Canfield to know about it."

Joanna knew that Frank Montoya would be looking at the phone records for both the gallery and Dee Canfield's house, but without Harve Dowd's tip, no one would have thought to check the pair of pay phones on Main Street.

Thanking Harvey Dowd for his help, Joanna stuck her head into the gallery long enough to let Casey Ledford know where she was going. Then she got back into the car and drove down to the post office, where two waist-high public telephones stood side by side. After jotting down all the numbers, she radioed them into Dispatch, asking Tica to pass them along to Frank Montoya so he could ask for phone logs as soon as possible.

With that call completed, Joanna started to return to Castle Rock Gallery but changed her mind. The more people who showed up at a potential crime scene, the greater the potential for contamination, and the longer it would take for Casey and Ken Junior to process the place.

Across the street, through a tiny park, and up a concrete stairway, Joanna glimpsed the creamy-lit facade of Bisbee's Copper Queen Hotel. Inside the hotel Joanna knew she would find Cornelia Lester. Latisha Wall's sister was someone who had yet to have a face-to-face visit from the Cochise County sheriff. Joanna owed the woman that much courtesy, and some information as well.

With a sigh, Joanna put her Crown Victoria in gear and headed for the hotel. Once there, she stopped at the desk and asked for

Cornelia Lester's room. "She's not there," the clerk responded. "She's right around the corner on the far side of the stairs."

Walking around the sheltering stairway, Joanna saw a large African-American woman sitting on a leather-backed chair speaking to someone. Reluctant to interrupt, Joanna paused for a moment—long enough to see that the person opposite Cornelia Lester was none other than Special Investigator Beaumont.

All afternoon, the man had dogged her heels. Now he was interviewing Latisha Wall's sister. Refusing to give way to a budding temper tantrum and steeling herself to be civil, Joanna stepped forward. "Good evening, Mr. Beaumont," she said as she walked past him. She stopped in front of the woman. "You must be Cornelia Lester," she said. "I'm Sheriff Joanna Brady. Please accept my condolences for the loss of your sister."

IF LOOKS COULD KILL, I would have keeled over dead when Joanna Brady walked into the lobby of the Copper Queen Hotel and shook hands with Cornelia Lester.

"Thank you," Cornelia said graciously. "I take it you and Mr. Beaumont here already know each other?"

Joanna nodded. "Yes," she said. "We've met." Her cool response was less than enthusiastic.

Settling into a nearby chair, Joanna leaned toward Cornelia as she spoke again. "I'm sorry to have to tell you this, Ms. Lester, but we've had another homicide this evening. Actually, I'm guessing that the death happened a day or so ago, but we've only just now discovered the body."

Cornelia Lester didn't blink. "Who?" she asked.

"Deidre Canfield."

"The woman who owns the gallery?"

Joanna nodded. "Yes."

"If she's dead, too," Cornelia speculated, "and if she and my sister were friends, then her death must have something to do with Tizzy's, don't you think? I'm sorry, Sheriff Brady. I mean with Latisha's. Tizzy is what we always called my sister back home. But tell me, please, is there any progress now?"

Joanna glanced at me before she answered. "Not much," she admitted. "We have only preliminary autopsy results for your sister at the moment. We believe she ingested some kind of poison, which may have been placed in your sister's iced tea."

"Who did it?" Cornelia asked. For her it was a simple question that should have had an equally simple answer—one Joanna Brady was currently unable to give.

"At this point, Ms. Lester, I'm afraid we have no viable suspects. My investigators are working on it, of course, but it's still very early."

"If it was in Tizzy's tea, could it be a random-tampering case that has nothing to do with Tizzy being in the witness protection program?"

I have to give the lady credit. Cornelia asked tough questions. Joanna shook her head. "We can't say one way or the other."

"What are the chances that this second dead woman—this Deidre Canfield who was supposedly Tizzy's friend—was somehow connected to the people who ran UPPI, the people Tizzy was so afraid were going to try to kill her?"

"That is a possibility," Joanna conceded. "So far we've found nothing that would bolster that theory."

"What about this?" Cornelia asked. "First they use Deidre Canfield to get to my sister, and then, with Tizzy gone, they get rid of Dee Canfield, too. Those UPPI folks are not nice people, Sheriff Brady."

"I'm convinced your sister was right to be scared," Joanna agreed. "But as for Deidre Canfield being tied in with them, that doesn't seem likely."

"What about Tizzy's boyfriend then?" Cornelia asked, switching directions. "What's his name again?"

"Jenkins," Joanna supplied, glaring at me. "His name is Bobo Jenkins, but I must object to Mr. Beaumont here giving you access to confidential information. He may be a special investigator with the Washington State Attorney General's Office, but he has no business . . ."

Oops. I should have come clean with Cornelia Lester and told her who I was. Now the cat was out of the bag. My ears reddened under her shrewdly appraising look.

"Mr. Beaumont?" she said finally. "Why, he never told me a thing about Mr. Jenkins. It was that nice man up at the antiques store. What's his name again?"

"Harvey Dowd?" I asked tentatively.

Joanna Brady shot another baleful look in my direction. I had noticed earlier that her eyes were a vivid shade of green. In the dim light of the hotel lobby, however, they looked more like chips of slate.

"That's right," Cornelia said with a nod that somehow conveyed she had forgiven me my sin of omission. "Harvey Dowd is the one. He gave me to understand that Mr. Jenkins has quite a temper. He told me about a serious confrontation of some kind up at the gallery the other day—serious enough that police officers had to intervene."

"That's true," Joanna said. "There was a confrontation. In fact, I'm the one who broke it up, but in Mr. Jenkins's defense, you have to understand that he had just learned of your sister's death—the death of the woman he had known as Rochelle Baxter and whom he had cared about deeply. When he discovered that Deidre Canfield still planned to go ahead with her grand-opening party, he was outraged. And when he learned Dee was raising the prices on the pictures . . ."

"Raising the prices?"

"Yes. Her position was that, with the artist dead, the few paintings that did exist would be that much more valuable. Mr. Jenkins took exception to that. He thought the show should be canceled and the pictures turned over to their rightful owners—the artist's family."

"He wanted the paintings returned to us?" Cornelia asked.

Joanna nodded. "That's what the big fuss at Castle Rock Gallery that morning was all about."

"He was trying to keep the gallery from selling them?"

"Yes," Joanna said. "So they could be given to you."

Cornelia Lester shook her head thoughtfully. "Mr. Dowd didn't say a word about that," she said, after a moment.

"No," Joanna agreed. "I'm sure he didn't, because he didn't know it."

Cornelia Lester sighed. "I've never met Mr. Jenkins, but when I do, I owe him an apology and my thanks. Now, if you'll both excuse me, I'd better go on upstairs and go to bed. My body's still on East Coast time. I'm running out of steam."

She used the arms of the deep leather chair to raise herself to her feet. "There's a lot more I'd like to discuss with you, Sheriff Brady, but not tonight. I'm just not up to it."

"I understand," Joanna said. "I know you already have my phone numbers. Feel free to call anytime."

Nodding, Cornelia started toward the elevator. As she rounded the stairs, she stopped and turned back to us. "By the way," she added. "I'm glad to know you and Mr. Beaumont are working on this situation together, Sheriff Brady. It gives me a lot more confidence that something will come of it."

Not wanting to be chewed up and spit out by Sheriff Brady, I stood up, too. "I could just as well be going," I said.

"No, you don't," she said. "I want to talk to you."

I sat back down and slumped down on the couch. *Here it comes,* I thought, remembering being hauled on the carpet by the daunting Miss Heard.

"How long have you been in town?" Joanna asked.

"Since around one P.M.," I said.

"And who all have you talked to since then?"

I pulled a tattered notebook out of my pocket and consulted the list of names I had jotted there. "Cornelia Lester, Harvey Dowd, Angie Hacker, Archie McBride, and Willy Haskins. Later on I spoke to your chief deputy Mr. Montoya and also to a reporter named Marliss Shackleford."

Sheriff Brady's eyes registered surprise when I mentioned the last name on the list. "You've talked to Marliss?" she asked.

"You know her, I take it?"

Joanna nodded grimly. "We're not on the best of terms."

I suppose I should have let it go at that, but I felt constrained to tell her the rest. "You should be aware that I met with her earlier this evening," I said. "Marliss introduced herself to me down at the crime scene, the one where you sent me packing. Then, a little while ago, she came here, to the hotel, and interviewed me."

"About?"

"She wanted to know why I was in town," I said.

"What did you tell her?"

"I told her I was sent as an observer for the Washington State Attorney General's Office. I doubt that was what she was really after, though. She seems to be under the impression that Ross Connors doesn't think your department can handle the Latisha Wall case. I believe her exact words were: 'Ross Connors has no faith in Sheriff Brady's ability.' Something to that effect, anyway."

"What did you tell her?"

"That both Mr. Connors and I thought you were doing fine." Joanna blinked. "Thanks," she said.

"There's something else," I added.

"What's that?"

"She started asking questions about the Bobo Jenkins interview."

"How did she know about that?" Joanna demanded.

"I sure as hell didn't tell her," I responded quickly. "I may be a royal pain in the ass as far as you're concerned, Sheriff Brady, but I know better than to compromise an ongoing investigation by leaking information to the press. The same can't be said for everyone in your department, however. Someone on your staff needs to learn to keep his mouth shut."

There was a long period of silence after that. The longer Joanna Brady went without speaking, the more I figured I had blown it for sure. If there had ever been a remote chance of the two of us working together successfully, it was gone for good.

"Thanks for telling me," she said finally. "I'm pretty sure I know who Mr. Big Mouth is, but I haven't figured out what to do about him."

"If I were you," I told her, "I'd kick ass and take names later."

She laughed then. "I'll take that suggestion under advisement." Her single burst of laughter seemed to put us on a whole new footing. "Cornelia Lester isn't the only one who needs to hand out apologies," she said. "I believe I owe you one as well."

"What for?"

"You've been in town for less than twelve hours, Mr. Beaumont. And yet, without any help from me or my people, you've managed to sort out most of the major players in this case."

"I used to be . . ." I began.

"I know. You used to work homicide at Seattle PD. I'm guessing you must have been pretty good at it. The truth is, we are shorthanded at the moment, so if you're still willing to help, please be at my office tomorrow afternoon at one. I'm creating a task force, and you're more than welcome to join it."

Nothing short of flabbergasted, I said, "I'll be there."

Joanna stood up then and held out her small hand with that surprisingly firm grip. "It's late," she said. "My daughter's dog had to be put down today. I should be at home with Jenny instead of out here traipsing all over the county. I'll see you tomorrow, then?"

I nodded. "One o'clock."

"Sharp," she added.

"I'll be there."

As she walked away, I was still shaking my head in utter befuddlement. It may have been my birthday, but I was no closer to understanding women than I was on the day I was born.

I sat for several minutes listening as the noise from the bar got louder and louder. It kept tugging at me. Finally, breaking free, I headed up to my room. Once there, I glanced at the clock. It was nearly midnight, but my night-owl grandparents would still be wide awake.

I dialed their number and was relieved when my new stepgrandfather, Lars Jenssen, who is also my AA sponsor, answered the phone. "Ja sure," he said. "If it isn't the birthday boy! Beverly tried calling you off and on all day, but there was no answer on your dang cell phone. She's in getting ready for bed. Hang on. I'll go get her."

"No," I said quickly. "Don't do that. This isn't that kind of call."

"You having a tough time?" Lars asked, immediately switching gears. "You thinking about having that first drink?"

"Yes," I admitted. "I am."

"Well, then," he said. "Let's talk about it."

And we did.

Fifteen

DRIVING UP TO THE HOUSE at High Lonesome Ranch, Joanna was vividly aware that with Sadie gone, neither of the dogs came bounding down the road to greet her. When she pulled into the yard, she noticed a light still burning in the window of Jenny's corner bedroom.

Butch was in bed reading when she went in to undress. "Did Jenny ever come out of her room?" Joanna asked, kissing him hello.

"Once," he said. "To feed Tigger and let him out. Other than that, I haven't seen her."

"Did she eat dinner?"

"Nope."

"Her light's still on," Joanna said. "Maybe I should go talk to her."

"Good idea," Butch said. "You can try, anyway."

Hoping Jenny might be asleep, Joanna opened the door without knocking. Inside the room, Jenny lay on the bottom bunk, one arm wrapped tightly around Tigger, who was curled up next to her. Tigger thumped his tail when Joanna first entered the room, but he didn't try to slink off the bed, where, under normal circumstances, he wasn't allowed.

"You awake?" Joanna asked, sinking into the creaking rocker next to the bed.

"I fell asleep this afternoon," Jenny said. "Now I can't sleep. I'm lying here, thinking."

"About Sadie?"

Jenny nodded. "She was just always here, Mom. I never thought she'd go away. She never seemed sick. She never *acted* sick."

"That's the good thing about dogs," Joanna said. "They don't complain. The bad thing is, they can't tell us what's wrong with them, either. And they don't live forever, Jen. What's important is what you said this afternoon. We loved Sadie and took care of her while she was here with us. Now we have to let her go. And you were wonderful with her, sweetie. No one could have done more."

"Really?" Jenny asked.

"Really."

There was a long pause. When Jenny said nothing, Joanna finally asked, "Are you hungry? Would you like me to fix you something?"

Jenny shook her head. "No, thanks," she said.

For a time after that the only sound in the room was the creaking of Butch's grandmother's rocking chair. Jenny broke the long silence.

"I think Tigger knows what happened—that Sadie's gone and she isn't coming back. Somebody told me that dogs don't have feelings like we do—that they don't grieve or feel sorry for themselves or anything. Do you think that's true?"

Joanna studied Tigger, who had yet to move anything other than his tail and his dark, soulful eyes. The usually lively dog was mysteriously still, as quiet as Joanna had ever seen him. If he wasn't grieving, he was doing a good imitation.

"I'm sure he does know something's wrong," Joanna said. "Maybe he's simply responding to your unhappiness, but I believe he understands."

"I think so, too," Jenny said. "He doesn't usually like to cuddle."

Neither do you, Joanna thought.

That was followed by yet another silence. At last Joanna sighed and checked her watch. It was after midnight. "All right, then," she said. "If you're not hungry, I guess I'll go to bed."

She got as far as the door before Jenny stopped her. "Mom?"

"What?"

"I think I know what I want to be when I grow up."

Joanna's heart lurched, grateful for this small connection with her grieving daughter. "What?" she asked, turning back.

"A veterinarian," Jenny replied. "Just like Dr. Ross. She couldn't fix Sadie—she couldn't make her better—but she was really nice to Sadie and to me, too. It was like, well, she really cared. Know what I mean?"

"Yes." Joanna returned to the bed and perched on the edge of it, close enough that she could rub Tigger's ears. "I know exactly what you mean, Jen," she said. "The way you love animals, I'm sure you'll be a terrific vet."

"Is it hard?" Jenny asked.

"Every job has hard things and good things about it," Joanna said. "I'd hate to have to put a sick animal down and then try to comfort the owner."

"How long do you have to go to school?"

"To be a vet? A long time. First you have to graduate from college, then it's just like going to medical school. To get in, you have to earn top grades in math and science, chemistry especially."

"Do you think I can do it?"

"You're a very smart girl, sweetie. If you set your mind to it, you can do anything you want."

AT A QUARTER TO TEN the next morning, as Butch, Jenny, and Joanna were ready to walk out the door for church, the telephone rang. "Here we go again," Butch grumbled, handing Joanna the receiver. "It's Lupe Alvarez," he said. "According to her, it's urgent."

"What is it?" Joanna asked.

"There's a lady here in the lobby," Lupe replied. "Her name is Serenity Granger. She's Deidre Canfield's daughter. The ME's office had the Cheyenne Police Department contact her last night. She wants to talk to you right away."

"All right," Joanna agreed. "I'll be there as soon as I can." When she turned to Butch, he was shaking his head. "Sorry," she told him. "You and Jenny go on without me. I'll join you as soon as I can."

"I won't hold my breath," he said.

While Butch and Jenny drove away in the Subaru, Joanna opted for her Civvie. Ten minutes later she entered her office through the back door. Once at her desk, she called out to the lobby. "Okay, Lupe," she said. "I'm here. You can bring Ms. Granger back now."

Knowing Dee Canfield, Joanna was surprised by her first glimpse of Serenity Granger. She was the exact antithesis of her mother's tie-dyed, let-it-all-hang-out splendor. Serenity, perhaps a few years older than Joanna, was tall and pencil-thin. She wore a business suit—the kind of smart, above-the-knee tailored model favored by the current crop of television heroines. The charcoal pin-striped outfit was complemented by matching two-inch gray sling-back pumps with an elegant Italian pedigree.

Joanna realized that Serenity Granger must have traveled most of the night in order to make it from Cheyenne, Wyoming, to Bisbee, Arizona, by ten o'clock in the morning. The woman should have looked wrinkled and travel-worn, but she didn't. The suit showed no trace of unwanted creases. The mass of bleached-blond curls that framed a somber face was in perfect order. Only her makeup, which had no doubt started out as perfection itself, was beginning to show a few ill effects. Her gray eye shadow was slightly smudged, and a speck of unruly mascara had dribbled down one cheek.

"I'm Sheriff Brady," Joanna said at once, standing up and offering her hand. "I'm so sorry about the loss of your mother. Please, have a seat."

"Thank you," Serenity returned.

Removing a small long-strapped purse from her shoulder, she eased herself into one of the captain's chairs and folded her well-manicured hands in her lap. "I know this is Sunday," Serenity began. "I'm sorry to interrupt your day off, but this is too important to let go until Monday."

"What's too important?" Joanna asked.

Serenity chewed her lower lip. "Please understand," she said. "This is all very difficult."

"I'm sure it is. Take your time, Ms. Granger. Can I offer you something to drink—coffee, water?"

"Water would be nice."

Without Kristin in the outside office, Joanna had no one to fetch it. "Hang on," she said. "I'll be right back."

When she returned a few minutes later, Serenity Granger sat

in the same position. Now, though, under her still-folded hands Joanna spied a single piece of paper that hadn't been there before.

"I suppose I don't have to tell you my mother and I weren't close," Serenity began again with a regretful half-smile. "We didn't have much in common."

"There's a lot of that going around these days," Joanna offered encouragingly. After all, when it came to mother-daughter relationships, she and Eleanor Lathrop weren't exactly shining examples.

"We were at loggerheads as long as I can remember," Serenity continued. "Whatever came up, we fought about it. My mother tuned in during the sixties, dropped out, and stayed that way. I couldn't wait to join the establishment. My mother never completed high school. I did four years of college and finished law school with honors in a year and a half. Mother never voted in her life. According to her, the Democrats are too conservative. Naturally, I'm a card-carrying Republican." She shrugged. "What else could I do?"

Joanna nodded.

"Anyway, for years we weren't in touch at all. In fact, for a time I didn't know if she was dead or alive. Then, about a year ago and out of the clear blue sky, Mother sent me an e-mail. She had come into a bit of money, from my grandfather, I guess. She said she was moving to Bisbee and getting ready to open an art gallery.

"I wasn't necessarily overjoyed to hear from her. For a while I didn't bother to respond, but my husband's a psychologist. Mel finally convinced me that the best thing I could do for Mother and for me, too, was to figure out a way to forgive her. Eventually I wrote back. We started by sending little notes back and forth. To my amazement, e-mail ended up bringing us closer than ever.

"I'm not sure how it happened, but for the first time I can remember we weren't at each other's throats. Maybe part of it was not being in the same household and having some distance between us. We'd talk about what was going on in our day-to-day lives. Even though I had been married for seven years, Mother had never met Mel. I told her about him, about our house and garden, and about both our jobs. Mel has a private practice in Cheyenne. I'm a corporate attorney for an oil-exploration company. I thought hearing that would freak her out, but it didn't. She never said a word.

"She told me about what it was like to live in Bisbee, about the little house she had bought—the first one ever—and about the new man in her life, a guy named Warren Gibson. As a kid, that was one of the reasons I despised my mother. There was *always* a new man in her life. They came and went with astonishing regularity. But I could tell from the way she talked about Warren, this time things were different. She really liked the guy; really cared about him. I think she was finally ready to settle down to something permanent, and she believed Warren Gibson was it.

"She told me about the work they did together on the gallery, getting it ready to open. She also told me about the upcoming showing of Rochelle Baxter's stuff. Mother was really excited about it and proud of having discovered someone she fully expected to turn into one of this country's up-and-coming African-American artists."

Serenity stopped long enough to sip her water before continuing. "She sent me this e-mail on Thursday afternoon. Unfortunately, I was out of town and didn't read it until yesterday."

Unfolding the single piece of paper that had been lying in her lap, Serenity Granger handed Joanna the printed copy of an e-mail.

Dear Serenity,

Something terrible has happened. Rochelle Baxter is dead, murdered. She died last night sometime. The grand opening of her show is tonight. The caterer will be here in a little less than two hours. I found out about Shelley too late to cancel the food. Since I have to pay for it anyway, I decided to go ahead with the party.

The problem is Warren. He and I were among the last people to see Shelley before she died. The cops wanted to talk to both of us. Detective Carbajal is with the sheriff's department. He told me this afternoon that they'll also need to fingerprint us since we'd both been at Shelley's place earlier in the day. We went there to collect the pieces from her studio to hang them here in the gallery.

When I told Warren about the fingerprint thing, he went nuts. We ended up having a huge fight. In all the months I've known him, I've never seen him so upset. He's off doing some errands right now. I've been sitting here thinking about all this—thinking and wondering.

Is it possible Warren could have had something to do with what happened to Shelley? I mean, we were both there in her house. I can't think of any other reason why the very mention of fingerprints would

The e-mail ended in midsentence. "Where's the rest of it?" Joanna asked.

"That's just it," Serenity returned. "There isn't any more. It's like Mother had to hit the 'Send' button in a hurry. Warren may have come into the gallery right then, and she didn't want him to know about her suspicions or about her sending them along to me.

"As soon as I accessed my e-mail yesterday evening, I started trying to call. I called both the gallery and the house several times and left messages. Naturally, there wasn't any answer. Then, an hour or so later, when a Cheyenne PD patrol car stopped in front of our house, I knew what was up. The officer didn't have to tell me Mother was dead. I already knew.

"So where's Warren Gibson, Sheriff Brady? I am convinced he

killed my mother, and he must have murdered that other woman as well. I want him caught."

"I can assure you, Ms. Granger, so do we. Now, please excuse me for a moment while I make a phone call."

Joanna picked up her phone. It was Sunday, after all. Frank Montoya could have been home or at church. On a hunch, though, she dialed her chief deputy's office number. He answered after half a ring.

"You'd better come into my office, Frank," she told him. "Dee Canfield's daughter is here. I'm sure you and Detective Carbajal will both be interested in what she has to say. Is Jaime in, by the way?"

"No," Frank Montoya said. "But he will be as soon as I can reach him."

It took only half an hour for both Frank and Jaime to converge on Joanna's office. For the next hour or so, they pumped Serenity for information.

"Did your mother tell you anything in particular about Warren Gibson?" Jaime Carbajal asked.

"Just that he was good with his hands. He could put up drywall, plaster, install wiring, and do any number of things she would have had to spend money on otherwise."

"She didn't say where he came from?"

"Not that I remember. At the beginning, I think she maybe hired him to do a couple of days' worth of odd jobs. Before very long, though, he had moved in with her. As far as Mother was concerned, that's typical. It also goes a long way to explain why I was a twenty-six-year-old virgin when I got married."

The sardonic self-deprecation in that sentence lodged like a sharp-edged pebble in Joanna Brady's heart. Dee Canfield and her daughter had spent a lifetime locked in almost mortal combat. Serenity Granger's strategy had been to look at what her mother did and then do the opposite. The same was true for Joanna and Eleanor Lathrop.

What will happen with Jenny? Joanna wondered. *Since I'm a cop, does that mean she's destined to end up a crook? Or will she really turn into a veterinarian?*

Joanna was drawn out of her reverie, not by the continuing questions and answers, but by a sudden urgent knocking on her office door. Why was it that just when she had something important going on—just when she needed a little peace and quiet—her office turned into Grand Central Station?

Not wanting to disrupt Jaime's interview with Serenity Granger, Joanna hurried to the door. Casey Ledford stood outside holding several pieces of computer-generated printouts.

"What is it, Casey? We've got an important interview going on in here."

"Yes, I know." Casey nodded. "Lupe told me, but this is important, too. I got a hit from one of the prints I took off a hammer I found in a drawer up at Castle Rock Gallery. Everything else was pretty clean, but whoever wiped the place down must have forgotten about the hammer or maybe didn't see it. Anyway, here's the guy's rap sheet. I thought you'd want to check it out."

Joanna took the paper and looked at the mug shot. The name said Jack Brampton, but the photo was clearly Dee Canfield's boyfriend, the man known around Bisbee as Warren Gibson. Joanna's memory flashed back to when she had last seen him, standing in Castle Rock Gallery, glaring threateningly at Bobo Jenkins and tapping the head of a hammer—perhaps the very same one—in the open palm of his hand. Brampton had served twenty-one months in a medium-security Illinois prison for involuntary manslaughter committed while driving drunk. He had previously worked as a pharmaceutical salesman.

That might be enough for him to know something about sodium azide, Joanna thought. *Enough to make him very dangerous.*

"Good work, Casey," she said. "Can I keep this?"

Casey nodded. "Sure. I'm making copies for everyone who'll be coming to the one-o'clock meeting."

"Terrific. Drop one off with Dispatch as you go. I want an APB out on this guy ASAP. He's got a good head start on us, so we may have a tough time catching up. We'll assume, for right now, that he's still driving Deidre Canfield's Pinto. It's distinctive enough that it shouldn't be hard to find."

While Casey hurried away, Joanna turned back into her office. The interview was coming to an end. Serenity Granger, purse in hand, stood just inside the door. "So you think it's going to be several days before Mother's body can be released?"

"Several for sure," Jaime Carbajal said. "First there'll have to be an autopsy. The medical examiner won't release the body until well after that. If I were you, I'd find a hotel room where you can settle in and wait."

"Any suggestions?"

"Probably the Copper Queen back uptown in Old Bisbee," he told her. "But regardless of where you stay, please let us know where you'll be."

Serenity Granger nodded. "Of course," she said.

Joanna wished Jaime Carbajal hadn't suggested the Copper Queen. Pretty soon everyone staying at the old hotel would be connected to this case, one way or the other. But she didn't voice her objection aloud. After all, the only thing Joanna wanted was for Serenity Granger to leave her office. The information about Warren Gibson's criminal past was far too important to blurt out with a civilian present, even if that civilian was vitally concerned with finding the person under investigation.

"I'll walk you to the lobby," Frank Montoya offered.

"Don't bother," Serenity said, turning him down. "I can find my way."

As soon as the door closed behind her, both Frank and Jaime turned to Joanna expectantly. "All right," Frank said. "Give."

Joanna handed him the paper. "Warren Gibson's real name is Jack Brampton," she said. "He's an ex–pharmaceutical salesman who's done time for DWI and involuntary manslaughter. Casey's made copies of the rap sheet so we'll have them available for the task force meeting at one. I want everybody there. I also want copies available of everything we have so far, including a written report of what we've just learned from Serenity Granger. By the way, Beaumont will be here for the meeting."

Both men looked at Joanna. "Since when?" Jaime asked.

"Since last night when I invited him," Joanna said.

Jaime shook his head. "Great," he muttered. "Guess I'd better get started typing my report, then."

Jaime stalked from the room. Joanna glanced at Frank to see if he shared Jaime's opinion about including Beaumont in the task force. If the chief deputy disapproved, it didn't show. He walked over to Joanna's desk and retrieved a pile of papers he'd brought along with him into her office.

"What are those?" she asked.

"Copies of everything we had up to this morning. Even with Beaumont included, there'll be enough to go around. I thought you might want to go over them yourself before the meeting."

"Thanks, Frank. You're good at keeping me on track. I really appreciate it."

"And then there's this." He removed a fat manila envelope from the bottom of the stack and passed it over as well.

"What is it?" she asked.

"A present," he said. "It's the information you asked me to track down on Anne Rowland Corley," Frank told her. "There's quite a bit of it—probably too much to read between now and one o'clock, but you might want to skim through some of it. If what I'm picking up is anything close to accurate, whoever sent Special Investigator Beaumont to Bisbee wasn't doing the poor guy any favors."

Joanna pulled out the topmost clipping and glanced at it. The article, dated several years earlier, was taken from the *Seattle Times*. It reported that a special internal investigation conducted by the Seattle Police Department had concluded that a deranged Anne Corley had died three weeks earlier as a result of a single gunshot wound, fired by her husband of one day, Seattle Homicide Detective J.P. Beaumont. The fatal shooting had occurred at a place called Snoqualmie Falls State Park. Anne Corley's death had now been officially ruled as self-defense, and Detective Beaumont had been recalled from administrative leave.

Putting the paper down, Joanna stared at her chief deputy. "It sounds to me like cop-assisted suicide," she said.

Frank Montoya shrugged his shoulders. "Or husband-assisted suicide," he said. "Take your pick. Now I'd better get going, too. I'm working on the telephone information you asked me to get, but weekends aren't the best time to do that."

He went out then, closing the door behind him. Meanwhile, Joanna shuffled through the contents of the envelope. Looking at the dates, she realized that at the time Anne Rowland Corley died, Joanna had been a working wife with a husband, a young child, and a ranch to look after. In addition to her full-time job as office manager for the Davis Insurance Agency in Bisbee, she had been making a two-hundred-mile commute back and forth to Tucson twice a week while she finished up her bachelor's degree at the

University of Arizona. No wonder Anne Rowland Corley's death hadn't made a noticeable blip on Joanna's mental radar.

As Frank had suggested, Joanna scanned several more articles from Seattle-area papers. Most of them were from immediately before and after the fatal shooting. One piece was a blatantly snide commentary from a columnist named Maxwell Cole connecting Detective Beaumont with a "mysterious lady in red." Finally, Joanna came to a much longer, denser article from the *Denver Post*. This one, running several pages in length, was an in-depth piece that had been part of an investigative series dealing with female serial killers.

A look at the clock told Joanna she was running out of time. Intriguing as the article might be, her first responsibility was to be properly prepared for the upcoming task force meeting. Thoughtfully, Joanna shoved the collection of papers back into the envelope, which she dropped into her briefcase.

From the moment Joanna had met J.P. Beaumont, she had thought of him as a smart-mouthed jerk. Last night, at the Copper Queen, when he had been straight with her and told her about his interview with Marliss Shackleford, she had glimpsed something else about him—that he was probably a good cop, a straight and trustworthy one.

Now, though, she realized there had been something else there as well, a certain indefinable something she had recognized without being able to put her finger on it, a sort of common denominator between the two of them that she couldn't quite grasp. Now she knew what it was. Beaumont's wife had died tragically; so had Joanna Brady's husband. Having survived that kind of event didn't excuse the man's smart-mouthed attitude, but it made it a hell of a lot easier to understand.

For the next while Joanna concentrated on reading the material Frank Montoya had brought her. Lost in her work, she jumped when her phone rang and was astonished to see that her clock said it was already twenty minutes to one.

"I'm guessing you won't be coming home for Sunday dinner, is that right?" Butch asked.

"I'm sorry," she said. "The time got away from me. I'm due to be in a meeting at one. Save some for me, will you?"

"I already did."

⁞⁞⁞⁞⁞⁞⁞

WITH LARS JENSSEN'S TIMELY INTERVENTION I managed to avoid that first drink. When I finally went to bed around one, I fell right to sleep. The problem is, the dream started almost as soon as I closed my eyes. It's a dream I've had over and over for years. Even in my sleep, it makes me angry. I want to wake up. I don't want to see it again, and yet there's always the faint hope that somehow this time it will be different. That it won't end with the same awful carnage.

I know from interviewing crime scene witnesses that human memory is flawed. Dreams, which are memory once removed, are even more so. The events of the few jewel-like spring days I spent with Anne are jumbled in my dreams, sometimes out of sequence and often out of sync with the way things really played out. The words we said to each other are hazy; the scenes slightly out of focus. Still, they always leave me wrestling with an overriding guilt and with the same unanswered questions: When did I fall in love with her? How did it happen? What else could I have done?

In the dream I usually relive feelings rather than what actually happened: The joy I felt when I asked her to marry me and she said yes. The amazement as I slipped my mother's treasured engagement ring on her waiting finger and saw how perfectly it fit. There's the fun of the surprise wedding shower the guys from Seattle PD threw for us down at F. X. McRory's and the blue-sky perfection of our early-morning wedding.

But then a cloud moves between us and the sun. The scene darkens. Sometimes I manage to wake myself up here, but it doesn't matter. When I fall back asleep, the dream will be there again, cued up and waiting at the exact same place.

I'm in the interview room on the fifth floor of the Public Safety Building, listening to that poor, terrified phone company service rep. "I left a message," he tells me hopelessly. "I left a message with your wife. Didn't you get it?" But, of course, I didn't get it. I didn't have a wife then—not until that very morning in Myrtle Edwards Park.

The scene goes darker still. I'm driving toward North Bend, toward Snoqualmie Falls, squinting through a daytime blackness no headlights can penetrate. I try to fight off the yawning chasm of despair that threatens to engulf me, because I know by then— know beyond a reasonable doubt—that Anne Corley is a killer. A murderer. People are dead, and it's all because of me. My fault. My responsibility.

And then I walk into the restaurant. She's seated across a crowded room from the door. Sometimes she's wearing her vibrant turquoise wedding dress. Sometimes she's in a jogging suit. Sometimes she's swathed all in black. This time it's the bright blue dress. Our eyes meet over the heads of the other carefree, unsuspecting diners. The look she gives me is electric, chilling.

This is another point in the dream where I sometimes manage to wake myself up. I used to have a drink—make that another drink. Now I go to the bathroom and have a glass of plain water. But it's no use. Whatever I do, I'm trapped in the dream's inevitability. When I close my eyes again, she's there waiting for me, beckoning to me from across the room.

The dream usually skips that last conversation. And I know why. Even when I'm awake, I can't remember it exactly, and I consider that a blessing. It would be too painful to remember. She simply stands up and leaves. As she maneuvers through the tables, I see the gun in her hand—a gun no one else can see—and know it as my own.

Next we're racing down the path toward the pool at the bottom of the falls. She's ahead of me. There are people in my way—gimpy, slow-moving tourists going up, coming down. I thrust past them, push them out of my way. And then we're at the bottom. She turns to face me. I see her raising the gun and feel the bullet smash into my shoulder. I fall—fall forever. And then, once I land, I fire, too.

I'm a good shot. An excellent shot. I shoot to disarm, not to kill. But she's standing on wet, moss-covered rocks. As I pull the trigger, she somehow loses her footing. She slips, and the motion moves her ever so slightly. My bullet misses her arm and slams into her breast. As she falls, a crimson stain blossoms across the fabric of whatever she's wearing.

In the Copper Queen Hotel that night, that's when I woke up—sweaty, shaken, and filled with remorse. I stayed awake for hours after that, fearing that the dream would come again the moment I closed my eyes. The sun was just rising when I finally went back to sleep. Thankfully, the dream did not return.

WHEN I FINALLY STAGGERED DOWNSTAIRS late that Sunday morning, I was as bleary-eyed and hungover as in my worst drinking and stinking days. I barely made it into the dining room

before they stopped serving breakfast at eleven. As soon as I finished eating, I headed for the Cochise County Justice Center. It
was just twelve-thirty when I arrived there for the one o'clock
meeting. Still not sure of what my reception would be, I opted for
being prompt. After all, Sheriff Brady may have relented enough
to allow me inside the investigation, but I didn't want to do anything that would screw things up.

The same lady I had met the day before, Lupe Alvarez,
manned the front desk. She greeted me with a smile. "Good afternoon, Mr. Beaumont. Sheriff Brady asked me to give you this to
use while you're here."

She handed me a badge that had my name on it, along with
the initials MJF. The other side contained a magnetic strip.

"What's MJF?" I asked.

"The Multi-Jurisdiction Force," Lupe explained. "When members of the MJF work joint-ops out of our building, it's easier to
give them badges so they can come and go as they please without
our having to buzz them in and out. The card works on all the
lobby security doors. Also the rest rooms," she added.

If I was being given my own rest-room key, I had evidently
arrived. "Thanks," I told her. "Now, where do I go?"

"The conference room," she said. "It's through that door and
three doors down the hall on the left."

Since it wasn't yet twelve forty-five, I figured I'd be the first to
arrive, but I was wrong. Sheriff Brady was already in the conference room. She sat at the head of a long table with several stacks
of paper lined up in front of her. She looked up at me curiously as
I entered the room. Her appraisal was so thorough that I wondered for a moment if my fly was unzipped.

"Good afternoon, Special Investigator Beaumont," she said,
motioning me into a chair. "You're early."

I took the seat she indicated. She slid one of the stacks in my direction.

"What you have there are copies of everything we've come up with so far," she told me. "You'll find crime scene reports, preliminary autopsy results, transcripts of interviews, an Internet treatise on poisons in general and sodium azide in particular. If we're going to be working together, you need to know everything we do."

"Thanks," I said, and meant it.

It hurt to have to haul my reading glasses out of my pocket, but I swallowed my pride and did so. The topmost report was the crime scene report from the Latisha Wall murder in Naco. I started to read, but stopped a couple of sentences into it.

"There is one thing," I said.

Sheriff Brady looked up from her own reading. Under her questioning brow, I caught a glimpse of the banked fire in those vivid green eyes. "What's that?" she asked.

"Since we're going to be working together, how about ditching the 'Special Investigator' crap? Most people call me Beau. Either that or J.P."

She studied me for a long time before she answered. "All right," she said finally. "Beau it is, and I'm Joanna."

Sixteen

WHEN I WAS IN the eighth grade at Seattle's Loyal Heights Junior High, my homeroom and social studies teacher, Miss Bond, encouraged me to run for student council. Unfortunately, I won. That year of attending regular and utterly pointless meetings doomed me to a lifetime of hating same. In my twenty-plus years at Seattle PD I had a reputation for dodging meetings—this very kind of meeting—whenever possible.

This particular task force gathering, however, was one I had actually wanted to attend. Since Joanna and I seemed to have a few more minutes before the others were due to arrive, I settled in and read as much of the handout material as I could. I wanted to be prepared. Before, Sheriff Brady's department had given me no information at all. Now, with someone obviously burning the midnight-copier ink, I'd been given far too much.

One by one, people wandered into the room and were introduced: Casey Ledford, the latent fingerprint tech; Deputy Dave Hollicker, crime scene investigator; and homicide detective Jaime Carbajal. The last to arrive was Chief Deputy Frank Montoya, but I already knew him. As they showed up, I was struck by how young they all were. I could just as well have wandered into a Junior Chamber of Commerce meeting. My understanding about Jaycees is that once a member hits the ripe old age of thirty-five, he's out on his tush. Self-consciously, I stroked my chin, making sure I had shaved closely enough that morning to erase the stubborn patch of gray whiskers that has lately started sprouting there.

I'm not sure what Joanna's team of investigators had been told previously about my presence in their midst. None of them went out of his or her way to make me feel welcome. I was grateful when Joanna Brady tackled that issue head-on.

"You've all been introduced to Special Investigator Beaumont," Sheriff Brady said when she stood up at the stroke of 1 P.M. "He's here as a representative of the Washington State Attorney General's Office, which has a vested interest in seeing that whoever killed Latisha Wall is brought to justice. Since it seems inconceivable that Latisha's murder and Deidre Canfield's death are unrelated, this is Mr. Beaumont's deal as much as it is ours. From here on, he's to be treated as a full member of this investigation. Any information you give me, you should also give him. Is that clear?"

Sheriff Brady's crew may have been young, but they were unarguably professional. Uneasy nods of assent passed around the table. None of them were thrilled to have an interloper among them, but no one raised an audible objection.

"Good, then," Joanna concluded. "Let's get started."

Clearly I wasn't the only one who had put in a relatively sleepless night. Deputy Hollicker looked especially bedraggled, with dark circles under bloodshot eyes. He had spent most of the night processing the Canfield crime scene down in Naco. Scanning through my pile of papers, I noticed that it didn't contain a written report from him about that. Bearing that in mind, I wasn't the least surprised when Joanna Brady put him in the hot seat first.

"I'm working on the paper," he said when she called on him. "I'm sorry my report isn't ready—"

"Never mind the report," Joanna Brady said, waving aside his apology. "Just tell us. Did you find anything useful?"

The CSI shook his head miserably. "Not really. Local kids have been messing around in those old cavalry barracks for years. I found all kinds of junk in there—trash, beer bottles, cigarette butts, and gum wrappers. It's tough to tell what, if anything, might be related."

"You did say cavalry," I confirmed. "As in horses?"

"That's right. The building where the body was found is on the site of an old U.S. Cavalry post that dates from the 1880s," Joanna Brady explained. "The crime scene is actually one of the old officers' quarters. What about the stables, Dave? Did you search them, too?"

If I had stumbled into a case where the crime scene turned out to be a cavalry post, maybe I was Rip Van Winkle in reverse.

Hollicker nodded. "Yes, ma'am. Every inch. Detective Carbajal thought we might find another body there—the boyfriend's, presumably. We didn't, though."

"No, I'm sure you didn't," Joanna said grimly. "There'll be more about Warren Gibson later. Go on."

"Deputy Howell and I brought back as much stuff to the lab as we thought might be relevant. Again, it'll take time to go through it all. I'll work on it as time allows."

"Did you talk to Doc Winfield?" Joanna asked.

Dave nodded. "Detective Carbajal and I both did. It was right after the ME arrived on the scene, so he didn't know much at that point. He did tell us, though, that he's reasonably certain Dee Canfield died somewhere else. The body was dumped there afterward."

"What about Dee's house out in Huachuca Terraces? Did either you or Casey get around to checking it out?"

Casey Ledford and Dave Hollicker shook their heads in unison. "Ran out of time," Dave explained. "I had a deputy put up crime scene tape. I'll go there later today, right after the meeting."

"Good," Joanna said. "Moving right along. Let's talk about Warren Gibson for a minute. Dave, you and Mr. Beaumont probably haven't heard about this yet, but Ms. Canfield's daughter from Cheyenne, Wyoming—a woman named Serenity Granger—came to my office this morning. She brought along a copy of an unfinished e-mail that her mother sent her Thursday afternoon. Ms. Granger didn't actually read the message until yesterday. You should have a copy of that along with your other handouts."

I shuffled through my paperwork until I located Deidre Canfield's unfinished missive to her daughter.

"If you check the time," Joanna Brady was saying, "it's listed as 4:10:26 P.M. Mountain Standard. Now look at the transcript of Jaime's interview with Dee Canfield. Look at the last two sentences right at the end."

After a little more paper shuffling, I located the right passages.

Detective Carbajal: Since both you and Mr. Gibson were in Latisha Wall's house yesterday, we'll need fingerprints from both of you.

Ms. Canfield: Yes, yes, of course. I understand. We'll take care of it right away, tomorrow probably, but not right now. The show's tonight. I really do have to get back up to the gallery now so I can be ready to meet the caterer and let her in.

That was the last entry. The transcript indicated that the interview terminated at 3:08 P.M. An hour and two minutes later, Dee had sent her daughter an incomplete e-mail voicing her concern that perhaps Warren Gibson had been involved in Latisha Wall's murder. I could see where Sheriff Brady was going with all this.

"Casey and Deputy Galloway spent a great deal of time last night and early this morning processing Castle Rock Gallery. A while ago, Casey got an AFIS hit on one of the prints she found there. The man everyone in Bisbee knows as Warren Gibson turns out to be a convicted felon named Jack Brampton. How about passing around copies of that rap sheet, Casey?"

As we say in the trade, "Bingo!"

Joanna Brady was totally in her groove by then. While the fingerprint tech slid pieces of paper out across the smooth surface of the conference table, Sheriff Brady continued without pause. "So we've put out an APB on Jack Brampton, aka Warren Gibson." She stopped long enough to give her chief deputy a searching look. "It did go out, didn't it, Frank?"

"Yes, ma'am," Montoya replied. "And I added that the suspect is most likely driving a 1970 red Pinto wagon."

Joanna frowned. "Red," she repeated. "Where did you get that information?"

Montoya bristled slightly at the impatient way she posed the question. I would have, too.

"Where else?" he returned. "From the DMV. That's the vehicle they show as being registered to one Deidre Canfield, 114 Cochise Drive, Bisbee, Arizona."

"The DMV maybe *thinks* it's red," Joanna told him. "But they're wrong. The last time I saw Dee Canfield's Pinto, it looked like somebody had used it for a drop cloth."

"What color is it then?" Montoya asked.

"All colors," she answered.

The chief deputy sighed. "All right, then," he said. "If you'll excuse me for a moment, I'll go amend that APB."

Frank Montoya stood to leave the room as Joanna continued. "The good news is, there aren't that many 1970 Pintos of any kind or color still on the road. If someone spots one moving under its own power, they're likely to let us know."

"Wait a minute," I said, opening my mouth for only the second time in the course of the meeting. "A 1970 Pinto? What kind of fuel does it run on?"

"Leaded," Joanna said.

"I didn't know you could still buy leaded," I objected.

"You can," she replied, "but only across the line in Old Mexico."

Frank Montoya was still lingering by the conference room door. "That's something then," he said. "If Brampton is using the Pinto as his getaway car, it's a pretty good bet he'll be headed south. I'll get on the horn to Border Patrol here about him, and I'll let the *federales* in Mexico know about this as well."

"Good idea," Joanna said. "Do it."

Meanwhile, I busied myself studying Jack Brampton's rap sheet. What stuck in my head was the fact that he'd served his time at a medium-security facility in Illinois. UPPI's corporate headquarters was based in Illinois. I wondered if there was a connection. I circled the name of the prison. When I came back to the discussion, Frank had returned and Joanna had moved on to another topic.

"For someone who claims he doesn't gossip, Harve Dowd from Treasure Trove is full of information," she was saying. "He told me last night he thought Warren Gibson was pulling a fast one on Dee Canfield. Harve is of the opinion that Dee wasn't Gibson's only romantic interest. He claims to have seen Gibson using the pay phones down by the post office on numerous occasions. Frank is currently in the process of checking phone records, but since his special phone company pal doesn't work weekends, it's taking more time than usual."

"Wait a minute," Jaime Carbajal said. "Does this mean we're dropping Bobo Jenkins as a possible suspect?"

"Okay," Joanna said. "Let's talk about him for the moment. What do we know?"

"That he was at Latisha Wall's home the night she died," Jaime Carbajal began. "We also know, by his own admission, that he and the woman he calls Rochelle Baxter had quarreled or at least had a disagreement earlier in the day. We also have his fingerprints on those sweetener packets from the kitchen."

Casey Ledford raised her hand. "May I speak to that? To the sweetener packets?"

Joanna nodded and all eyes went to the fingerprint tech. "Dave and I examined the crime scene evidence from Latisha Wall's kitchen. It's true Mr. Jenkins's fingerprints are on the sweetener packets. They are. But the physical evidence—the way the fingerprints are layered on the glass and bottle—would indicate that Ms. Wall drank iced tea and Mr. Jenkins had the beer."

"See there?" Jaime said. "What did I tell you? He poured the sweetener in her tea and then sat right there and watched her drink it. What a hell of a nice guy! And then, on the Dee Canfield part of the equation, we know Bobo was adamantly opposed to her plan to go through with the show despite Latisha Wall's death. Sheriff Brady, you witnessed some of that yourself on Thursday morning at the gallery."

"You're right about that," Joanna conceded. "Bobo Jenkins was at the gallery, and he was very upset. Do we have any idea where he was or what he was doing between three and five on Thursday afternoon?"

"He claims he was at home and alone the entire afternoon," Jaime answered. "That's in the transcript of the interview Frank and I did with him on Saturday morning. He told us he stayed home all day, trying to come to grips with what had happened. Of course," the detective added, "at the time we spoke to him, we were only aware of the Latisha Wall incident. We had no idea Dee Canfield was also dead, so there was no reason to check on his whereabouts or movements the day after what we assumed to be a single homicide."

"Did he come right out and actually *say* he was home alone?" Joanna asked.

Jaime scanned through the transcript. "Here it is, right here. Yes, that's what he said, but I'll go uptown a little later. I'll talk to Bobo's neighbors and see what they have to say."

"All right," Joanna said. "You do that." Then she turned to Chief Deputy Montoya. "In the meantime, Frank, while you're dealing with the phone factory, have a go at Bobo's phone records as well. If he happened to be on the phone making calls between three and four o'clock Thursday afternoon, that would tend to corroborate his story even if no one was there with him at the time."

That intrigued me. Just because Bobo Jenkins was a suspect in one homicide, Joanna Brady wasn't giving her people carte blanche to turn him automatically into prime-suspect material in the second death as well. In other words, rather than looking for the quickest way to clear cases, Sheriff Brady was prepared to take the time and make the effort to find out what had really happened. I liked that about her. Respected it.

As Joanna Brady fired off one question after another, I felt as though I had been transported back to the fishbowl at Seattle PD with Captain Larry Powell popping questions left and right to see if his detectives were making any progress or doing something to earn their keep.

I sat up straighter and paid closer attention because I was beginning to suspect that perhaps Sheriff Joanna Brady was my kind of cop after all.

JOANNA LOOKED DOWN AT THE CHECKLIST she had scribbled off in advance of the meeting. "So," she said, crossing off another item. "With the next-of-kin notification out of the way, what does Doc Winfield say about scheduling the autopsy?"

"He'll do it first thing tomorrow, and he'll give me a call beforehand," Jaime Carbajal replied. "The good news is that Ernie will be back on duty tomorrow morning. Once he's back on board, maybe I can have him handle the Verdugo boys' interviews. At least I'll have some help covering the bases."

"Or Mr. Beaumont could help out," Joanna suggested quietly. With Jaime looking mutinous, she moved to lessen the tension. "Hey, Frank," she added. "Next time Ernie asks for a whole week off, let him know he's not allowed to leave town until after he checks with our upcoming homicide scheduler."

They all laughed at that, even Jaime. The atmosphere in the room relaxed noticeably.

"All right," she said. "Now for our chemistry lesson."

WE SPENT THE NEXT HALF HOUR hearing all about something called sodium azide. Joanna had mentioned it prior to the meeting. Rather than show my ignorance, I had said nothing. It turns out that as far as sodium azide is concerned, ignorance is bliss. Just hearing about the stuff was enough to scare the crap out of me.

Frank Montoya had tracked down an Internet article that explained how various poisons, sodium azide included, present. An ingested poison often exhibits a delayed reaction. The victim isn't affected until the substance is absorbed into the bloodstream. Inhaled sodium azide goes into the lungs and directly into the blood, where its molecules bond with oxygen molecules and render the oxygen unusable.

The information in Frank's article was already more than I wanted to know, but it did explain the time lag between when Latisha Wall drank her tea and her death sometime later. What Dave Hollicker had to say about sodium azide's ready availability was horrifying.

"Wait a minute," I interrupted, minutes into his lecture. "You're saying this stuff—this incredibly dangerous stuff that isn't even illegal—can be found in damned near every two-car garage in America?"

"That's right," Hollicker agreed blandly. "Those canisters are in every car with air bags."

"So the next kid who gets pissed off at his English teacher in Podunk, USA, can slip some of it into her coffee and knock her off just like that? This is nuts, totally nuts! And nobody's doing anything about it?"

"Not so far," Dave Hollicker said. "According to what I've learned, there's currently no plan to regulate sodium azide in any way or even to add a marker substance."

About that time there was a knock on the conference room door. "Come in," Joanna called.

Lupe Alvarez stuck her head inside. "Rick Orting, the dispatcher for the city of Bisbee just called, Sheriff Brady. Someone from Phelps Dodge is reporting finding an abandoned multicolored Pinto."

A charge of excitement surged around the room. "Where is it?" Joanna demanded.

"Between the end of Wood Canyon and Old Bisbee," Lupe replied. "It's on one of those company roads, the ones that go out to PD's new drilling sites north of Lavender Pit. The Pinto's rear axle is broken. A day-shift watchman found it a little while ago when he was out doing his rounds."

"Thanks, Lupe," Joanna said, then turned back to her team of investigators. "Okay, Jaime. You, Casey, and Dave get on this right away." Without another word, the three of them hustled out of the room.

"What about me, boss?" Frank Montoya asked.

"Even if you're dealing with second-stringers, you stay here and keep after the phone stuff. We need that information."

"And me?" I asked. "What am I supposed to do?"

"You're with me."

"Why?"

"So I can keep an eye on you. You're part of this investigation, but I don't want to spend the entire afternoon giving you directions and guiding you from one place to another."

"I have a map . . ." I began.

"Forget it. Just go get in the car."

"Yours or mine?"

The disparaging look she gave me told me the question was unworthy of being dignified with an answer. "Come on," she said.

Rather than going out through the public lobby, Joanna hustled me first to her private office and then out a door that led directly into the parking lot. I started toward the Crown Victoria I knew to be hers.

"Not that one," she said, stopping me. "We'll take the Blazer."

We walked two rows into the parking lot, where she climbed into the driver's seat of an SUV that had definitely seen better days—from a physical-beauty point of view. However, a powerful engine sprang to life the moment she turned the key in the ignition. The term "ugly but honest!" came to mind.

We drove into town and back toward Old Bisbee. At the far end of the huge layered hole in the ground she explained was Lavender Pit we came to a spot where a group of cop cars, lights flashing, had converged alongside the road. Some of the vehicles were marked CITY OF BISBEE; others, SHERIFF'S DEPARTMENT. They were grouped around the entrance to a freshly graded dirt road that led off between the red-rock hills.

We were pulling over to check things out when a call came in over the radio. "Sheriff Brady?"

"Yes, Tica," she responded. "What is it?"

"I have Burton Kimball on the phone. He needs to talk to you right away."

Joanna sighed. "Look, Tica. I'm really busy at the moment. . . ."

"He says it's urgent," Tica insisted. "Is it all right if I patch him through?"

"I suppose so," Joanna agreed grudgingly. "Go ahead."

"Sheriff Brady?" A male voice roared through the radio. Despite having been filtered through both a telephone receiver and the radio, his words buzzed angrily in the air.

"What in the world are you and your people trying to pull now?" he demanded. "I can't believe you'd stoop so low that you'd go to such incredible lengths. Really, Joanna, I always thought you were above this kind of stunt."

Whoever Burton Kimball was, he was pissed as hell. In the course of the previous twenty-four hours, I'd seen some pretty strong indications that Sheriff Brady has a temper. I fully expected her to cut loose and give the guy as good as she got. She surprised me.

"Slow down a minute, Burton," she returned mildly. "What are you talking about?"

"Someone has broken into my client's house and planted what looks like a cache of drugs here," he replied. "If you think you can get away with that kind of nonsense . . ." He paused as if searching for words. "I tell you, Joanna, I'm outraged about this—absolutely outraged!"

She and I hit on the word "drugs" at the same time, and we both jumped to the same conclusion. Why wouldn't we? Drug or not, sodium azide was the topic of the moment. A few minutes earlier we'd been sitting in a conference room learning all about it.

It was interesting to realize once again that when Joanna Brady was upset, her voice went down instead of up. "What drugs?" she asked urgently but softly. Sitting right next to her, I could barely hear her, but Burton Kimball heard.

"How would I know?" he snapped back. "I didn't taste it, if that's what you mean. I wouldn't know what cocaine tastes like if it walked up and hit me in the face, but since this is a white powder, cocaine is my first assumption."

I watched while every trace of color drained from Joanna Brady's face. Her voice didn't change or falter. "This white powder," she said calmly, "where exactly is it?"

"In my client's laundry room," Burton Kimball replied. "Bobo went out there this afternoon to do some laundry and found it sitting there, right in plain sight on the dryer. It's in a box that's been wrapped in duct tape and hooked up to the dryer vent. When he called to tell me about it, I advised him to leave it alone. I tell you, Joanna . . ."

"Where are you right now?" Joanna interrupted.

"Where am I?" Burton Kimball returned. "Where do you think? I'm at my client's house, and you can bet I'm staying here until someone comes to collect this stuff and take it away."

"Whereabouts are you in the house?" Joanna prodded.

I had to give the lady credit for staying cool. By then she had put the idling Blazer in gear. We were back on the road, speeding toward Old Bisbee.

"In the kitchen," he said. "Talking to you on the phone."

"What about Bobo?" she asked. "Where's he?"

"Right here with me. Why?"

"Good," she said. "Now listen to me, Burton. Listen very carefully. Whatever's in that box in Bobo's laundry room wasn't planted by anyone from my department. But I suspect that it is dangerous, probably even deadly."

"What is it, then, some kind of bomb? Is it going to explode?"

"No, nothing like that. But don't interrupt. I want you both to leave the house, Burton. Immediately. Go outside and stay out. I'll be there in a few minutes. In the meantime, don't go near the laundry room, and whatever you do, don't touch that box."

"I hope you're not trying to pull a fast one here, Joanna," Burton Kimball warned, but his tone of voice had changed slightly. The naked urgency in her orders had commanded his attention.

"All right," he relented, backing down. "But if you even so much as try using this as evidence against my client without having a properly drawn search warrant . . ."

Joanna started to lose it. "I don't give a rat's ass about evidence," she interrupted. "I'm trying to save lives here. Now get the hell out of that house, Burton, and take Bobo Jenkins with you."

She ended the call and tossed me the microphone.

"What?" I said.

"Call Dispatch back," she ordered, switching on both lights and siren. The calm voice she had used to address Burton Kimball was replaced by that of a drill sergeant barking orders. "Tell them we need the state Haz-Mat team at Bobo Jenkins's place on Young-blood Hill. Tell them you and I are on our way to secure the scene."

"Which is where?"

"On Youngblood Hill."

"I know that. What's the address?"

Joanna Brady shook her head in disgust. "For crying out loud!" she exclaimed. "I have no idea, but since it'll take the Haz-Mat team a good hour and a half to get here from Tucson, we should be able to figure out the address between now and then. Maybe somebody with half a brain can look his address up in the phone book!"

I punched the "Talk" button on the microphone. As I gave Tica the necessary information, it occurred to me that I wasn't the only person in that speeding Blazer who should have invested a few hundred bucks in a Dale Carnegie course.

With lights flashing and siren blaring, we screamed into the old part of town and turned right up a narrow, one-lane strip of steep pavement. The sign said "O.K. Street," but there was noth-ing okay about it. Calling it a goat path would have been closer to the mark than calling it a street. Then, about the time I was sure the Blazer was going to scrape off both its mirrors, we met a vehi-cle coming down. A silver-haired lady, driving a Pontiac Grand Prix with Nebraska plates, backed out of a parking lot beside what was evidently a small hotel and started in our direction.

She looked a bit surprised when she realized a cop car with flashing lights and a blaring siren was aimed right at her, but instead of stopping or returning to the parking lot, she kept right on coming, motioning for us to move over and get out of *her* way. Somehow Joanna managed to do exactly that, tucking the Blazer into an almost nonexistent wide spot.

"For God's sake!" I demanded. "Isn't this a one-way street?"

"For everyone but the tourists!" Joanna muttered. The woman in the Pontiac edged past us, waving cheerfully and smiling as she went. "Lights and sirens must not mean the same thing in Nebraska."

"Sheriff Brady," the dispatcher called, interrupting Joanna in midgripe.

Not wanting her to take her eyes off the road, I picked up the mike. "Beaumont here. What is it?"

"City of Bisbee wants to know what's going on, so I told them. They're sending backup for you. And I have that address on Youngblood Hill for you now."

Joanna Brady didn't look as though she needed to be told where she was going, and right that minute I was too busy hanging on for dear life to take notes.

"As long as the Haz-Mat guys have it," I said. "I think we're fine."

We came to a real wide spot in the road where several cars were parked at haphazard angles around the perimeter. Joanna threw the Blazer into "Park" and jammed on the emergency brake. She paused long enough to retrieve a pair of worn tennis shoes from the floor of the backseat. After changing shoes, she leaped out of the car and started down a winding street that was even steeper than the one we'd been on before. The posted sign here said "Youngblood Hill." Glad to be ignorant of the street name's origin, I tagged after her.

The pockmarked, broken pavement was scattered with loose gravel. The surface was an open invitation for broken legs. Or ankles. It was all I could do to keep from falling ass over teakettle.

Halfway down the hill was a blind curve. I expected Youngblood Hill to be a one-way street. No such luck. Rounding the curve, we came face-to-face with a city of Bisbee patrol car nosing its way uphill. About that time Joanna Brady turned left, darted under an archway, through a wrought-iron gate, and up an impossibly narrow concrete stairway. I went after her. Taking both age and altitude into consideration, I didn't even try to keep up. The best I hoped for was not to die in the process.

Hearing footsteps behind me, I looked back. Right on my heels came a beefy young man in a blue uniform. The Bisbee City cop had left his idling patrol car sitting in the middle of the street and charged after us. He outweighed me by forty pounds, but by the time we reached a small terrace of a yard, he was only a step or two behind me. My chest was about to burst open. He hadn't broken a sweat.

The new arrival was Officer Frank Rojas. I stood aside long enough to let him hurtle past me and catch up with Sheriff Brady. Since we were obviously inside city boundaries, I expected an immediate outbreak of jurisdictional warfare. I've seen it happen often enough. I know of numerous occasions in the Seattle area where bad guys have gotten away because cops from neighboring suburbs weren't necessarily on speaking terms. In Bisbee, Arizona, that was evidently not the case.

"What do you need, Sheriff Brady?" Rojas asked.

"To secure the residence," she gasped. That made me feel a little better. At least I wasn't the only one having trouble breathing.

"Anyone inside?"

Joanna glanced at two men who stood together in the far corner of the tiny front yard—a rangy African-American in a T-shirt,
shorts, and tennis shoes, and a white man in full Sunday go-to-
meeting attire—gray suit, white shirt, and tie. His once highly polished shoes now sported a layer of red dust. I assumed the guy in
the suit to be the attorney, Burton Kimball. That meant the other
one was Bobo Jenkins, Latisha Wall's boyfriend.

The man was big and tough, and I wondered how he felt about
being called Bobo. Someone tried to pin that handle on me once
when I was in fifth grade. I creamed the guy. I hoped Mr. Jenkins
didn't mind. Despite Archie's description of Bobo as a sort of gen-
tle giant, Mr. Jenkins looked as though he was more than capable
of taking care of himself when it came to physical combat.

"No," Joanna told Rojas. "As far as I know, no one's inside."

"What seems to be the problem?"

"Dangerous chemicals," she answered. "We've called for the
Haz-Mat team from Tucson. You take the back of the house,
Frankie. Make sure no one enters. And whatever you do, don't go
near the dryer vent."

Frank Rojas didn't question her orders. "Yes, ma'am," he said.
Without another word, off he went.

Seventeen

BOUT THEN THE MAN IN THE SUIT charged across the yard to meet us. From the irate expression on the attorney's face I doubted Burton Kimball would be nearly as tractable as Officer Rojas had been.

"All right, Sheriff Brady," Kimball snapped. "As you can see, we did what you said. We're out of the house. Now how about telling us what this is about? If the white powder in the box isn't a drug, what is it?"

Joanna took one more deep breath before she answered. "I'm guessing it'll turn out to be sodium azide," she answered. "It's a deadly poison. We have reason to believe Latisha Wall died as a result of sodium azide poisoning."

"Never heard of it," Kimball grunted.

"Not many people have," Joanna agreed.

"What is it?"

"It's the propellant used to deploy air bags in vehicles," she explained. "Sodium azide is more toxic than cyanide. It has no known antidote."

Bobo Jenkins spoke for the first time. "Did you say Shelley was poisoned?" he croaked. "How's that possible?"

"We believe the fatal dose was placed in something she drank," Joanna answered. "Most likely in her iced tea."

"But how . . ." Bobo began. Then his face changed as he put it together. "The sweetener packets!" he exclaimed.

Joanna gave him a searching look. Finally, she nodded.

As I said, Bobo Jenkins was a big man. His arms and legs bulged with muscles. As the awfulness of the situation sank in, his knees seemed to buckle. He staggered unsteadily over to the porch steps and dropped down onto the topmost one.

"But I'm the one who put the sweetener in her tea," he blurted out. "Two packets. That's what Shelley always took in her iced tea. Two packets. Never any more; never any less. Does that mean I'm the one who killed her?"

"Enough, Bobo," Burton Kimball interjected. "Don't say anything more. Not another word."

If Kimball's stunned client heard his attorney's objection, he paid no attention.

"And that's what you think is here in my house right now, in the box in my laundry room?" Jenkins continued. "You think it's the same thing? The same poison?"

By then, Kimball was practically beside himself. "Mr. Jenkins, please. No more. Sheriff Brady, you haven't informed my client of his rights. I must ask that you refrain from asking any more questions, the answers to which may be prejudicial. . . ."

Ignoring the lawyer, Joanna sat down on the porch step next to Bobo Jenkins. "Tell me about today," she said quietly.

"Today?" He gave her an anguished look, as though not quite comprehending the question.

"Tell me everything that happened," she urged. "Everything that led up to your finding the box."

He sighed and shook his head. "Last night I couldn't sleep." He said. "I kept tossing and turning and thinking about . . ." He paused and swallowed hard before continuing. ". . . about what had happened. I couldn't believe I'd lost Shelley just like that. I still can't believe it. Sometimes it seems like it's got to be some awful nightmare. Eventually, I'll wake up and she won't be gone.

"Anyway, after lying in bed for hours, I finally got up about three o'clock this morning. I dressed and went for a run. I ran all the way down to Warren and back. By the time I finished, the sun was just coming up. I showered and went to bed. I finally fell asleep after that and didn't wake up until a little while ago. I went out to the kitchen to put on some coffee. While I waited for the coffee to finish, I decided to start a load of clothes. That's when I found that box—a duct-taped box I'd never seen before—sitting there on top of the dryer. The flexible vent duct is connected to it."

"Did you touch it?"

Jenkins shook his head. "Give me some credit. I'm smarter than that. The box has a window in the top that's covered with plastic wrap. As soon as I saw the white powder in it, I called Mr. Kimball."

"Why?"

"Are you kidding? When Jaime Carbajal and Frank Montoya interviewed me yesterday morning, they didn't give out any details, but I could tell from their questions that I was under suspicion—that they thought I was somehow responsible for Shelley's death. Now I know why. You must have found my fingerprints on the sweetener packets, since I'm the one who poured them into her glass."

Ignoring that, Joanna responded with yet another question. "When you saw the box, what did you think was in it?" she asked.

Jenkins shrugged. "I assumed it was cocaine. I figured someone was trying to frame me for dealing drugs or something worse."

"But why would you think someone from my department placed it there?" Joanna asked.

He shook his head as though no explanation should have been necessary. "You're not a black man considering running for public office in this country," he said softly. "You're not being paranoid if people really are out to get you."

I had been listening to all of this and trying to keep my mouth shut. Now, though, I couldn't resist putting in my two cents' worth. "Look. If someone planted the box in Mr. Jenkins's house, how was it done? Any sign of a break-in? It takes time to rip off a dryer duct and reconnect it."

"I don't lock my doors," Bobo said. "I never have."

Burton Kimball looked distinctly unhappy about the way the conversation was going, but there wasn't much he could do about it. Nobody paid any attention to him, least of all his client.

"You said you were making coffee," Joanna mused thoughtfully. "What do you use in it?" she added.

It seemed like an off-the-wall question. At first I couldn't see where she was going. Bobo Jenkins seemed puzzled as well. "What do you think? Coffee and water," he said. "What else is there?"

"I mean, how do you take it?" Joanna asked. "Black, or with cream and sugar?"

"Sugar but no cream," he said. "I'm lactose-intolerant."

"Where do you keep your sugar?"

"In the fridge," he said. "If I leave it out on the counter or table, I sometimes have problems with ants. Why?"

Then I understood. The white powder in the duct-taped box. It would have taken time, effort, and ingenuity to put sodium azide in sweetener packets. By comparison, putting a few spoonfuls of it into a sugar bowl would be simple—and just as deadly.

At that moment a deputy I didn't know—an officer named Matt Raymond—hustled up the steps and into the yard. "What's happening?" Joanna asked.

"Detective Carbajal says it's confirmed. The abandoned car definitely belongs to Dee Canfield. It's on a road that winds through the hills and ends up about half a mile east of here, on the far side of B-Hill."

I had noticed a big whitewashed "B" on one of the hills as I drove into town for the first time. Now I realized that Bobo Jenkins's home was on one of the flanks of that selfsame hill. Half a mile away wasn't very far.

"Which way was the Pinto going when they found it?" Joanna asked. "In or out?"

"Out," the deputy returned. "Detective Carbajal says it looks like the driver was attempting to turn the vehicle around so he could head back to the highway when he got hung up on a boulder. Broke the axle right in two."

"Thank God for small favors," Joanna said. "We'd better get the K-9 unit out there on the double."

"Already done," Officer Raymond said. "Deputy Gregovich and Spike are on their way.

Nodding, Joanna turned back to the attorney. "Look, Burton," she said, "we've called in the Haz-Mat team. The fewer people we have hanging around when they get here, the better. How about if you take Mr. Jenkins and go someplace else for a while? Let me know where you are. Someone from the department will notify you when it's safe for him to return home."

"I'll be only too happy to," Kimball said, still sounding slightly miffed. "Come on, Bobo. Let's get out of here. We wouldn't want to be in anyone's way."

JOANNA BRADY WASN'T GOOD AT WAITING; she never had been. As the minutes ticked by, she paced back and forth in Bobo's small terraced yard. If her suspicions proved correct, her jurisdiction had been plagued by two murders and an attempted homicide in less than a week. Right that minute, the only thing working in her favor was the fact that the supposed getaway car— Dee Canfield's aging Pinto—had finally come to grief. Had it not been for that, Warren Gibson would have been long gone. Then again, with as much of a head start as he'd had, maybe he'd made good his escape after all.

It didn't help that J.P. Beaumont sat on the porch staring at her and watching her every move as she anxiously paced the confines of the yard. The last thing she needed right then was an audience.

"Sit down," he suggested. "Take a load off."

But Joanna didn't want to sit. She didn't want to be patronized, either. "I'd rather stand," she said.

Across the yard, Matt Raymond's radio crackled to life.

"What is it?" she demanded.

The deputy listened for a moment, holding one finger in the air. "It's Detective Carbajal. He says the K-9 Unit has found two separate trails. One seems to head in this general direction. The other one heads back along the road and out to the highway."

"Have them follow that one," Joanna said at once. "Let's try to see where the SOB went."

When she glanced back at Beau once more, she noticed he had taken his packet of Xeroxed reports out of his coat pocket. He unfolded the pages, put on a pair of horn-rimmed reading glasses, and began studying the pages, occasionally making notes.

At least he finally quit staring at me, Joanna thought as she checked her watch for the third time in as many minutes. At this rate, the hour-and-a-half wait for the arrival of the Haz-Mat team was going to take a very long time.

Several long minutes passed without a word being exchanged. Beaumont finally broke the lingering silence. "Could you do me a favor?" he asked.

"What's that?"

"It says here that Jack Brampton was incarcerated in the Gardendale Correctional Institute outside Elgin, Illinois."

"Right."

"I need to find out if that's a state- or privately run facility."

"Frank Montoya's your guy," Joanna said. She removed her cell phone from her pocket, punched up Frank's direct number, and handed it over to Beau. He looked down at it in baffled silence, as though he had never seen a cell phone before in his life.

"The number's already programmed in," she told him impatiently. "All you have to do is hit 'Send.'"

Beaumont shot her another dubious look and then did as he was told. A moment later he was explaining to Chief Deputy Montoya what was needed.

Joanna glanced at her watch once more. Time was passing, but not nearly fast enough. She listened to Beau's part of the conversation with only half an ear. The call had barely ended when another one came through. She took the phone from Beau's hand and answered the call herself.

"What is it, Jaime?" she asked.

"Sorry, boss," he said. "It's a dead end. Spike led us right back here—to the highway. That's where the trail stops. Brampton got into a vehicle and rode away."

"Have Terry and Spike go back to the Pinto and try following the trail in the other direction," she ordered. "I want to know where that one goes as well. In the meantime, send Casey out to Dee Canfield's house. I'll need Dave up here so he can handle the chain of custody on whatever evidence the Haz-Mat guys turn up."

She ended the call. Beaumont had obviously been listening. "If the killer got in a car and rode away," he said, "that probably means one of two things."

"What would those be?" Joanna asked.

"Either Jack Brampton has an accomplice who came and picked him up, or else he hitched a ride with some poor innocent passerby who's going to wind up being our next victim."

"Great," Joanna muttered. "Just what I want to hear."

About that time the first member of the moon-suited Haz-Mat team came huffing up the stairs. "I'm Ron Workman, the team captain," the leader announced to everyone in the small yard. "Who's in charge here?"

Since Deputy Raymond's was the only visible uniform, the question was addressed to him. The deputy nodded in Joanna's direction and she stepped forward.

"I am, Mr. Workman. I'm Sheriff Joanna Brady."

The man gave Joanna a skeptical top-to-toe appraisal, from her grubby tennis shoes to the skirt, blouse, and blazer she had dressed in for church. He seemed less than thrilled at the idea that she was in charge.

Workman peered around the yard. "I was told we'd find a hazardous material situation here," he said. "What is it, some kind of false alarm?"

By then three more moon-suited guys had crowded into Bobo Jenkins's tiny front yard. They stood in a clump like a bunch of stranded astronauts waiting to see what would happen.

It would have been nice if Workman's dismissive attitude hadn't been quite so blatant. Joanna had dealt with similar reactions for years; they still irked her.

"It's no false alarm," she assured him crisply. "The hazardous material is inside the house. In the laundry room you'll find a box we suspect contains sodium azide. The box is hooked up to the dryer vent."

That got Mr. Workman's attention. "Sodium azide?" he demanded. "My God, woman! Do you have any idea how dangerous that stuff can be?"

"As a matter of fact, I do," Joanna said sweetly. "That's why we called you."

"Where is it?"

"Around back. A uniformed officer is standing by at the back door—"

Not waiting for her to finish, Workman motioned to his team. "All right, guys. Let's get moving."

"Stop," Joanna barked. "That's not all."

A moment earlier, Workman had been prepared to write the whole thing off as a false alarm. Now he scowled impatiently at the delay. "What then?" he asked.

"Your team is to remove and examine all open food containers, including the contents of all sugar, flour, and salt containers. We've had one homicide due to sodium azide poisoning and suspect we may have another. In the first case, the poison was concealed in sweetener packets. My concern is that here it may have been used to contaminate other foodstuffs. So, although this is primarily a hazardous-materials operation, it's also a crime scene investigation. I want photographs and a properly documented evidence log."

"I was told no one here was hurt," Workman objected. "In fact, I asked the dispatcher specifically, and he said—"

"You're right, no one *is* hurt here," Joanna corrected. "Not at this location, but only because we got lucky. Let me remind you, however, Mr. Workman, that two other people *are* dead. If you find any trace of sodium azide in the food inside the house, that adds one count of attempted murder as well."

"All right, all right!" Workman conceded grudgingly. "I get the picture." He turned once again to his waiting crew. "Okay, guys," he said. "Move it."

One by one, the Haz-Mat team disappeared into the house.

"Good work," Beaumont said after they left.

Joanna turned on him. "What do you mean?"

He grinned at her. "You know exactly what I mean. You chewed that poor guy up and spit him out. He never even saw it coming."

The next thing Joanna Brady knew, she was grinning, too.

"Something's bothering me," he said, when the lighthearted moment had passed.

"What's that?" she asked.

He reached into his pocket and pulled out a cell phone that was very nearly a duplicate of her own. "How come yours works and mine doesn't?" he asked.

"Oh, that," she says. "It's a Dual-NAM phone."

"What's that?"

"Two numbers and two cell-phone providers. I got tired of all the dropped calls. Now I'm hooked into the system down in Naco, Sonora, as well. They have a stronger signal. . . ."

"Is that why I keep ending up with the recording in Spanish?"

"Right," she said. "And you're going to keep on getting it until you're on the other side of the Mule Mountains."

Shaking his head, Beau pocketed his phone. "Sorry I asked," he said.

SOMETIME LATER, THE FIRST OF THE HAZ-MAT crew members emerged from the house carrying several tightly closed stainless-steel containers. It was an hour after that when the last of them, Ron Workman, stepped out onto the porch. Divested of his moon suit, he stopped in front of Joanna and handed over an evidence log as well as a fanfold of Polaroid prints.

"Whoever your guy is, he knows what he's doing," Workman told Joanna as she studied the pictures.

"What makes you say that?"

"If he hadn't known something about sodium azide, he'd most likely be lying dead in there, too, since just breathing this stuff can kill you." Dave Hollicker was standing nearby. Remembering her crime scene investigator was lucky to be alive, Joanna shot him a meaningful glance. Dave nodded and said nothing.

Workman continued. "He jury-rigged himself a laminar-flow fume hood. Attached a cooling fan from a computer to one side and cut a hole big enough for his hands in the other. With his hands inside, the two openings would be almost the same. He also cut holes into the top and made Saran Wrap windows so he could work with his hands inside the box and still see what he was doing. Then he sealed all the seams with duct tape. And—voilà. There you have it—the same kind of equipment we use when we're working with hazardous materials in the lab, except ours sets the state back a bundle of money. What your guy used was crude but effective."

"And portable," Joanna added.

"That, too," Workman agreed. "Whenever he was working with it, he would have connected it to an outside vent."

"It's hooked to the dryer vent so he wouldn't end up breathing it himself."

"Right."

"Did you dust for prints?" Joanna asked.

"Not yet," Workman told her. "When we get back to the lab, we'll dust the box and the food containers we took, but for the rest . . ."

"That's all right," Joanna said. "My people will handle it. How much sodium azide did you find in there?"

"In the box?"

She nodded.

"Plenty," Workman answered grimly. "More than I wanted to see. If your suspicions about the sugar and flour are correct, he had enough to do some real damage."

"How long will it take you to find out about the sugar and flour?" she asked.

"Not long," he said with a shrug. "A day or two. I'll be in touch as soon as we finish the analysis."

Joanna wanted to grab the man by his shoulders and give him a shake. She wanted to flood Workman with the same kind of urgency she felt, but he didn't have people in his jurisdiction dying right and left. He didn't have some nutcase walking around his town carrying God knew how much more sodium azide. But Joanna understood she had already pushed him just getting him to create the evidence log. If she said much more, it would likely slow the process rather than speed it up.

"Thanks," she said. "I'm sure you'll do your best."

I GOT A KICK OUT OF WATCHING it go down. It occurred to me while Sheriff Brady was nailing Ron Workman's feet to the floor that even though the Haz-Mat squad leader was a good twenty years younger than Harry I. Ball, the two men were cut from the same cloth.

Most people are under the mistaken impression that sexism is limited to old farts like Harry and me. They think one of these days all of the old guys will die off, sort of like the dinosaurs did, and the problem will disappear from the face of the planet. I have bad news for those folks. Since Ron Workman wasn't a day over thirty-five, they probably shouldn't look for it to happen anytime soon.

The Haz-Mat guys and Deputy Hollicker were packing up to leave when Joanna's cell phone rang again. She answered and then handed it over to me. "For you," she said.

"I've got two things to tell you," Frank Montoya reported excitedly. "Number one: I checked on that Gardendale Correctional Institute you asked me about. It's private, not public, owned and operated by UPPI."

"And the other?"

"I've finally managed to get a hold of some of the phone records we need. I started with the pay phones down by the post office, and I've found something very interesting. There are three long-distance calls that were placed from one of those phones to Winnetka, Illinois, on Thursday. One was at eleven-twenty. The second was at three forty-six, the third at three-fifty. The first two went to the offices of a law firm named Maddern, Maddern, and Peek. The last one was to the residence of someone named Louis F. Maddern, the Third. That call lasted for close to ten minutes. Does the name 'Maddern' ring a bell?"

"Not to me," I told him, jotting the information into my notebook. "Never heard of the guy or the law firm, either one."

"It could be nothing," Frank was saying. "Since Brampton is evidently from Illinois, it could be Maddern is a friend or a relative. But still, the timing . . ."

I was doing some dot-connecting. Frank Montoya was right. The timing of the calls was critical. Vital, even. One had been placed in the morning, probably shortly after the end of the donnybrook at Castle Rock Galley. The second two had been placed within minutes of Brampton's finding out he was about to be fingerprinted in regard to the Latisha Wall homicide. If he'd had something to do with her death—if he was in any way responsible—he might have been operating in a state of near panic about then. Everyone pretends that detectives solve cases by virtue of pure skill and dogged determination. The truth is, we usually catch crooks because they make stupid mistakes.

"This is good stuff," I told him. "Thanks."

"I thought you'd like it," Frank replied.

I started to hand the phone back to Joanna, then changed my mind. "Could you check on one more thing?" I asked.

"What's that?" Frank returned.

"UPPI and the state of Washington are currently involved in some upcoming litigation. How about checking to see if a company named Maddern, Maddern, and Peek is representing in that case."

"Sure thing," Frank said. "I'll see what I can do." I heard someone speaking to Montoya in the background. When he returned to the radio mike, his voice crackled with new urgency. "Have the Haz-Mat guys left yet?" he demanded.

I looked around. The yard was empty. While we talked, Joanna had evidently followed Ron Workman and his crew back down to the street. "I'm not sure," I told him. "If they're not already gone, they're packing up to leave. Why?"

"Somebody'd better grab them before they do," Frank Montoya returned. "Casey Ledford just radioed in from Dee Dee Canfield's house out in Huachuca Terraces. She says there are clear signs of a struggle in the living room, and there are traces of a white powder on the furniture and in the rugs. She's evacuated the place and is awaiting Haz-Mat assistance."

Before the call even ended, I was thundering down the stairs, looking for Joanna Brady. Ron Workman was shaking her hand and about to get into his truck when I caught up with them. I gave her Frank's message, which she immediately passed along to Ron. He took the news of this additional Haz-Mat site with all the eye-rolling good grace of a fifth grader who's just been told the principal has canceled recess.

"Where's this one?" he demanded.

"A few miles from here," Joanna said. "You'll get there faster if I lead the way."

With that, Joanna Brady struck off up the street toward the parked Blazer. Since I was currently without wheels of my own, I jogged along. If where we were going was "a few" miles away, I had no intention of walking.

Riding through town, I was struck by the general junkiness of the place. Homes and businesses alike seemed to have collections of old cars, washing machines, refrigerators, and other rusty equipment that defied identification moldering around them. Evidently the city of Bisbee wasn't big on litter patrol.

The route we took around the traffic circle and out of town was familiar. We'd gone that way the day before when I had followed Joanna's Crown Vic to Naco. This time, though, we blew straight through that critical intersection. Half a mile later, we turned left into a little subdivision of humble-looking late-fifties bungalows, complete with what looked distinctly like another hazardous material—asbestos siding.

Dee Canfield's house was the most beat-up place on the block. A seven-foot-tall chicken, made of soldered-together scrap metal and too tall to fit under the low-slung front porch's overhang, stood sentry in the middle of a weed-clogged front yard.

Joanna parked on the street. While she hurried off to confer with her deputies and the Haz-Mat guys once again, I stayed put. I didn't have the patience or the inclination to go hang around another crime scene. Playing fifth wheel and staying out of the way of the people who are doing useful work doesn't suit me.

That's how come I was still in the car and half-dozing when the radio call came in from Frank Montoya.

"Sheriff Brady," he asked. "Can you put Beaumont on?"

I picked up the radio. "I'm here," I said. "What's up?"

"Maddern, Maddern, and Peek may not be representing UPPI in Washington State, but they are in several other jurisdictions—Missouri, Arkansas, and Pennsylvania, to be exact. The law firm UPPI is using in Washington is actually McRainey and Dobbs. They're located in a place called Bellevue."

My heartbeat quickened. It may have been entirely circumstantial, but here was a connection—a real connection—between Latisha Wall's killer and UPPI. I could hardly wait to tell Ross Connors that I was making progress.

"Thanks, Frank," I said. "Thanks a lot. I'll let Sheriff Brady know right away."

But before I did that, I picked up my cell phone. Without thinking, I dialed the attorney general's cell phone number, only to discover I had once again been captured by that Spanish-speaking babe from Old Mexico.

"Damn!" I exclaimed, whacking the phone on the dashboard in utter frustration. *What's the point in packing the damned thing if it doesn't work most of the time?*

Climbing out of the car, I went looking for Joanna Brady.

"What now?" she asked when I interrupted her yet again. I was going to ask to borrow her phone, but she looked so harried that I simply passed along what Frank Montoya had told me. "I need to get back up to the hotel," I added. "I want to call my boss and let him know what's happened."

"Sure," Joanna said. "Go ahead." With that, she turned once again to her officers.

"But I don't have a car," I objected.

Shaking her head, she reached in her pocket and found a set of keys, which she tossed over to me. I caught them in midair. "Go get your Kia," she said. "Leave my Blazer at the department. You can leave the keys at the front desk."

"But how will you get back?" I asked.

"Don't worry. Somebody here will give me a ride when we finish up." With that Joanna turned away and returned to her huddle with Workman, Hollicker, and the others.

I didn't fault her for rudeness. Cops working crime scenes don't have time to observe all the Miss Manners rules of polite behavior. Joanna Brady was working a crime scene and, as it turned out, so was I.

Eighteen

FTER DROPPING OFF JOANNA'S BLAZER, I took the Kia and headed for the hotel. It was early Sunday evening. With the weekend over, parking was a little less scarce than it had been the day before. I walked down the hill and up the steps in early evening twilight.

Entering the Copper Queen, I was intent on going straight to my room and calling Ross Connors, but Cornelia Lester was in the lobby. She caught my eye and flagged me down before I could make it to the elevator. She sat on one of the deep leather couches before a cup-and-saucer-laden coffee table. Walking toward her, I realized she wasn't alone. A grim-faced Bobo Jenkins was there, with her, along with a blond-haired woman in a business suit. The blonde appeared to be crying.

"You know Mr. Jenkins, don't you?" Connie asked.

"Yes, I do."

Bobo Jenkins and I shook hands.

"And this is Serenity Granger," Connie continued. "She's Deidre Canfield's daughter. Serenity, this is Mr. J.P. Beaumont. He's a special investigator for the Washington State Attorney General's Office."

The other murder victim's daughter, I realized. *No wonder she's in tears.*

Serenity Granger pulled herself together. "Hello," she said.

"I'm so sorry about your mother," I said.

She nodded. "Thank you," she murmured.

"Won't you sit down?" Cornelia Lester asked.

What I wanted to say was, *No, thanks. I have to go up to my room and make some phone calls.* But I didn't want to be rude. Here were three grieving people, two black and one white—all of them bound together by tragedy and loss—who had found the strength of character to offer comfort to one another in a time of trouble.

I understood the kind of limbo they were in. They were stuck between knowing their loved one was gone and being able to deal with it. Their lives had been put on hold by officialdom. There would have to be questions and interviews and autopsies before bodies could be released. Only then would they be free to observe the familiar rituals of funerals and memorial services that precede any kind of return to normalcy.

Under those circumstances, it was impossible for me to walk away no matter how much I might have wanted to. I sat.

Cornelia Lester was clearly in charge. "Can we get you something?" she asked. "Coffee, tea, a drink? The waitstaff has been kind enough to serve us out here. It was far too noisy in the bar, and we weren't interested in food."

"I'm fine," I said. "Nothing for me."

"Have you heard if they're finished with Mr. Jenkins's house yet?" Cornelia asked. "Sheriff Brady said someone would let him know when it's safe for him to return home. So far he's heard nothing."

That was hardly surprising. Once the second call came in summoning Joanna to the new Haz-Mat site, the sheriff had a readily understandable excuse for not getting back to Bobo Jenkins. I also knew that, although the Haz-Mat guys were gone, Casey Ledford, the fingerprint tech, probably hadn't had a chance to go through Bobo's house yet, either.

"She's pretty busy," I said. "Another call came in."

Bobo's eye drilled into mine. "You mean I can't go home yet?"

"I don't think so. You'd probably be better off renting a room. Maybe you should bunk in here with the rest of us."

There was plenty I could have told them, but not without raising Joanna Brady's considerable ire. I sat for a while making appropriately meaningless small talk. When a waitress from the dining room came out to refill coffee cups, she asked me if I wanted something. I took that as a sign I had done my bit and was free to escape.

"If you'll excuse me," I said. "I need to make some phone calls."

As soon as I shut the door to my room, I hurried over to the desk. I dragged the raggedy list of Ross Connors's telephone numbers out of my wallet and dialed his home number first. I recognized Francine Connors's voice as soon as she answered the phone.

"Is Ross there?" I asked.

"Yes, he is," she replied. "May I tell him who's calling, please?"

"Sure," I said. "Tell him it's Beau."

I hate waiting on phones even when it's on somebody else's nickel. It seemed like a long time before Ross Connors came on the line, but then again, the AG and I aren't exactly pals. I had never been invited to his residence down in Olympia, but I assumed from the considerable delay that it had to be a fairly large place with lots of distance between phone jacks. Eventually, Ross's hearty baritone boomed into my ear.

"Beaumont!" he exclaimed. "What's the news?"

"Not good, I'm afraid," I told him. "It's looking more and more like whoever did this went to great effort to frame Latisha Wall's boyfriend."

"Damn!" Ross Connors said.

"But wait," I added, "there's more." I must have sounded for all the world like an agitated announcer hawking television's latest 1-800 fruitcake invention. "You remember that second homicide I told you about, the one I said could be related?"

"The one Sheriff Brady threw you off?" Connors asked.

"Right. It turns out the second victim was a good friend of Latisha Wall's. Her name was Deidre Canfield. The prime suspect in that case is a guy named Jack Brampton. Ever heard of him?"

"Not that I remember."

"Bisbee's a small town," I explained. "A snoopy neighbor let on that this Brampton character routinely used a pay phone down near the post office. Our informant was under the impression that Brampton had a girlfriend on the side."

"Do people do that in small towns?" Connors demanded with a chuckle. "Are they so bored that they have to report on pay phone use, for Crissake? What about cell phones? Do they call in if someone uses one of those, too?"

Right that minute I didn't feel like explaining the difficulties of cell-phone usage in Bisbee, Arizona. Instead, I forged on. "We suspect that Brampton used one of those phones three times on Thursday, once in the morning and twice in the afternoon, the second time was within minutes of his learning that Cochise County investigators were going to fingerprint him as part of the Latisha Wall investigation."

"Get to the point," Connors urged.

"The calls went to someone in Winnetka, Illinois, at a law firm called Maddern, Maddern, and Peek. One of Maddern, Maddern, and Peek's big-deal clients happens to be UPPI, and Brampton did time in a UPPI facility when he was convicted of involuntary manslaughter."

There was stark silence on the other end of the phone, a silence so complete that I wondered if maybe I'd been disconnected. Finally, Connors said quietly, "There really is a leak, then."

"No shit," I agreed.

"I'll have to bring the feds in," he added.

It was a statement, not a question. My response should have been an unequivocal and resounding yes, but I said nothing, letting Ross Connors draw his own conclusions. There was another long pause. Finally, he took a deep breath.

"All right, Beau, here's what we're going to do. I know how this must look to you, but I'm going to let sleeping dogs lie for another day or so. I don't want to do anything prematurely. So far this all sounds pretty circumstantial. You keep right on doing whatever it is you're doing, and keep me posted on anything else that comes up. I'm not going to make my move until after we have rock-solid evidence."

What more do you want? I wondered.

Thinking about it, I figured Connors needed the extra time to come to terms with his changing reality. It also occurred to me that he might be looking for a way to cover his own butt. Still, the man was my boss, and he was calling the shots. If he wanted to wait for more damning information before nailing his own people, that was entirely up to him.

"Sure," I said coldly, "I'll be in touch," And we signed off.

I put down the phone and gave myself the benefit of a long,

hot shower. Then I lay down on the bed with every intention of watching television. I saw a few minutes of *60 Minutes*. It wasn't even dark yet before I was sound asleep.

Anne Corley stopped by to visit and woke me up around three. In the wee small hours of the morning I was once again wide awake and sleepless in Bisbee, Arizona. But I wasn't mulling over the increasingly complicated aspects of the Latisha Wall and Deidre Canfield cases. No, I was thinking about something else. Someone else. I was thinking about a little girl named Anne, growing up in a house with a developmentally disabled sister she was unable to protect from their pedophile father and with a mother who didn't believe—who wouldn't believe—anything of the kind could happen under her own roof.

No wonder the Anne I had known had been so terribly damaged and hurt. She had been an incredibly beautiful but broken bird. No wonder I had loved her.

IT WAS TEN O'CLOCK THAT NIGHT when Joanna Brady finally dragged herself into the house at High Lonesome Ranch. Jenny was already in bed. Joanna was rummaging through the refrigerator for leftovers when she spotted a bottle of champagne and two glasses sitting on the table in the breakfast nook.

A broadly grinning Butch Dixon appeared in the kitchen doorway. "What's this?" she asked, nodding toward the bottle.

"Nothing much," he said casually, but Joanna knew at once that wasn't true. The man looked so pleased with himself she thought he was going to burst.

"What nothing much?" Joanna asked.

"I had a call from an agent today," he beamed. "Her name is

Drew Mabrey, and she wants to represent me. She says she thinks she knows an editor who's looking for something just like *Serve and Protect*."

Joanna slammed the refrigerator door shut, hurried over, and planted a congratulatory kiss on her husband's lips. "That's great!" she exclaimed. "Wonderful! What else did he say?"

"She," Butch corrected. "The agent's a woman."

"Did she tell you how good it was?" Joanna continued. "I told you it was good, didn't I?"

"Yes." He smiled, heading for the champagne. "I think you did say something to that effect. That it was all right, anyway."

Joanna glared at him in mock exasperation. "I never said anything of the kind and you know it. Now tell me. What did she say?"

"Like I said before," he told her, carefully loosening the cork. "Drew loves it and wants to handle it, but there's a problem."

"What? Tell me."

"It's my name."

"Your name?" Joanna asked, mystified. "What's wrong with your name?"

"Drew said she almost didn't bother to read it because it came under the name F. W. Dixon."

"So what? Those *are* your initials. It *is* your name."

"But it's also the pseudonym of the author who wrote the Hardy Boy books, remember?"

"So?"

"Drew said that while she was growing up, she had to go visit her grandmother in Connecticut every summer. Her grandmother kept trying to get her to read her old Hardy Boy mysteries. Drew ended up hating them."

"So drop the initials then," Joanna advised Butch. "Write under the name of Frederick Dixon. What's wrong with that?"

"There's a difficulty there, too," Butch said. With a practiced hand he poured champagne into the glasses, doing it slowly enough that no liquid bubbled over the sides. "Drew says that with all the humor in the story it's really more of a cozy than a police procedural. She says male readers don't buy cozies; women do, and most cozies are written by women."

"What are you supposed to do, then?" Joanna asked.

"She wants me to change my name to something 'less gender-specific' were the words she used. Something like Kendall Dixon or Dale Dixon or Gayle Dixon."

"The agent wants you to pretend to be a woman to fool your readers?"

"And the editor, too," Butch said. "She wants me to pick a name before she submits the manuscript to anyone."

"What do you do when it comes time for an author photo?" Joanna asked.

Giving her the champagne, Butch shrugged. "I give up. I guess we'll cross that bridge when we get to it."

Joanna raised her glass in a toast. "Well, here's to you, then," she said with a smile "Or to whoever you turn out to be."

"So tell me about your day," Butch said as they settled into the breakfast nook to sip their champagne. "I knew you'd never make it to church."

WHEN JOANNA ARRIVED AT WORK the next morning, Kristin Gregovich was nowhere to be seen, but the conference room down the hall was already crowded. Frank Montoya, Ernie

Carpenter, and Jaime Carbajal were seated around the table. J.P. Beaumont, however, was among the missing.

"Welcome home, Ernie," Joanna said, making her way to her usual chair. "Turns out we need you."

"So I hear," he said.

For the next forty-five minutes they each briefed Detective Carpenter on everything that had happened. Then, when Jaime left for the medical examiner's office and Ernie went to handle the interviews with Eddie and Marcus Verdugo, Joanna retreated to her own office. She was surprised Kristin hadn't called in to say she would be late. Nevertheless, having worked all weekend long, Joanna appreciated the absence of that first load of morning mail. It meant her clean desk could stay that way awhile longer.

Reaching for her briefcase, she withdrew the first thing that came to hand—the envelope containing the Anne Rowland Corley materials. The first article she removed from the envelope was the one from the *Denver Post* titled:

THE FEMALE OF THE SPECIES
CAN BE DEADLIER THAN THE MALE

Conventional wisdom holds that serial killers are usually disaffected white males. But what happens when women turn deadly? How do they differ from their male counterparts, and how are they treated by the criminal-justice system?

In this series of six articles, award-winning *Denver Post* staff writer Susan DePew focuses on six notorious female killers, each of whom escaped detection far longer than she should have due to the fact that law-enforcement agents weren't looking for murderers from the second sex.

Today's installment deals with Arizona copper heiress Anne Rowland Corley, whose jet-set lifestyle underpinned a decades-long pursuit of misguided vigilante justice, which ultimately ended in her own death as well as in the deaths of at least two innocent people.

On a sunny May morning six years ago when Anne Rowland Corley married her second husband, Jonas Piedmont Beaumont, the groom was a homicide detective with the Seattle Police Department. The bride told the presiding minister that she intended to continue using the name of her first husband, Milton Corley, a Phoenix-area psychologist who had died several years earlier.

Hours after the wedding ceremony in one of Seattle's waterfront public parks, Anne Rowland Corley was dead of a gunshot wound received during a fatal shoot-out with her new husband. Her death was subsequently ruled self-defense. It was only afterward that the truth about Anne Rowland Corley's life of homicidal vengeance began to surface.

Serial killers often manifest their murderous tendencies early on. Stories abound of how an adolescent history of torturing and killing small animals is an early indicator of a troubled youth who may well end up becoming a serial killer. But Anne Rowland Corley skipped that intermediate step. At age twelve, she went straight for the gusto and allegedly murdered her father. Not that she was ever convicted or even tried for that offense.

Roger Rowland was the well-heeled heir to a pioneering Arizona copper-mining fortune who carried on a family tradition of hands-on involvement in the mining industry by moving his young family—a wife, Anita, and two daughters, Patricia and Anne—to Bisbee, Arizona, where he oversaw one of the family holdings.

Patty, the older of the two and developmentally disabled, died at age thirteen in what the Cochise County coroner's report declared "an accidental fall" in the family home. A few days later, Roger Rowland was dead as well, as a result of what was officially termed "a self-inflicted gunshot wound."

That double family tragedy was made worse when, prior to her father's funeral, Rowland's younger daughter, Anne, rocked the official boat by insisting that she had shot her father because he had been molesting her sister. The molestation allegations were never substantiated. Instead, twelve-year-old Anne Rowland was shipped off to a private mental institution in Phoenix, Arizona, where she remained for more than a decade.

While hospitalized, Anne Rowland came under the care of Dr. Milton Corley. She was released shortly after her mother's death, and, at age twenty-four, she married Dr. Corley. She remained with him until his death seven years later. Corley suffered from colon cancer but he, like Anne Rowland Corley's father, died of what was subsequently ruled to be a self-inflicted gunshot wound.

Dr. Myra Collins, a longtime friend and colleague of Milton Corley, says that even at the time she doubted Corley would have taken his own life, but no one was interested in hearing what she had to say. They still aren't.

"By that time Anne was the sole heir to her father's fortune," Dr. Collins stated. "She also picked up a nice piece of change when Milton died. She had the financial resources to hire high-powered attorneys and to get away with murder, which I continue to believe to this day is exactly what she did."

When asked if she thought Anne Rowland Corley was responsible for her father's death years earlier, Dr. Collins replied, "Anne always claimed she was the one who killed him. No amount of so-called treatment ever made her retract that statement. She was a smart, beautiful, and utterly ruthless young woman. I never had any reason to doubt what she said."

After Milton Corley's death, his widow lived a shadowy, vagabond lifestyle, never staying long in any one place. Her bills were sent to Scottsdale-area attorney Ralph Ames, who handled her finances and paid the bills as they came in, leaving her free to come and go as she wished.

People who had dealings with her during the next ten years said she looked like a movie star, drove a series of bright red Porsches, and stayed only in first-class hotels. It is also thought that she left behind a trail of murder.

Her victims were most likely people free on bail and awaiting trial in cases of suspected child abuse. Local law enforcement agencies, freed of the necessity of trying, convicting, and incarcerating yet another pedophile, were usually happy to close the books on those cases after only cursory investigations.

After Anne Rowland Corley's death, there is some sketchy evidence that her widowed husband and her longtime attorney contacted several jurisdictions around the country, quietly closing several of those far-flung cases.

In one of them, Jake Morris, a forty-six-year-old drifter suspected of kidnapping and raping a six-year-old girl, was shot dead in Bangor, Maine. In another, twenty-three-year-old Lawrence Kenneth Addison, suspected of luring and molesting numerous children who lived near his parents' home in Red Bluff, California, disappeared on a sunny Friday afternoon. His body was found two days later at a deserted I-5 rest area.

In both of those cases, witnesses mentioned something about a stranger—a good-looking woman—who was seen talking to both victims shortly before their deaths, but no one ever bothered to track her down. She was never thought to be a viable subject. Since there was no communication between the two affected jurisdictions, no one ever made the connection or noticed the similarities.

"That doesn't surprise me," Dr. Collins says. "There are plenty of male chauvinist homicide detectives out there who don't believe women are smart enough or tough enough to be killers."

Both Anne Rowland Corley's widower and her long-term attorney refused to respond to repeated requests for interviews in conjunction with this story. Perhaps the possibility of a series of wrongful-death suits contributed to their reticence.

Anne Rowland Corley usually dispatched her victims with a single bullet to the head. She believed in being up close and personal with her victims. Once her identity was established, some local police investigators in those far-flung cases admitted that she had befriended officers in both locations as a way of gaining information and access to her intended victims. She did so by claiming to be writing a book on convicted child molesters, although no such manuscript has ever surfaced.

Her use of subterfuge may well account for the ongoing conspiracy of silence on the part of many police agencies involved. Although there are no doubt other cases to which Anne Rowland Corley was connected, it has been impossible to track down any additional ones in which she was directly involved. Only a diligent search of public records finally uncovered the list of acknowledged victims that accompanies this story. It's likely there are other victims whose cases remain unsolved.

Six years ago, as a homicide detective for Seattle PD, J.P. Beaumont was investigating the abuse and death of a five-year-old child, Angela Barstogi. Suspects in that case included the child's mother, Suzanne Barstogi, and the mother's spiritual adviser, Michael Brodie, a dictatorial, self-styled religious leader whose followers in a sect called Faith Tabernacle did whatever he required of them.

Like his counterparts in Bangor, Maine, and Red Bluff, California, Detective Beaumont found himself befriended by a disturbingly beautiful woman who expressed an interest in the case. Shortly thereafter, the two prime suspects were found shot to death in a Seattle-area church. A day later, a man who turned out to be the real killer in the Angela Barstogi homicide investigation was also found murdered. Hours later, Anne Rowland Corley herself was shot dead.

"This was clearly a woman who felt violated and betrayed by the very people who should have protected her," says August Benson, professor of criminal psychology at the University of Colorado. "When the people who should have offered protection failed her, Anne Rowland Corley took matters into her own hands."

Joanna paused in her reading and glanced at the accompanying photo and the sidebar. The Anne Rowland Corley pictured in a posed black-and-white portrait was a lovely young woman with long dark hair and a reserved smile.

No wonder cops talked to her, Joanna thought. *And no wonder J.P. Beaumont fell so hard.*

Joanna was about to return to her reading when the phone rang. "Sheriff Brady?" Tica Romero, the day-shift dispatcher, asked.

"Yes. What's up?"

"We've got a situation unfolding just west of Miracle Valley, out by Palominas. An unidentified intruder walked up to what he thought was an unoccupied house. He broke in and stole some food from the kitchen of Paul and Billyann Lozier's place on River Trail Road. Then he went out to a corral, saddled up one of their horses, and took off. Billyann's mother, Alma Wingate, was in an upstairs bedroom and saw the whole thing. Unfortunately, she didn't have a phone with her at the time and couldn't call 911 until after he left."

"Undocumented alien?" Joanna asked.

"I don't think so," Tica replied. "For one thing, the guy on the horse seemed to be headed south, not north. For another, from the description Mrs. Wingate gave me, the suspect might very well be the guy on our APB. She said he was tall and skinny, with a single gray braid hanging down the middle of his back."

"You're right," Joanna breathed. "Sounds like Jack Brampton."

"I've got units on their way," Tica continued, "but they're clear over by Benson. It'll take time for them to reach the scene. The problem is, the border fence is only four miles away, and it looks like that's where the perp is headed. As of now, he's got a ten-minute head start."

Joanna Brady was already on her feet. "Give me the address," she urged. "We'll get on this right away. I'm a lot closer than Benson. I'll take a couple of cars and a squad of officers along with me. Thanks for letting me know, Tica. And how about calling out Terry Gregovich and Spike? If we lose him, Spike may be able to track him down."

"Will do," Tica said.

Pulling on her Kevlar vest, Joanna raced to the conference room. "Okay, guys," she announced. "On the double. Somebody who looks like Jack Brampton just stole a horse from a corral between Palominas and Miracle Valley. According to an eyewitness, the guy who did it is headed for the Mexican border. Let's get rolling."

I CAME DRAGGING IN LATE, feeling like hell and ashamed to think that I had overslept—again. By the time I showed up, I had already missed the morning briefing. Frank Montoya introduced me to a guy named Ernie Carpenter, Detective Carbajal's homicide counterpart, who had evidently just finished interviewing the two little boys who had found Dee Canfield's body.

Ernie Carpenter was around my age, which made him by far the oldest officer I had met in the Cochise County Sheriff's Department. He was a big bear of a man with a pair of bushy eyebrows and a knuckle-crushing handshake. In other words, Ernie was my kind of guy. After introductions were out of the way, Frank Montoya passed both Ernie and me two tall stacks of computer-generated printouts.

"What's this?" I asked.

"Background on your friends at UPPI," Frank told me. "I downloaded it from the Internet and thought you might find it interesting. They're even more litigious than I thought they were when we found out about that law firm in Illinois yesterday."

As I settled in to read, I realized this was information I should and could have had from the beginning. If Ross Connors had wanted to keep a lid on things, he couldn't have chosen better when he entrusted the problem to Harry I. Ball and me. Of the two of us, I'd be hard-pressed to decide which one was less likely to go surfing the Internet.

But, as Frank Montoya said, the material was interesting. UPPI had ventured into prison construction and management when the field was booming, but whoever drew up their business plan had failed to predict the sudden drop in crime at the end of the nineties that would leave them holding thousands of unoccupied and shoddily built prison beds.

To make up for their own bad planning, they had tried to staunch the flow of red ink by filing breach-of-contract suits in twelve different states, all of them still pending. Although one article hinted that at least one UPPI executive was suspected of having links to organized crime, no firm connections had ever been established.

Lost in the material, I paid no attention as people came and went from the conference room. Ernie Carpenter and I were the only ones left when Joanna Brady burst in a while later to tell us that something was going down at a place called Palominas. When she first mentioned a stolen horse, I thought she was joking. But as soon as she said the suspected horse thief was most likely Jack Brampton, Ernie and I dropped what we were doing and headed for the door.

I was two steps down the hallway when she stopped me. "Wait a minute, Beau," she said. "Where's your vest?"

"Not on me."

"You'd better go see Frank Montoya then," she said. "You're sure as hell not riding along without one."

"But . . ." I began.

"No buts," she said. "My way or the highway."

With that, she turned and sprinted away, leaving me with a whole mouthful of unspoken arguments still superglued to my tongue.

Nineteen

B Y THE TIME JOANNA NEARED PALOMINAS, she had
learned from Dispatch that the backup cars Tica had called
for, although en route, were still ten and twelve miles away,
respectively. The assets she had brought with her from the
Justice Center—the two cars driven by Detective Ernie Carpenter
and Chief Deputy Frank Montoya—were the only immediate
help she would have at her disposal. She had expected someone
else to show up as well.

"What happened to Beaumont?" she demanded into her
radio. "He was supposed to come with Frank."

"By the time Frank was ready to leave, Mr. Beaumont was
nowhere to be found," dispatcher Tica Romero told her.

Just as well, Joanna thought. "What about Deputy Gregovich?"
she asked. "Is he on his way?"

"I still haven't been able to locate him," Tica said.

"Keep trying."

Joanna swung the Blazer off Highway 92 and onto the short stretch of paved street that ran through Palominas. Overall, the tiny community ran along the highway and was far longer than it was wide. At River Trail Road, where she had turned off, the town was barely two lots deep. The pavement ended just beyond the second house. Now she sped down the dirt road that ran alongside the eastern bank of the north-flowing San Pedro River. The turnoff to Paul and Billyann Lozier's place was half a mile south of town.

With Joanna leading the way, the three patrol cars pulled into the Loziers's yard, spewing dust behind them. Eighty-two-year-old Alma Wingate met them on the front porch. She was a frail-looking woman, thin beyond belief, and leaning heavily on a cane, but her blue eyes sparkled with determination.

"Thank God I had my cataract surgery," she exclaimed as Joanna sprinted onto the porch. "Otherwise I wouldn't have been able to see a thing. When he broke in, I hid in a closet and didn't come out until I heard the screen door slam shut. I went to the window and saw him grab Princess—that's Billyann's horse, and she loves that animal to pieces—then I knew I had to do something."

The frightened woman's words poured out in a torrent. "Please, Mrs. Wingate," Joanna interrupted. "Slow down. Which way did he go?"

Alma pointed a shaky finger. "That way," she said. "Toward the river."

Joanna nodded wordlessly at Frank, who sprinted off in the direction of the river, following a trail of fresh hoofprints.

"Do you know if he was armed?" Joanna asked.

Alma nodded. "Must be," she said. "I just checked. The door to my son-in-law's gun cabinet is smashed to smithereens. I don't know what all's missing. You'll have to ask him."

"Look," Joanna advised. "You should probably go back inside the house and stay there. Backup officers are on the way, but in the meantime, you need to be safe."

"You think he's dangerous then?" Alma demanded. "I thought he was just a dirty low-down horse thief."

"I'm afraid this guy's far worse than just a horse thief, Mrs. Wingate," Joanna said as Frank came racing back toward the house. "Much, much worse."

By the time Joanna had guided Alma Wingate safely into the house, Frank was leaning against his Civvie, gasping for breath. Ernie had disappeared.

"He went down into the riverbed and turned south," Frank reported. "It's a good thing we didn't come with sirens blaring. It looks like he's walking the horse rather than running her."

"Where's Ernie?"

"He's going to move south, sticking to the riverbed to make sure he doesn't turn out somewhere between here and the border. I've put in a call to the *federales* across the line in Old Mexico. They're sending a squad of agents over from Naco. They should be here within fifteen minutes. I told them someone would meet them where the river crosses the border."

Knowing her own lack of proficiency in Spanish, Joanna had no doubt about who should be at the border to meet the *federales*.

"Do it, Frank," she said. "I'll drive along the riverbank and see if I can spot him somewhere between here and there."

Frank nodded. "Be careful," he warned. "There's lots of thick cover in there, places where he could hide and see you without being seen."

"You be careful, too," she told him.

Moments later, with tires spinning in the dirt, both cars swung out of the yard and headed south. A quarter of a mile down the road, Joanna stopped and got out. Crouching behind the trunk of a cottonwood tree, she used a pair of binoculars to peer up and down the river. Even though there was no movement in the dry bed of the river, she could make out the pattern of blurred hoofprints that said a horse had recently passed that way.

Parallel to her and across the river, a cloud of fast-moving dust rose skyward. She didn't remember there being another road over there, but obviously one existed nonetheless.

Whoever you are, she told the faceless driver in that invisible vehicle, *just stay the hell out of our way.*

With that, she jumped back in the Blazer and headed south again. As she drove she was glad she'd had the good sense to use lights only; no sirens. Out here in the silent desert, Jack Brampton would have heard those sirens from far away and would have known they were coming. This way, there was still a chance of surprising him.

Joanna stopped for a second time and got out, crouching in the dead grass, keeping under cover. And that's when she heard the sound of sirens, wafting up from the south. The *federales* were coming, all right, with their sirens blaring to kingdom come!

"Damn," she muttered. "Damn! Damn! Damn!"

GRUMBLING UNDER MY BREATH, I went looking for Frank Montoya. It turns out he did have a vest, but it wasn't my size. He said he thought there were larger ones back in the supply room, but since he was on his way to Palominas, I'd have to have one of the clerks in the lobby get it for me. By the time I had the blasted thing in my hand and made it out to the parking lot, everyone else, including Chief Deputy Montoya, was long gone. So much for hot pursuit!

"Damn!" I hurried back into the lobby. "Where's Palominas?" I demanded.

"West of town, on Highway 92," the clerk told me. "It's beyond Huachuca Terraces. Do you know how to get there?"

I'm a native of Seattle. There, geography poses no problem. I know the streets and my way around them. In Bisbee I was totally useless, but the name Huachuca Terraces sounded vaguely familiar. I was pretty sure that's where Dee Canfield's house was located.

"Thanks," I told her. "I think I can find it."

Racing back out to the parking lot, I jumped into the Kia and wound it up as fast as it would go. If somebody gave me a speeding ticket, it was just too damned bad, although the idea of getting a speeding ticket in a Kia might have been worth it. Then again, out here in the world of the Wild West, where crooks used stolen horses instead of getaway cars, maybe state patrollers just shot speeders instead of handing out tickets.

Retracing the route Joanna Brady had driven the day before, I was relieved when I finally saw a sign that read: PALOMINAS, 10 MILES. I knew then that I was on the right track. And with the Kia running on the flat and wound up to a full eighty-five miles per hour, I knew that meant I was six minutes out.

Driving through the desert, I looked ahead. In the distance I saw a long meandering line of greenish-yellow autumn-tinged trees stretching south to north. Near that line of trees I saw what appeared to be a cluster of buildings. That must be the town of Palominas, whatever that means.

Isn't that some kind of horse? I wondered.

Crossing a railroad overpass, I caught my first glimpse of flashing red lights as the fast-moving police cars ahead of me swept into that tiny community. I was thrilled to think that I was actually closing the distance between me and them. They had all left the Justice Center a couple of long minutes before I did. Maybe my Kia wasn't so terribly lame after all.

Soon I was near enough to tell that the rearmost vehicle was signaling for a left-hand turn. About that time, however, I met a pair of oncoming dodoes who never should have been issued driver's licenses. As soon as one guy pulled out to pass, the other one sped up, thus making the passing process take far longer than it should have. As they rushed toward me side by side in both lanes, I started looking for somewhere to hit the ditch and dodge out of the way. Finally, at the last moment, the passing car gave up and pulled back into the right-hand lane. By the time I looked again, the police cars had disappeared.

As I entered town, I slowed down. When I reached what I assumed to be the correct intersection, I turned left. After a hundred yards or so, the pavement ended and I bounced down a narrow, rutted cow path without another vehicle in sight. I stopped finally, rolled down the window, and listened. I was hoping for sirens. I saw clouds of dirt billowing skyward east of me, but I heard nothing, at least not at first. But then, very, very faintly, I did hear a siren. Not the standard kind of siren we use here in the States. No, this one had a decidedly foreign flavor to it.

I was watching the clouds of dust off to my left and listening to the siren when it finally hit me. I had made a mistake and overshot the turn. The action was there, all right—to the south and east of where I was.

I pulled ahead, looking for a place to turn around so I could go back the way I had come, but then I stumbled on another dirt road. This one, little more than a two-wheel track, was even narrower than the one I was already on, but at least it wandered off toward the southeast, the same general direction I wanted to go. So I went that way as well.

The Kia and I were tooling along just fine until we came up over a ridge and dropped down toward that line of trees I had seen earlier. I knew now for sure that the trees marked a riverbed. In fact, I remembered flying across a bridge back on the highway immediately after I had been looking for a place to ditch. There had been a sign attached to the bridge announcing the name of the river that ran under it, but I didn't remember the name, and I hadn't spotted any water, either.

Where I come from, rivers usually contain water. Actually, in the Pacific Northwest, it's a rule.

Whatever the unknown river's name might be, water wasn't required. What it lacked in moisture, however, it made up in sand—loads of it. Ahead of me, the bone-dry riverbed was a good fifty yards wide. On the far side of that long expanse of sand I spotted another narrow set of tire tracks. It seemed reasonable to assume that those tracks might be a continuation of the road I was on.

I paused long enough to consider my options. Going back and taking the other road would use up the better part of half an hour. By then, whatever action there was across the river would be over and done with. If I could cross the sand, though, I might be able to catch up with Joanna and the others before I missed out; before they had Jack Brampton handcuffed and thrown in the back of a patrol car.

Naturally, my low-priced rental Kia wasn't equipped with four-wheel drive. Even so, I thought that if I built up a good-enough head of steam before I hit the sand, maybe momentum would carry me across.

That was the plan, anyway, and that's exactly what I did. I shoved the gas pedal all the way to the floor and charged into the riverbed. I was doing fine. In fact, I probably would have made it to the far side without a hitch, except for one thing. All of a sudden, right in the dead center of the sand trap, a horse and rider appeared out of nowhere. They came galloping down the riverbed straight at me.

When I finally realized that the crazy bastard on the horse was headed right for me, I took my foot off the gas and slammed on the brakes. The Kia stopped dead. At the same time, something smashed into and through the windshield. It smacked into the shoulder rest of the passenger seat only a foot or so from where I was sitting. Simultaneously, a spiderweb of tiny cracks spread across the windshield's safety glass.

By then I had seen the gun and understood that the son of a bitch on the horse was shooting at me—shooting to kill! Covering my head, I dived for cover and put the Kia's engine block between me and any more flying bullets. Even muffled by sand, I could hear the thud of the horse's hooves as it pounded by. I waited until I couldn't hear it anymore. Only then, with my small backup Glock in my hand, I cautiously raised my head and peered out.

Off to the south, the riverbed curved slowly to the left. Horse and rider were fast disappearing around that bend. By then, they were already far beyond the range of my wimpy backup handgun. Shaking my head in disgust, I climbed out of the car. I plowed through deep sand in my once pristine Johnston and Murphys and surveyed the damage. The windshield was a goner. Both axles were buried up to the hubs. It would take time and a well-equipped tow truck to dig me out.

I set out to finish crossing the river on foot. A stiff wind blew from the south, kicking powdery sand into my eyes. As I walked along, half-blinded by the sand, I heard Joanna Brady's voice calling my name.

"Beaumont, what are you doing down there?" she demanded. "Are you hurt?"

Looking up, I caught sight of her. She stood on the edge of the far bank. The top of her Blazer was barely visible in the background. It hurt my pride to admit it—hurt like hell, in fact—but I had to do it.

"I'm stuck," I called back, "but the guy on the horse went that way." I pointed to what I assumed was downriver, although I learned later it was actually up.

Joanna turned her back on me and disappeared from view. I figured she would leave me stranded and go after Brampton without me. Instead, moments later, the speeding Blazer hurtled down the bank. Instead of setting out across the expanse of treacherous sand, she stayed near the edge, where the sand was covered with what looked like a cracked, hard-baked crust.

"Come on," she yelled, motioning for me to join her. "We haven't got all day! The border's only a mile away."

Running through sand is a joke. My feet sank up to my ankles with every step. I've always assumed that quicksand is wet. This was dry, but it was treacherous as hell. I finally lost one shoe altogether and had to go back to retrieve it. At last, shoe in hand, I caught up with the Blazer, wrenched open the door, and clambered inside.

"Did you get a good look at him?" she demanded.

That morning, in the conference room, I had studied Jack Brampton's mug shots. "It's him, all right." I panted. "Believe me, he is armed and dangerous."

*

"No kidding," Joanna said.

There was no time to look at him as Beaumont slumped in the

passenger seat. Her eyes were glued to the riverbed. Sticking to the shelf of caliche, she headed south.

"The bastard tried to kill me," Beaumont grumbled. "Shot the hell out of my windshield. I'm lucky he didn't take me out, too. By the way," he added in what sounded like a grudging afterthought, "thanks for the vest."

"You're welcome," she returned. "And don't worry. Brampton won't get away. Frank went on ahead. He's meeting up with some *federales*. They'll be waiting at the border."

"Right," Beaumont said. "I heard them."

"So did Brampton," Joanna said grimly.

They drove in silence after that. Periodically the narrow shelf of caliche would give way to sand. When they hit that, it took all of Joanna's considerable driving skill to keep the Blazer moving, even *with* four-wheel drive. She was paying attention to the sand directly in front of them when Beaumont yelled, "There he is."

Ahead of them, Joanna caught sight of the galloping horse and rider. The little mare, laboring through the treacherous, knee-deep sand, was struggling to maintain the pace. Beyond Princess, Joanna spotted the string of fence posts that marked the international border. Unfortunately, Frank Montoya and his promised squad of *federales* were nowhere to be seen.

Knowing Brampton was almost at the border, Joanna stomped on the gas and the Blazer shot forward. Then, unexpectedly, the horse stopped. She stopped abruptly, but her rider didn't. Jack Brampton kept right on going. He tumbled headfirst over the horse's neck and shoulders and then over the fence, where he lay still in the sand.

Tossing her head, Princess wheeled around and started back toward the Blazer. Meanwhile, Joanna jammed on the brakes, stopping twenty yards downriver from the fallen man.

"Hit the dirt!" she ordered. Drawing her weapon, she flung herself out of the Blazer and down onto the sand. On the far side of the Blazer, J.P. Beaumont followed suit.

Princess trotted back toward them and then stood still once more, with her trembling legs spread wide apart and her head drooping. She was close enough to the Blazer that Joanna could hear the exhausted horse's snorting and labored breathing. Lying flat on the ground, Joanna wriggled a pair of binoculars out of her pocket and looked through them. On the far side of the fence, Jack Brampton lay in a crumpled heap on the ground.

"Freeze!" Joanna shouted. "Don't move."

Brampton complied with the order. Joanna and Beau watched for half a minute and detected no sign of movement.

"Closer?" Beaumont asked.

Joanna nodded and stowed the binoculars. "Go!" she said.

With their weapons drawn, they advanced again. When they ducked for cover the third time, Brampton still hadn't moved. "He's either knocked out cold or he's dead," she said.

Before they moved forward that last time, a gust of wind blew down the bed of the river, bringing with it a sudden flurry of movement. A cloud of something seemed to rise up ghostlike out of the ground beside the fallen man. It floated toward them, eddying in the breeze. As the mini–dust devil came closer, it separated itself into individual pieces of paper. Only when one of them landed beside her did Joanna realize it was a twenty-dollar bill— one of hundreds of other bills, twenties and fifties and hundreds— spiraling through the air.

Blood money, Joanna thought.

Still the suspect didn't move. "Shall we take him?" she asked.

Beaumont nodded. "Let's."

"Go!" she ordered.

Joanna and Beaumont scrambled to their feet simultaneously and rushed toward Jack Brampton. When they reached the border fence, they stopped. On the far side of it their murder suspect lay lifeless on the ground, his neck twisted back toward them, his eyes open but unmoving. Still strapped to his body was a torn backpack leaking money.

"He must have thought Princess was a jumper," Joanna Brady muttered as she reholstered her weapon. "Lucky for us, it turns out she wasn't."

Twenty

HINDSIGHT IS ALWAYS twenty-twenty. What Joanna Brady and I probably should have done the moment we saw Jack Brampton was grab him by his legs and drag his body back under the fence. Unfortunately, we were so relieved to be alive that neither of us figured that out until it was too late. By then, the *federales* had arrived on the scene, and all bets were off.

I worked the Seattle PD Homicide Unit for the better part of two decades. In all that time, I never had to bring a dead suspect's body back across an international border. I was about to get a first-hand lesson, and it wouldn't be pretty.

Sheriff Brady spoke. Frank Montoya translated. The *federales* listened and shook their heads. One of them caught sight of the packets of money spilling out of the fallen backpack. At that point the head-shaking became even more adamant. I believe the applicable term would be "No way, José." Right then I knew how it was going to play out. Without the personal intervention of Vicente Fox, or even God himself, Jack Brampton wasn't coming back across the border anytime soon. Neither was the money.

Frustrated beyond belief, I went plowing back down the river, gathering hundred-, fifty-, and twenty-dollar bills as I went. I had a whole fistful of them by the time Joanna Brady, her face clouded with anger, caught up with me. I glanced back at what should have been an official crime scene in time to see the Mexican officers summarily load Jack Brampton's body onto a stretcher and cart him away, right along with his backpack.

"Which do you want to take back?" she demanded. "Princess or the Blazer?"

"Princess?" I repeated.

"The horse," she said impatiently. "The horse's name is Princess."

I had far more faith in my ability to drive a Blazer than I did with my skill on a horse. For one thing, just inside the border fence on the U.S. side, I had spotted a reasonably serviceable road-way someone had carved through the desert. I suspected it had been put there for the convenience of passing Border Patrol vehicles and agents, and it looked to be in better condition than either of the narrow tracks I had driven on earlier.

"I'll drive," I said. "What about the money?" I added, showing her the wad of bills I held in my hand.

"Give it to Frank," she said. "He'll have deputies gather what they can and bring it back to the department. I'll be more than happy to put it in the confiscated-funds account."

Without another word, Joanna tossed me the keys, then she stalked off toward the Blazer. Once there, she pulled a gallon-sized plastic bottle of water out of the luggage compartment and poured it into a hard hat she evidently kept on hand in an equipment locker. Holding the water-filled hard hat in front of her, she moved cautiously toward the horse, making soothing clucking sounds as she did so.

As a city-born-and-bred boy, I figured the animal would take off. Instead, Princess pricked up her ears, trotted straight over to Joanna, and gratefully buried her muzzle in the water. By the time Princess had drunk her fill, Joanna had the creature's bridle firmly in hand. Without a word, Sheriff Brady vaulted easily into the saddle. As she rode past, she tossed me the hard hat.

"Put it back in the Blazer, would you?"

"Sure thing," I said.

Watching her ride away, I remembered what Harry I. Ball had said all those days earlier about Joanna Brady being a latter-day Annie Oakley. As it turned out, he hadn't been far from wrong.

⁜⁜⁜

JOANNA DELIVERED PRINCESS BACK to the Lozier place. By then someone had contacted Billyann Lozier at work, and she had come home to be with her mother. Alma Wingate, worn out by all the excitement, was back up in her bedroom lying down. Billyann was ecstatic to see Princess. She ran across the road to greet them when Joanna and the horse emerged from the riverbed. With tears running down her cheeks, Billyann Lozier buried her face in the horse's long black mane.

"Thank you so much for bringing her home, Sheriff Brady," Billyann murmured. "Thank you, thank you, thank you. After what Mother told me, I didn't think I'd ever see Princess again."

"You're welcome," Joanna said.

Returning the horse safely was the single bright spot in the day's events. Joanna should have been happy knowing that Jack

Brampton was done for. He would never be able to harm anyone else. The problem was, he had died without revealing anything about the people he had worked for—the people who had provided the money that the wind had blown out of his backpack. As far as Joanna was concerned, the job of apprehending the killer was only half done.

Not only that, but from the ham-fisted way the *federales* were handling the situation, Joanna doubted she and her investigators would learn anything more from the effects on the dead man's body. Plus, she didn't even know if Jack Brampton had gone to his death with an additional supply of sodium azide still in his possession, although Frank had apprised the Mexican officers of the possibility.

It was only when Joanna was standing in Paul and Billyann Lozier's front yard that she realized one of the backup deputies she had summoned had yet to appear. The others had both been sent down to join Chief Deputy Montoya and Ernie in searching for more of the scattered money. The K-9 Unit, however, wasn't with them.

Once Beaumont handed over the keys to the Blazer and they were headed into town, Joanna got on the radio to Dispatch. "Tica," she said, "whatever happened to Deputy Gregovich? He never showed up."

"He's at the hospital," Tica Romero replied. "At least Deputy Gregovich is. I don't know about Spike. Kristin's about to have her baby."

"Oh," a relieved Joanna said. "That explains it."

Minutes later, while requesting a tow truck to come to retrieve Beau's damaged Kia, she turned to him and asked, "Where should they take it?"

"I have no idea." He shrugged. "The rental agreement's in the glove box. Have the tow-truck driver call Saguaro Discount Rental in Tucson and ask them where they want it. Unless you need it for evidence, that is. If so, you can take it back to your department and have someone dig the bullet out of the passenger seat."

Joanna shook her head dispiritedly. "Why bother?" she asked. "The shooter's dead and you're not. I don't see any point in wasting time or energy on it."

"Makes sense to me," Beaumont agreed.

Sensing that he wasn't any happier about the situation than she was, Joanna drove for several miles without saying anything more.

"I'm sorry we didn't catch him," she said at last. "If your boss thought we were incompetent before—"

"Ross Connors didn't say anything of the kind," Beaumont said quickly. "And just for the record, neither did I."

"Thanks," Joanna said, and meant it. "What'll you do now?" she asked. "Head back home?" She was wondering if he'd say anything more about Anne Rowland Corley. He didn't.

"Probably," he answered. "With Brampton dead, there's not much reason to hang around any longer. Although, since Frank went to the trouble of getting those phone logs, I should finish going over them before I leave. I'll catch a plane back to Seattle tomorrow sometime."

Riding Princess back to the Lozier place had given Joanna time to mull over what she had read earlier in the *Denver Post* article. She wanted to talk to Beaumont about it, but her office at the Justice Center was the wrong place to broach the subject. She glanced at her watch.

"It's after one now," she said. "I'll probably have to spend the afternoon on my knees, begging the governor of Arizona to work with the governor of Sonora to get Jack Brampton's body shipped back to the States. To do that, I'll need patience, strength, and food. How about grabbing some lunch?"

"Fine," Beaumont said. "As long as you let the state of Washington buy."

Feeling a little underhanded, Joanna stopped at Chico's in Don Luis. Once inside, she ordered tacos for both of them. Her choice of food was actually a test, and Joanna liked the man better for contentedly munching his way through a plate loaded with Chico's luncheon special.

"Tell me about your wife," Joanna said quietly as Beau mopped up the last few crumbs of shredded beef and cheese that lingered on his plate.

When he raised his eyes to look at her, J.P. Beaumont's gaze was suddenly wary. "Which one?" he asked, but it was only a defense mechanism. They both knew Joanna was asking about Anne Corley.

"The second one," Joanna said.

"What do you want to know?"

"I've read the *Denver Post* article," she told him. "Frank downloaded it from the Internet."

"Damn his computer anyway!" Beau muttered. "Why the hell couldn't he mind his own business? You, too, for that matter?"

"It *is* my business," Joanna said. "You asked me about her, remember?"

His expression softened a little. "Well, yes. I suppose I did. I just haven't had time . . ."

"As I was reading through the article," Joanna continued, "something kept bothering me."

"What's that?" She heard the tightly controlled anger beneath his question.

"How many cases were there?" she asked. "Besides the two mentioned in the article and the three victims in Seattle, the article hinted there were others. Were there?"

Beau paused before he answered. Finally he nodded. "Several," he said. "It really doesn't matter how many. Ralph Ames and I worked with the various jurisdictions and cleared the ones we knew about—the ones Anne had kept a record of. There was no need to make a big deal of it."

"The article implied that you did it quietly because you were worried about a flurry of wrongful-death suits."

"That's not true," Beau replied shortly. "Anne was dead, for God's sake. Just as dead as Jack Brampton back there in the riverbed. Ralph and I did it that way so Anne's name wouldn't be dragged through the mud any worse than it already had been."

"Anne's name?" Joanna asked. "Or yours?"

Beaumont's face fell. Finally, he nodded bleakly. "That, too," he admitted.

"My father used to be sheriff here," Joanna said. "Did you know that?"

"I saw the picture and the name in the display case out in the lobby. I assumed the two of you might be related."

"Dad always maintained that Anne Rowland got away with murder. He said that by claiming she was crazy and locking her up in a mental institution, Anne's mother, Anita Rowland, caused a miscarriage of justice."

"No," Beau said quietly after a moment. "You're wrong there. That's not where justice miscarried. What Anne's father had done to her big sister—what Anne had been forced to witness as a little girl—drove her over the edge. By the time she killed her father— which she readily admitted—she really was crazy. Locking her up was the right thing to do, but they never should have let her loose. If the legal definition of insanity is an inability to tell right from wrong, Anne never was cured. She was able to see how other people's actions might be wrong, but never her own."

"How did she get out then?" Joanna asked. "Why was she released?"

"Because she conned Milton Corley the same way she conned me."

"The article hinted she might have had something to do with her husband's death as well."

"Yes," Beau said softly. "I'm sure she did. Milton Corley was dying of cancer, but she helped him along. She told me so herself that last day, the day she tried to kill me, too."

The man's anguish was so visible, Joanna felt ashamed of herself for prying. "I can see this is terribly hurtful for you," she said. "I'm sorry I brought it up."

"No," he replied. "Don't be. It's okay. If I hadn't wanted to talk to someone about it, I wouldn't have mentioned her to you that first day. It's just that sometimes I feel as though Anne never existed at all, as though she's a figment of my imagination. I knew her for such a short time, you see, and . . ." He shook his head and didn't continue.

Joanna slid across the cigarette-marred bench seat. "Come on," she said gently. "We'd better go."

WHEN WE GOT BACK TO THE JUSTICE CENTER, I went straight to the conference room. I was glad no one else was there. I needed some time alone. I sat down in front of the stack of phone logs and put on my reading glasses, but I made no effort to read. The conversation about Anne had rocked me. I was filled with the same kind of apprehension I had felt that May morning as I had driven to Snoqualmie Falls, and in countless dreams since—that there was more to learn about the woman who called herself Anne Corley—more than I would ever want to know.

Finally, because I had to do something to keep from losing it, I picked up the first of the telephone logs.

In terms of excitement, examining telephone logs is right up there with watching paint dry. Or maybe playing with Tinkertoys.

When I was a kid being raised by a single mother in Seattle's Ballard neighborhood, we were poor as church mice. One year for Christmas my mother came home from the local Toys for Tots drive with a Tinkertoy set. That's what I got for Christmas that year—Tinkertoys and a plaid flannel shirt Mother made for me. I remember hating to wear the shirt to school because other kids knew it was homemade.

But the Tinkertoys were a hit. I loved putting the round sticks into those little round knobs with the holes and making them jut out at all different angles. Telephone logs are a lot like that. The numbers are the little round knobs with holes in them. The calls that travel back and forth between them are the sticks.

The first knob was the pay phone that had been used to make the three separate calls to Winnetka, Illinois, on the day Deidre Canfield disappeared. But Frank Montoya is nothing if not thorough. Based on Harve Dowd's observation that Jack Brampton had used the phones on numerous occasions, Frank had collected phone logs for both of the post-office pay phones over a period of several months—for as long as Jack Brampton had been in the area. Scanning through those, I found two more calls had been placed to Winnetka, Illinois—both of those to the offices of Maddern, Maddern, and Peek.

The next set of knobs were the two phone numbers in Illinois. Because of the volume of calls, I started with the log for the residence number first. The logs were arranged in order of the most recent calls first. I worked my way down list after list after list until I could barely see straight. Until I felt myself starting to doze in the chair. And then I saw it. The words "Olympia, Washington," leaped off the page and brought me bolt upright and wide awake.

The call had been placed two months earlier at ten o'clock in the morning and had lasted for forty minutes. Excited now, I scanned faster. Three weeks before that was another call. A month before that was another. All of the calls were placed to the same 360 prefix number. Shaking my head, I extracted my wallet from my pocket and pulled out the list of telephone numbers, and there it was. That 360 number was the unlisted home number for Ross Alan Connors.

"What the hell does this mean?" I asked myself aloud.

Actually, the answer seemed pretty clear. I remembered that long empty silence when I had told Ross about the phone calls to the Illinois law firm. Now I had to face the possibility that Washington State Attorney General Ross Connors was actually involved in the plot that had resulted in the death of his own witness.

I've never been long on patience. Cooler heads might have paused for a moment or two of consideration. Not me. There was a phone on a table at the far end of the conference room. I grabbed the receiver off the hook and dialed in Ross Connors's office number, only to be told he was out to lunch. Next I tried his cell phone. As soon as he answered, I heard the tinkle of glassware and the muted hum of background conversation. Connors was in a public place—some fine dining establishment, no doubt—and most likely with friends or associates. It wasn't the best venue for me to try forcing him to tell me the truth, but I wasn't willing to wait any longer. If my boss was a crook, I wanted to know it right then so I could deliver my verbal resignation on the spot.

"Beau," he said when he recognized my voice. "I really can't talk right now—"

"Sorry to interrupt your lunch, but the suspect we were looking for, Jack Brampton, is dead," I told him. "He died this morning making a run for the Mexican border. I thought you'd want to know."

"You're absolutely right!" Ross Connors exclaimed. "I do want to know about that. Good work. Anything else?"

"Answer me one question," I growled into the phone. "Why didn't you come clean with me when I told you about Maddern, Maddern, and Peek? Louis Maddern is obviously a friend of yours."

He excused himself from the table and didn't speak again until he was outside the restaurant. "Louis really isn't a friend of mine," he said. "The Madderns are closer to Francine. She's known Madeline since college, since she was Madeline Springer, in fact. The girls were sorority sisters together. Lou can be a bit of a pill sometimes, but I suppose he's all right. Why? What's going on?"

Sorority sisters, I thought. *That might explain those widely spaced, long-winded phone calls. It could be they were nothing more than that, the totally harmless chatting of a pair of old friends, but still . . .*

"Probably nothing," I said.

"Well," Connors said. "I should get back to my guests. I'll be back in my office about three. Why don't you give me a callback then."

"Sure," I told him. "Will do."

I put down the phone. I've spent most of my adult life working as a homicide detective, and I can usually spot a liar a mile away. J.P. Beaumont's gut-instinct opinions carry about the same weight in a court of law as polygraph results do—which means they're widely regarded as totally unreliable.

The problem for me right then was that my gut instinct didn't think Ross Alan Connors was lying. True, he hadn't answered my question in front of his guests, but nowadays that was considered to be polite cell-phone behavior. Still, he had sounded glad to hear from me and delighted that Jack Brampton had been run to ground. He didn't sound to me like someone with some dark, hidden secret.

I should have been ecstatic about thinking my boss wasn't a crook after all, but I wasn't. Because if his relationship to Madeline and Louis Maddern was totally harmless, then I was getting nowhere fast.

I went back to my place at the table and returned to the telephone logs. The law firm logged hundreds of phone calls a day, which meant I was dealing with a huge stack of pages. I lit into scanning them with renewed vigor, but instead of starting from the most recent ones, I decided to go to the end of the list and begin there. Halfway through the fourth page, Olympia, Washington, began appearing again. Not one call or two, but dozens of them, some only a minute or two long, some that lasted for forty or fifty minutes.

That pattern was obvious almost immediately. None of the calls were placed earlier than 11 A.M. central time, which would have been 9 A.M. Pacific. And none were placed later than 5 P.M. Pacific. And, although they all went to the same number in Olympia, it wasn't one of the numbers I had on my Ross Connors contact list. I guessed then where this was most likely leading, but before I did anything about it, I wanted to be absolutely sure.

Twenty-one

ONCE BACK IN HER OFFICE, Joanna immediately tried reaching Governor Wallace Hickman, only to be told that he wasn't in, who was calling, and he would call her back. *Not likely,* Joanna thought. She'd had previous dealings with Wally Hickman in a case that had reflected badly on one of the governor's former partners. With that in mind, she doubted the governor would be eager to return her phone call—no matter how urgent.

The surface of Joanna's desk was still unnaturally clean. While she waited, Joanna took messages off the machine. One was from Terry Gregovich. "Sheriff Brady, sorry I didn't call in earlier. Kristin went into labor and there was too much happening. Kristin is fine. We think Shaundra is, too, but she had some breathing problems. Dr. Lee is having her airlifted to the neonatal unit at University Medical Center in Tucson. Kristin went with her in the medevac helicopter. Spike and I are going along, too, but we're driving, not flying. I'll let you know how things are as soon as I know anything."

As she erased that message, Joanna said a small prayer for the whole Gregovich family.

Next came a call from Joanna's mother. "Hi," Eleanor Lathrop Winfield said airily. "George and I are planning a little dinner get-together for Friday evening. We wanted to know if you and Butch could come."

The fact that Eleanor had finally unbent enough to call her son-in-law Butch rather than insisting on using the more formal given name of Frederick still gave Joanna pause.

"He said there wasn't anything on his calendar, but that I should check with you," Eleanor's message continued. "Grown-ups only this time, but Jenny won't mind. She'd probably rather be with Jim Bob and Eva Lou anyway. Let me know. We'll get together around six and eat at seven or so."

Joanna groaned inwardly. This would be one of her mother's command performances. Since Butch had already said they were free, Joanna probably wouldn't be able to dodge it. She made a note in her calendar, then called Eleanor back and left a message that she and Butch would indeed attend.

The next voice she heard was Marliss Shackleford's. "I under-stand you'll be speaking to a high school career assembly later this week," she said. "I wanted to put an item in my column about that. I was also wondering if you have any comment on the fact that Deputy Galloway has officially declared that he's running for sheriff."

With a decisive poke of her dialing finger, Joanna erased that message without bothering to jot down the number. She had sus-pected it was coming. Still, now that Ken Junior's candidacy was evidently official, Joanna felt a sudden flash of anger toward

Deputy Galloway. She had allowed him to continue with the department when others might have manufactured reasons to let him go. He had repaid Joanna's kindness by undermining her administration in secret. Now his opposition had gone public.

If he had made a public announcement, it was probably in that day's edition of *The Bisbee Bee*. Under normal circumstances, Kristin would have placed the paper on Joanna's desk with any pertinent articles marked with Hi-Liter. But Kristin wasn't here. Wanting to know exactly what candidate Galloway had to say, Joanna called the mail room and spoke to the clerk, Sylvia Roark.

"Kristin Gregovich is out today," Joanna said into the phone. "Would you please bring the admin mail down to my office?"

Minutes later Sylvia Roark appeared in the office doorway, wheeling a large metal cart that was filled to the brim with a mass of papers. Joanna was surprised when she saw it. She had often objected to the piles of paper Kristin Gregovich routinely brought into Joanna's office and stacked on her desk, but she had no idea that the relatively small piles that actually appeared had been culled from this kind of daunting heap.

"What should I do with it?" Sylvia asked.

Sylvia was a mousy, painfully shy young woman with bad teeth and ill-fitting clothing who came and went from the mail room on a daily basis without exchanging a word with anyone. She spent most of her work hours closeted in the mail room. When not actively dealing with mail, she hunkered over a computer and transferred cold-case information from microfiche into files that could be accessed via computer.

"I'm going to need you to sort it for me," Joanna said.

Sylvia's face turned crimson. "But I don't know *how!*" she objected.

"Then you'll have to learn," Joanna told her firmly. "Make five stacks. One for junk mail, one for magazines, newspapers, and newsletters, one for Chief Deputy Montoya, one for me, and one for don't know. I'll help you sort through the don't-know stack later."

"But doesn't Kristin do that?"

"Kristin just had a baby," Joanna said. "Until she's back on the job, we'll be counting on you."

"All right," Sylvia said, backing up and scuttling toward the hallway. "I'll take it back to the mail room and sort it there."

"No," Joanna said. "That won't do. Use Kristin's desk. And if the phone rings while you're there, you'll have to answer it."

"But . . ." Sylvia began.

"Please," Joanna insisted. "I need your help."

Nodding, Sylvia pushed the cart closer to Kristin's desk. Joanna didn't want to spook the young woman further by looking over her shoulder as she set about doing an unfamiliar task. Spying a copy of *The Bisbee Bee* near the top of the pile, Joanna grabbed it, then retreated to her office and closed the door.

✸✸✸✸✸✸✸✸

WITH THE NEW UNIDENTIFIED number in hand, I left the conference room and went looking for Frank Montoya. The desk outside Sheriff Brady's office was almost buried under stacks of paper. Seated there was a young woman I hadn't seen before. When I asked if Chief Deputy Montoya was in, she didn't answer. Instead, she ducked her head and pointed.

When I entered the chief deputy's office, Frank was on the phone patiently explaining to an out-of-town reporter that, until the dead suspect's relatives had been contacted, he was unable to release any further information.

"How's it going?" he asked, when the call finally ended.

I handed him a sheet of paper on which I had written the unidentified number, the next cog in my telephone Tinkertoy trail. "Can you find out whose phone number this is?" I asked. ·

"Sure," he said. "It may take a few minutes."

"Good," I said. "I'll be in the conference room."

⋮⋮⋮⋮⋮⋮

THE HEADLINE JOANNA SOUGHT was in the right-hand bottom corner of the *Bee*'s front page:

DEPUTY KENNETH GALLOWAY
OPPOSES SHERIFF BRADY

"Crime rates may be down in the rest of the country," Cochise County Deputy Sheriff Kenneth Galloway declared yesterday while throwing his hat into the ring in the race for sheriff. "But here, on Sheriff Joanna Brady's watch, it seems to be going in the opposite direction."

Citing increased numbers of undocumented aliens who are flooding into the county, Galloway says sheriff's deputies are often outgunned and outnumbered. "We don't have the manpower to deal with UDAs and with our regular law enforcement responsibilities as well. Sheriff Brady hasn't done enough to increase staffing to deal with this ever-growing problem."

That was as far as Joanna could bear to read. Increased staffing simply wasn't possible in the face of lower tax receipts and across-the-board budget cuts. It was easy for someone outside the process to point a finger and call her incompetent, but Ken Junior wasn't the one who had to face up to the board of supervisors and try to balance the budget. She tossed the paper aside.

She had already decided she would run again. With the next election still more than a year away, she hadn't wanted to start campaigning quite so early. But if Kenneth Galloway was already out on the stump, she would be forced to follow suit. That meant organizing a committee, raising funds, and doing appearances, all while doing her job.

For several minutes she sat brooding, wondering where she'd find the time and energy to do both. Gradually, though, her thoughts shifted. She was mentally back at Chico's and analyzing the conversation she and Beau had shared there. She recalled the man's painful admission about how Anne Rowland Corley had conned him and others; about how the real miscarriage of justice hadn't been in confining a twelve-year-old to a mental institution but in releasing her years later.

Joanna had dropped the offending copy of *The Bisbee Bee* on top of the serial-killer piece from the *Denver Post*. Now she unearthed the article and scanned the timeline sidebar that had accompanied the feature article. It showed when the child Anne Rowland had been shipped off to Phoenix and when she had been released.

With a growing sense of purpose, Joanna picked up the phone and dialed Frank Montoya's office. When he didn't answer, she tried Dispatch. "Where's the chief deputy?" she asked. "Is he still out at Palominas?"

"No," Tica Romero said. "I think he's out in the lobby talking to some reporters. Want me to interrupt?"

"Never mind," Joanna said. Her next call was to Ernie Carpenter. "When did Bill Woodruff disappear?" she asked when he answered.

"Who?"

"Bill Woodruff. You remember him. He used to be the Cochise County Coroner."

"Oh, that Bill Woodruff," Ernie said. "Sure, I remember him.

That's a long time ago. I was a brand-new detective back then. Woodruff went fishing down at Guyamas and never came back."

"That's what I remember, too, because Dad was sheriff," Joanna said. "But wasn't there something about Woodruff having a 'side dish' somewhere down across the line in Old Mexico?"

"Sounds familiar," Ernie allowed.

"Do you remember any of the details?"

"Like I said, it's been a long time," Ernie said.

"Yes," Joanna said. "It has. Thanks."

She hurried to the office door. Sylvia Roark was still pulling envelopes out of the cart. "How are you doing?" Joanna asked.

"Okay," Sylvia mumbled.

"Not on the mail," Joanna corrected. "I mean, how are you doing on the microfiche project?"

"I can't do anything on it if I'm here," Sylvia sputtered. "I thought you said I should—"

"Not right now," Joanna said quickly. "I don't mean today. I mean in general. How far have you gotten?"

"Only the mid-eighties, I guess," Sylvia said. "I'm working backward, and it takes time, you know. I can work on it only an hour or two a day, but I'm doing the best—"

Without waiting for Sylvia to finish, Joanna headed for the mail room. Tucked into a far corner sat the clumsy old microfiche machine next to its multiple-drawered file. Pulling out the one marked "1979–1981," Joanna settled herself in front of the screen and went to work.

⁂

I SAT IN THE CONFERENCE ROOM twiddling my thumbs for the next twenty minutes. Finally Frank Montoya showed up.

Wordlessly he handed me back the piece of paper on which I had scribbled the unknown telephone number. "Who's Francine Connors?" he asked.

"The Washington State Attorney General's wife," I told him. "Why?"

"I'd say the man has a problem then," Frank Montoya replied. "The cell phone in question is registered to her."

Frank exited the room, leaving me feeling as though he had poured a bucket of cold water down my back. Ross Connors had been looking for a leak in his department and among his trusted advisers. It was clear to me now that the problem had been far closer to him—in his own home! Francine Connors had been carrying on a long-distance relationship with the husband of one of her friends. In the process, she had not simply betrayed her husband, she had also helped murder Latisha Wall.

I popped my head back out of the conference room. Chief Deputy Montoya had not yet made it to his office. "Hey, Frank," I called. "One more thing."

"What's that?"

"I'm going to need a log on that one, too."

"No kidding," he replied. "I've already ordered it. I'll bring it to you as soon as I can."

While waiting, I struggled with my conscience, wondering what to do. Under the circumstances, nothing seemed clear-cut. Was my first responsibility to my boss? Did I have an obligation to call Ross Connors and tell him my as yet unproved suspicions? But if I did that, wasn't I dodging my responsibilities to Latisha Wall? Most of my adult life has been spent tracking killers. If Francine Connors had betrayed a protected witness's whereabouts, then she was as guilty of Latisha Wall's murder as the man who had poisoned her.

Francine Connors was the dishonorable wife of a man sworn

to uphold the laws of Washington State. How would Ross Connors react? Would he listen to what I had to say and do what had to be done, or would he try to save his wife? In a tiny corner of my mind, I wondered if that was why I was here. Was it possible Ross Connors already had his own suspicions about Francine's possible involvement? Had he sent me to Arizona hoping against hope that I wouldn't discover the truth about what had gone on? Was that why, when I first brought up Maddern's name, Ross had said so little?

Finally, I picked up the phone in the conference room. Pulling a battered ticket folder out of my pocket, I dialed the toll-free number for Alaska Airlines.

"When's the next flight from Tucson to Seattle?" I asked.

"There's one this afternoon at three-thirty," I was told. The conference room clock said it was already ten past two. I was a good hundred miles away from the airport and without a vehicle. "That one won't work," I said. "When's the next flight?"

"Tomorrow morning at seven."

I reserved a seat on that flight. I had finished and was putting the phone down when Joanna Brady appeared at the conference room door. She stepped inside, flipped up the OCCUPIED sign and pulled the door shut behind her. Her face was set; her eyes chips of dark green slate. Something was up.

"Did Frank tell you?" I asked.

"Tell me what?"

"He's waiting for the next set of telephone-toll logs, but it looks as though my boss's wife has been carrying on a clandestine affair with one of UPPI's big-name attorneys back East. I'm guessing that's how they learned of Latisha Wall's whereabouts. As soon as they knew, they must have sent Jack Brampton here to rub her out."

Joanna relaxed a little. "You've caught them then," she breathed, but she didn't sound nearly as pleased about it as I would have expected.

"Frank's the one who did it," I said. "I've never seen anybody who can work with the phone company the way he does."

Joanna nodded absently, as though she wasn't really paying attention. She had taken a seat at the conference table. Sitting directly across from her, I noticed a long, jagged scar on her cheek for the first time. She probably usually covered it with makeup, but now her face was pale. The scar stood out vividly against her white skin, making me wonder what had caused it.

"What's wrong?" I asked.

Joanna put a slim file folder down on the table, but she made no move to hand it to me. "You said earlier that you and Anne Rowland Corley's attorney . . ."

I wished she wouldn't keep using Anne's maiden name. I hated having Anne's name linked to her father's.

"Ralph Ames," I supplied. "The attorney's name is Ralph Ames."

"That the two of you cleared all the cases," she continued.

"That's right."

"But you didn't come here," she said. "You didn't clear any cases here."

It was a statement more than a question. My heart gave a lurch.

"As far as we knew there weren't any cases here," I said, "other than Anne's father, that is. With the whole family dead by then . . ."

"You said she kept a written record?"

"Yes, in the form of a manuscript. Why?"

"Was Bill Woodruff's name in it?" Joanna asked.

"Bill Woodruff? Not that I remember. Who's he?"

"You mean who *was* he," Joanna corrected. "Years ago he used to be the Cochise County Coroner—before he disappeared, that is. He wasn't declared officially dead until three years later, but I'm sure now that he died much earlier than that. He was also the man who ruled Patty Rowland's death an accident and Roger Rowland's a suicide."

She spun the file folder across the table to me then. "Check the dates yourself," she added. "Bill Woodruff disappeared within three weeks of Anne Rowland Corley's release from the hospital in Phoenix."

Joanna left the room, leaving me to pick up the pieces of my heart. In the file I found several pages copied from a missing persons report. From the bare bones of what was written there I learned that Bill Woodruff had gone on a fishing trip to a town in Mexico, where he was reportedly seen in several bars in the company of a young woman—a strikingly beautiful young woman—after which neither of them were ever seen again.

I'm always accusing Maxwell Cole of editorializing. Since he writes a newspaper column, I suppose he's entitled to put his opinions right there in print for all to see. But the truth is, cops editorialize, too. Couched in the supposedly nonemotional declaration of fact and allegation that passes for cop-talk and cop-write, I recognized what the long-ago investigator had obviously concluded. A few terse but nevertheless disparaging remarks about Bill Woodruff's wife, Belinda, revealed the investigator's opinion that the missing man might well have had good reason to walk away from a shrewish, carping wife—walk away and simply disappear.

Unlike that original investigator, I saw Anne Corley's troubled face leap toward me out of the telling words in the report: "strikingly beautiful." That was Anne, all right—strikingly beautiful.

And ultimately dangerous. Bill Woodruff must have thought he was about to get lucky and have himself a harmless little fling. I'm sure he had no idea he was dealing with the now-grown and incredibly vengeful little girl his official reports had once betrayed.

That much Anne had told me herself. Her written manuscript had alleged that her sister Patty hadn't really died as a result of an accidental fall. She had been tortured and abused and finally savagely beaten. And both of Anne's parents, along with her father's cronies—the police chief and the local coroner—had conspired together to cover it up, just as Anita Rowland and Woodruff had concealed Anne's role in her father's supposed suicide.

It's hard to be angry with someone who's been dead for years. But I was. A riot of fury boiled up in my heart because Anne had done it to me again, damn her! She had left me a manuscript that, according to her, told me the whole truth. Clearly she had left out a few things—a few *important* things—and had suckered me one more time. And that brought me back to the central question I have about Anne Corley: Did she ever really love me, or did I just make it all up? Because, if she had loved me, wouldn't she have told me *everything*?

There was a discreet tap on the door. I looked up from staring at a paper I was no longer seeing as Joanna Brady came into the room, once again closing the door behind her.

"I'm sorry," she said. "I assumed you knew, but I can see from your face—you had no idea."

I shook my head. "It happened within weeks of her being released from the hospital, just prior to her marriage to Milton Corley," I said. "How do you suppose she did it? How did she pull it off?"

Joanna shrugged. "I have no idea," she said kindly. "But

remember, we could both be wrong. We don't have any actual proof. It might have been someone else."

I wasn't prepared to give either Anne or me that kind of break. "No," I said. "I don't think so."

"Then you're right," Joanna said finally. "The real miscarriage of justice happened when they released her. And you were right about something else, too," she added. "Look."

She'd been holding something in her hand, but I had been too preoccupied to notice. Now she passed me a new set of phone logs. Putting on my reading glasses, I scanned through the listings. They included literally dozens of phone calls from Francine Connors's cell phone to Winnetka, Illinois. Some I recognized as going to Louis Maddern's office number, while a few of the others went to his residence. Most of them, however, had been placed to a third number I didn't recognize.

"Maddern's cell phone?" I asked.

Joanna nodded. "You've got it," she said. "Frank just checked."

The last call had been placed on Sunday night. Looking at the time, I realized it had been placed within minutes of my call to the Connors's home. That one, lasting over an hour, originated from Francine's cell phone. After that there was nothing.

I closed my eyes and tried to remember exactly what had gone on during that critical call. I was sure Francine Connors had answered the phone and had asked who was calling. Had I told her who I was? I couldn't remember, but I wondered now if she had somehow stayed on the line and listened in on my conversation with her husband. I tried to recall exactly what Ross had said. The only thing that stuck in my head was that he had planned on calling in the FBI to track down the leak.

Bearing all that in mind, there could be no question about

what I had to do next. "May I use this phone?" I asked, although I had already used it once without having asked for Sheriff Brady's permission.

"Sure," Joanna said. "Go right ahead. Do you want me to leave?"

"No," I told her. "That's not necessary."

I searched through my wallet until I once again located the list of Ross Connors's telephone numbers. By then I should have known them by heart, but I didn't. I dialed his office number first.

"Attorney General Connors's Office," a crisp voice replied. "May I help you?"

"Mr. Connors, please."

"I'm sorry, he's not in. May I take a message?"

"No," I said. "That's all right."

I dialed his cell-phone number. After ringing several times, the call went to voice mail. Hanging up, I tried the home number last. A woman answered. I wasn't sure, but the voice didn't sound like Francine Connors's voice.

"Ross, please," I said easily, hoping to pass for an acquaintance if not a friend.

"He's not here," the woman said, her voice quavering slightly. "He's at the hospital. I'm Christine Connors, Ross's mother. Is there a message?"

"Hospital?" I asked. "Has something happened to him? Is he ill?"

"Oh," she said. "You must not have heard then. It's not Ross. He's fine. At least he's okay. No, it's Francine."

"What about her?"

"She's dead. She and Ross went to lunch together. He had a wonderful time, and he thought Francine did, too. But then, when she came home, and, without even changing her clothes, she went out in the backyard and just . . . just . . ." Christine Connors stifled a tiny sob. "The gardener was working out front. He heard the shot and came running. He called an ambulance and they took her to the hospital, but they couldn't save her. I can't imagine why she'd do such a thing. I just can't."

I was stunned. I remembered the sound of tinkling glassware in the background—the sounds of fine dining at a luncheon meeting. I hadn't thought that Francine might be there, but she must have been. And from that and the call on Sunday night, she must have known the jig was up.

"I'm sorry," I murmured into the phone. "I'm so very sorry."

"Well, if you'll leave your name, I'll be sure to let Ross know you called."

"No," I told her. "Don't bother. I'll be in touch."

When I put down the phone, Joanna Brady was staring at my face. "She's gone, isn't she?" she said.

IN NO MORE THAN TEN MINUTES, J.P. Beaumont looked as though he had aged ten years.

"Is there anything I can do?" Joanna asked.

Beaumont shook his head. "I don't think so," he said. "No, wait. There is something. I'm going to need a ride. First I have to go to the hotel and check out. Then I need a lift as far as Tucson. My plane's first thing tomorrow morning."

"Come on," Joanna said. "We'll take my Civvie."

Beaumont followed her through the building and out the office door without exchanging a word with anyone. Only when he was fastening the seat belt in Joanna's Crown Victoria did he have second thoughts.

"That was rude," he said. "I should go back in and tell Frank how much I appreciated his help."

"Don't worry," Joanna told him. "I'll pass it along."

"He's a good man to have on your team."

"Yes," she agreed. "I know."

When they reached the entrance to the Justice Center, Joanna sat there, hesitating, even though there was no traffic coming in either direction. Finally, making up her mind, she turned left.

"Wait a minute," Beau objected. "Where are we going? I thought the Copper Queen was the other direction. I need to check out."

"We're taking a detour," Joanna told him. "There's something I want to show you."

After heading east for a mile or so, she turned right onto a road labeled WARREN CUTOFF.

"What's Warren?" he asked.

"It's another Bisbee neighborhood," she explained. "Until the 1950s, when Bisbee was incorporated, Warren and all these other places were separate towns."

"Oh," he said and lapsed into silence.

Coming into town, Joanna turned right at the first intersection and then gunned the Civvie up and over two short but relatively steep hills. At the top of the second one the road curved, first to the left and then back to the right. Beyond the curve, Joanna pulled over onto the shoulder, stopped the car, and got out. Beaumont followed.

"What's this?" he asked.

Joanna pointed to a massive brown stucco mansion lurking behind a curtain of twenty-foot-high oleander. The house stood at the top end of what had once been the lush green of Vista Park. Now the park was little more than a desert wasteland—a long, desolate expanse of dry grass and boulders with houses facing it on either side.

"I thought you'd want to see this," Joanna told him quietly. "This was Roger Rowland's house. It's where Anne Rowland Corley grew up."

She saw him swallow hard. Tears welled in his eyes. A sob caught in his throat. There was nothing for her to do but try to comfort the man. As she wrapped her arms around him, hot tears dribbled down his cheeks and ran through her hair. His arms closed around her as well. As they stood there holding each other, it seemed to Joanna like the most natural thing in the world.

Twenty-two

I DON'T KNOW WHAT came over me. It was more than a momentary lapse. I remember crying like that when my mother died of breast cancer, and again when my first wife, Karen, succumbed to the disease, too. But Anne Corley had been gone for a very long time.

I should have thought that by now the hurt of losing her would have been scabbed over and covered with a protective layer of scar tissue. Still, seeing the house she grew up in—a mansion of a place that must have seemed more like a prison than a home—hit me hard. It sat there obscured behind a thick, decades-old oleander hedge. That planted green barrier had provided far more than simple privacy for the troubled family that had once lived behind it. Evil, murder, and incipient insanity had resided there along with the woman I loved.

It was only when I started to pull myself together that I realized I was standing in broad daylight with both arms wrapped tightly around Sheriff Joanna Brady. And with her arms wrapped around me, too. It was a shock when I noticed I didn't want to move away. Pulsing electricity seemed to arc between us.

I started to push her away, but she wouldn't let go. Then a call came in on her car radio.

"Sheriff Brady?" the dispatcher asked.

With a sigh, Joanna loosened her grip on me and returned to her Crown Vic. "What's up?" she asked.

"I have Governor Hickman on the phone. Do you want me to patch him through?"

While Joanna talked to the governor, trying to convince him that he needed to negotiate with Mexican authorities for the return of Jack Brampton's body, I stood beside the car and tried to get a grip. Several cars rolled past, slowing when they saw the Crown Vic with its flashing yellow hazard lights pulled over on the narrow shoulder. To a person, every driver eyed me curiously, probably trying to figure out what kind of miscreant I was. Fortunately, they couldn't tell by looking.

I remembered all too clearly that it was only due to some Bis-beeite's nosiness that we had come to focus our investigative efforts on Jack Brampton and his suspicious pay-phone calls. If making a simple phone call had been enough to raise an alarm, what would people think if they had observed my unexpected and entirely unauthorized embrace with the sheriff of Cochise County? I also wondered how long it would take for that juicy tidbit to become public knowledge.

It probably already has, I thought grimly. I didn't know Marliss Shackleford well, but I guessed that would be just the kind of item she'd love to lay her hands on. Even so, I still wanted to hold Joanna Brady again and feel her surprisingly strong body against mine and her curved cheek grazing my shoulder.

When she finally ended her radio transmission, I climbed back into the car. "What'd the governor have to say?" I tried to sound nonchalant, but I was embarrassed and ill at ease. She'd been nothing but kind—offering me comfort and a shoulder to cry on. Obviously, I had taken it the wrong way—read something into it that hadn't been intended.

"He'll see what he can do," Joanna said without meeting my gaze.

"In other words, you're supposed to take an old cold tater and wait."

"I guess." Joanna sighed. "We'd better go," she said.

"You've got that right."

She shot me a defiant look then. Her green eyes pierced right through me. "I'm not sorry," she said.

I was astonished. What did *that* mean? That the flash of desire I had felt flowed in both directions? That right there in broad daylight, Joanna Brady had wanted me as much as I wanted her? *Unbelievable!*

"I'm not, either," I agreed, and that was the truth. Sorry didn't apply. Confused? Yes. Concerned? You bet; that, too.

Joanna was driving again, faster than she should have. I watched the speedometer spike upward—ten miles over the posted limit. Ten, then fifteen, then twenty.

"Maybe we should slow down," I suggested quietly. She jammed on the brakes hard enough that the seat belt dug into my collarbone. The truth is, I wasn't talking about the car—and she knew it.

It's probably a function of age rather than wisdom, but I've finally outgrown my need to play chicken the way we used to down along the railroad tracks in Golden Gardens when I was a kid. My need for Joanna Brady was a speeding locomotive. It was time to get the hell off the tracks or pay the price.

Another call came in on the radio. "Sheriff Brady?" I recognized Frank Montoya's voice.

"Yes."

"Serenity Granger is here at the department," Montoya said. "I told her Jack Brampton is dead. I also told her that, although we can't be absolutely sure at this point, we're fairly certain he's the one who murdered her mother. Serenity wants to know if it's possible for her to have access to Castle Rock Gallery. While she's here waiting for Doc Winfield to release Deidre Canfield's body, she wants to clear up some of her mother's affairs. Latisha Wall's paintings were on consignment. Serenity wants them crated up in time to ship home with Cornelia Lester. She's worried about a liability problem if something were to happen to them.

"I told her that the house out in Huachuca Terraces is clearly a crime scene and that's still off limits, but I agreed to check with you about the gallery."

"What do you think, Frank?" Joanna asked.

"Those paintings are probably worth some serious money," he returned. "Sentimental value to the family would make them priceless. If we force Serenity to leave them hanging in the gallery and something does happen to them—if they end up being damaged in a fire or stolen—we could end up being liable, too."

"You don't think releasing them will have an adverse effect on the rest of the investigation?"

"I can't see that it will."

"All right, then," Joanna said, making up her mind. "Tell Ms. Granger to go ahead. Someone will have to go to the gallery to let her in, but we should probably have someone on-site while she's doing the packing just in case something turns up."

"Okay," Montoya said. "I'll handle it." He paused for a moment. "By the way," he added, "I heard about Ken Junior. Don't worry."

"Thanks," Joanna said. "I'll try not to."

I had heard the name Ken Junior mentioned in passing several times. I knew he was a member of Joanna's department, and I wondered if something had happened to him.

"Ken Junior is one of your deputies, isn't he?" I asked, trying to steer the conversation into less dangerous territory. "Did he get hurt or something?"

"He's running for office against me," Joanna replied. "That reporter you met, Marliss Shackleford, is a great supporter of his."

I may have had to deal with Maxwell Cole on occasion, but not while I was running for public office. "Not good," I said.

Joanna put down the microphone and glanced at me. "I suppose you think returning the paintings is a bad idea."

"No," I replied. "Not at all. Returning them to their lawful owners is the right thing to do—the sooner the better."

Another radio call came in. I was grateful for the continuing interference. It was giving me time to pull myself together.

"Sheriff Brady," the dispatcher said. "Is Mr. Beaumont with you?"

"Yes. Why?"

"The tow-truck driver is on the line. He was on his way to pick up Mr. Beaumont's vehicle, but the car-rental agency needs a form signed before the driver can pick it up and take it back to Tucson. He wants to know where Saguaro should fax the form."

Joanna had already offered me a lift to Tucson, but if I accepted it, God only knew what would happen. My mother struggled to raise me to be a "good boy," and good boys don't do the kinds of things I wanted to do with some other man's wife.

When Joanna handed me the microphone, I took the easy way out of what could have been a bad situation for all concerned.

"Have Saguaro fax me the form at the Copper Queen Hotel," I said. "And tell the driver that when he comes to pick up the form, he'll need to pick me up as well. He can give me a ride back to Tucson right along with the car."

At that very moment, Joanna's Crown Vic was pulling into the loading zone in front of the hotel.

"You're turning down my offer of a ride?" she asked.

I nodded. "I think it's for the best. Don't you?"

She bit her lower lip. I wanted that lip about then, wanted to feel it against mine and taste the remains of the lipstick she had bitten off. But her lips were forbidden fruit for me, just as mine were for her.

"Does that mean we're supposed to pretend that what happened back there didn't happen?" she demanded huskily. "Or maybe I'm wrong. Maybe I made the whole thing up, and it didn't happen after all."

"No," I told her evenly. "It happened, all right—it happened to both of us."

"What does it *mean*, then?" She seemed close to tears.

I wavered between what I wanted to do and what I needed to do. Between right and wrong. Good and evil. Between my mother's long-ago admonitions and the burning present. I tried to ignore the craving I felt. And the need.

"We're comrades-in-arms," I said at last. "We've been through a tough three-day war. Being on a battlefield together makes for strong connections. They're not meaningless, but they don't necessarily last forever. What happened to us back there isn't worth risking the family you already have or hurting the people you love. The war is over, Joanna. This old soldier needs to go home now, and so do you."

I reached out, clasped her hand—the one without the wedding ring—and shook it. "You're doing a fine job, Sheriff Brady. Best of luck to you. Keep up the good work."

"Thank you," she said softly. "I guess."

I opened the car door and stepped out into brilliant sunlight. I stood on the curb and watched her drive away. She didn't wave, and she didn't look back.

※※※※※※※

TWO HOURS LATER A STILL-SHAKEN Joanna Brady ventured into Castle Rock Gallery, which was bustling with activity. Detective Carbajal had been dispatched to unlock the door and then stand by and observe the proceedings. Bobo Jenkins, however, had drafted Jaime into the work crew. Armed with hammer and nails, the two men worked together, busily fashioning sturdy crates from sheets of plywood and lengths of two-by-fours.

One by one, Serenity Granger and Cornelia Lester removed the framed paintings from the walls, brought them to the construction zone, wrapped the artwork in bubble wrap, and slipped them into newly made crates. As they worked, Cornelia related stories about the people pictured on the various canvases—the absent loved ones whose lives Latisha Wall had so carefully recreated with brush and pigment. Working like that while listening to Cornelia's stories was a balm that seemed to help all three hurt and bereaved people begin to come to grips with their losses.

Banished to the sidelines and nursing her own hurt, Joanna felt let down and useless. She was relieved when Ernie Carpenter came looking for her.

"Hey, boss," he said, peering at her face. "Are you all right?"

"I'm fine," she said impatiently. "What's up?"

"We finally finished scouring the San Pedro for money."

"How much did you come up with?" she asked.

"Six thousand and some," he answered.

"There was a lot more than that in Brampton's backpack," she told him. "Do you think that's his pay for making the hit?"

"Seems likely," Carpenter answered. "The people Jaime and I have talked to who knew Jack Brampton said he was usually dead broke. If it hadn't been for Dee Canfield putting a roof over his head, the man would have been living on the streets."

Joanna was struck by a sudden inspiration. "Let's say he got paid twenty thousand," she said. "If I'm the guy paying for a hit, I sure as hell wouldn't want to cough up that kind of money until I was sure the job was done. Latisha Wall died on Wednesday night. Today is only Monday. So who sent Brampton the blood money, and how did it get here?"

"FedEx?" Ernie suggested. "Either that, or UPS."

But Joanna's mind was on that pair of pay phones that stood outside the post office—the phones Jack Brampton had used often enough to arouse Harve Dowd's suspicion.

"The post office has next-day delivery," she told Ernie. "Do you have any friends who work there?"

"Moe Maxwell retired."

"Ask him anyway. He may still be able to ask around and find out whether or not any packages came in for Warren Gibson on Friday or Saturday. Tell him it's an informal inquiry only. If it looks like a yes, we'll get a warrant."

'An hour later, when Joanna drove into the yard at High Lonesome Ranch, Tigger came racing out to meet her. She felt a tug at her heart to see that Sadie wasn't with him, but it was reassuring that the younger dog was picking up the pieces and going on. That was what she had to do, too. She had lost something—missed something—even if she wasn't sure what.

Slanting late-afternoon sunlight glinted off the house's tin roof. The surrounding trees were only now beginning to change color. Fall was definitely on its way.

Opening the back door, she welcomed the steamy warmth of a kitchen replete with the comforting aroma of baking meat loaf. She found Butch and Jenny in the combination living and dining room. Jenny was sprawled on the floor talking on the telephone while Butch worked at his computer on the dining-room table. Once inside, Tigger raced to Jenny and curled up next to her, letting her use his shoulders as a shaggy, pit-bull/golden retriever pillow.

Joanna started for the bedroom but paused long enough to give Butch a peck on the cheek as she went by.

"How'd it go today?" he asked, not taking his eyes off the screen or his fingers off the keyboard.

"Okay," she said. "I think we got him."

"Great," he said. "Not bad for a girl."

She gave his shoulder a friendly whack and then continued into the bedroom, where she removed her uniform and locked away her weapons. When she returned to the living room, Jenny was still on the phone, but Butch's computer was closed. She saw him moving back and forth in the kitchen, carrying dishes from cupboard to table.

He brightened when she came into the kitchen. "So tell me

about your day," he said, handing her three glasses. "I've already heard the condensed version. Now give me the real story."

Half an hour later, Jenny finally put down the phone and came into the kitchen, "Oh, Mom," she said, "I almost forgot. Somebody called while I was talking to Cassie. He wanted me to give you a message."

"Who was it?"

"I can't remember his name now. Ron something. He said to tell you that you were right and there was something—I don't remember that word, either—in the sugar."

"Ron Workman," Joanna said. "And sodium azide."

"Right," Jenny said. "It seemed like a funny kind of message. What does it mean?"

"That we got lucky," her mother replied. "Very, very lucky."

LATE THAT NIGHT—LONG AFTER DINNER was over and the dishes had been washed and put away—Joanna lay in bed. She had felt a sudden magnetic attraction to J.P. Beaumont. But lying next to the soothing warmth of Butch Dixon's sleeping body, Joanna finally began to see that instant of connection for what it was and what it was not.

Butch's presence in her life had blessed Joanna with a kind of calm stability she had never known before, not even with Andy. He offered her the loving creature comforts of warm meals and clean and folded laundry. He listened to her troubles and talked her through moments of self-doubt. He loved Jenny. He loved High Lonesome Ranch. And he loved Joanna.

With a cringe that made her blush in the dark, Joanna thought about that time, a few months earlier, when she had suspected

Butch of having renewed an affair with an old flame. Joanna had been quick to jump in with all kinds of wild accusations. Now she herself had come close to starting something with someone who, just a few days earlier, had been a complete stranger. In both instances, nothing untoward had happened, but in Joanna's case, it had been close—far too close. If J.P. Beaumont had been any less of a man than what he was . . .

It was time, Joanna decided, to pay attention to the essentials in life—to the things that were worth keeping; worth treasuring. Things people like Bobo Jenkins and Latisha Wall would never have a chance to share.

In the dark, she snuggled closer to Butch. "You awake?" she asked.

"I am now," he grumbled sleepily. He reached over and pulled her close. "I don't understand it. How can you get by on so little sleep?"

"I've always been that way," she said. "It drove my mother crazy."

"I can see why," he said. "Now what's happening?"

"Remember what you wanted to do in the family room?"

"I wanted to do it in the family room?" he asked, rolling over onto his back. "When?"

"Not that." Joanna giggled. "I'm talking about the train track."

"Oh, right, the train track. You said you didn't want it."

"Well, I've been thinking," she said, "and I've changed my mind. If it's not too late, we should put the track in after all."

"I thought you said it was weird and you wanted normal."

Joanna sighed. "We're not normal. Why should our family room be any different?"

"Well, then. If you're sure you don't mind."

"I told you. It's fine."

"Great, then, we'll have trains. Oh, by the way. I forgot to tell you. We agreed on Gayle."

"Gayle what?"

"Gayle Dixon. My pen name. Drew and I finally worked it out today. She's sending me an agency contract for me to sign and rewrite suggestions. When those are done she wants me to send the manuscript back under the nom de plume of Gayle Dixon."

"I still think it's strange that you have to change your name."

"So do I," Butch agreed. "But you'll still love me, won't you? Even if I turn into someone named Gayle?"

"As long as Gayle keeps the same meat-loaf recipe."

"The name may change," Butch said, chuckling. "but the food is bound to remain the same. Now, is that the only reason you woke me up—to talk about model trains?"

"Maybe not the only one," she told him.

"Show me," he said.

THE TOW-TRUCK DRIVER was kind enough to drop me off at some anonymously forgettable, cheapo motel close to the airport. The next morning I took the motel shuttle to catch my plane. Surprisingly enough, the early-morning flight to Seattle was almost deserted. The Husky fans had evidently all gone home to Seattle, and I had no idea who had won or lost the game.

I had a whole row of three seats to myself. With no one crowding me and no one to talk to, I had plenty of time to think. With some effort, I managed to keep my mind off both Anne Corley and Joanna Brady.

I had yet to speak to Ross Alan Connors, but that was my first priority. As soon as I landed at Sea-Tac, I rented a car and drove straight down to Olympia. On the way, I called the office and spoke to Barbara Galvin, Unit B's office manager.

"Where are you?" she asked. "Still in Arizona?"

"I'm on my way home," I told her.

"Did you hear about what happened to Ross Connors's wife?" Barbara asked.

"Yes, I did. In fact, that's why I'm calling," I told her. "I need his address. I want to send flowers."

"You don't have to do that," she said. "The whole squad is chipping in and sending a single arrangement."

"I want to do my own," I said.

"Well, okay, then," she agreed. "Suit yourself."

She gave me an address on Water Street. Once I arrived in Olympia, I wasn't surprised to find the attorney general's home was within easy walking distance of the capitol complex. The house wasn't quite as imposing as the one Anne Corley had been raised in, but it came close. Built of red brick and boasting a genuine slate roof, it was a showy kind of place, with a three-story round turret on one side. The expansive yard was surrounded by an ornamental iron fence with a bronze fleur-de-lis topping every post.

Up and down the narrow street, late-model upscale cars—Mercedeses, Jaguars, and an understated Lexus or two—were parked on either side. When I rang the bell, a uniformed maid answered the door. I gave her my card. Minutes later, I was led inside. Hearing voices in the living room, I was a bit miffed at being directed away from the piss-elegant crowd that had come to mingle and comfort Ross Connors in his hour of need. Underlings like J.P. Beaumont, however, were shunted away from other, more important, guests. As I allowed myself to be unceremoniously herded up the staircase that wound through the turret, it irked me that Ross was keeping me out of sight and out of mind.

Imagine my surprise, then, when I reached the small single room at the top of the stairs and discovered that Ross Alan Connors was already there before me, all alone and seated at a battered, old-fashioned teacher's desk. Windows in the room offered a panoramic view of the water hinted at in the street name. But if you're used to looking out the window at the majesty of Elliott Bay, the puddle that is Capitol Lake doesn't count for much.

But just then Ross Connors wasn't enjoying the view such as it was. In fact, I doubt he even saw it. When he rose to meet me, I was shocked by the haggard look on his face and the dark hollows under his eyes. His normally florid complexion was sallow and gray. There was no trace of the man I knew as a high-flying lawyer and glad-handing politician. Ross Connors was a doubly defeated man, bereft and betrayed. Unfortunately, I knew exactly how he felt because I had been there, too. My heart ached with sympathy.

"Hello, J.P.," he said somberly. "I didn't know you were back."

"I came straight here. I'm so sorry about Francine. . . ."

"I know, I know," he said impatiently, brushing aside my condolences. "Sit down." He motioned me toward a sagging, butt-sprung leather recliner that could have been a brother to the re-covered wreck in my own living room. "Who told you about it?"

"Your mother. I talked to her yesterday afternoon."

"Oh," he said.

Not knowing what to say next, I waited for him to continue.

"She left me a note," Ross Connors said finally, his voice brittle with emotion. "She said she listened in the other night when you and I spoke on the phone. She was sure that once the FBI got involved, the whole thing would come out. She said she couldn't face it."

He paused. I knew what *it* was—knew what he couldn't bring himself to say, so I helped him along.

"I know she was involved with Louis Maddern," I said quietly. "It's all in the telephone logs. I can show you. . . ."

"That no-good son of a bitch!" Connors muttered fiercely. "It must have been going on behind my back for years, and I never figured it out. How could I have been so stupid that I never had a clue? But somebody else must have figured it out—someone who works for UPPI. Maddern, Maddern, and Peek didn't get that big piece of UPPI's business by random selection, J.P. They figured out that that worm Louis Maddern might be able to deliver something more valuable than legal representation and, God help me, he did!"

"Latisha's whereabouts," I supplied.

Ross nodded miserably. "I didn't even realize I had said anything. It must have slipped out. Francine and I didn't have any secrets from each other, at least . . ." We both saw heartbreak where that sentence was going. He broke off and didn't finish.

Half a minute later, he continued. "One way or another, Louis must have weaseled the information out of Francine. Once she put it all together and realized it was her fault that Latisha Wall was dead, Francine couldn't live with herself. She was Louis Maddern's lover. She was also his partner in crime, but until Sunday night, I don't think she had any idea. Then yesterday, at lunch . . ."

Again he broke off and couldn't go on.

"Ross, I'm so sorry. I didn't know she was with you at lunch."

"It's okay," he said. "It's not your fault. You didn't say anything out of line. Francine knew me very well. She must have read it in my face."

He fell silent. We sat without speaking for more than a minute. "It's such a shock. I'm still ragged around the edges," he said at last. "All those nice people downstairs. They want to tell me how sorry they are—how much they care—but it hurts too much to hear it. That's why I'm hiding out up here, where no one can find me."

I wondered if changing the subject would help. "There's something I don't understand," I said. "Why did UPPI need Latisha Wall dead? What made her so important? You told me yourself there's enough evidence available in the form of depositions that even if she weren't here to testify at the trial . . ."

It turned out I was right. Bracing anger flooded across Ross Connors's face.

"Latisha Wall was supposedly under our protection!" he growled, sounding more like himself again. "My protection! She was a single protected witness in a single case. Right now UPPI has lots of other cases hanging fire, and there are lots of other witnesses who are expected to testify against them. How many of them will still be tough enough to stand up and speak out if they know they're in mortal danger? How many other employees or ex-employees will be willing to put their lives on the line and come forward to testify?"

The man's anger and anguish were both palpable. "I'm sorry," I said.

He nodded. "So am I."

I had been told no official report was expected on my trip to Arizona. And Ross Connors had plenty of reasons to bury what I had found out right along with his wife.

"Should I write a formal report?" I asked.

He took a deep breath, straightened his shoulders, and looked me straight in the eye. "You bet," he said. "Type it up and send it through the regular chain of command. If it gets leaked, too bad. My first instinct was to cover up this whole thing, but I'm not going to. Francine is dead, by God! I want the world to know who did this to her and why."

And in that moment, I realized I was glad Ross Alan Connors was my boss and proud that my name had been added to the roster of his Special Homicide Investigation Team. He may have been a politician, but he was also a good man who wasn't afraid to make a tough call when the situation required it.

"There's something else," I said.

"What's that?"

"What do you know about sodium azide?"

He frowned. "Never heard of it. Why, should I have?"

"Yes," I told him. "And here's why."

AS I DROVE TO SEATTLE FROM OLYMPIA, I called Harry I. Ball on my now-working cell phone. He told me to take the rest of the day off.

"That's big of you," I said. "Especially considering I've been working my butt off almost round the clock for the last three days."

"Don't start," he warned. "I don't wanna hear it."

I returned the rental car to the airport and climbed into the Belltown Terrace limo I had summoned to drag me home. By 2 P.M. I was in my recliner, thinking.

I had told Ross Connors about the dangers of sodium azide, but what about the dangers of love? Latisha Wall and Bobo Jenkins had fallen in love, and he had unwittingly poisoned her. After years of playing the field, Dee Canfield had gone for a guy she thought was finally the love of her life, and Warren Gibson had snuffed her out of existence. Francine Connors had betrayed her husband for a fling with Louis Maddern, and now a widowed Ross Connors was imprisoned in his turret, nursing a broken heart.

And then there was me. J.P. Beaumont and Anne Corley. J.P. Beaumont and Joanna Brady. Anne had been a case of fatal attraction, and Joanna might have been.

Without realizing it, I drifted off, and all too soon the dream came again.

At first it was the same as it's always been, and I tried to fight it off. Anne Corley was striding toward me across a grassy hill in Mount Pleasant Cemetery. But then I noticed something different about her. This particular Anne Corley had bright red hair and amazingly green eyes.

Once I realized that, I didn't bother trying to wake myself up. For the first time ever, I just lay back and enjoyed it.

Author's Note

IDEAS FOR BOOKS come from strange places. *Partner in Crime* had its origins in reading an article on the dangers of sodium azide I discovered in my University of Arizona alumni magazine. From that article and from subsequent research, I've come to believe that the widespread availability of this hazardous and so-far uncontrolled substance poses a real threat to the safety of far too many people.

When used as intended to inflate air bags in automobiles, the substance is transformed into a harmless nitrogen-based gas. Originally, the idea was that the unused air bags and canisters would be removed from wrecked vehicles and recycled, but in the real world, that's not happening. No one wants to risk his own life or the lives of his family members to somebody else's cast-off air bag. As a result, tons of unused and unsecured containers of this deadly, poisonous, and easily water-soluble compound are readily available. They lie, unguarded and unsecured, in junked cars and on junkyard shelves all over the country. And that's what worries me.

I completed writing this book prior to September 11, 2001, when the world suddenly became a vastly different and more dangerous place. I'm hoping that somewhere there's a courageous lawmaker who'll be willing to take on the automotive industry and introduce legislation requiring that all air bags in vehicles must be deployed and the sodium azide rendered harmless at the time the vehicle is scrapped.